Born in Paris in 1947, Christian Jacq first visited Egypt when he was seventeen, went on to study Egyptology and archaeology at the Sorbonne, and is now one of the world's leading Egyptologists. He is the author of the internationally bestselling RAMSES series, THE STONE OF LIGHT series and the stand-alone novel, THE BLACK PHARAOH. Christian Jacq lives in Switzerland.

For the Love of Philae

Christian Jacq

Translated by Marcia de Brito

POCKET
BOOKS

LONDON · SYDNEY · NEW YORK · TORONTO

First published in Great Britain by Pocket Books, 2003
An imprint of Simon & Schuster UK Ltd
A Viacom Company

3 5 7 9 10 8 6 4

Simon & Schuster UK Ltd
Africa House
64–78 Kingsway
London WC2B 6AH
www.simonsays.co.uk

Simon & Schuster Australia
Sydney

A CIP catalogue record for this book is available from
the British Library

ISBN 0-671-02858-8

Typeset by SX Composing DTP, Rayleigh, Essex
Printed and bound in Great Britain by
Cox & Wyman Ltd, Reading, Berkshire

For the Love of Philae

'I touch the heavens,
My head pierces the firmament.
I scrape the belly of the stars,
And I shine with their light.
Overwhelmed by celestial joy,
I dance with the constellations.'

Text found in the eternal abode of
Prince Sarenput, at Aswan

1

The stars danced in a lapis-lazuli sky. Isis, the High Priestess of the temple of Philae, contemplated their light, a light that issued from the depth of the universe. It revealed the presence of immortal kings in the heart of infinity.

Although the new religion had conquered the whole country, the souls of long-gone pharaohs still protected the sanctuary where the great goddess watched over her last followers; around fifty men and women who, six centuries after the birth of Christ, lived according to the laws of the faith of the ancient Egyptians, immersed in the purity of an immemorial rule. The sacred mountain of Philae continued to resist, lit daily by the fiery orb which rose from the Levantine East. In the middle of a jumble of rocks, the sacred island of Isis emerged like a green paradise, surrounded by high walls. An enduring old legend said that to look at this fortress was to open the door to the Gods.

The young woman, dressed in the traditional white dress, heard the birds in the aviary chirping under the shade of an acacia tree. Light would soon prevail over darkness. From its hard granite pedestal, softened by a luxuriant vegetation sprinkled with date palms, the island stood defying Theodore, the powerful bishop who was both the temporal and the spiritual master of this forgotten region in Southern Egypt, at the bottom end of the Empire. Beyond it lay the unknown, danger and barbaric peoples.

Christian Jacq

Isis perfumed her short hair, black as jet, and walked towards Emperor Trajan's pavilion. Built to welcome the divine barge, the structure, with its elegant long columns, was unfinished; the priestess saw in this a message of hope, a task to pursue, even though destiny seemed hostile. How could the daughter of the Elder of the community and the most brilliant disciple of the House of Life admit that Egyptian civilization would one day disappear, crushed under the weight of a dogma that would not hesitate to use violence to impose itself?

Even if the enemy threatened, he would always encounter the walls of the temple, the ultimate reminder of the primordial bastion where life had first sprung from stone and sand to create the luxuriant hibiscus with red corollas, the blue clematis or the bougainvillaea with its pink garlands. Pushing back the branches of a sycamore tree, Isis made her way to the riverbank. The steep drop was like the end of the world, but it was just the edge of the gorge where the Nile flowed between increasingly narrow banks before losing itself in the turbulence of the first cataract. This launched rapids over the rocks and around the small islands. Isis loved this grandiose spectacle. She let herself be seduced by the mountains made of red sand, the ochre desert, the eternal stones. Nothing about this landscape ever changed. The power of primordial times, of glorious eras, of giant architects who built the most accomplished of cultures, could be felt here. Philae was the heart of the first province of Egypt; from her the revivifying flow of the vintage sprang, from her happiness would be reborn.

Isis needed the solitude of dawn to become imbued with the essence of the goddess whose name she bore. It was a mysterious dew born of the communion between heaven, earth and the temple. In the same way that the austere rocks were tamed by the sacred island's mesmerizing enchantment, the young priestess wanted to tame the hostile forces which had led Christian armies to the gates of the last Egyptian sanctuary. She would show she was worthy of the goddess who had chosen to incarnate at Philae.

Isis sat by the water. A soft wind enveloped her like a shawl; under her naked feet the earth was already warm.

How she worshipped this isolated place, this temple lost in the middle of these waters and reefs, this sandstone hymn to the invisible power, this joyous song chanted by the queen of stars! She had come into the world here, in the birth chamber.

She had learned to read, write and count in the House of Life, and had been initiated into the Lesser Mysteries at the age of sixteen, before developing her spirit to soar like the wings of a bird, and to know the illumination of the Greater Mysteries necessary to carry the weight of leadership. But how could she ignore the convulsions of the outer world? The Byzantine occupation was as violent as the Roman one. Bishop Theodore was the power in the city of Elephantine* and he had forced the conversion of the scribes, the boatmen and the peasants. They were now constrained to forget their roots and to behave like obedient Christians.

Today, old age weighed down the Elder. It was up to Isis to continue the fighting and protect Philae from being attacked. The new fanatics dreamed of taking over the temple and its riches. She counted on the moderation of the Bishop, an Egyptian who had been won over to Christ's cause.

When the old man died, another high priest would have to be found, capable of reigning with her. She could not help thinking of Sabni, a young man with a severe countenance and high forehead. He had too often been in her thoughts in the last months, so much so that she had felt disturbed while performing the rites. In her eyes, Sabni possessed the qualities this post required. Nevertheless, she could not help wondering if she was surrendering to a passion.

The sound of sistrums† echoed throughout the still air. Isis came back towards the temple. Two old priestesses were leaving the house of worship, handling the musical instruments

*Town which was situated opposite modern Aswan.

† Sistrum; a jingling instrument used by the Ancient Egyptians in the worship of Isis.

3

whose metallic ring kept away the night demons who tried to penetrate into the walls of the building. One held a sistrum with small branches supporting copper serpents. Another sistrum was like a handle-shaped column, topped with a head of the goddess of love, Hathor. They too had put on their festive habits. As they saw Isis approach, they bowed. In spite of her youth, the High Priestess inspired respect; smiling, never raising her voice, she was endowed with the innate dignity characteristic of high-ranking Egyptian women, whose beauty has been immortalized in thousands of low-relief sculptures. Isis's beauty was luminous, the mere sight of her was a balm to anguished souls. The adepts of the temple who bore the sacred title of 'brother' and 'sister' had decided to stay on in the island and they knew that their safety depended on her.

The sun rose above the eastern mountain and its fire spread throughout the sky. A procession of adepts crossed the threshold of the Ptolemy Euergetes gate. Leading the way was Sabni, tapping out the rhythm of the march with a long gilded wooden cane. Behind him came the Elder, supported by the perfumer and the slaughterer, followed by a retinue composed of the priestesses, and the priests with their shaved heads. They carried statuettes of the divinities, gold and silver vases, sceptres and coffers made of wood. These precious objects, preserved in dark crypts and chambers, were brought out into the light of day, according to an age-old ritual.

Isis had decided to organize this ceremony during a period of torrid heat, in which, with a splendour that aroused great envy in the neighbouring land, only the island of Philae remained luxuriantly green. Around it the landscape was arid, with abrupt slopes, arid rocks and barren earth, dried by the disease-laden southern wind. Soon, when the river tide was at its lowest level, the Nile would reveal the cataract and the rocks over which no boat could travel. In Elephantine, people found it more and more difficult to breathe. Death lurked and preyed on infants and old people.

Isis noticed signs of exhaustion among her brothers and

sisters. The strength of her father, the Elder, was declining. He was past eighty-five and feared that he would not reach the age of wise men, one hundred and ten years. Yet, he continued to show a brave face to the world, as if the terrible pains in his chest were but an illusion. Isis was afraid that in spite of all the care bestowed upon him, the end was near. But he might overcome adversity once again, as he had done so often in the past.

The High Priestess waited for the procession at the entrance of the pavilion. When Sabni came forward through the fourteen columns, guiding the cortège dressed immaculately in white, Isis made way for him. The community laid down the sacred objects. After one year of usage, the energy with which they had been charged during the previous ritual was spent. Only the sun would once again restore their effectiveness and render them capable of transforming ugliness into beauty. The master of the ritual recited:

> *'How radiant is your countenance, Divinity of Light,*
> *When with your own hands you mould matter*
> *To fashion gods, humans, animals and all Creation.'*

For three thousand years the ancient hymn had been chanted on similar occasions. Listening to it, Isis made up her mind to act on the decision she had been pondering on for weeks.

'Regeneration by light must be accompanied by an outing of the holy barge. Our ancestors did this and so will we.'

The community's beautiful serenity was broken; disapproving whispers pervaded the crowd. A gleam of excitement flashed through the eyes of the Elder.

'High Priestess,' said Sabni respectfully, 'this project seems very daring; we no longer have the right to leave the island; we have information that troops are stationed in Elephantine; we would be putting ourselves in great danger.'

'We have to start a resistance movement. None of the peasants who work on our lands are Christians. They were

5

baptized by force, with a sword on their necks; if the barge of the goddess remains invisible, Egypt will continue to die.'

'The enemy has the power.'

Isis turned towards the Elder.

'We should not risk the lives of lukewarm individuals,' he cried in a buoyant voice, 'they are too unsavoury, even for jackals.'

The High Priestess took her father's hand.

'You who do not know fear, be the guardian of this temple. Keep the older ones at your side; I only want volunteers who are conscious of the danger. Even if we are destroyed, this place must go on existing.'

2

The community still had several barges. Even though the teams of shipwrights and the naval shipyard were now remote memories, two adepts still saw to the upkeep of these priceless treasures. One of them was moored in front of Trajan's pavilion, far from the usual pier, so as not to draw the attention of occasional bystanders. Ten priests went on board. Sabni was carrying a miniature sacred barge, with its prow in the shape of a lotus flower. With a frowning look, he tried to dissuade Isis from undertaking this expedition; but the High Priestess settled at the prow savouring the feeling of the breeze on her face. The short trip, from the island to the deserted bank, seemed to augur victory. Philae was breaking the invisible fortress that prevented communication with the outer world; the emblem of the goddess would reappear before her subjects who had been cut off from her presence and condemned to despair.

A shepherd, standing at the top of a hill, was the first to see the procession. He saw it setting out from the embankment, with Isis leading the way. Full of joy, he ran to tell the peasants, bent over in work on a neighbouring field that had escaped the drought. One labourer jumped on his donkey, and riding at full speed went to spread the good news.

The cortège reached the rocky esplanade that dominated the town. Isis was moved when she saw the suburbs of Elephantine. The large southern city was now just a garrison

7

Christian Jacq

town abandoned by the gods, a profane territory where the temples had been ransacked. Sabni had difficulty hiding his anguish, but he too felt the intense joy of escaping confinement, of seeing once again the place where he had been born, and of hoping that his country might have a different future.

Worried, the priests looked right and left, fearing the intervention of the armed forces, which had a reputation for being ferocious. Step by step, they gained renewed courage. They crossed the first vineyard where, among the vines, grew some date palms. They were convinced that nothing could hold them back. The goddess's barge, lit by the rays of a hot sun, protected them. They carried on without haste, adopting the solemnity which was characteristic of the processions within the temple. They felt that if only they could reach the first farmhouses at the end of the path, the whole of Egypt would welcome them. Isis would proclaim the return of traditional faith, and happiness would be theirs once more.

About ten fierce-looking peasants barred the way. Sabni entrusted the sacred vessel to his followers and stood near Isis, who did not stop. The men, unarmed, fell to their knees; the High Priestess made them stand up again.

'The Goddess is nourished by your trust, not your humiliation.'

The peasants joined the priests. One of them started singing a song whose words he no longer understood; it praised the ripening of the barley seeds, and gave thanks to the benevolence of heaven. A priest took up the refrain and his brothers followed suit. When they came to the first fortified camp barring access to the town, a unified powerful voice arose from their breasts. As the procession went by it was joined by gardeners, itinerant pedlars and boatmen. They left their work to be part of this re-conquest of Elephantine.

Isis prayed; she sang a hymn to the divine mother very gently, trying hard to resist a growing feeling of elation. Why had they waited so long, if assailing the town was so easy? The number of the devotees of the goddess grew continually.

8

Women and children dared to leave their house and join in the celebration. It was as if the old gods were returning, as if Egypt was resuscitated. Sabni did not participate in the cheerful atmosphere; the songs and joyous cries did not reassure him. He kept his eyes on the path where two patrolling soldiers armed with spears had just come into view.

The young man shuddered: these were not peasants who had been conscripted, but well-equipped mercenaries supervising the customs post, exacting taxes and escorting the convoys carrying food. Their main task was to enforce law and order no matter the cost in human lives. Their bodies were covered by leather breastplates and leggings, their heads were hidden by helmets with two openings for the eyes. They handled both the pike and the double-edged axe with great ease. The people hated and feared these barbarians, who came from Asia.

The procession carried on to a rough brick-built fort, whose main aspect faced south, from whence rebellious Nubian tribes had come many years ago. The sinister structure, a symbol of the bishop's power, was linked to watchtowers patrolled by the military detachments that supervised frontiers, roads and quarries.

By entering once again into Elephantine, the community would give a breath of new life to the whole of Egypt. In a few weeks, everyone would know that the Goddess had left the sacred island to reopen the ancient sanctuaries and revivify the sleeping cults. There would be celebrations everywhere. Once again there would be rejoicing during the festival of heaven and earth.

Four soldiers in rags ran towards the cortège. They took off their papyrus boots and threw away their short blunt swords. Dirty and dishevelled, these men lived off money demanded weekly from their own families, from whom they had been torn to become policemen under the orders of the foreign mercenaries.

Desertion had started. Two, three hundred men . . . Sabni

gave up counting the allies who, taking off their Christian rags, freed themselves and spoke from the heart. They regretted having doubted. Now they knew that no oppressor would succeed in killing Egypt's soul.

How beautiful Isis looked in that moment of triumph! Calm and resplendent, she commanded with grace. She was fragile, yet indestructible. Sabni had admired her for so long that he was surprised to find his feelings had become even more ardent. The deference in his manner was mingled with a passionate feeling that he still refrained from expressing. Could this possibly be love? How could two beings so dissimilar come together in love: Isis, the heiress of a long line of illustrious Egyptian queens, and Sabni, a modest priest of humble origin?

The attack came from the rear. Entranced in their delirium, the pilgrims had not noticed the rapid encircling manoeuvre. The orders the mercenaries had were clear: no disturbance was to be tolerated. Ordinarily, they chastised a drunk or caught a desperate peasant fleeing to escape from slavery and poverty. This time the situation was much more worrying: a riot, a rebellion against the established order. Furthermore, the sentinels themselves had assisted the desertion of several policemen, who had joined the agitators. Consequently, the instructions were carried out with the ultimate severity.

The first row of mercenaries attacked with bow and arrow. The arrows pierced the backs of Isis's followers. With their axes the soldiers chopped the arms and noses of the wounded. Then they disembowelled the last of the rebels. In a few minutes the surveillance troops had control of the terrain.

Those who had believed in the restoration of the great goddess lay slaughtered and covered in blood on the ground. Only one of the priests had lost his life, and he lay with his throat cut; a mistake due to an over-zealous soldier, who had remembered too late the recommendations of the Bishop: to spare the life of the men and women dressed in white robes.

The men quickly disrobed the dead priest and dressed him in a dirty peasant tunic.

Isis, Sabni and the other members of the religious community were escorted back to their barge. Crushed, they heard the cries of the deserters as the mercenaries hung them by their feet and poured molten lead on their testicles. The tortured were then burned; the smoke that drifted towards the blue sky marked the end of the insurrection.

An officer picked up a small model of a barge with a prow in the shape of a lotus flower. Disappointed by the absence of gold ornaments, he shattered it with his boots, scattering the bits among the loose stones.

3

Prostrated at the feet of a column in Trajan's pavilion, Isis had fasted for two days. The bewildered community waited for their High Priestess to come out of her silence. The Elder, who was confined to his bed, no longer spoke. The ritualist was content with repeating the texts that recounted the numerous offerings to the divinities, so as to preserve the tenuous link uniting Egypt to celestial harmony. There was complete silence around the temple, as if a general lethargy had contaminated its walls, indifferent to the sweetness of the day.

Sabni placed a goatskin full of water before Isis.

'No one holds you responsible for the death of our brother. He knew the risks, just like the others.'

'The Bishop promised that the lives of the members of our community would be spared. All those poor people murdered, such terrible fury unleashed on them . . .'

'Theodore has always kept his word. It was an accident.'

'Are you sure?'

'I intend to find out.'

'How?'

'By meeting Theodore.'

'You are not allowed to leave the island.'

'As a priest, but who will suspect a peasant?'

'Too dangerous.'

'It is essential.'

'What if I forbade you to go?'

'I would obey, but we would suffer unbearable anguish.'

Isis stood up. It was hard for Sabni to resist rushing to her and taking her in his arms! She admitted that he was right. When the land was divided, the Bishop had not confiscated the temple's patrimony. Although not as rich as it once was, it still owned and cultivated fields that continued to feed the community. Each peasant was convinced that, if the goddess received the best part of the harvest, his fate would improve. The Bishop turned a blind eye and the economic system continued to work as it did previously: foodstuffs were brought to the temple, then blessed by the High Priestess, and redistributed.

'Another important matter compels me to go to Elephantine without delay.'

'What important matter?'

'Our faithful Mersis has not sent us his usual message. There are soldiers on the banks and no fisherman can venture near our waters.'

Mersis, an Egyptian whose name meant 'The Red One', was one of the Bishop's trusted men. An old convert, he could not bear to see the ancient cults disappear. He wanted to save Philae and always conveyed information to the community that was essential to its survival.

'How will you get there?'

'I will swim up to the first frontier post. It is only guarded by peasants recruited by force, and who spend their time dozing or playing dice. Then I will borrow the ferryboat. In Elephantine, I will wait as long as it takes to be able to meet Theodore alone.'

Isis turned to Sabni. In her eyes, there was both disquiet and tenderness.

'So we don't have a choice . . .'

'I am your servant. You are the soul of Philae.'

'Return quickly, Sabni.'

Sabni swam easily across the small stretch of water that separated the island from the barracks where the so-called customs men piled up crocodile carcasses and second-rate Nubian loincloths.

Nobody went to this sinister place where there was nothing to steal; in the distance, just before the first cataract, Sabni noticed the fortifications of the large customs post on the frontier between Egypt and the South. Lit by torches, it was in a state of round-the-clock vigilance during the low tide period. The occupants did not fear raids by black tribes, as the last attacks had occurred over ten years ago. What they had to protect against pillage were the treasures piled up in the warehouses: bags full of gold, ivory, ebony wood and wild animal skins. After having been catalogued and evaluated, these goods were traded in the busiest market in the country. The custom officials attended to the caravans that came from Africa, levied taxes and guaranteed the security of the goods before they were negotiated.

Philae no longer possessed enough silver coins to trade for that precious metal used to cover the statues of the gods and the doors of noble residences. Feeling melancholy, Sabni delved into the dark waters. As a child, he had so often played on those banks and cliffs that he was familiar with their smallest pebble. Certain paths, which looked easy to tread, concealed some mortal traps; many Byzantine soldiers had broken their necks by forgetting that the stones were precariously balanced and could give way and hurtle down the sandy slopes at any moment.

He took off his peasant tunic and slept on top of a hill, under a pink granite boulder. Awoken by the glimmer of dawn, he dressed and walked down calmly to the dock where a crowd of people gathered. The trip by barge to and from the island of Elephantine where the Bishop lived was free; sheep, calves, donkeys, labourers taking provisions to the master of the land and to the garrison, were all packed together aboard. Sabni took a heavy basket off an old woman heaving under the weight of bunches of onions. She had to deliver them to the market stalls built on the southern point of the island. Walking beside her and talking, he could easily be taken for a devoted son helping his mother. The soldiers and policemen did not question them. They passed near the famous well where the Greek Eratothenes, in 230 BC, confirmed the measurement of the earth's circumference established by Egyptian sages.

In this region, during the summer solstice, luminous solar rays fell vertically and illumined the hand of the sundials without a trace of a shadow, an excellent point of departure for the calculations of ancient surveyors.

Most houses had changed their terraces for roofs made of plaster. Some of them had been completely destroyed, a stern reminder of the punishment inflicted on those who obstinately refused conversion. The old home of the Egyptian governor who was hostile to Christianity was deserted. Its façade, lacerated and sullied, evoked the face of a tortured dissident.

Sabni accompanied the old woman to the grocer's stall. The Lebanese owner was always ready to sing the praises of Byzantium and the wisdom of the invader. The cousin of an officer, he had bought a lot of land. To cultivate it, he exploited with impunity several families who, were it not for him, would have died of hunger.

Exhausted, the onion-seller asked Sabni to carry her bag, although it was now considerably lighter. She lived in a poor neighbourhood and had to go every day to her small plot of land on the East bank. During the hot season, she worked by night. Her husband was dead, and her two sons were stationed in Asia. She had a hard time making a meagre living.

The house, with its low roof, was situated in a dark and muddy alley, and was built with sun-dried earth bricks. On the brownish unkempt façade there was a tiny window made of wooden trellis. Sabni and the old woman went up three worn steps, She put an old rusty key in the lock; she had the illusion that this wobbly bolt would offer her some protection. Inside, there were two small rooms with some broken-down furniture. The old woman slumped on the floor made of beaten earth.

'Who are you?'

15

'Do you really want to know?'

She closed her eyes.

'You don't have the manners of a peasant, your voice is poised like a priest's . . . I remember the peaceful words that the adepts of Isis would profess when they came out in procession, before the Bishop forced them to remain on the island. They had calm gestures, like yours.'

'Those times have gone. I am here to enlist in the army. Farewell.'

The old woman kept her eyes half closed. To denounce a priest would bring her a handsome sum. She would have enough to eat for many months.

4

Alongside the Bishop's residence was the tallest dovecote in the Elephantine region. Pigeon excrement was a valued and efficient fertilizer, especially for the vineyards. The building where the master of the province lived boasted of two floors and a terrace. Sabni knew it well; before its present owner, it had been the home of a judge and his family, whose children often played with the young Theodore and with the future priest of Isis.

Every day, about ten servants cleaned the reception room, the bedrooms, the kitchen, the washroom, the porticoes and the pantry. Sabni thought at first that he might join them, but there were soldiers checking their identity. Therefore, he slipped in among the team that cared for the farm, where there were often new hired hands.

All day long Sabni took care of the pigs, geese and chickens. He had worked as a farmhand at the temple, before being admitted into the school for scribes. He exchanged a few words with his colleagues, without actually mixing with them; when they left the farmyard, he stayed behind and remained inside when they locked up for the night.

When night fell, he slipped into the cellar through a low window with shaky bars. He crept through two rows of jars filled with fine wine, then went up the stairs that led to the ground floor. The office of the Bishop was on the second.

Christian Jacq

Sitting down at his ebony wood desk Theodore checked the accounts by the light of two oil lamps.

'Come in, Sabni. You crept in very silently, but I was expecting you. After such dramatic incidents, I felt sure you would come.'

Isis's follower came into the room. It was filled with papyrus documents carefully rolled up in their cases. Theodore loved order; he detested clutter and negligence. Although he reigned over a squad of secretaries, he continued to file his documents himself. A tireless worker, he allowed himself very little rest. At thirty he already looked like a mature man, exhausted by shouldering too many responsibilities. Sabni, who was only two years younger, looked like a youth compared to Theodore, whose elongated face, bald temples and gauntness gave him an appearance of great severity. As an adolescent, he had envied his companion's beauty, his joyous and triumphant nature.

'Sit down on the cushions and savour these succulent figs. I have to finish a report, for God had no mercy, entrusting me with the government of the province. The emperor's civil servants only nurture their own sloth.'

By looking at his quarters no one would guess that Theodore was of Egyptian origin. He loved Byzantine robes with violet hems and golden floral embroideries. Mosaics depicting scenes from Greek mythology covered the walls; Greek inlaid work decorated the furniture; the glasses and the crockery came from the Eastern Empire. Sabni despised this excessive refinement, but he was hungry.

He savoured several sweet figs, which had practically no pips. They were prized by highly placed officials.

'A priest has been killed, Theodore.'

'Officially, he is considered a deserter. That version is preferable.'

'You had promised.'

'And you had promised not to leave the island under any circumstances; simple people were killed because of you.'

18

'Try to understand our position.'

'It is you who must realize that Philae violates God's law and that of men, and has done so for too long. Are you aware that Constantine II ordered the closure of pagan temples from the year 356 after the Saviour's birth, that Christianity is the state religion since 380 AD and that heretic cults are forbidden since 392 AD?'

'Rome fell in 410 AD,' Sabni reminded Theodore. 'Its fall proves that the Christian belief can perish and that the most pitiless tyranny can collapse.'

'The Eastern Empire now carries the torch. Philae only subsists in a dream that threatens to become a nightmare. Why don't you agree to convert?'

The Bishop turned towards the Egyptian priest.

'We are friends and the gods are dead. It is the true faith, which now reigns over the world. Christ will receive you in his Church, you will finally know peace . . . and so will I.'

There was a gleam of hope in Theodore's eyes. Whereas the West, still recovering from the fall of Rome, was writhing under barbaric convulsions, Constantine's legacy, the rich provinces of Asia Minor, of Syria and Egypt, elevated the Eastern Empire to the rank of humanity's leading light. Byzantium, the new Rome, held the keys to civilization. Only Alexandria tried to rival Constantine's capital, which it did by laying its riches at the feet of the Patriarch, an adept of the monophysite doctrine, according to which the divine nature of Christ had integrated His human nature. Although condemned by the Emperor, the Egyptian idiosyncrasy still flourished. Theodore as bishop should fight it with more energy, but another adversary, Philae, still worried him: the last of the pagan temples was still active.

'I will never be converted,' Sabni, with the calm certitude of an unshakeable faith.

'I have just signed a new decree, on the Emperor's orders. Every baptised person who practises an ancient rite, even in secret at home, will be condemned to death. Read it.'

19

Christian Jacq

Sabni deciphered the text, written in Greek, Latin and Demotic,* so that no one could allege their ignorance of the document. The illiterate would be gathered in public places where the herald would solemnly announce the warning:

'Regardless of family, rank or dignity, whether he be invested or not with authority or public function, whether he be well born or of modest condition, with a high or humble fortune, no one may perform any sacrifice, in any place or city, to symbolic objects; nor may he make any offering. Anyone who does is to be denounced.'

Sabni rolled up the papyrus.

'So this is your new weapon, informers. Don't worry, I am not baptized. Hearts have become greedy, there is no more kindness. Evil is the order of the day. Criminals have the law on their side and each person goes about with eyes cast down: the country is at the mercy of those who hate it.'

'Don't be obstinate.'

'Time is just an illusion. In today's disgrace lies tomorrow's happiness.'

'You are underestimating how vicious your enemies are. The cohorts of priests who invaded the ancient tombs will not tolerate Philae's existence much longer. At every meeting, their representatives demand the exile of the community and the destruction of the temple. I try to hush up the presence of the last pagans under my jurisdiction, but your stupid procession has completely undermined my efforts.'

'Isis worships the heavens and banishes demons. She persecutes no one. Her love will pervade.'

'You are a man of another age, Sabni. Isis . . . a forgotten ghost.'

'Why is your God so bloodthirsty? Why does he enslave so many countries?'

*Demotic alphabet – the alphabet used by the laity and the people of Egypt as distinguished from the hieratic on which it is based.

'And why do you worship deities which have the body of a man and the head of an animal?'

'That argument is unworthy of you, Theodore. In an animal, a divine force is incarnate; we don't adore idols, but we recognize the message contained in symbols.'

The Bishop left his desk and sat opposite his friend. He accepted the figs that were being offered to him and poured some white wine into two silver cups.

'Would you at least consent in venerating the Lord on Sundays, an obligatory holiday?'

'Every day should be sacred. The ritual is never interrupted; each dawn brings the rebirth of creation. Why privilege Sunday?'

'You speak as if the world had not changed! The voice of pharaohs has been silenced for ever.'

'But Philae remains. Come to the island, Theodore; come and meditate in the square, by the shade of the columns. Walk through the rooms and the chapels, read the hieroglyphs engraved on the walls, feel the serenity that emanates from Isis, the celestial queen.'

For a moment, Sabni thought the Bishop would follow him and open his heart, even if only for a pilgrimage to the mysteries of the goddess. If Theodore was once again touched by the magic of the temple and the last community, then there would be hope.

'You're a child! Do you know that Philae is full of diabolical characters, of goddesses whose tight dresses reveal their breasts? Do you know that their dress is so transparent it does not even hide their intimate parts and that their jewels and ornaments are an insult to the poverty of the just? A bishop who would venture into that brothel that you call temple would immediately be damned.'

'Wasn't it the apostle Paul who wrote: "Woman was created for man, and she is the reflection of man"? If you consider woman to be so diabolical, then why admit that Christ was born of the Virgin Mary? Joseph, Mary, Jesus . . . are they not the trinity Osiris, Isis, Horus?'

'You're blaspheming.'

'And you're repeating a dogma you only believe in half-heartedly.'

'You're mistaken. I believe that there is only one God, the Father, from whom all things are born. It is He who has designated me to be the servant of His Church; my duty is to protect the faith and fight against misdeeds.'

'You're also head of an army of deacons, civil servants and administrators, you possess an incalculable amount of land and properties, you demand taxes which increase poverty. Your religion is cruel; it admits no other truth except its own. Only slaves follow it. The faith of the pharaohs was neither missionary nor conquering: the only thing that mattered was the conversion of the heart. It was the initiation into the divine treasures that generated a deep change in the depths of each being.'

'The sacraments have replaced initiation.'

'They do what they are told like sheep. They have your Revelation instead of developing themselves.'

'Their sincerity is just as genuine as the one professed by the last of Isis's adepts.'

'Serve Christ then, if that's your vocation, but at least grant my community the right to live; it is the embodiment of a spirituality that will allow tomorrow's world to be reborn.'

The Bishop raised his hands in a beseeching gesture.

'I am begging you, Sabni! Persuade the High Priestess not to sink further into folly. As for you, at least pretend to want conversion. I will carry the weight of your lie and implore God's forgiveness.'

Sabni stood up and Theodore followed suit. The two men looked at each other and felt the bond of their eternal friendship.

'I will not renounce my religion, Theodore.'

'History is against you.'

'Numbers and power also, and they are wrong.'

'Together we would have surmounted every obstacle and recreated paradise in this region.'

'There is Philae already, protect it. Our survival depends on your vigilance.'

Theodore turned and took a papyrus from the box reserved for urgent matters.

'Yesterday's incidents force me to take certain measures. The inhabitants of the island must become workers like the others. They must provide the soldiers of the station with free clothes: first delivery is to be next month.'

'That's impossible. Our two old weavers are almost senile and the other members of the community are assigned other urgent tasks.'

'In that case, I will suppress the donation of linen to Philae.'

'We were counting on the next one to manufacture some robes.'

'What do I care? The subjects of the Empire do not go around in white robes.'

Theodore started writing again.

'Will you grant me a pass?'

'You were never here, Sabni.'

The Bishop dipped his quill in a pot filled with black ink and wrote out in Greek the formal definitive ban forbidding the delivery of linen to the pagan temple.

5

Without a pass, Sabni was like any outlaw. The patrols that supervised the streets of Elephantine would demand to know his profession, his place of work and the name of his employer. He had hoped to obtain more substantial help from the Bishop. But that was the Bishop's way of teaching him a lesson. Alone in a hostile town, he had to escape the patrols and get back to Philae. It was impossible to leave by the farmyard, for the exit was guarded.

Sabni glanced for the last time at the Bishop's window, lit by the flickering gleam of the lamps, and climbed over the parapet of the terrace and on to the roof. He observed the alleys: there was not a soldier in sight. With the help of an arch formed by a climbing vine, Sabni worked his way down into a small square filled with detritus. He went on his way, from building to building, distancing himself from the town centre.

All he had to do now was to reach the riverbank by the old temple gardens; there he could find some abandoned boats that lay rotting and were rarely used. He avoided an alley and took a small path along which were the ransacked domiciles of the priests of the Ram God. He edged his way along the walls and ruins, coming closer to a potter's workshop on the Nile bank. On top of a window there remained a lintel made of cedar wood. The ornamental tiling and limestone wall facing had been ripped off. Despite the scattered piles of bricks, Sabni could still detect a large room with niches that had once sheltered the domestic divinities to whom, in the old days, families would address prayers morning and night.

He crossed the threshold of what had once been a door and thought that, in less than one hour, he would be back on the island.

'Don't move. You are under arrest.'

From the debris emerged about ten helmeted soldiers, who pointed their swords at him.

'If you try to run away we will kill you.'

Sabni turned. Other soldiers blocked his way. He stood still. The commander of the patrol, a Byzantine with a curt and dry manner, came forward.

'Who are you?'

'A peasant.'

'What is your name?'

'I cannot remember . . .'

'What are you doing here? Don't you know this is army territory?'

'I was lost.'

The commander circled around Sabni with his sword in the air, as if he was looking for the best place to pierce his flesh.

'Are you a Christian?'

'Who isn't?'

'Have you been in prison?'

'No.'

'Take him away.'

Two soldiers took Sabni and pushed him before them. He did not resist and was dragged to the guard's post at the barracks. Hidden behind a militiaman, an old onion-seller looked at the patrol commander and nodded her head when Sabni passed.

The suspect was thrown into a cell with walls made of crude sun-baked bricks and a floor made of beaten earth. The ceiling was so low that Sabni could not stand up. When the heat was at its warmest, he would suffocate. He sat in the posture of the scribe and emptied his spirit of all agitation. The Elder had taught him how to situate himself outside immediate events, to become almost a stranger to himself so as to orient his thoughts better. The young man then forgot the fetid place he was in, the comings and goings of soldiers, the noise of the camp. The fear he felt slid over his skin like drops of water and fell from him.

How could he warn Isis? To escape seemed impossible. He would have to bribe one of the soldiers and ask him to convey a message to Philae. But he had nothing on him to give. Would he find a charitable being in this wild pack of wolves? Nobody brought him anything to eat or drink. In the middle of the afternoon, Sabni felt his tongue swell and his muscles contract. An infantryman pulled him out of the cell by his left arm; Sabni stumbled, his legs gave out. He regained his balance with some difficulty. Then folding his head high, he went forward. He was poked in the back and walked faster. Someone pushed him into an old office with derelict walls; some engraved tablets lay in disorder on a chest. The infantrymen made way; a superior officer came in, he was about fifty years old. His right cheek bore a scar, his nose was broken, the man showed all the signs of having been involved in numerous combats.

He closed the door with a kick.

Sabni drew back.

Then the two men fell into each other's arms.

'Mersis!'

'It was the old woman that denounced you. That is why my men arrested you.'

'As one of Isis's priests?'

'As a brigand; at least that is the term used in the complaint lodged against you. Drink this.'

The captain offered Sabni a goblet filled with fresh water.

'Did you take the risk of writing the text yourself?'

'The clerk of the court obeys me. I still have some power in this garrison. Perhaps not for much longer: the future seems rather sombre.'

Captain Mersis hit the wall with his fist.

'The Prefect, Maximin, arrives tomorrow, leading five hundred men. Four hundred infantrymen and one hundred horsemen; an elite troop, a formidable reinforcement to add to the mercenaries and those who are forced to enlist. I have orders to put the barracks in pristine order and make the weapons shine.'

'Why this show of force?'

'For the final pacification of this region.'

'What about Philae?'

'I don't know, but the surveillance of the island will be reinforced. I will no longer be able to send you daily messages.'

'The Bishop is forbidding the donation of linen.'

An expression of deep pain creased the rough features of the captain.

'The robes of the priests . . .'

'We will look after the ones we already have.'

The soldier was deeply upset. Death left him indifferent, but he was really touched by the ceremonial beauty of a ritual.

'That Theodore is a monster.'

'Is he on good terms with Maximin?'

'They don't know each other. But it is known that the prefect is a very despotic man.'

'The Bishop will not like that.'

'Luck may yet smile on us.'

'Those hundreds of soldiers . . .'

'Philae would not justify such an army. There must be another reason.'

The captain could see none. For a long time now, even the hint of a rebellion had been uprooted like an old vine. The fortresses on the frontier between Egypt and the South had crushed all control of the empire: the pagan temple of Philae.

'You must no longer lay yourself open to peril, Mersis. If it becomes known that you help us . . .'

'I'm not afraid of my destiny. You will remain in prison

until tomorrow morning; the interrogation that I have just put you through proves your innocence. At the abandoned dock, you will find an old boat, it should carry you halfway. Then you will swim. I will try to send you a message by pigeon as soon as I know more about the situation; but the best messengers, those who can fly by night, are requisitioned by the Bishop. For now, forgive me, but no suspect emerges intact from this office.'

Mersis hit Sabni several times, then violently opened the door and threw his victim outside, crying out in pain.

'Put this thief back in his cell. The little ruffian needed a lesson.'

6

With numb fingers, the Elder sculpted a figurine in olivewood. He did not have proper control of the chisel and scratched the back of his hand with it, but he was so absorbed in what he considered an essential task that he was oblivious to the pain. Sabni watched him in silence. Since his return to Elephantine, he described the situation to both Isis and her father. Furious, the Elder had come out of his muteness and taken the young man to the temple's library.

'A time will come when the Gods will leave the earth and regain the heavens; strangers will disfigure our country. This place, the most sacred of all, will be covered with corpses and tombs. Nothing will survive, except a few signs engraved in stone: thus speak the prophets. I do not accept their curse, I will fight to the end!'

The old man continued to carve the statuette. He gave it the rough form of a human being, covered it with a cloth and placed it on a table where there was a clay incense burner and an oven made of coarse bricks. He threw some charcoal and some balls of goose fat into it.

'Everything is ready. We just need to light the fire and pronounce out loud the name of our enemy and throw his effigy into the furnace. The adversary will be destroyed. Ah, I was forgetting . . .'

The Elder unrolled a virgin papyrus.

'Take this inkpot and use the ink; they have never been used. Write the name of Bishop Theodore.'

'I refuse.'

'Why?'

'This magic is in vain.'

'It has been efficient thousands of times.'

'Theodore is not our enemy. He may well be the only one capable of saving us; it's not him that we should do away with, but the whole Empire with its cohorts of soldiers. No magic can do that.'

The Elder threw the statuette in the furnace, which he did not light.

Maximin, the Prefect, a portly sixty-year-old with a round face and a shiny, oily skin from an unguent he used to look younger, entered Elephantine on horseback, at the head of his troops. This was his way of showing that he was taking charge immediately and had unchallenged power from now on. The authorities of the region would submit to his will without delay.

Behind him came a fierce army, well equipped and well nourished. The four hundred infantrymen had new leather breastplates, clean tunics, coats and boots. The one hundred horsemen were mounted on vigorous horses. Each soldier received two daily rations, which consisted of bread, meat, wine and oil. Their pay allowed the wiser ones to economize a little gold. Syrians, Greeks, Romans, Asians and some Egyptians composed the ranks of that cohort now in charge of pacifying once and for all this region whose latent insubordination exasperated the Emperor.

The mission was not to the Prefect's liking. He would much rather be in Alexandria, which he loved, with its luxury, its women, the banquets and the soft sea breeze. It was the first time, after fifteen years spent in Egypt, that he had gone so far south. The heat exhausted him, the stark rocks and the arid landscape of the cataracts evoked a terrible loneliness. Only the centre of Elephantine, with its planted trees and gardens, had some charm. But Maximin would quickly tire of this provincial backwater. Already, he yearned to leave. Luckily his task would be easy and quickly accomplished.

He was astonished to see how well turned out the troops who were paying homage to him were. Infamous rumours spoke of a group of poor devils in rags, incapable of fighting. In reality their clothes and their arms were just as good as those of the arriving troops. The Bishop who was responsible for the garrison had done a good job.

The Prefect refused the help the footsoldier was offering him to get down from his horse. Despite his relative corpulence, he boasted about being in great shape physically, something that a life of pleasure had not altered. Theodore came to greet him. The two men saluted each other.

'You are welcome, prefect Maximin.'

'Congratulations, Monsignor. Order is not a vain word in Elephantine.'

'Discipline is a virtue that Our Lord loves A meal awaits you; no doubt you would like to bathe first.'

'Yes, indeed. The journey was long and dusty.'

Maximin tasted the delights of a hot perfumed bath. The hot water circulated in ancient plumbing that the Bishop had preserved scrupulously.

Theodore had as many followers as adversaries. He was considered the most remarkable of Egyptian prelates and an excellent administrator. His ambition was as powerful as his faith; he was the absolute master of the South, and no doubt expected to be given new responsibilities. He had been described as a rough and cold man, yet Maximin found him to behave with great courtesy. The meal was worthy of the best-kept tables: white melon, fish from the Nile, roast lamb, green vegetables, goat's cheese, peaches, figs and pomegranates. The cook had used spices with an expertise that enchanted the palate. The wines, a local red and a white from the Delta, would not have been out of place at a banquet given by the

31

Emperor. The Bishop did not eat much. After so many mediocre inns along the way, Maximin indulged his hearty appetite.

'You are an astonishing individual, Monsignor. A well-groomed army, a sumptuous house, an exceptional cook . . . don't you feel stifled in this provincial backwater?'

'I was born here.'

'Does that matter? I could not wait to leave my native North African village.'

'This land is rough, but it is not without riches.'

'There is a part of that wealth which the Emperor considers he has been deprived of for far too long: the Nubian gold. For over a year now, no shipment of gold had been received in the capital.'

'The orders I had were to reinforce the vigilance at the frontiers, to discourage any attempts at invasion. The caravans can no longer penetrate into the gold-producing regions. The black tribes would massacre them; I do not have the authorization to organize an expedition.'

'I have. General Narses will lead this army to Nubia, while I stay here and verify your accounts and your administration.'

The Bishop looked embarrassed.

'You're looking for trouble. There are insurmountable difficulties.'

Angered, the prefect banged down his cup abruptly on the solid acacia wood table.

'You refuse?'

'I will gladly put my office at your disposal; you can examine all the administrative documents at your leisure. It is the Nubian expedition that concerns me.'

'How can a bunch of savages resist an experienced army?'

'Experienced or not, it will have to go through the cataract first.'

Maximin wiped his forehead with a handkerchief.

'Nobody mentioned this hurdle in Alexandria . . . Kindly explain.'

'This is the low-tide period; one can see the rocks. No vessel would risk navigating through that labyrinth; if you persist with your project, more than three-quarters of your men will perish.'

The strategy experts who had never seen the cataract had only taken the military reality into account.

'When the flood comes, will we be able to surmount this obstacle without difficulty?'

'Not during the first days; after that everything will depend on the intensity of the inundation; if it is too weak, the water will barely cover the most dangerous rocks. If it is too violent, the waters will provoke whirlpools that even the best sailors will not manage to avoid.'

Maximin was shattered: How many months would go by before the Emperor could be satisfied? What sanctions would he suffer if he failed? This mission which looked so easy was turning into a nightmare.

'You can count on my total support,' promised Theodore. 'If your stay here must be lengthy, then I will do everything in my power to make it as pleasurable as possible. My secretaries and my staff will satisfy the least of your desires.'

'There's something else . . . The Emperor has received complaints concerning a small group of pagans who refuse to convert.'

'That is correct.'

'Where do they live?'

'On the island of Philae, lost in the middle of the current. It is an isolated place. No one goes there.'

'Is there a temple?'

'Yes.'

'Why have you not closed it down? Its very existence is against the law.'

'I am aware of that, but I hesitate to use force; Philae does not disturb the population. The fifty pagans who live on that island, far from public attention, are condemned to extinction. The majority are harmless elderly people. Their children were converted a long time ago, some of them are soldiers; how can I send them to attack their own parents?'

Maximin poured himself some more red wine.

'I am not partisan to violence . . . The conversions to Christianity have already caused many deaths, not to speak of the suffering caused by previous persecutions. But this situation is unacceptable: couldn't you chase these people away without manhandling them?'

'Try to understand them: they're dreamers, nostalgic for the past. Many were born on the island, have lived there all their lives, and wish to die there. Soon the temple will revert to the Church. Compassion dictates my attitude.'

Maximin thought that was a strange position for the Bishop to take; his reputation was that of an inflexible man, not accustomed to being crossed and a stickler for law and order. Was he covering up some crucial information?

'Philae is therefore the only pagan temple that is still active?'

'Active is too strong a word: lethargic would be more appropriate.'

'Is the island easy to get to?'

'Yes, one can, by boat, but . . .'

'Is it no longer part of the Empire's territory?'

Theodore did not answer.

'I will go to Philae,' announced Maximin. 'Show me where your office is, Monsignor.'

7

Sabni supported the Elder, who relished the delights of his daily walk under the covered portico, between the alighting platform and the first pillar, enjoying the coolness of this cloister where so many sages had meditated. He lingered over the ceremonial texts and the divine figures that covered the walls and columns. On these, the pharaoh dialogued with gracious young women whose harmonious bodies manifested the love of the earth for the celestial powers. Despite the pain in his old joints, the old man was jubilant.

'A moment spent serving God is more bountiful in riches than the whole existence of a wealthy man. A day spent making offerings is more fruitful than all the treasures in the world. That is what my father repeatedly told me, after having heard it from his own father; and you, Sabni, will you pass on these words?'

'My the Goddess give me the strength to do so.'

The Elder stopped and looked at the sky.

'Today the event that will decide the future of this community will take place. Observe the sun . . . it's up to him to make his voice heard!'

A new strength dwelt in the old man's limbs, giving him the energy to walk for longer than usual. Sabni, who felt oppressed, did not dare question him. The Elder also had a premonition that the following hours would be unlike anything he had lived through before.

The two men made their way to the south-western part of the island, where the pavilion of Nectanebo I stood out above the water. In the past great barges drew alongside the quay. They transported the people who came to work in the temple for one week before returning to the mainland. The gallery had once been filled by a female orchestra, whose melodies welcomed visitors to the island. Now it was almost in ruins. The two small obelisks erected opposite the southern façade of the pavilion swayed on their plinth.

The Elder sat on top of the stairs that led to the water, facing the island of Biga, sacred territory where Osiris rested. No lay person was allowed to set foot on it. After a long rest, the Elder said that he wanted to go and walk on the portico once again; he looked out on to the landscape of water and rocks. His face betrayed intense disappointment.

'My sight is going, my ears are deaf, my strength is leaving me, my mouth can no longer utter words, my bones are painful and my thoughts unclear; would I be capable of interpreting an omen if one came? I have but one joy left and that is my daughter. Did you know that Isis belongs to the noblest lineage, that she is a descendant of Cleopatra, the last of the great queens? She dreamt of rebuilding the pharaoh's empire.'

The Elder was immersed in his memories and the name of his daughter kept recurring.

Sometimes his sentences were incomprehensible. He mixed real words and imaginary ones, moving through the past in turmoil of dying hopes.

Staring fixedly, he suddenly stood up.

'Look! Look at the Sun!'

From the blinding light came a flock of wild ducks in a triangular pattern. The leader plunged towards Nectanebo's pavilion; the others followed his movement with grace. Sabni left the colonnade to observe the admirable ballet. The mallards changed direction and whirled above him.

'The omen!' shouted the Elder.

The birds, flying in a triangle once again, regained height

and flew off into the blue sky. The old man fell into the arms of the young man.

'The sign I was waiting for . . .You will be the Head of the community.'

Sabni's enthronement ceremony started in mid-afternoon. An owl hooted. That prodigious sign validated the Elder's decision. Isis had given her approval. The community was gripped by an unexpected exaltation. It felt young again, inebriated with joy. The naming of a new communal leader, called to form with Isis the symbolic couple who would reign over the island, would guarantee the perennial continuity of the cult. The rooms of the temple had been cleaned, the weeds removed; even the old and the sick had given their utmost to make this event memorable. Even if certain linen robes were threadbare or had holes in them, they were resplendently white after having been washed repeatedly. There was not one ritual object that had not been cleaned and dusted, not a statue which had not had its original beauty restored. The temple was ready to welcome its master.

Sabni had spent the night meditating; he understood neither the Elder's choice nor Isis's approbation. The Head of a community should be a sober man, serene, distanced from any passions, attentive to the divine word, detached from himself. To guide a community whose members were older and more experienced than himself seemed an impossible task. Therefore, he experienced extreme anxiety in the hours that preceded the ritual of the entry into the temple. Two Elders came to remove him from the cell where he had been locked in. They led him to the northern part of the covered gallery, between two obelisks, facing the first pylon, whose massive walls rose about twenty metres high. Some steps led up to the closed door; it opened slowly, as the priest conducting the ritual announced in a powerful voice the coming of the new leader recognized by the community. Before taking the path of transformations, Sabni observed the towering figure of the

Pharaoh: brandishing the white club, the sovereign crushed the skulls of his enemies, visible and invisible, re-established order out of chaos and enlightened the forces issued from darkness.

From that moment onwards, the world outside the temple ceased to exist. Gone was Christianity, the Byzantine invader, the occupation army. Only the sacred island subsisted, preserved from misfortune and destruction.

On the plinth, pot-bellied figures with sagging breasts symbolozed the fertilizing powers of the Nile and lovely young women represented the provinces, laden with an abundance of foodstuffs to be offered to the divinities.

Obeying the order of the ritualist, Sabni stood still by the large pillar, between the broad towers where goddesses incarnated, nurturers of the newborn sun. An unknown energy penetrated the body of the postulant; from the stones a new benevolent light radiated.

A man with a jackal head came towards Sabni; carrier of the mask of Anubis, the one who opens paths, the priest guided the adept to the second pillar. The axis of the temple was revealed. The monumental doors moved a fraction, offering a glimpse of a spiral form, the matrix of the temple, which was drawn upwards towards the imperishable stars, to the north of the universe.

Sabni crossed the courtyard bordered to the west by the ambulatory of the birthing room; at the top of the capitals was a smiling Hathor. The sculptor had carved her face in different expressions: happiness, joy, pleasure, tenderness, creating a melody in animated stone. Engraved on the face of the second pillar, the Pharaoh asserted his presence once again; he triumphed over the powers of the nether regions for all eternity. The priest with a jackal head was replaced by his brother with a falcon mask; from now on Horus guided Sabni's steps.

Once through the door, having gone past the large rock sculpted in the shape of a stele on which Ptolomy VI listed donations to the temple, the future Head of the community discovered a room with ten columns. Palm tree green sprouted from the capitals, bluish vegetable stems linked the silvery gold of the floor to the ceiling covered with open-winged vultures. Multicoloured ribbons held together flower bouquets and bunches of red and yellow papyri, giving a certain rhythm to the scenes of offerings to the gods. Those columns, alive with rising tree sap and covered with gold leaf, brought to life the ritual celebrated by the hieroglyphs, whose radiating energy dated from primordial eras when the gods were alive, evoked in the annals of the temple. Sabni saw the Elder. He managed to stand without his walking stick and presented the young man with a loincloth similar to those worn by the kings of Egypt when they celebrated rituals in places of worship.

'Take off your linen robe; thanks to this garment your function will become apparent to all.'

Horus and Anubis stood one on each side of Sabni. They purified his naked body by sprinkling it with fresh water, then the Elder draped the great linen cloth around the High Priest's loins and folded the pleated extremity on to itself to form a prominent tongue which allowed the robe to be fastened. The cloth, passed between the legs and wrapped three times around the body, was held by a leather belt. The hand of the Elder had not trembled.

Sabni felt that it was the end of his carefree youth; this simple loincloth made him a part of an uninterrupted lineage of leaders of the community.

'You will subdue the infidel. Their race will be humbled, their children sacrificed and their women will become sterile, the statues of the gods will be set upright. The country will laugh again, thanks to the sovereign born of the sun. We will see the end of our misfortune; our land, the nurturer, will give sustenance to those who love life. The dead will resurrect to take part in the joy regained. Go, Sabni, and fulfil this destiny for us.'

The Elder removed the two locks that closed the door to the sacred throne. The mysterious place where the divine power

39

was concentrated was immersed in darkness. A few rays of light came from high window slits.

The god Thoth, with an ibis head, and Sechat, the sovereign of the House of Life, wearing a panther skin, took the High Priest by the hand. They made him go through the ambulatory which gave access to the vestment room, the treasure rooms, the purification chamber and the offerings chamber. Then they escorted Sabni to the Holy of Holies, normally barred, bolted and secured by two locks. Thoth spoke:

'The height of the temple is in consonance with wisdom, its width is in accordance with the law of numbers and its proportions respect the harmony which is above. Become the foundation stone of this edifice, penetrate the mystery.'

The divinities vanished, and silence enveloped the sanctuary.

Sabni pulled the bolts and, laying them on the floor, pushed open the last door.

A light blinded him: the granite shone with a silvery glow that mingled with the gold embellishment of the naos.* At the top of the monolith, sacred cobras spat out protective flames; on the plinth, the Pharaoh held up the great vault of the heavens.

When the awe subsided, he saw her. Dressed in a white, clinging tunic, wearing a large gold necklace around her neck and a lapis-lazuli tiara in her hair, Isis stood on the corner of the naos; she released the gold catch which held the door of the shrine where the statue of the goddess kept watch, her eyes permanently open.

'I am Isis, the mother of God, the queen of the heavens, sovereign of the sacred land. I have brought life into existence through what my heart conceived, I have given birth to the gods, shown the way of the stars, regulated the course of the sun and the moon, taught humans the initiation to the

*The sanctuary or principal chamber of a Greek temple, containing the statue of the deity.

mysteries, chased the demons, abolished the laws of the tyrants, put in order what no folly will disrupt. My love has made the earth bloom, the wind blow softly, the heat warm gently and the Nile abundant. I bestow the gold of the sky and good fortune on whoever worships me. Be the guardian of these riches, Sabni, High Priest of the community of Philae.'

Placing her hand in Sabni's, she led him out of the sanctuary. The young man was trembling. His life was no longer his, but he would live side by side with this almost unreal woman who was giving him her trust.

The community had assembled by the second large pillar; as soon as they saw the couple, they were acclaimed and their power recognized as legitimate. Then Sabni unfolded the papyrus containing the Law which governed everyone, poor or rich, noble or peasant.

Then Sabni read aloud: 'You who perform the rites and guard this temple, do not permit any impious individual to enter into it. No one can enter, if they are not righteous. May the offerings be taken to the gods, so that this land is blessed with peace and happiness forever. You who follow the path of light and watch over this temple, where the Principle resides, may your souls be replenished, rejoice! Life is in God's hands, happiness is held in his fist. I will personally banish the garrulous and the violent ones, for the harmony of the community is our kingdom. Fraternal love is the only enduring monument. Let us go forth without fear in our hearts to meet the impending trials and if they become too heavy, let us increase our daily offerings.'

Facing Sabni, the Elder welcomed him.

'You who are now our leader, take every opportunity of acting with justice so that your conduct is beyond reproach. Great and powerful is the Rule. It has not been disturbed since the time Osiris; when the end comes, the Rule will endure.'

8

Sabni lay down on the warm stones near a pool of fresh water and under the cool shade of a date tree. At the end of his initiation and after the discovery of the closed temple where he would henceforth celebrate the cult with Isis, Philae's newly appointed High Priest was overcome by a great lassitude. The Elder had been mistaken: he was not worthy of guiding the community. He drew up his loincloth, feeling that somehow this gesture lent him an authority, which he did not possess. Surely his predecessors had felt great exaltation during the ceremony, and not this enormous weight that seemed to paralyse him.

A warm and perfumed liquid spread over his chest. Opening his eyes, Sabni saw Isis. She held a flask tinted with yellow, with a long dark green neck, and poured a small trickle of amber-coloured liquid, smelling of jasmine. The young man surrendered to the pleasurable sensation, which relaxed his muscles and soothed his tiredness.

'This is the last recipe that our brother, the perfumer, perfected just before he died. He took the formula with him to the land of silence.'

Sabni wished that the balm would continue flowing and soothing him for ever; his skin absorbed it avidly, trying to retain the fragrance that streamed over his body. Dusk was falling. Sabni could not take his eyes off Isis, whose face mingled with the soft light of the sunset; it had been a while since she put down the perfume flask and its top in the shape of a palm leaf.

'Let's go in,' she said. 'I must show you the text of the founding of the temple.'

They sat in a small room situated behind the eastern plinth of the first large pylon, by the side of the library. That was where the archives were kept, on papyri and leather rolls. Isis poured sesame oil into the reservoir of a terracotta lamp, verified that the airing vent was not obstructed and pulled the woven linen wick out. She lit it. Sabni held the handle and illumined a yellowing papyrus that the High Priestess took out of a long chest resting on lion feet. She unrolled it carefully.

'Here is Philae's birth charter, signed by Imhotep.'

'The creator of the step pyramid?'

Isis nodded.

Incredulous, Sabni read the short document, written in the perfect hand of a scribe living in the time of the Old Kingdom. It proclaimed the sacred character of the island, the place where the first royal couple had come together. Isis and Osiris had revealed the laws that governed architecture, music and agriculture to the people who lived on the banks of the Nile. Imhoptep, a sage among sages, requested that his successors embellish Philae and that they celebrate the cult of the great goddess until the end of time.

Sabni kissed the papyrus.

'You are the High Priest of this community now. May you never betray the master mason.'

Isis put the treasure back in its case. When leaving the room of the archives, Sabni lingered over a relief sculpture that occupied the lower part of the wall. A grotesque and yet disquieting figure, with the head of a monkey, wearing a striped bonnet. He had two almond eyes framing a thick nose, a mouth open to reveal teeth carved into a sharp triangle, a bearded chin, muscled torso, huge sexual organ.

'What's this monster?'

'A Blemmye.'

'An imaginary being?'

'A member of a black tribe that lives in the inaccessible territories in the great South, beyond the cataract. These dark-skinned people hate the Christians. They worship the god, who has a chapel in our temple. His favourite offering is the fruity wine of Nubia, which they brought in great wineskins. Before we were born, with my father's permission, they valiantly fought the Roman armies to come and worship their deity. They are very attached to the sacred character of the island of Biga, where Osiris rests, because by the side of Osiris lies Mandulis, their celestial master, the lord of the secret sanctuary of living souls, and the brave lion who protects them from infidels. The fortification of the frontiers ruined their plan for the liberation of the province.'

'Are they really this ugly?'

'This is a caricature, made by one of our sculptors who was wounded by a Blemmye archer. Fierce warriors, in the heat of the battle, they no longer distinguished between allies and enemies; perhaps their race is extinct.'

'Are you sure?'

'It's no use dreaming, Sabni. We can only rely on ourselves, we are on our own.'

The High Priest knelt down to examine the barbaric features, synonymous with hope.

'Beyond the fourth cataract . . . the roads are unknown. As High Priest, you have to devote yourself to the defence of the sacred body of the community; to abandon Philae and risk your life is forbidden to you. Forget the idea of this wild adventure.'

None of the brothers were young enough to tread African routes and surmount four cataracts. Feeling frustrated, Sabni surrendered to reason; the idea of a Blemmye ally vanished as quickly as it had come.

'You should sleep. At dawn, you will direct your first ritual.'

'I would love . . .'

She put a finger on her lips.

'It is time to be silent.'

Isis vanished into the night, a white apparition whose luminous trace lingered in the darkness. Sabni wished that she had stayed longer, he wanted to tell her all about his distress, he needed a reassuring presence. But she retreated into a haughty solitude, more inaccessible than a fortress, leaving him, the High Priest, and her, the High Priestess, strangers to one another, prisoners of their office. Their position was truly ephemeral. The bishop could do away with it just by waving his staff. How much longer was Isis going to pretend that Philae could survive? Sabni hated himself for having these miserable thoughts. He would only attract the disdain of the one he loved so inadequately. Added to his anxiety, he now felt a cowardly discouragement, due to his wavering and indecisiveness. He, a High Priest . . . what a charade! Nevertheless, he had taken his vows before Imhotep. That oath had bound him to a task beyond his strength and shackled him to a duty with chains that no amount of will could shatter. Sabni was no longer free to live as he pleased, to give in to his impulses. Given that he no longer had a choice, he wondered if he would ever experience the serenity of those who are enlightened, because they no longer have any outward expectations.

A piercing scream broke the peaceful silence of the island. It came from the west bank, near Hadrian's portico. There were no fortified walls at that point. Sabni hurried. He heard a cry for help.

The moonlight revealed a horrible scene: a dishevelled man was violently punching a weaver. The woman's face was covered in blood. Suddenly, she stopped wailing. Her assailant was pulling her by the hair, when Sabni forced him to let go.

The maniac smelt terrible; he had vermin running all over his skin, covered in red patchy scabs. The High Priest recognized one of the friars who had been imprisoned in the Egyptian tombs after having desecrated religious images and

45

set fire to the chapels. Several members of the community ran to the scene, torch in hand. The toothless wretch tried to bite Sabni, who had no trouble pushing him away.

'Kill him!' shouted one of the sisters.

The aggressor had attacked Philae single-handed; he had rushed down along the bank to his raft made of wooden branches and palms.

'You are all going to die,' he prophesied, 'all of you!'

9

At dawn, Isis and Sabni entered the closed temple to awake the great goddess who resided in the heart of the sacred shrine. The High Priest lifted his hands in adoration; Isis stood behind him and energized the back of his neck.

'Hail, oh Winged Disk,' exclaimed the High Priest. 'You who are born of the primordial ocean, creator of gods and father of men, unique being whose form remains a mystery, sculptor whom no one has ever portrayed. You who travel throughout eternity and bring joy to the whole world: for You each day is but a moment.'

The High Priest pulled the bolt, thus symbolically removing the finger of Seth, master of the tempest and of the power that had to be contained by the rite. He had to heal Horus's eye by opening the dark abode from which the light of the goddess emanated.

'I see your secret,' exclaimed the High Priestess. 'For you I unite heaven and earth.'

Neither Isis nor Sabni could stop thinking about their sister who had been seriously injured. The High Priest had refused to let the community lynch the friar, who in the end had run away shrieking abominations.

Sabni made an offering to the goddess's soul, a modest round bread. Altars covered in victuals were now a thing of the past, as were the processions carrying fresh meat, sweet-smelling and vivid-coloured vegetables, and vessels full of wine. The abundance of days gone by gave way to the recital of texts inscribed on the walls. Animated by the power of words, the hieroglyphs became gold and silver, animated with fatted oxen and incense vapours.

Isis took the statuette out of the naos and exposed it to the light of a lamp. After having crossed the nether regions of the earth, the power would materialize in the stone, where the energy that was indispensable to the temple would be stored. It would circulate on its reliefs, on the engraved signs, and would animate them with an eternal life energy.

The High Priestess perfumed the effigy of Isis, nourished by the subtle reality of the offering, then closed the doors of the naos once again.

Isis and Sabni left the venerable shrine, walking backwards, bowing to the divine presence before greeting one another. The High Priest, who had performed the age-old daily movements taught by the first pharaohs, took the hand of the young woman. He wanted to share with her the emotion of his first ritual. Their fingers intertwined, hesitant at first. Sabni wanted to speak, but Isis bade him to be silent. Together they went through the room with painted columns and passed the door of the second large portal. A bright sun invaded the inner courtyard enclosed by the first portal.

'The first column on your right is damaged, you should restore it.'

Sabni agreed enthusiastically. He had a proven talent for drawing and painting.

'I will gather the sisters at the Nectanebo pavilion,' Isis announced. 'We should examine the texts relating to the return of the distant goddess; we have been neglecting this myth for far too long.'

Surrounded by women who had devoted their lives to the temple, Isis co-ordinated the work. The reader suggested a few sentences from the story, each sister gave her interpretation, the High Priestess corrected and guided. Just before their noon meal, Isis realized that there had not been a novice for a very long time in the sorority. The Bishop had forbidden young girls to leave their family for a period of probation at the temple. The minimum age among the sisters was now over fifty. The masculine brotherhood was not any different, it had also suffered because of the same ecclesiastical law which condemned Philae to oblivion through a dearth of new adepts. The only woman of childbearing age was Isis. But her station forbade it; her family, her children, were the community.

One of the sisters stood up and pointed towards the blue water.

'There, look, a boat!'

Frightened, she gripped the arm of the High Priestess, who gently pushed her away.

'Go back to your houses.'

'But what about you?'

Isis's smile was like an order; the sisters dispersed, the stronger ones sustaining the invalids. The High Priestess went to the end of the pier.

The vessel with a white sail was already quite close to the island, carrying around twenty soldiers. At the prow, draped in a red tunic embroidered with gold thread, stood the Prefect Maximin, his eyes scanning Philae. Soon, his eyes met those of Isis. Neither one showed signs of weakness. When the boat drew up alongside the quay, a youthful soldier threw a rope, which the young woman grasped firmly.

'This island is sacred territory. No non-believer can set foot here without my permission.'

Maximin tried to leave the deck and Isis barred his way. Despite the sweetness of her face, the High Priestess looked fierce and determined. She would fight no matter what, even knowing she was already defeated.

'Philae is Empire territory. I am the Prefect Maximin, sent by the Emperor.'

'If you wish to pay homage to the great goddess, she will welcome you; come alone and unarmed.'

The soldiers stood still, waiting for their orders. Hitting a woman would not enhance the dignity of a high commissioner.

'I accept.'

Isis tied the rope to a mooring picket, then helped the Prefect climb over the parapet. The contact of Isis's arm, soft as silk, troubled him.

'Welcome to Philae, here you will enjoy peace of the heart. Do not raise your voice. The goddess loves tranquillity.'

Isis herself took his sword out of its scabbard and put it on the floor. The Prefect just watched, mesmerized by the vision of the great colonnade that dominated the river and led to the first massive pylon.

The serenity and nobility of the place bewitched him: he could feel the pulsating vibration of a living entity hidden in the stone. Discovering the ritual scenes interrupted by windows with a view of the water and the rocks, he was moved by the magnificence of those ancient figures representing the power of the Egyptian pharaohs, masters of the greatest empire in the world. For a moment, he thought they would come to life, leave the wall and reclaim their lost kingdom.

As Maximin touched the sculptures he felt the energy of the stone. He unwittingly became an accomplice of the king immortalized by the sculptor. How would he have served such a sovereign, how would he have administrated the provinces and their abundant riches? The truth about the time he lived in suddenly struck him violently: he lived in mediocre times, with no genius; the grandeur he had always dreamed about was here in this imprisoned island.

'Would you allow me to visit the rooms of the temple?'

Isis opened the door of the main entrance portal. In the inner courtyard were assembled the brothers and sisters; Maximin looked at these men and women of another age who were hostile to the expansion of the Christian faith. Why did they not run away, and return to their families after accepting to convert to the new faith? He felt like shouting at them the truth about the ruthless world outside this protected enclave, a world rigid with intolerance. But he did not utter a word. The dignity of his consenting victims, their noble serenity disoriented him. They had engendered a universe that was autonomous, immune to the one that they rejected. What if they were right, if the temple's existence were to prove essential, more crucial than that of the Empire?

The Prefect suddenly felt faint. He climbed the steps leading to the second large portal, half open, and leant against the wall. An acrid sweat dripped down his forehead into his eyes.

'This temple must be destroyed. It violates the law.'

Isis, standing at the centre of the courtyard, just smiled. The power that Maximin thought he possessed was crumbling at his feet.

He felt bereft of strength, drained of all his aggression, almost docile. The magic of Philae, the enchantment of the great goddess . . . only madmen would have given credit to these superstitions. Yet he was bowing before a woman he could just strike down with the back of his hand.

To escape her, he forced his entry into the inner temple. Kneeling before a column, a young man with a noble forehead was adding touches of colour to worn motifs. On a palette carved with small indentations he had mixed chalk with gypsum to obtain a brilliant white. Azurite provided a deep long-lasting blue. The artisan was restoring the crown of a goddess, after having readjusted the gold-headed pegs that upheld a gold plaque covered in hieroglyphs.

Maximin took a few steps towards the inside of the room filled with painted columns, and was overwhelmed by the myriad colours everywhere. Every inch of the walls and columns was covered in a wonderful panoply of deities, protective ganii and scenes of offerings made to the gods. The temple spoke and taught through these images. The painter's lively palette animated even the smallest detail. No Greek, Roman or Byzantine artist had acquired such absolute mastery.

'You must leave this place,' said Sabni, 'it is not open to lay or profane people.'

Maximin ought to have punished such impudence, but he

51

Christian Jacq

just obeyed. Retracing his steps, he stopped before Isis and looked at her for a long time.

When the Prefect boarded the vessel, the soldiers thought he looked strange. Pale and trembling, Maximin uttered orders to sail: the invasion of Elephantine would not take place.

10

Up before dawn, Bishop Theodore reread the report sent to him by a soldier who was a member of Maximin's escort on his visit to Philae. His mission was to spy on the Prefect, to observe his manner and what happened around him. From what Theodore was reading, it looked as if Maximin had taken leave of his senses. On his return from Philae, he had locked himself in his room in the vast official mansion assigned to him. Disoriented, his escort returned to the barracks. Already rumours were spreading that the Prefect, bewitched by Isis's followers, had gone mad and was preparing to wage war against the Christians. Everyone remembered the wave of persecutions that had decimated whole villages. Hermits would soon be rallying the faithful on the mountains; they would go so far as to form militias armed with pitchforks and pickaxes that the Bishop's troops would have to fight. A civil war among Christians . . .

Theodore was wary of the arrival of this Prefect who ignored the realities of the South, but had not expected his behaviour to become so disastrous so quickly. What a victory for Philae! Because of Maximin, the island emerged from the silence in which the Bishop had so successfully held it hostage. It rose once more as a danger that must be suppressed as quickly as possible. How would he manage to contain the anger of his fellow Christians and save Sabni? All things considered, Theodore felt he must visit the Prefect.

Contemplating the silver hues of the Nile in the first hours of the morning and the cliffs that became tinted with the orange red of the early sun when they awoke from the night, Theodore understood how much he loved this land.

None of the followers of Isis responded to this beauty with as much fervour as he, the servant of God, who was incarnate both in the solitude of the desert and in the luxuriance of vegetation. A God who forged both hell and heaven in the same landscape, who delineated every path, the way of hope and of repentance. Philae, the last heresy, the last bastion that resisted the wave of Christianity which spread over the world, had to survive as a symbol of a vanquished pagan faith and a token of the Lord's mercy. The ignorant of yesterday would be the believers of tomorrow.

The moment the Bishop went through the gate and entered the garden that surrounded the Prefect's villa, one of his couriers caught up with him and delivered a yellowing papyrus fragment. Theodore recognized the seal of the temple. Before deciphering it, he had to speak with Maximin.

According to his servants, he was still asleep. Nobody dared interfere when the Bishop pushed the door of the bedroom. Maximin was lying on a low bed, staring fixedly at the ceiling decorated with interlaced vegetal motifs. For a moment, Theodore thought he was dead; but no, the Prefect was breathing.

'It's you, Monsignor . . . At such a late hour . . .'

'On the contrary, it's very early. I had to see you.'

'Philae . . .'

'Yes, of course, Philae.'

'The temple must be saved.'

'Are you really bewitched?'

The Prefect sat up and looked at the Bishop, with feverish eyes.

'Have you ever been in love?'

'Marriage is not forbidden to me, but I have other concerns. What love could compare with the love of God?'

For the Love of Philae

'The love of a woman.'

'Isis?'

'You have never seen her, Monsignor . . . You have not desired her mouth, her breasts, her body . . . You have not felt her smile as a calling to experience supreme ecstasy, her presence fills one with overwhelming joy and happiness. She bears the same name as the goddess. What if . . .'

'You are delirious.'

Maximin stood up.

'That is what true love is like . . . a delirium that leads to transcending oneself, a fire that burns so that one can be reborn. I thought I knew women, Bishop. I have seduced dozens, of all ages and races . . . But, this one! I am like a child before her. Not a gentle infant, but a capricious youth, burning with desire.'

'The trip exhausted you. The sun is dangerous at this time of the year.'

Maximin ate a few dates and helped himself to a glass of milk.

'Don't take me for a madman. I am still a statesman.'

The Bishop breathed a sigh of relief. Maximin would not give in to his passion.

'What characterizes a statesman,' continued the Prefect, 'is the capacity to change his mind at the right moment. I wanted to close down the temple of Philae; I had forgotten Isis.'

'How do you intend to proceed?'

'Let us re-establish the privileges of the island.'

'That would be a dramatic error. The Christians would not stand for it.'

The Prefect turned to face the Bishop.

'Is that a threat?'

'If you want to save Philae, make sure that its existence is forgotten.'

Maximin smiled in a strange way.

'That will be difficult.'

'Why?'

'Because Isis will be my spouse. And the spouse of a Prefect

55

has to have what she pleases! She will never abandon her temple; it must therefore be restored so that it regains its former glory.'

'Would you go against the Emperor's orders?'

'That is my business. The interview has come to an end.'

The message bearing the temple's seal announced Sabni's elevation to the rank of High Priest of Philae's community. Due to this investiture and the privileges attached to it, the new master of the island requested an audience with the Regent of Elephantine, Bishop Theodore. The text, written in hieroglyphs and in Demotic, superbly ignored Greek. Philae dealt on an equal footing with the established power, as if the temple had a legal status.

Sabni was becoming as mad as the prefect. His title had made him drunk with power; he obviously felt projected outside his time, into a mythic era that seemed more real than the present. Theodore suddenly felt trapped; to save his childhood friend was still a mandatory duty, but the difficulties and dangers loomed larger than ever. First, he must neutralize the Prefect, then bring Sabni back to his senses. After having acquiesced to the latter's request, the Bishop granted an audience to General Narses, a colossal man with a square face and a chin that sported a fine black beard. The rigid posture of the military man was accompanied by an imposing presence, despite the absence of his left arm, lost in hand-to-hand combat with an Egyptian who refused to yield up his farm to the army. Narses enjoyed an excellent reputation. The Emperor appreciated his rigour and loyalty, his soldiers worshipped him. His long career had never been tainted by failure. Opinionated, meticulous, he never became implicated in a situation without carefully studying it. Some would have judged his spirit rather narrow and his intelligence mediocre, but the Bishop had his own opinion.

Theodore remained seated at his desk. Narses, standing, kept his eyes slightly downcast.

'Are you enjoying being in Elephantine, General?'

'I am here to follow the orders of the Prefect, that is all.'

'Your stay may be longer than originally planned. Has he sent you a message?'

'We don't communicate much. He commands, I obey.'

'Is that how it is going to be with me?'

'You are responsible for the permanent military force. We are therefore duty bound to collaborate.'

'That is my intention; have a seat.'

'I prefer to stand.'

'A little wine?'

'Never.'

The Bishop stood up.

'Come, General. Let's go on to the terrace.'

Surrounded by high parapets, the flat roof of the Episcopal mansion overlooked the whole city. Narses, beside Theodore, contemplated Elephantine, the grouped white houses, acacia bushes, palm groves, fortified barracks and the high cliffs of the Nile. Although no emotion registered on the General's countenance, the Bishop could feel that he was moved. How could anyone remain indifferent to such a spectacular view? From that moment onwards, Narses felt he wanted to protect that province, that landscape painted with the colours of eternity and to spend his old age there in peaceful retreat. He, who had always been an itinerant soldier, felt that he had finally found peace.

'You are an honest man, General.'

'That is my reputation.'

'How do you evaluate the Prefect's attitude?'

'He is my superior.'

'Are you a good Christian?'

Narses replied haughtily: 'Do you doubt it?'

'Maximin's behaviour ought to shock you.'

'It is not up to me to venture an opinion.'

Narses consented to sit on a stone bench, under the shade of a climbing vine.

57

'You have too much experience, General, to neglect the genius of a place. Elephantine is very attached to the purity of its Christian faith.'

'And yet it tolerates a Jewish community and the existence of the last pagan temple.'

'I detest fanaticism. I believe in the conversion of hearts and work tirelessly to that end. Why not let the avatars of the past die a natural death? Time will act more efficiently than force; but we have to be careful not to fan the flame at the moment of its death.'

'Could you not warn the Prefect?'

'That would be a lack of respect for the hierarchy.'

'Did you know that he has fallen in love with Philae's High Priestess and that he intends to give back to the island the privileges that were legally withdrawn?'

The military man shuddered.

'You . . . Aren't you exaggerating?'

'To lie would be a sin, and to deny the truth would be equally wrong. If we don't intervene, we run the risk of witnessing the awakening of many passions.'

Narses lost his composure. This conversation was very disturbing. He did not like arguments and avoided diplomats. The Bishop's revelations were beyond the call of duty. To revolt against a superior was equivalent to high treason; to get involved in bloody conflicts with the population was repulsive.

'Let's hope that Maximin will recover some lucidity. We trust him, you and I. I will continue to take care of Philae. In a few days, I will grant an audience to the community's High Priest. You are the only person who knows that and I would like this information to remain confidential.'

Narses did not reply. That silence made him the Bishop's accomplice.

11

As Sabni had requested, the boat from Philae stopped mid-stream, halfway to the bank. The High Priest jumped on to a ship carrying some of the Bishop's soldiers. They took him to the entrance of the temple, the largest pharaonic building in Elephantine, now in ruins. The pillars were shattered, the drums of columns sawn off, fragments of carvings and sculptures strewn on the floor like the abandoned, dismembered parts of a gigantic body. The sanctuary of the lord of the cataract and of the water, carrier of floods, had been devastated first by the Romans, then by the Christians. According to the sorcerers, the place was haunted by ghosts armed with knives. Nobody was supposed to believe in those fables; and yet the ruins were deserted. No Egyptian would venture there. As for the Byzantine invaders, they had no taste for that sad past. Neither the Bishop nor Sabni feared the ghostly envoys of the Ram god. The first because he would confront them with Christ's cross, the second because he knew the right formulas to appease them. The two friends were certain that in this place they could enjoy the utmost privacy, away from any indiscreet eavesdropping. They sat side by side on the corner of a fallen naos made of pink granite.

'So, you have accepted the post of High Priest.'

'Yes, the elder asked me to and Isis approved.'

'How am I going to fight this new folly? Philae has had no

High Priest for the past twenty years! One would swear that you are trying to resuscitate the community.'

'That is my sole duly: to transmit the rites that our ancestors have handed down to us.'

Theodore picked up a fragment of granite and threw it into the distance.

'You are like that stone: incapable of moving at will, a slave of the hand that holds it. You are the useless principal of an army of old men at death's door; if your foolish letter had fallen into the hand of the Prefect, you would already be in prison.'

'My dignity as principal . . .'

'It is non-existent, Sabni! I am the only religious authority in this region.'

'You reign over the Christians, I rule over the Egyptians. No matter what their numbers are, nowadays we are equals. That is why I expect a favourable answer to my request.'

Relinquishing the idea of being able to jolt Sabni out of his dream, the Bishop listened to him in astonishment.

'Some parts of the temple are badly in need of restoration. For the ceilings, I need palm tree trunks which we will saw ourselves. Acacia and sycamore wood are essential for the doors; some Asian pines will be used for the restoration of the liturgical chests. I will also need about a hundred sandstone blocks. I will give you the dimensions of those.'

It was Sabni's turn to pick up a piece of granite from the floor.

'Was your church not built on a rock?'

Deep lines carved the Bishop's face.

'Why are you provoking me?'

'I made an official request.'

'Did you think for one second that I would grant it?'

'I won't give up. I will persuade you.'

'Wood and stone are rare materials, very expensive ones, reserved for the army and for official buildings only. I am accountable for them to the Prefect.'

'The temple belongs to the Goddess; it is only to Her that we, both you and I, are accountable after our journey on this earth. Her abode must be the most beautiful, the richest; no material is too precious to honour her.'

'God does not inhabit a temple, Sabni. He inhabited man so that man could become God: "Nor is it I who really lives. It is Christ who lives in me."'

'What vanity! The adoration of the individual is a supreme betrayal of Christianity. He is not divine, Theodore. Neither you nor I exist in the image of God; only the temple, built according to the Rule, is the symbol of the Divine Principle.'

'You have enclosed God in the temple, I have set him free. You confined him to a handful of initiates, I have revealed him to all men.'

'By espousing the mediocre and the masses, by ignoring people's efforts to transcend themselves, you conquer like a warlord.'

'The individual must show his weakness, wrote Paul, so that the strength of Christ may descend upon him.'

'Paul . . . It is because of him that your religion has become full of fanaticism and dogma. There is nothing worse than converted oppressors.'

'Your criticism is sterile. The One who was sent to this world was a stranger to it before His birth. He became man without ceasing to be God. From her entrails, like a star plucked from heaven, Mary gave birth to Him in divine gestation. A new light was born, there is no denying it.'

'Mary is the daughter of Isis, who tomorrow or in two thousand years will once again guide the world towards faith without dogma.'

'Thanks to some initiates without a future?'

'Remember the Scriptures: just one will suffice.'

'Isis, the goddess, is dead. Your last believers will disappear.'

'Is this the famous tolerance that you preach?'

'I want to save you and your community, not the funereal

ideas that poison your spirit. When you are delivered, the real faith will enlighten your hearts.'

'That faith has sown blood and tears. Byzantium is as cruel as Rome. In the time of the pharaohs, Egypt was beautiful, rich and happy. From the peasant to the King, everyone lived in communion with the sacred Principle, the credulous through an intermediary statue, the wise through contemplation of a hidden light in the temple. Look at my country, Theodore, just take a good close look at our country . . . miserable, exploited, ruined! The canals are no longer drained, the fields are no longer irrigated, the rich are like wild beasts, violence triumphs, the villages are dirty and full of vermin, corruption has dethroned law. Where is the potter god who, with his robust arms, inundated Egypt with victuals? Remember our Rule: give bread to the hungry, clothe the naked, provide a barge to whoever cannot cross the river, a coffin to the one who does not have a son to make it. Today, men mistake ignorance for wisdom and regard what is harmful as useful. They live off death, they gorge on it daily. Are you satisfied, do you give thanks to your God?'

'Creation is imperfect.'

'Humanity soils it. The Pharaoh created heaven and earth, with ceaseless toil; by making each man believe that he carries God within, you drive the world towards the worst kind of conflict.'

'Christ teaches us to love our brothers, you are forgetting that.'

'The Greeks are satisfied with beautiful words. Egypt demanded action, beings who desired to fashion themselves by cutting stone and wood. To close the temples is to make the most vital spring dry up.'

'Could it be that pagan Egypt is the mother of the world?'

'If you were not convinced of that, would you still remain here?'

The Bishop looked at the landscape around him. On the horizon, he could see the heap of boulders that formed the cataract. The temple of Knum still breathed out its sanctity; a breath, so tenuous that it was barely perceptible, drifted among the sculpted capitals and dislocated columns.

'Why don't you destroy Philae, Theodore?'

'Because you are my friend.'

'Isn't there another reason . . . Could it be that you are trying to preserve the last vestiges of your past?'

The Bishop held his face in his hands.

'That procession . . . and now the title of high Priest, the dangerous activity you want to undertake . . . why are you making my task so difficult?'

'To make you choose.'

'Sabni, you must know when to stop, before it is too late. Maximin's army is not a mirage. I am forced to obey it.'

'I trust you. You obey no one but yourself. Will you grant me the stones and the wood that I need?'

'No. Let Philae fall in ruins, that will be my greatest joy.'

'We will be seeing each other soon, Theodore.'

Sabni distanced himself with a calm and assured step. The Elder had not been mistaken: the young man had indeed the stature of a High Priest.

12

The month of May was coming to an end. It was harvest time, and the peasants threshed and gathered under a baking sun. A question haunted their spirits: just what would be the quality of the next flood? Would the bishop be able to attract the favours of the spirit of the river and master it, as had the pharaohs and the high priests of Isis? From conversations in the street Theodore was conscious that he was the cause of widespread anxiety. People had their supper quite late, chatted outside by their doorways, taking in the fresh night air. But games and jokes dwindled as the decisive moment approached, the time that would decide the destiny of an entire people during the coming year: would there be prosperity or famine? Unease grew. Here and there fights broke out, brutally repressed by the soldiers. Many could not sleep. Mad men crossed the villages predicting terrible calamities. The astrologers, whose art had been condemned by the Church, kept quiet.

Maximin invited the authorities of the province to a banquet worthy of the most sumptuous receptions held in Alexandria. There was not a deacon, a high-ranking officer, a rich land-owner who failed to respond to the invitation. To make such an ostentatious act of allegiance was a clever way of ensuring that his privileges were consolidated and also of coveting further riches or favours. Theodore admired Maximin's ability; he knew each person's career and gratified his guests

For the Love of Philae

by addressing appropriate personal comments to each one. In less than three weeks, he had studied the Bishop's archives. Those who had bet on his rapid decline were disappointed. During his periods of isolation, the Prefect had learned all there was to know about the local upper classes.

Wine and beer were served in abundance. Dozens of varieties of fish and meat were presented to the guests, who also gorged on fruits and sweet pastries. When dawn was about to break, Maximin asked the Bishop to follow him into his office.

'You have drunk nothing, Monsignor.'

'My station requires that I stay sober, yours does not. And yet you have not tasted those excellent vintages.'

'The time for pleasure will come later.'

The vast room where the Prefect worked rather closely resembled, in its layout, the one Theodore occupied.

'I have admired your sense of administration, Monsignor. To tell the truth I have never seen better. You will forgive me for imitating you.'

'I feel honoured.'

'Such rigour is sometimes a disadvantage.'

'How so?'

'I quickly observed that all the notables of the region are under your influence. At least half the land belongs to you.'

'To my church,' rectified Theodore.

'Your policy of buying land is developing at an accelerated pace, you feed and clothe the soldiers posted in Elephantine. Anyone who dared attack or oppose you would be eliminated very quickly.'

'Why would anyone attack a man of God? I love this province. My aim is to make it prosper, is that such a fault?'

'Having just finished a first audit of your accounts, I have no reason to reproach you. You are more competent than the Emperor's treasurer. In Byzantium you would be a minister; you probably have the stuff of a future Patriarch of Alexandria. But there is a trait of conduct that I disapprove of.'

65

'Which one?'

'Why do you persecute Philae?'

Theodore clutched his cross in his right hand.

'A ban on the delivery of linen, refusal to provide wood and stone to restore the building . . . I have read your decrees.'

'They are not confidential. The bearers of news proclaim them in public places.'

'You are submitting that community to a veritable torture.'

'Those reproaches are surprising. Do I have to remind you that they are pagans?'

The Prefect began nervously pacing up and down the room.

'I have been forced to support your decisions.'

'You don't have a choice. They correspond to the Emperor's wishes.'

'But not to mine.'

Theodore did not hide his indignation.

'Is that really you, the faithful servant of the Empire, expressing himself like this?'

'There is a fact that astonishes me: you do not close that temple, whereas you could order a quick and definitive evacuation of the place. There is, therefore, something restraining your animosity. As for me, I wish to obtain Isis's favours. As we are accomplices in this, let us save time and find a satisfactory solution for both of us.'

Theodore spent the night at his desk, unable to sleep. He classified some documents, studied the city's budget for the months to come, verified the list of his lands and prayed to God.

The names of the heavily indebted were underlined in red ink. Once again, he would resort to soldiers to recover the missing funds. That the Prefect examined his administration did not bother the Bishop, who, by temperament and because he expected that kind of inspection, had made a habit of concealing nothing. The whole of his business was carried out within a legal framework whose resources he made use of with extreme skill. The danger was elsewhere: Maximin was losing his mind. His folly seemed all the more dangerous because it was profound, he looked like someone who was totally in control and master of his actions. And yet his obsession with Isis was so total that it went as far as making him betray his duties to the Emperor. Such absurd passion was bound to fail. A passion which rendered Maximin as uncontrollable as a straw in the wind. Because of the love he felt, Philae was becoming an object of conflict. The temple that Theodore had managed to plunge into a protective shadow, almost into oblivion, now emerged into the forefront of events.

Maximin was now nothing but an adolescent ready to be taken over by his emotions. His feelings for the High Priestess cancelled out his past. Isis, so beautiful, so attractive, so full of the magic of the goddess that she worshipped! The Bishop understood his bewitchment. The danger was that he might arouse the anger of the Christians, which he, Theodore, would not be allowed to repress.

He no longer had any influence over Sabni. On becoming High Priest, his friend had changed. He took his duties seriously and harboured many illusions, dreaming of impossible exploits. Did Isis encourage suicidal acts or did she respect measure and silence, her strongest weapons? Theodore regretted never having met her. In their mutual solitude, a mute dialogue had occurred. At a distance, they perceived each other's intentions; but Sabni and Maximin spoilt the game.

Was Philae a part of himself? Was this pagan temple the symbol of a faith that he could not pluck from his deepest self? These questions were senseless. By converting to Christianity, he had changed his life. Immersed in Christ, he devoted his life to the establishment of a solid and long-lasting doctrine that would keep even the most stubborn of men from error.

Theodore felt that there were many trials ahead. He did not fear them. He would deliver his friend from a tragic end, convert Philae without using violence and neutralize Maximin. God was on his side, and he would vanquish.

13

In the middle of the month of June, on a very hot day, the Nile changed its colour. The water became brown, and the flow of the river increased. It carried mud and silt. Agricultural work stopped. In Philae, Isis observed Sirius, the main star of the Dog Constellation, whose rise announced the start of the flood, said to be nourished by the sweat and the lymphatic glands issuing from the murdered body of Osiris. When his spouse cried and lamented his death, the marriage would once again be celebrated, this time in the heavens, and the land of Egypt would be inseminated.

The Bishop requisitioned an agricultural task force, farmhands, itinerant salesmen and artisans, to drain the canals and clean the irrigation basins where the excess water would be retained. In most provinces these difficult tasks were neglected, whereas in the time of the pharaohs this work would be carried out regularly, making of Egypt an immense oasis in the heart of the desert. More than half of the cultivated land had been lost; subject to taxes it no longer inspired devotion from the peasants ever more oppressed by a callous administration. Theodore fought this injustice in his own way. Certain parts of the region of Elephantine were like paradise on earth, the legacy of royal dynasties. Work and money were not enough; men badly needed to feel the enthusiasm of faith. Who, if not Christ Himself, could offer them that inner flame?

A week after the beginning of the rising of the water,

Theodore and Maximin went down the ninety steps of the Nilometer staircase. On the walls, the cubit graduation allowed them to measure the height of the flood. In that well made of stone, thanks to the carved inscriptions, one could tell the height of the water in previous years. Everyone knew the litany of these measurements by heart. Twelve cubits meant famine, thirteen equalled hunger, fourteen signified happiness, fifteen, the end of the people's worries and finally sixteen equalled perfect bliss. Theodore leant on the humid wall and consulted the opposite one and verified that the present mark was one cubit under the previous one. Past experience warranted prediction.

'What is your conclusion?' asked Maximin anxiously.

Doubtful, the Bishop redid his calculations.

'Tell me, please!'

'I keep getting preposterous results. I will come back tomorrow. The water will have risen by then.'

The following day, and the one after that, Theodore obtained the same results. Faced with the Prefect's insistence, he had to reveal his thoughts: one must expect the worst.

Everyone watched the river, hoping in vain for the majestic waters to overflow with great zest, mounting the banks and splaying over the fields, transforming the valley of the Nile into a lake from which would only emerge the villages built out of the rocks. People hoped that the spirit of the Nile would leap out of the water and assail the heavens, drown the rats and vermin, purify the water, deposit the silt and prepare for the sprouting of the wheat, the symbol of Osiris's rebirth.

But the level of the waters remained abnormally low. If the Bishop had not been mistaken, it would not reach eleven cubits; there would be a terrible famine. Theodore called a meeting of the Council. The Prefect joined the local dignitaries.

'Do we have grain reserves?'

'They are almost spent.'

'Due to lack of foresight?'

'The last floods have been mediocre. The Empire has imposed heavy taxes on us.'

'What about other foods?'

'Alexandria is bleeding us.'

The Prefect issued emergency measures. The army should be provided for first; come July, only the soldiers would eat their fill. The food supply for the province would be shared among the high-ranking officers, who would think mainly of their troops. The population was indignant. All they had left to eat were dried figs and stale bread.

On the last day of July, Maximin summoned the Bishop: all hope of a good flood was now lost. Children and old folk were dying in great numbers. The law-enforcing troops had had to suppress two attempted riots, one in a village near the cataract, the other in one of the suburbs of Elephantine. There had been around ten civilian casualties according to the soldiers, and about two hundred according to the populace.

Theodore noted that the Prefect's aids were as lazy as they were incompetent. This was not surprising, since the Bishop himself had recommended them. The surest way to isolate Maximin was to surround him with staff mediocre enough to give him the illusion of being the sole master of Elephantine. Anyone unfamiliar with the interior of the province would get lost in the bureaucratic maze of its administration. Byzantium had added so many laws to those enforced by Rome that only the Bishop could still find his way through this veritable labyrinth. Theodore inundated the Prefect's office with useless reports; the busier he was, the less preoccupied with Philae.

Beside Maximin was General Narses with his finely cropped black beard. The Bishop felt both men's hostility. He had not managed to throw them against one another, and now they would probably both turn against him. Theodore was the perfect scapegoat in the present untenable situation.

'The people are disgruntled, Monsignor.'

'The soldiers will take care of that.'

'Do we have a rebellion on our hands? Are we going to have to crush it?'

'The emperor would detest that kind of incident.'

'I will maintain order, but this catastrophic drought is demoralizing the troops under General Narses.'

The General acquiesced.

'There are rumours that Elephantine has been cursed.'

'Some of my men are very superstitious and lend an ear to the prophets of doom; rumour has it that the wrath of the ancient gods caused this famine.'

The Bishop looked at the two men with severity.

'Naturally, both of you reject such far-fetched tales.'

Neither the Prefect nor the General answered. Maximin broke the silence.

'A riot would compromise the mission that the Emperor assigned to me.'

'What do you suggest?'

'I have walked in the streets; the townspeople spoke to me. To chase away the evil spirits, let us ask Philae's High Priestess to help us. She knows the formulas that will make the waters rise: she must celebrate the ancient ritual.'

'Black magic is punishable with death,' objected Theodore. 'I have spent years and years trying to eliminate those wretched practices; are you saying you would dare to revive them, despising both divine and human laws?'

'These are exceptional circumstances,' replied the Prefect.

By giving Isis the opportunity to prove her powers and show that the traditional religion had survived, he counted on attracting her favours.

'Are you aware of the risks?'

Maximin softened his tone.

'How could a young, disarmed woman threaten public security? The people love superstition: her appearance will calm them. Afterwards she will return to the island.'

'You are underestimating the purity of Christian faith; it will not tolerate such an affront.'

'I am a Christian,' recalled Maximin. 'Isis will not convert anyone. Although she is a recluse, she still has a great deal of prestige. She will be our ally for one day, she will serve the cause of peace. We will announce to the Emperor that this region has totally surrendered.'

'You are mistaken. Isis will not make a pact with you; she will take advantage of what you are offering to proclaim that the goddess is all-powerful. The consequences . . .'

'Are you so uncertain of your flock's faith?'

'Weeds grow quickly.'

'We must close ranks.'

'I am not sure I can help you.'

Maximin frowned.

'It is not the man of the church I am addressing, but my subordinate. I would consider a refusal the equivalent of desertion.'

Narses put his hand on his sword. The Bishop knew he would not hesitate to use his weapon against him.

'Your fears are unfounded,' Theodore declared coldly.

14

Wearing a long white robe, Isis disembarked at the foot of Elephantine's tallest hill. General Narses and a squad of soldiers guaranteed her protection. The infantrymen had evicted about ten hermits who lived in nearby caves; incarcerated in the barracks, they would know nothing of the ritual celebrated by Philae's High Priestess. Isis had accepted the Prefect's proposal in exchange for some victuals. Several members of the community were wasting away; some no longer had the strength to work.

Before Isis's departure, a boat carrying vegetables, fruits and flowers had drawn alongside the bank at the temple; Sabni had taken charge of the unloading. While the brothers and sisters enjoyed their first substantial meal in a fortnight, the High Priestess left the island to face the unknown. She had opposed her father, who was certain that Maximin was laying a trap for her; but the Prefect had already kept his word by resuming the supply of foodstuffs to the island.

From the top of the hill, the view was grandiose. The river meandered slowly around the steep rocks. In the distance the city shone in green and white colours. At this time of year the lack of water produced dark patches in the fields; everywhere the desert was gaining ground.

'Splendid country,' said Maximin, his hands crossed behind his back, facing the horizon.

'The gods chose to live here,' replied Isis, standing beside him.

The infantrymen were standing well away and would neither hear nor see them. The Prefect did not dare look at the young woman whose mere presence set his blood on fire; the pain was both atrocious and delicious.

'The flood will be too weak, millions of people will die of hunger. There will be no harvest, the blades of wheat will dry up; already infants cry and old men are laid low. The area is teeming with vermin.'

'It is too late.'

'Do the tears of the goddess not bring about the flood?'

'We have let the right moment pass.'

'Is there a ritual that could remedy this?'

'Organize a procession, make offerings to the river of meat, cakes, fruits and female statuettes for it to inseminate. That was the essential ritual when the river started changing colour.'

'Is there nothing else we can do?'

'There is one other thing. Imhotep did it more than three thousand years ago when a terrible drought endangered his throne: go to the source of the Nile.'

'It's a legend,' cried Theodore. 'The source of the Nile is not in Elephantine!'

Maximin was not deterred.

'What our eyes observe is often illusory; Isis states that the power of the river is hidden in a grotto, near here. You obstructed the entrance.'

'That was an imperative measure. The pagans used to meet there every year, before the beginning of the flood, to celebrate satanic rites.'

'The High Priestess is willing to go there and pray to the genius of the Nile.'

'I refuse to be dragged into this masquerade.'

'Millions of lives are at stake. The very existence of your

province depends on the flood. Let Isis act; she holds keys that we no longer possess.'

'You are a Christian, and yet you speak thus!'

'This is an emergency, as you well know. Let us clear the entrance of that grotto.'

'A mouth to hell . . .'

'Now, no superstitions, Bishop.'

'Is this an order?'

'To be executed without delay.'

She was the High Priestess. He was the Bishop. She did not lower her eyes like a good Christian; Theodore forgot the sermon he had prepared.

There was no exchange between them, for they wanted to complete the task that brought them together, in a forced alliance, rapidly.

Where the grotto was located was a secret of State known only to a few. Situated on the extreme eastern point of the island and protected by a rocky spur, it had just one narrow entrance by which only a slender person could enter. Only Maximin, Theodore, Isis and a stone-cutter had taken the small forgotten path that led to it. They pushed away branches and weeds before coming to a small esplanade hidden by six-metre-tall papyrus plants. Isis guided her adversaries through a maze where even the most able of adventurers would have got lost. The sight of the sanctuary of the ram god, who liberated the flow of waters by raising his sandal, made Isis's heart leap with joy. This was the only place in Elephantine she knew; her father had brought her here thrice before the Bishop banned access to it.

Theodore ordered the stone-cutter to remove the blocks that he had piled up in order to hide the entrance. When it was clear, Maximin became impatient.

'Are you going in, Isis?'

'Not before the sign is given. One cannot address a god with human words.'

The stone-cutter sat down a little further away. The High
Priestess stretched her arm inside the grotto, and fetched out
two small vases. One contained water from the heavens, the
other water from the Nile. She put one on each side of the
entrance. The Bishop was feeling uncomfortable and kept
touching the cross he wore on his chest, as if ready to ward off
the devil who might appear at any moment.

'How long . . . ?'

'I don't know.'

A lengthy hour went by. Once his irritation had died down,
Maximin savoured the sweetness of the hour. He admired Isis;
she resembled Cleopatra, whose portrait hung in the dining-
room of the old Alexandrian families, but her face had greater
perfection and finer features. Her solar purity made her even
more desirable, and so unlike any other woman. To contemplate her was already like making love to her, with the
infinite respect of the most ardent of passions. Isis belonged to
him; she would be no one else's.

Theodore hoped that the event he feared so much would not
occur. Without a sign, the High Priestess would not enter the
grotto and the Church would not be humiliated. Isis was very
serene, her hope was becoming certitude. Not only would
Philae not be destroyed, but it would resume its original
function: to instruct adepts, initiate them in the mysteries and
transmit spiritual values. Under these circumstances why
should divine will not manifest? She was fighting a silent
battle, with no weapons, no apparent wounds; perhaps the
future of the temple of Philae was at stake here.

Isis and the Bishop defied each other openly for the first
time. They respected and feared each other. The beauty of the
young woman ravished Theodore. Inwardly, deep down, he
understood the Prefect's foolish impulses. The prelate became
conscious of her implacable will. She was a born leader. If
Sabni had the intelligence to listen to her, they would form a
couple capable of incredible feats, to the point of being a
menace to civil stability.

Isis was surprised to find such a powerful adversary, whose capacities were far more impressive than his reputation. As well as being a leader, he had the malleability of a politician allied to the formidable strength of a believer. An implacable enemy, he would behave with the dexterity of an experienced warrior, totally merciless.

'The sign,' said Isis calmly.

Maximin followed her eyes: on the grotto's soil, a viper undulated.

The High Priestess knelt and with a brisk movement caught the back of its head. Instinctively, the Prefect drew back. Brandishing the struggling creature, Isis stepped forward towards the entrance of the grotto; Theodore barred her way.

'I forbid you to use the symbol of the devil!'

'The serpent is not evil, he is born of the earth regenerated by the waters. I must take it to the genius of the Nile, alone, in silence and in respect for the hidden god.'

'The fish of Christ has vanquished the demon's reptile. This magic is illusory and dangerous. The Bishop of Elephantine will not let it pass and no satanic ritual will sully this city. Go back, all of you!'

Amazed at the Bishop's vehemence, the Prefect gave in.

Isis threw the viper into a papyrus bush.

'Block that accursed opening,' ordered the Bishop to the stone-cutter. 'May the memory of this place be lost for ever.'

The Bishop fell to his knees and, brandishing his cross, exorcised the pagan lair.

15

The wine harvest started at the end of the month of August. No song rang through the vineyards, usually so joyous. The country was preparing to face the consequences of the weakest flood of the last two hundred years. The Bishop would be forced to levy the quantities of wheat and barley demanded by the Empire. There would be nothing left for the inhabitants of the province, and the rodents spared by the meagre flood would then attack the agricultural products and the orchards.

What had happened at the site of the holy grotto, where the secret sources of the Nile were? For some, Isis had tried in vain to calm the wrath of the god; for others, Theodore had dried the flow of the water by murdering the spirit concealed in the river. Some thought that neither the High Priestess nor the Bishop had ever gone to the sacred place, the exact location being forgotten long ago. The office of the Prefect denied that Maximin had played any role in this tale invented by slanderous folk. As for the only witness, the stone-cutter, no one had ever seen him again in Elephantine. Only General Narses knew that the Bishop had exiled him to the oasis of Khargeh, from whence he would not return.

The Prefect, shut away in his house, hated himself. Why had he behaved like a coward, why had he disappointed Isis whose accusing eyes he could still feel, humiliating him? What did he really desire, he wondered? He felt lost, inconsistent. A new feeling invaded Maximin, over which he had no control whatsoever.

Used to leading men, he no longer commanded himself. His temples pounded continually, as if prey to a merciless insect that gave him no rest. His infatuation for Isis had ruined a career dedicated to public order and service of the State. With just a few glances, a self-contained attitude, so noble that nothing seemed to trouble her, yet so very provoking to Maximin, she had completely seduced him. Every hour that went by, her very absence, made her all the more indispensable yet even more unattainable. The Prefect was used to picking women like ripe fruit. The High Priestess had ripped his heart out, she had opened a gaping void where a tempest now raged. Uprooted, Maximin felt growing within him a stranger who, with a reckless joy, destroyed his old attitudes.

Occasionally the prefect managed to deal with his daily obligations. The Bishop plied him with detailed reports on the arable patches of land, the irrigation basins, the transportation of foodstuffs; each document specified the difficulties with a minutiae that was worthy of the most punctilious Alexandrian clerk. Distracted, Maximin's thoughts were quickly elsewhere, in a flash he would conjure up Isis's face. How could he make her notice him?

To occupy the island would be easy; but if he acted thus, he would lose her. He must find a way to marry her and make her love him.

More than half the farming land was left uncovered by the waters; it would be useless to sow on cracked soil. The peasants had started leaving their land and crowding into the suburbs of Elephantine. During a High Mass, the Bishop had implored the Lord to give his faithful followers the necessary strength to overcome adversity, and then he had distributed food in equal parts. Philae received its share, as if the temple were a simple village under administrative jurisdiction.

The vision of that country parched and burned by the sun, of the slopes with their ochre tints gliding into the Nile, a river too weak to rise and cover its banks, incited a grand project: to go forth and plunder Nubian gold. That would please the Emperor. He would give Isis a part of the precious metal, the flesh of divine statues. Philae would shine as it had in the past. Maximin had found his wedding gift.

He called Narses, ordered him to prepare the troops and assemble ships that could cross the cataracts.

The soldiers were thankful for an opportunity to break their idleness, and were almost immediately ready for war. But the General came up against the corporation of boatmen, which gave him only three vessels, all in a state of disrepair. The others belonged to the Bishop.

Furious, Maximin burst into the prelate's office. Theodore was busy trying to solve difficult irrigation problems.

'I demand that you give me all the vessels you have.'

'They are essential to the life of the city.'

'Do not oppose my will; I will cross the cataract.'

'The Nile is too shallow. You will fail.'

'I will cross it.'

'No boatman will agree to be your guide.'

'I will officially requisition them.'

The population gathered around the steep banks bordering the maze of rocks. The river, whipped up by gusts of wind, crashed violently against the rocks, dousing them in foam then baring their pointed edges, before receding to form unpredictable swirls. The Bishop had refused to attend the departure of the expedition; despite grave warnings, the Prefect had obstinately insisted on going ahead.

The soldiers were divided among the heavy, difficult to manoeuvre barges; the Prefect, after having examined the vessels at his disposal, had chosen this type of vessel because of its stability. At the prow, a boatman would test the water with a long pole.

As the first barge was launched into the water to face the cataract, cries of encouragement rose from the crowd.

Maximin's enthusiasm was proving contagious. Many now thought the exploit was possible, even if older people still considered the expedition folly. The Prefect and General Narses watched the scene from a hillock. The boatman, an experienced professional, managed to avoid a huge rock almost totally submerged in muddy water and side-tracked a whirlpool, but the barge found itself engulfed in a narrow channel, hitting a granite block. Narses's throat tightened. The pilot, manoeuvring with dexterity, went along with the increasingly violent current; when exiting a second channel, the river seemed more peaceful. Maximin began to believe he had won his bet.

The prowman relinquished his attention too soon. When he caught sight of the flat rock just beneath the surface, he no longer had time to warn the pilot. Letting out a scream, he dropped the pole and plunged sideways. The barge smashed into the obstacle, rebounded and capsized. Several soldiers were crushed, others drowned. The two barges that followed were abandoned by their pilots and met the same fate. Narses watched, helpless, at the death of his men. Maximin shut his eyes.

More than two hundred soldiers disappeared into the cataract's snares. These were experienced warriors, worthy members of the Roman legions at the height of the Roman Empire, heroes who had come through the worst battlefields unharmed. Brave men, coming from all four corners of the Empire, had stupidly perished in that rocky chaos.

Despite the loss of half of his army, Narses did not feel bitter about Elephantine. He was a zealous military officer and yet was becoming detached from his office. Little by little, he was drawn into meditation for ever longer periods, contemplating an overheated desert bareness where the noise of past battles was lost.

Narses's road stopped here. He had enlisted voluntarily at the age of twelve. Since then he had roamed the provinces of the Empire looking for glory. Destiny had generously fulfilled

81

his desire. This new campaign was designed to confirm his prestige with the Emperor, who was to have given him an honorary post in Byzantium in preparation for a golden old age. But Narses did not want to leave Elephantine; the capital's intrigues and opulence no longer interested him. The peace for which he had fought was to be found here in a desolate landscape where man was the intruder.

Maximin did not blame anyone for the disaster. Face to face with the General and the Bishop, he recognized his error. Refusing to linger over failure, he revealed his plans: to organize a new expedition as soon as possible.

'None of my men will leave barracks,' said Theodore. 'It is my duty to watch over the security of those in my diocese.'

After long hesitation, the Bishop tore up the report that he had intended to send to Byzantium denouncing the Prefect and his conduct. This strategy would engender Maximin's recall to Byzantium as well as a long enquiry by magistrates and military personnel. Theodore felt he should act alone and get rid of his adversaries without anyone's help.

'Your attitude does not surprise me, Monsignor. The General and I will bring back the gold from Nubia.'

'Don't even think about it,' advised Narses.

Amazed, Maximin turned towards his subordinate.

'How dare you?'

'I have the right to challenge your authority.'

'Only in cases of mental unbalance.'

Narses and the Bishop looked at each other. They were accomplices now. the Bishop ignored whatever reasons might have led to this unexpected reversal, which he would exploit without hesitation.

'Who would testify to such mental derangement?'

'Be careful, Bishop, one word from me and . . .'

'We will not go to Nubia,' said Narses firmly.

'You are delirious, General.'

'The cataract is impassable. We should be able to navigate ourselves through but we are not capable of doing so. I cannot let the other half of my army perish. Rather than that, I would appeal to the power of the judiciary to intervene.'

Maximin managed to contain his anger. 'The judiciary powers . . . in other words the Bishop!

'What do you suggest?'

'We shall wait, as long as is necessary.'

'But the gold . . .'

'The Emperor will understand. We are at the mercy of the Nile and its whims; write a report along those lines and I will countersign it.'

'Do not mention any loss of life', recommended the Bishop. 'I will also omit it. Elephantine is far from Byzantium . . . If strange rumours reach the Emperor, we will deny them. Those men died of ill health, officially: a year of poor floods, epidemics that reap havoc among the population . . .'

The Prefect hesitated. The proposition of the Bishop presented just one disadvantage: it forced Maximin to become his accomplice.

'What do you think, General?'

'The worthiest man can make a mistake. I am ready to forget the whole misadventure.'

'On what condition?'

'That I be appointed permanent chief of the Elephantine garrison.'

'You wish . . . to live here?'

'I have stated my desire. Now it's up to you to make the official request to the Emperor, with the Bishop's blessing.'

'I need to give it some thought.'

The General and the Bishop left the prefect's office. Maximin realized how little he knew about his fellow men. That was another illusion he would have to relinquish. Narses, that sombre man, cold as the snow on the mountains of Asia, that intransigent soldier so content to follow orders, had fallen in love! He had found his paradise and wished to sacrifice his career to it.

Luckily, Theodore and Narses were not plotting against Maximin; the General had been converted by this southern province. This miracle would serve the prefect's interests well. Narses would remain faithful to the status quo and protect both Philae and the Christians.

Theodore's sense of diplomacy filled him with relief.

The Bishop had no desire for open conflict. Even though Philae might prove a point of discord that did not mean that they could not find certain common ground. A man privileged enough to have God's attention should be able to reach an understanding with an emissary of the Empire.

The horizon was clearing. There was just one distressing question left: Maximin would not be able to offer Isis the Nubian gold.

16

Isis had learned to truly know each member of the community; she was able to assuage their doubts and encourage their hopes. Sometimes an attitude, a simple gesture, was enough to unravel a difficulty. Despite all this, the librarian's behaviour surprised her. This fifty-year-old plumpish woman had a very jolly temperament at times verging on the facetious. No pain would stay with her for long; living among ancient texts and caring for rolled papyrus documents, she had acquired a sturdy and debonair balance.

Each morning, Isis talked with her. For many months Isis had been studying the return of the distant goddess. According to the tradition, she would add her own formulas to the words previously used and wrote 'another way of saying' in the margin, to single out her own contributions. From the beginning, Egypt had never suppressed a perception of the absolute characteristic of a particular time. It refused to build on a definitive truth and preferred to structure thought like a pyramid, adding stone after stone.

Extremely tense, the librarian crushed the corner of a papyrus. Frightened, she ran to the door of the library; coming back to the middle of the room, she searched along shelves filled with books. Isis grasped her by the shoulders and forced her to calm down.

'Are you ill?'

The sister lowered her head and tried to run away; Isis held on to her tightly.

'Explain yourself.'

'It's too horrible. I have committed the most terrible transgression . . .' She burst into tears.

'Is it so terrible?'

'I have difficulty talking about it even with you. And yet . . .'

'And yet . . .'

'The whole community will see it. I . . .'

She bit her lip so hard that she drew blood, before the truth cried out.

'I'm pregnant.'

She waited for the High Priestess to condemn her. Isis took her hands tenderly.

'I was careless,' she confessed. 'I thought it was no longer possible. The brother who keeps the monastery accounts and I have known each other for so long . . . I did not want this to happen, I swear! Now, I will be expelled from the community.'

'Do not presume to know what the decision of the Ruling Chamber will be.'

'Our law knows no exception.'

'Philae is a small sacred island in a profane world. We must take that into consideration.'

The kindness of the High Priestess reassured the librarian. Her reassurance vanished when she entered into the Chamber of Maat, Ruler of the Universe. She stood facing the court, composed of the Elder, Isis and Sabni. The latter spoke: 'If the Temple's rules, which only imposed chastity during short periods preceding initiations, informed the sisters that it would be best not to have children and forbade it for the High Priestess, it did so at a time when there were many neophytes asking to be admitted. Since Philae is now condemned to perish in isolation, why refuse this child, whose sole presence is symbolic of the future? The librarian sister and the

accountant brother shall live together under the same roof.'
The Elder, deprived of his voice once more, nodded his head.
Isis embraced her sister.

As she left the Ruling Chamber, Isis was approached by
Ahoure. She had now become a ritualist; after having made
her way up through the temple's hierarchy, she often played
the role of spokeswoman for the community before Isis.

'Our sisters were worried about the sentence.'

'What about you?'

'I knew you would show clemency.'

Ahoure, who was over forty, had a strong presence. Though
robust and stocky with square shoulders, she was feminine and
sometimes excessively coquettish, with a penchant for wearing excessive make-up. Although she was not a confidante,
Isis had tended to rely on her. She felt supported by this
woman, who was a tower of strength even during the most
tempestuous times.

'To break with her would have weakened our community.
We should help each other. To ostracize our brothers and
sisters would take us nowhere.'

'Even if one of us is a traitor?'

'How can you even mention such a crime? As our spiritual
guide, I thought you trusted us implicitly.'

'The enemy is drawing near the temple,' warned Isis.
'Tomorrow, we will be at war; will all the adepts have the
courage to fight and sacrifice their lives?'

'You have no right to doubt that.'

'You are reassuring, Ahoure.'

'I am lucid, Isis. Philae is our most precious treasure, the
last symbol of a golden age. Who would be so foolish as to
renounce it?'

Not a breath of wind troubled the moonless night. On the
southern corner of the monumental colonnade, below
Nectanebo's pavilion, the water lapped against the embankment. Sabni looked over in that direction, glimpsing the black

87

barge that had quietly arrived. Its only occupant, Captain Mersis, had moored it behind a rock.

'Why come in person?'

'I can no longer trust anyone. The General keeps the garrison under constant scrutiny; he is suspicious. The atmosphere has really changed, there is no laughter any more. To compete with General Narses, the Bishop imposes permanent discipline on us; it seems that there is a conflict brewing between the two factions.'

'That is good news.'

'Do not rejoice yet. I am worried, very worried. The Bishop, the Prefect and the General meet often. After the failed attempt to launch the expedition to Nubia, their only concern seems to be Philae.'

'Have they taken any decisions?'

'I really don't know.'

'Perhaps they are planning some other ventures.'

'Let's hope so. There is a strange decree about sanitary measures.'

'An epidemic?'

'Apart from rampant hunger, there is no trace of it. No doubt it is an invention of Maximin's to justify the death of his soldiers; the Prefect is a crafty, venomous man.'

'He seemed very impressed by the temple when he came to visit Philae.'

'I would not rely on that. Who is he really? Nobody knows. His career is everything to him. This posting in Elephantine is just a stepping stone. If destroying Philae means promotion, he will not hesitate. I'm telling you, I'm afraid of what might happen. My soldier's instinct is rarely mistaken. Your community had better be ready to flee.'

Isis woke Sabni in the middle of the night.

'My father is dying.'

The High Priest hurried to the Elder's house, a small white two-storey house built to the right of the landing quay, facing

the temple. The old man was lying on a narrow bed, his arms
inert by his side; his face showed no suffering, but his eyes
looked tired and spent. With an imploring stare, he looked
forward to the rest death would bring, taking him to a paradise
where, along canals with fertile banks, trees and flowers grew
and the souls of the blessed wandered. The Elder's right hand
gripped Sabni's wrist. His lips trembled, trying to utter words.
Isis helped her father to sit up.

'Pursue wisdom, my children, search for it with all your
might, until death comes to you with the smile of the Western
Goddess who will take you to our ancestors' paradise. She was
with us always, before fear struck at the heart of our harvesters
and ploughmen. Do not cry for me, but for Egypt from whence
divine light is departing. Re will have to create the world once
again. The light of the solar disc is dim, thick clouds cover it,
men are blind and deaf. Soon the river will dry up, its course
will stop and the fertile lime will not reach its banks. Fish and
birds will die. Other invaders will impose their law and despise
our temples. Everywhere, tumult will reign. Everywhere, blood
will be shed for a piece of bread. There will be pained laughter,
famished bellies, sons will take up arms against their fathers,
brother will kill brother, and evil will replace virtue. Thieves
will govern and cheat. Our country will be so afflicted that the
weak will become powerful to oppress those yet weaker than
they. The city of the sun, Heliopolis, where the Gods were
born, will be buried under the weight of hatred and folly. It was
once so noble, this land of ours, as beautiful as the morning
star, as sweet as the dew from heaven, tender like the perfume
of the first day of the year. By espousing the fruitful river it
provided all that was needed to build festival altars; papyrus
bushes, blue and white lotuses. Do you remember Isis? I have
sailed to the island where your mother waited for me, with
perfumed hair, under a sacred *persea* tree. She was so beautiful
and her eyes spoke of love. My hand will guide you, she
promised, your happiness will be my sole concern. I can go to
her now, my daughter, because you too know the way.'

'Please stay,' begged Isis. 'We need you so much.'

'Today death is before me, offering healing and deliverance. It will divest me of the old age that has become unbearable. My body will disappear but my spirit will not abandon you. Persevere . . . continue the work of Imhotep!'

The name of the great sage was the last word the Elder pronounced. His mouth remained half open, his eyes fixed. Isis pressed the head of the deceased to her bosom; Sabni gave him the kiss of peace.

'Now, we are alone,' he said to the High Priestess.

After having announced the Elder's voyage to the community, a happy adventurer gone to travel the beautiful paths of the next world, Isis ordered the brother in charge of mummification to get to his work.

Isis was violating the law. The Bishop had expressly forbidden this ancient practice. When someone died, the first step was to remove the deceased person's name from the list of taxpayers, the second was to pay for a tomb in a legal cemetery. The brother who was brutally murdered during that tragic procession was buried in a common pauper's grave. The Elder deserved a dignified resting-place.

The adepts bathed in the purification basins and rubbed oil on their bodies. The brothers did not shave. With a silex knife, the mummification expert opened the left flank of the corpse resting on a stone slab. He had extracted the entrails and managed to extract the brain through the left nostril with the help of a metal hook. After cleaning the abdomen with palm wine, he plunged the body into *natron* to dehydrate the flesh. That divine salt transformed the washed and dried mortal remains into the body of Osiris.

Isis put a small gold pillar, a *djed,* under her father's neck, a symbol of the stability of the resurrected god after many trials, and a vulture made of precious stones, evoking the celestial mother. She covered the peaceful face with a fine layer of gold, as well as the hands and the feet. The head was crowned with flowers.

Sabni anointed the mummy with aromatic oils, then wrapped it with small bandages doused in resin and bitumen. Where the heart was, he placed a scarab, the symbol of perpetual metamorphosis. A veil constituted the last shroud. The sarcophagus was the vessel carrying the dead one, summoned to roam eternally in the heavens.

The Elder's name and his titles were inscribed on binding cloth, as were citations from the Pyramids' Texts, the most ancient of sacred books. Going back to the eve of civilization, these texts had come to light four thousand years ago in the pyramid of King Una. Transmitted from House of Life to House of Life, from sage to sage, from scribe to scribe, they had remained as the eternal fountain of knowledge taught to the adepts. They gave the traveller to the other world the name of the thresholds to be crossed.

The mummy was carried to the roof of the temple, to a chapel decorated with scenes representing the stages in the resurrection of Osiris. The soul of the Elder savoured the last taste of the earth's sun before immersing itself in the energy of the primordial ocean.

After a moment's silence around the sarcophagus, the community went down the stairs that linked the roof to the room with the painted columns.

The ritualist chanted, 'Neither stop drinking nor eating, continue to live happy days, unite with the Goddess, follow your heart. Just ones who follow the divine path will not be reproached. The West where you are resting is a peaceful land; the silent one will find the spring there. You will forget what is useless and temporary, you will remember your name and take your place at the banquet of the Gods.'

The sarcophagus was buried under the pavement, facing the first large pylon. Huge stones would forever hide the Elder's resting-place. His funeral, worthy of his rank, would allow him to present himself majestically before the luminous assembly of the resurrected adepts. When the paving stones were put down again, Isis collapsed. But she refused to cry, to scratch the stone with her bare fingers and to wail in despair like the weeping mourners whose screams attracted the compassion of the Gods.

She would never get used to her father's absence. He was irreplaceable. He had taught her everything, from the simplest games when she was a child to the most abstract concepts. She owed him the smallest and the greatest joys. Once he had mourned the death of his spouse, when Isis was only three years old, he had devoted himself to guiding his daughter, teaching her no other discipline than the mysteries and the respect for the Rule of the temple.

The High Priestess had neither the right nor the leisure to linger over her pain. The community needed her reassuring presence. Ahoure would have liked to comfort her, but she could not utter a sound. Any words would have been futile. In moments like this, Isis seemed distant from her sisters. Her soul roamed in those secret regions where the nocturnal sun travelled in search of rebirth. The High Priestess wandered inside the temple. Her father had taught her that it had been erected when the earth was still in darkness, before any creature, plant, stone or animal had yet manifested. She went into the workshops, the bakery, the purified slaughter house, explored the great stone building where, in happier times, numerous staff prepared delicious meals for the table of the god, before eating the blessed food, fortified by the Creator's thoughts. She walked along the wall of the birth sanctuary, where the Goddess Isis suckled her son Horus with the milk of the stars, a divine nectar that made Him as luminous as the primordial light.

The High Priestess stopped before the large stele made of granite, built in front of the Eastern jetty by the second large pylon. Her father had taught her to read the text on the submission of the Dodekaschoinos region, comprising a stretch of Lower Nubia. The owner of vast areas of fertile land, the temple of Philae paid homage to the Pharaoh, who was depicted on every scene, sculpted in relief on the walls. Immutable, grandiose, indifferent to profane time, with his head in the heavens and his feet on earth, the Pharaoh saw into the other world, whose energy was the lifeblood of the community. He guided its steps, treading the invisible path, on the uncertain road of suffering, through the follies of the present time. A time which forgot that, without the presence of a sanctuary at the entrance and the heart of the city, barbarism would condemn men to crawl in their own squalor.

The Elder had refused to submit to the invaders, who reduced body and spirit to slavery, with the tenacity of those old chiefs who grew stronger as those hunting them grew more numerous. He continued to defy death and preserve the sacred site. His mummy would henceforth be at the threshold of the temple.

Isis went into the large courtyard.

Suddenly, she made out a strange silhouette.

A very young boy, around fifteen years old, came towards her, naked and drenched. Exhausted, he wavered. She approached.

'Who are you?'

'My name is Chrestos. I swam here. I want to be initiated into the mysteries.'

17

'Where are you from?'

'Elephantine. My father wanted to force me to enlist. I ran away. I will not be a soldier, but a priest serving Isis.'

Skinny, almost sickly, the boy had obviously spent all his physical energy to reach Philae. Incapable of standing any longer, he fell to his knees. Isis called for help. Sabni came to the rescue with some other brothers, who clothed Chrestos with a loincloth and gave him some bread.

'I don't know how to swim very well, but I'd rather have drowned than be imprisoned in the barracks. I want to live here.'

'We don't have the right to keep you in Philae.'

'It is my father's soul who guided this postulant,' said Isis. 'Do you really wish to know the mysteries?'

Chrestos's face lit up.

'Every night I dream of the temple. I have asked a thousand questions, but received no answers. People have tried to discourage me. Some say that Philae is a lair of devils, others a magician's den. You are both feared and hated. A shepherd reassured me and told me to follow my intuition. There, he said, pointing to the Holy Island, is where the last spring of wisdom flows. The day it dries up, the world will flounder in darkness.'

Sabni had followed the same path, taken the same steps and pronounced those very words. Only a violent and imperious

For the Love of Philae

inner fire could open the doors of the community. But Chrestos was a fugitive; his presence in Philae would give rise to police intervention.

'I vote for his admission,' said Isis, whom the boy was devouring with his eyes.

If the High Priest disagreed, then the request would be rejected without an appeal. Neither Sabni nor Isis could take a decision without the other's consent.

Sabni abandoned the idea of presenting the reasonable views that Isis knew so well, and chose to retire, leaving Chrestos to hope. As Isis did not move, he chose to emulate her. This was, no doubt, his first test; he knew he had infinite patience, as he had come this far and reached his goal.

When the High Priest returned, carrying a jug full of water, Isis felt a deep happiness; it was one of those moments whose intensity would endure beyond death. Celebrating the welcoming rite, Sabni washed the feet of the neophyte.

'The ritualist is preparing a bed for you. In your cell, the light will shine during the night. You will offer a libation to the gods because you owe them your life. Tomorrow, at dawn, you will confirm your commitment; if you renounce, you will have to leave immediately.'

The night proved to be Chrestos's accomplice. Isolated at the heart of the temple, free of any profane worries, he meditated all night, mesmerized by the flame of the lamp. His spirit danced and merged with the eternal secrets of the place. Time vanished, his soul was happy, his heart leapt with a joy which would remain in his heart, an eternal sun whose light vanquished the darkness. The night was his ally. There were none of the promised ass-headed demons armed with knives, only reassuring shadows. The adolescent felt them friendly and closer than parents and friends. Chrestos had found his true home. The austere walls became his confidants. The silence, filled with the voices of wise men, carried him in a dream that was as tangible as the stones of the temple of Philae.

95

How beautiful the dawn of his initiation would be!

'Do you wish to join our community?' asked Sabni.

'If you guide me on the path of life, I will give you my life.'

'Turn your face to the sun. Do not enter the temple in a state of impurity, neither a liar nor greedy be. Respect the Rule without fail. Do not reveal whatever you have understood the mysteries to be. Do not conceive destructive thoughts in your heart. Renounce your own will to fulfil the Principle. The community will protect you and will open the doors of the sanctuary if you show yourself worthy of the tasks assigned to you. You will purify yourself three times a day with water, you will nourish yourself with moderation, you will guard the integrity of the temple, our most precious possession. Do you accept to honour these duties?'

'With all my heart.'

'Receive therefore the welcome that makes you a brother.'

Sabni and Chrestos congratulated each other. Isis kissed the boy, leaving his cheek wet with her tears. How warm and sweet it felt, that liquid which greeted the birth of an adept! The Elder had successfully transformed his death into a miracle.

'From now on, you must show courage.'

'No one will accuse me of cowardice.'

'Like all brothers, you must be circumcised.'

The boy lifted his chin. The butcher dabbed his sex with an anaesthetic ointment and cut the foreskin. He could not help letting out a cry.

The birth of a brother was celebrated with a banquet, unfortunately a rather frugal one. Nevertheless, the last jugs of wine were produced from the temple's cellars, now almost completely depleted. Each person present swore secrecy. No lay person was to know about Chrestos's presence in Philae.

Isis wondered about his name: it was strangely analogous to Christ's, the god of Christianity, that religion bent on destroying the temple at Philae. She thought it a truly strange omen.

When the festivities were over, the brother guarding the landing quay warned Sabni that a boat was approaching. On board were two soldiers. The High Priest recognized them: they were part of the squad that had escorted him to the temple.

'The Bishop wants to speak with you. Come with us.'

'Theodore, you mean?'

The prelate had foreseen that question. One of the soldiers exhibited the cross the ruler of Elephantine usually wore. Reassured, Sabni climbed on board.

He was immediately beset by sudden worry. Was the flight of Chrestos known?

Not a word was uttered during the crossing to the deserted quay where the Bishop waited. He took Sabni to a palm grove, a place of meditation and leisurely walks beneath the shade of large palm trees that created cool and calm atmosphere.

'I have some bad news.'

'For you or for me?'

'Don't be ironic, Sabni. Whatever may be said in Philae, I am not responsible for such measures.'

What did the Bishop have in mind? By granting initiation rites to someone who would be branded a fugitive, Philae was committing a very serious transgression.

'The Emperor demands the whole of the papyrus harvest,' revealed Theodore. 'I will minimize the quantities reaped, but I am forced to suppress the allotment of stems destined for the temple.'

After experiencing great relief, came indignation.

'You know very well that we need the papyrus as a support for writing, to make mats, baskets, to make ropes, sandals and other goods.'

'I know, but the decree is signed by the Emperor's own hand; the Prefect is already organizing transportation.'

'Are we at least allowed access to the forest, to the north of Elephantine?'

97

'It is now a military zone. Soldiers have taken it over and any civilian presence is forbidden.'

'To deprive us of papyrus . . . Who would have thought such cruelty possible?'

'A Christian does not fear suffering; Christ suffered for humankind, Osiris did not.'

'Osiris taught us resurrection. Pain is not a path to fulfilment, it is just pain. To endow it with any kind of virtue is but a fraud.'

'The kingdom will come soon. The race, which came from the Divine Fish, will be admitted; their heart will be strong, for the Lord, whose words are sweet honey, will bring them nourishment. You are my friend. Accept conversion and you will become my brother. What does the papyrus allowance matter? God is closer to you than you could possibly imagine.'

'If that is so, then it is not God. The creative power cannot be closed to mankind. Men can be but an expression of that power, in a distant, often perverted, manner. Only the Rule of Temple can rectify that. Remember the words of our forefathers: the twisted wood, abandoned in the field, will dry up and finish in fire. If the hand of the artisan, guided by God, picks it up, he will set it upright and make a sceptre of it, for the sage to handle.'

'Only a trusting faith will guide you to the truth.'

A ray of sun broke down through the palms illuminating the two men.

'Grant us a few stems, Theodore. We will use them to make our last documents and inscribe our most important rituals on them.'

The Bishop hesitated; Sabni would not entreat him further.

'Go to the warehouse and fill your boat. Whatever you can carry will be yours.'

18

After a thorough inspection of his elite corps, General Narses mounted his horse and galloped to the cataract. Every evening, he stopped by the same granite rock beneath which the water whirled angrily. Sitting on the flat top, sometimes splashed by a wave, he contemplated the sacred river on which the very prosperity of Egypt depended. It was there, faced with that mineral barrage, that it asserted its great, unflagging strength. Untameable, it carried at will the silt-laden mud. Why was it being so avaricious this year? The answer was a secret only known to the heavens, where the great waters were held before they were released to carve a groove in that earth so beloved of the gods. Narses was getting used to expressing his doubts. He could not bear certainties any longer, to foresee, to organize, it no longer interested him; he was happy to accept the uncertainties of the Nile and to surrender to the river without putting up a fight!

Tomorrow, no doubt, he would have to take the dangerous paths that led to Nubia and fight there. Thanks to this bad flood season, the South remained inaccessible. Destiny had reserved him a precious gift, he would only take advantage of it if the situation took a turn for the worse. That the Bishop and the Prefect should want to neutralize each other was to his advantage.

His request for a transfer, supported by Maximin, had been sent to Byzantium. He did not have much hope of approval.

The Emperor would believe it a whim. It would remind him of Nubia's gold and he would then name the General head of an expedition party leaving for Asia. For the first time in his life, Narses prayed from the bottom of his heart: he implored these deities of the cataract to form an unsurpassable barrier for ever.

The man, well dressed and with a large belly, presented himself at the police station quite drunk. He screamed and gesticulated. The police officer threw him out, but he returned, adamant that he would lodge a complaint. His purpose was something to do with the Prefect and the Emperor. One of the militiamen recognized him: a madman, head of the fig merchants' guild. He could, if he so wished, block all fruit deliveries to Elephantine. Feeling incompetent to deal with such a person, the police officer took him to the barracks, where he was received by a specialist in such difficult cases, Captain Mersis.

'My name is Apollo.'

'You're drunk.'

'I have my reasons, captain.'

'Against whom do you want to lodge a complaint?'

'Against Philae.'

This was no doubt an overwrought Christian; Mersis took it calmly.

'Philae does not exist.'

'What are you saying? . . .'

'The temples were closed a long time ago.'

'Not that one!'

'Legally, it was. It is a disused building.'

'What about the community which lives there?'

'We have no knowledge of it on our records.'

'But they pay taxes, as you well know.'

'I'm afraid taxes are not my concern.'

'You're mocking me . . .'

'I am simply stating an administrative fact.'

Apollo sneered maliciously.

'When a peasant abandons his field and runs away . . . surely that is considered a crime?'

'Yes, punishable with imprisonment.'

'And even with forced labour?'

'In some cases.'

'One of my employees is just such a case. You should arrest him.'

'What is his name?'

'Chrestos, my son.'

'Your son!'

'That is my business. He left my house to go to the temple; Isis's adepts have given him shelter. I am lodging a complaint against them. I want Chrestos back and their condemnation, all of them!'

'You have to fill in a form.'

'I have the time.'

'Do you know how to read and write?'

'Only how to count.'

If what Apollo was saying was true, Philae had compromised its very existence. Mersis had to find a solution to this problem immediately.

'When will you send your soldiers to the island?'

'We have to follow certain procedures. Are there other plaintiffs?'

'No, just myself. Is that not enough?'

'Have you spoken to anyone about this flight?'

'No one. I was too ashamed. I preferred to get drunk. Now, I want revenge!'

'Do you have any proof that your son is really hiding on the island?'

'I am certain of it. He refused to enlist as a soldier. Since he was a boy, he has wanted to join the brotherhood of the temple.'

'So you do not have concrete proof.'

'Search the island.'

'In what capacity is Chrestos employed to work on your land?'

Apollo blushed.

'What do you mean, in what capacity?'

Mersis took a wood tablet from a shelf. He engraved a few Greek letters on it.

'Does your son have the status of a slave on your land?'

The merchant lost his temper.

'He's my son! You're offending my family!'

'If he is a free worker, why is he not mentioned on the list of tax-paying citizens?'

'Captain, he's only a child . . .'

'But old enough to do forced labour. You should have declared him for income tax purposes, no matter what age.'

'You said taxation was not your department, remember?'

'I will convey the information to the official responsible. All I need do is add your name to this tablet.'

'I will risk . . .'

'Life imprisonment?'

'Perhaps we could strike a deal.'

'Why not?'

'What do you want?'

Mersis pretended to think about it.

'You drop your charges, you forget about Chrestos and, above all, you entrust me with some silver coins. The army is poor.'

Apollo emptied the purse he was carrying on his belt.

'Will that be enough?'

Mersis bent down and counted.

'If you were to bring me a few extra coins, we would become the best of friends. I would even forget that you have a son.'

Apollo grumbled. The captain broke the wooden tablet. He would send this small contribution to Philae, for whose dwindling resources it would be a small fortune.

*

The best jeweller in all Elephantine was finishing a finely wrought bracelet. When the Prefect Maximin entered his workshop, he was both flattered and worried. What could this important state dignitary want? If it was a requisition, he would have come with a patrol.

The artisan bowed.

'I am your humble servant, sir.'

'I've heard that your jewels are incomparable.'

'You flatter me.'

'Show me your masterpieces.'

Nervously, the artisan opened a wooden coffer. He then placed a necklace and a few wrist and ankle bracelets on a piece of white linen.

'Admirable,' said the Prefect.

19

Chrestos was making rapid progress. In the morning, he worked with wood and stone in Sabni's company. After the meal at noon, Isis taught him to read hieroglyphs and gave him writing lessons; she guided his hand, taught him to draw with a continuous line without trembling into a bird's wing, a human leg, or a sealed papyrus. Then the new adept listened to the lessons given by the maker of unguents before paying attention to the knowledge imparted by the ritualist. His thirst for knowledge seemed unquenchable and he never seemed to get tired. Just after the evening meal, he went on the roof of the temple where Isis showed him how to decipher the message of the stars.

That night, the High Priestess could not conceal her weariness. Chrestos, conscious that he was perhaps being inopportune, asked fewer questions. Beside Isis, he enjoyed the silence of the night that protected the sanctuary, but he could not keep quiet for very long.

'I am so happy, Isis.'

'The temple is the joy of the heart. There is no greater happiness.'

'You seem tired.'

'You're being very indiscreet.'

'Your strength is our strength. If you weaken, what will become of us?'

'The future of the community does not depend on one person.'

'Today, it does. I have not been here very long. I know that if you and Sabni were to disappear we would flounder.'

'That is quite an assertive statement, neophyte.'

'I have eyes to see and I refute hypocrisy.'

'Let's look at the stars again. Listen to the voice of our ancestors transmitted in with the light. May our futures be as full as theirs; the truth they conveyed to us remains the most fabulous of our treasures, because it guides our thoughts towards true wisdom.'

The baker and carpenter brothers requested an audience with the High Priest. Sabni saw them in the Elder's house, which was now his. The two men, both in their sixties, sometimes contested the decisions taken by the High Priestess but kept it to themselves. When they took a stand together, it meant they had thought about it for a long while. Sabni dispensed with polite social graces.

'Speak.'

'You first,' said the baker to the carpenter.

'It's a bit difficult . . . could you help me?'

'We are brothers. Nothing should embarrass you.'

The two looked alike: they had round faces, sharp eyes, thick lips, double chins, wide chests and short thick legs.

'It's true,' recognized the baker, 'sometimes it is difficult . . .'

The severity with which Sabni looked at them was intimidating. The carpenter came to his friend's rescue.

'We are brothers and should tell each other everything. Isis has made some serious mistakes: the procession, the visit to the grotto . . . Our prestige is tarnished. As High Priest, you have to take some measures.'

Satisfied with his intervention, he spoke up.

'We accept to fight against the Bishop, on condition that we do not take unnecessary risks. You are a friend of Theodore's:

rid us of Isis, she is dangerous. Two people governing is one too many; she can take care of the rituals.'

'Do other brothers share your point of view?'

'We are the most experienced.'

'Did Isis not refuse your initiation into the mysteries of the covered temple?'

Neither the baker nor the carpenter replied.

'I had access to the reports written by the Elder and the High Priestess. You, by making a bench, and you, by baking a croissant in a fancy shape, thought that you were the authors of a masterpiece required by the temple's Rule. Your work was an insult to the community. As for your knowledge of hieroglyphs, it remains superficial. It is your incompetence that you have made a show of. Do not count on my indulgence: nothing justifies your laziness. Fulfil your daily duties and get rid of the rancour corrupting your thoughts, otherwise you will make no progress.'

The two brothers looked at each other, puzzled.

The temple community of Philae did not starve. With the silver coins that Captain Mersis donated, Sabni bought a significant quantity of wheat. Boats brought it to the island at dawn, before the patrols started to monitor the riverbanks.

Chrestos's enthusiasm proved quite contagious, and the old brothers, despite their years, started to clean the relief sculpture eroded by the winds of sand. Philae, invigorated by this new energy, concentrated less on her problems and breathed a new life. The sisters mended the musical instruments, wove white robes with the little linen that was left and washed the pavement of the birth chamber, where, in a few months, a new adept would be born. The community emerged from the lethargy that some had believed would mean its end. From dawn to dusk, the High Priest went from chapel to courtyard, from room to crypt, encouraging, counselling, verifying. As soon as a task was finished, he suggested another one, even more demanding.

Isis made progress in her study of the ritual of the distant goddess. She felt her work would not be in vain, because soon the community would try to make that ceremony come alive. Several times she caught her mind wandering off. She thought of Sabni, of his capacity to get projects to completion. Would it suffice to change a worn out-group into a lively brother-hood? The coming of Chrestos, an announced birth . . . The signs multiplied. After so many years branded with the seal of despair, Isis saw a much happier future ahead; she felt like abandoning herself to these trusting feelings, she wanted to share her doubts and her dreams with Sabni. When would he be ready to understand that?

Chrestos deciphered the lines of the ancient text written by a pharaoh for his son:

'The agitated man breeds confusion in his community. Become vigilant and do not pander to your pleasures, lest you cause misery to your soul. At the hour of judgement, the heavenly court will be merciless. In its eyes, your life is but an hour. Dare to take the most difficult paths; they will guide your spirit to wisdom. God knows the one who toils for his glory. Become a builder. From your effort joy will be born, the joy of wisdom.'

The neophyte rolled the papyrus carefully.

'Can a man attain such an ideal state?' he asked Sabni.

'Our fathers did. If this temple exists, it is because they lived heaven on earth.'

'And yourself?'

'I am a young High Priest as inexperienced as the novice addressing me. Our rank is different, but the magnitude of our task is the same.'

'You have spent many years in Philae.'

'You possess the burning fire of the apprentice.'

'Does it dwindle later?'

'It transforms and increases. It becomes less violent and yet more powerful. There comes the moment of certainty, like a sun that never sets. I hope you will have that experience, Chrestos. You will then belong both to this world and to the next; God is in the light of the temple, and we are that temple, with our ancestors and our successors. May your intelligence perceive my words and may your actions bring them into effect.'

'What about you, Sabni, do you listen to your heart?'

'Does my teaching disappoint you?'

'On the contrary, it surpasses all that I had hoped.'

'Then why do you ask such a question?'

'I am very young and I have no right to speak to you in this way. But the community would be much stronger if . . .' Chrestos hesitated. He was going too far.

'What is your advice?'

'Do not neglect those who love you more than they love themselves.'

The new adept regained his composure and drew some hieroglyphs on a pottery slab. He concentrated on sketching a chair with a high back, symbol of the goddess Isis.

The Prefect alighted near Trajan's kiosk, where the boatman drew in the floating white sail billowing in the wind. No escort had accompanied Maximin on this trip. As soon as he set foot on the island, he was intercepted by Sabni, who had been told by the watchman of his arrival.

'I want to speak to the High Priestess.'

'She is working with her sisters.'

'Please, tell her I am here.'

'First, promise me you will not take another step.'

Sabni behaved as if he was the leader of an invincible cohort who feared nothing from one of the Emperor's envoys. He humiliated Maximin. Throughout his career Maximin had never tolerated the slightest ungracious remark regarding his station; in this case he felt that Isis was worth the most painful sacrifice.

108

'You have my word. Hurry.'

Sabni walked slowly towards the door situated by the first pylon, earning himself Maximin's total loathing with every unhurried step he took.

The Prefect waited for over an hour under the burning sun, which he did not seem to notice. As soon as he saw Isis, a celestial vision, the temple became paradise once more.

'Here, I brought you a present.'

Maximin opened the jewel box. The gold jewellery shone in all its splendour.

'They are magnificent,' said Isis, 'and would do honour to the statues of divinities.'

'I meant you to have them.'

'In the old days, I would have worn them during the great feasts that were held, for the High Priestess had to present herself as the most beautiful of women, without forgetting that her riches came from the temple and should be returned to it.'

'We will celebrate new festivals. These jewels can herald them if you accept to become my wife.'

Taken aback by his own audacity, Maximin did not dare to look at Isis. He feared a peremptory refusal. The voice of the High Priestess remained calm and sweet.

'My calling and the temple's Rule forbid me a profane marriage.'

'The custom is obsolete. When you become my wife, Philae will live again.'

The Prefect immediately regretted the menace contained in those words. It might be interpreted as blackmail and keep Isis from him.

'You love Philae, Isis, and I love you.'

The brothers and sisters assembled under the columns and wondered what the reason for this visit from the Prefect could be. Ahoure proposed that they intervene violently. There were enough of them to throw their enemies into the Nile. Sabni told her to be quiet. Upset, the ritualist retired to her cell.

'Look at those timorous creatures,' said Maximin, pointing

109

to the community members. 'I am the only person who can deliver them from their anguish. For the love of Isis, to win your affection, I will ensure the perennial existence of the temple of Philae.'

The expression on the face of the High Priestess remained inscrutable. Was she waging an inner battle? That she did not vehemently repudiate his proposition reassured the Prefect; no doubt he had somehow managed to open a decisive breach.

'I will be back, Isis. Above all, do not betray me.'

20

The documents preserved in Philae did not specify the names of which sages to invoke so that the ritual of the distant goddess would be effective. Isis believed she knew where she might find them: in one of the tombs on the western bank of the Nile, dug during the Ancient Empire to honour the memory of the explorers of the unknown paths of the great South. Abandoned a long time ago, the site had become the ground for erring souls. To go there meant taking the kind of risks that the High Priestess was not meant to take. Nevertheless, Sabni could not dissuade Isis or reason with her. The future of Philae depended on this ritual being celebrated. It would breathe new indispensable energy into each community member. Isis was convinced that the event would unveil a whole new world to her. Sabni had to give in, but he refused to let her go alone. They warned the old weaver woman who, in their absence, would see that the brothers and sisters went about their tasks as usual.

They left the moment the top of the hills became tinted with the pink hues of early dawn. Sabni manoeuvred a light barge in the early morning wind that breathed over the silvery water. Like all sons of the province, Sabni had learned to sail when very young; he had often played at jumping from one boat to another as, at maximum speed, they raced along the currents. To navigate using such currents required long practice. Sabni sailed carefully around the island of Elephantine, passed in front of the fortified granite walls that protected the small forts spaced out along the coast, and pointed the prow towards the western flank of the mountain. After hiding the boat among the reeds and having made their way through the vegetation, the couple alighted by the long steep ramps that had served to pull the sarcophagi to the entrance of the tombs.

Sabni had brought a model boat in the shape of an antelope to offer the god of the dead, the only inhabitant of that silent, isolated region. The climb was long and difficult; the sand slid from under their feet, every step required effort. Once up on the rocky platform, Sabni pulled Isis up by her hands. His jerky movement threw her against him and they remained in each other's arms for a few moments. Noticing his confusion, she drew away gently.

They sat down to catch their breath. At their feet the holy river flowed by; it bathed several small islands, before flowing majestically towards Philae and throwing itself on the rocks of the cataract. The sky was very still, filling their eyes with a deep blue. White sails cut across the river: a boat filled with peasants and animals was leaving the eastern bank. A couple of peregrine falcons flew towards the rising sun.

'Our life should resemble this river, Sabni, eternally faithful to its nature and constantly renewed.'

'We are imperfect and infirm.'

'We serve a goddess.'

Isis, mother of God, ornament of the sky, fecundity of the fields, growth pervading the world with its beauty, perfume of the temple, mistress of joy, rain that turns the grass green, sweet lover . . . Had these aspects of Isis reincarnated in this woman who stood by Sabni's side, with her jet black hair that outshone the night, her nature more tender than ripe grapes and fresher than the water from the well, her teeth whiter than the milky way, her face sweeter than the choicest fruit in the orchard, her legs more slender than those of a gazelle? Such was the Isis who had initiated Sabni in his role, and inspired him to transcend himself.

'Let us look for the tombs.'

Following a path lined with stones along the top of a cliff, they penetrated the abandoned vaults. They were often confronted with desolate scenery. Burned chapels with their walls blackened by smoke, statues decapitated or broken. The low-relief sculptures had been wrenched out or whitewashed. But some eternal abodes had escaped the fury of Christian iconoclasm. The walls were decorated with hunting and fishing scenes, with banquets, tournaments and games, all with their colour still intact. They recalled happy times of former days and conquerors of unexplored lands come back to Elephantine to enjoy a happy old age. From the top of their tombs, they contemplated forever the serene landscape where their time of wandering the earth had come to an end. They had offered the gold from Nubia to the gods and in return the gods had given them glory and fortune. From inside the western mountain an inscription on one of the walls showed precious stones flowing in waves, hidden among the papyrus bushes and over the temple doors.

When Sabni read the inscriptions narrating the exploits of the conquerors of the great South, he admired their courage and will to win through. On a stele relegated to an obscure corner, Isis perceived the fine semblance of the goddess of the cataract wearing the crown of reeds. Reading the text, she revived the words spoken by the spirit of the river: 'For you I will make the sap of life rise, the flowers will grow, the harvests golden, the stones rejoice and the heart of men full of joy.'

Isis felt herself being carried by another force that drew her close to Sabni. Still, she resisted. She had to think of the sepulchre where the divine names were inscribed, the ultimate words of the ritual. At the end of a colonnaded courtyard there was a rectangular entrance. Sabni went in first. Up to that moment, no nasty encounter had hampered their quest. Nevertheless, the High Priest remained cautious. Some of the Christian hermits were fervent enough to attack the visitors to these tombs which they considered to be the mouths of hell.

The High Priest came back, meekly. Isis stood beside him and gripped his arm. Pressed against one another, they had the feeling of treading the narrow path leading to the kingdom of the next world. On both sides, white statues with green or black faces and with fixed eyes contemplated them, smiling.

The couple drew close together and went forth, among those ancestors immortalized in the joy of resurrection. Three steps led to a chapel decorated with a banquet scene. Perennial delicacies covered the banquet table of the one who was recognized as being a just man by the tribunal of the other world. Columns of hieroglyphs evoked the communion of Isis's followers, at the moment when the goddess, after her exile in the depths of Nubia, returned to Philae.

'The answer is here, Sabni. Present our offering.'

The High Priest placed on the ground the model boat shaped like an antelope that he had brought from Philae.

'The guardians of this abode are multiples of Osiris. He is one and many, that is his secret: one thousand faces for just one heart. He will invoke the distant goddess for us. A god will call on his goddess, she will hear his voice and return to her abode.'

They took their place on the stone bench, guests of an immobile feast with immaterial delicacies. Isis's quest had come to an end. Sabni felt that he could finally ask her the question he was obsessed with.

'What did the Prefect want?'

'He asked me to become his wife. In exchange, he would protect Philae and satisfy my desires. The future of the temple would be guaranteed. Should I accept?'

Sabni stood up and impulsively took her in his arms.

'The Rule forbids it.'

'It says that your main duty is to protect the community.'

'I love you, Isis. I love you with all my heart. It is our union and only our union that will preserve the temple from being destroyed.'

He lowered the straps on the golden shoulders.

'We are not allowed to have children.'

'It is beyond me. It's you and only you that I desire.'

The white dress fell at Isis's feet, unveiling her high breasts, her jet-black sex and her long legs. She took Sabni's tunic off. He caressed the small of her back and kissed her neck. When their lips met, he bent her backwards tenderly. The sap that flowed in Isis's body had the ardour of a newborn sun and the softness of honey.

She lay on the stone floor, among the rows of the many forms of Osiris, and he espoused her desire. In the happy silence of the eternal abode where the resurrected couple continued to feast and where the dead communicated with the living, they discovered the golden light of a dazzling love, such as the flame that comes up at dawn, at the heart of the Orient.

21

Evening fell. Isis and Sabni were drunk with the ecstasy they had experienced in the tomb of their ancestors. Despite the longing they still felt in their bodies, they thought of Philae. Only the future of the temple mattered. Their lives as adepts shunned personal ambition. They had learned to fight it, to renounce and be free of such feelings. Passion did not obliterate years of asceticism. It exalted their voyage together towards the invisible, in love, now they were but one body and one soul.

Sabni was the first to emerge from the tomb. The moon was shining and the stars, luminous doors, lit up the firmament. The High Priest took a deep breath, inhaling the still air of the night, and entrusted his enthusiasm to a universe woven by goddesses and fashioned on his wheel by the potter god Knum.

No sooner had he crossed the threshold than a violent wooden club struck into his stomach doubled him over in pain. The assailant, a monk with long hair, cried out in joy. He hit Sabni again. The High Priest threw himself sideways, grabbed the extremity of the club and disarmed his attacker. The Christian monk, despite his wrath, realized that he was not up to fighting Sabni and broke off, fleeing into the night.

Isis came up to Sabni.

'Are you hurt?'

'Let us go home.'

From the boat, they contemplated the steep Western cliff,

buried in bluish obscurity. The entrance of the tomb had disappeared, hidden by the darkness. Only the ramps leading to the summit were visible. Locked in the tombs remained the secret of a love experienced in a realm beyond time.

According to custom, Sabni took Isis in his arms and crossed the threshold of the Elder's old house. In the eyes of the assembled community, they became man and wife. There was no need for any written document, their commitment was now established in law.

All the brothers and sisters enjoyed that moment, but for Chrestos it brought particularly intense emotion. Was he not somewhat responsible for this marriage that the adepts considered blessed? By their union, Sabni and Isis proclaimed the freedom of the temple even in the very heart of a hostile world.

The betrothed slept under a fishing net of fine mesh, used as a mosquito net. When they awoke they each felt completely happy just to find the other there by their side.

'We have to be careful of Maximin,' Isis recommended.

'Is he that much in love?'

'If he knew about us . . .'

'We are all vowed to secrecy. Trust me.'

She nestled against his chest, trusting.

Ahoure put some eyeshadow on and some incense perfume. She sometimes reproached herself for this tendency to be so coquettish, but the Rule did not forbid the sisters to be beautiful. She was amused when some brothers fell in love with her, but they did not distract her from her work with the rituals. She boasted of her excellent memory and a knowledge of the rites as perfect as that of Isis. She did not envy the High Priestess her post, for she knew that all the worries that went with it far outweighed satisfaction. Yet she was well aware that her strong shoulders bore a good part of the weight of the community. Usually, Ahoure felt that Isis made the right decisions. Yet this time she felt that Isis had not taken the time to think over how such a marriage would take the adepts down a dangerous path. To criticize the High Priestess took the kind of courage that some would qualify as impudence. The ritualist, convinced of her own lucidity, did not hesitate.

In the orchard of the temple, Isis studied the ancient feast rituals; birds played around her. On the island nobody chased or hunted them. One of them, with a silvery head and yellow breast, landed on the shoulder of the High Priestess, pecked at her hair anointed with myrrh and flew to a persea tree where sparrows were nesting.

'What do you want, Ahoure?'

'This marriage, is it not too hasty?'

'Are you afraid that Sabni and I will coo like a pair of doves and forget our sacred duties?'

'Of course not. But the Prefect . . .'

'His passion worries you?'

'Why neglect it?'

'Would you wish that I become his wife?'

'If that sacrifice were to save the temple and the community . . .'

Isis lifted her eyes towards the top of the persea with its heart-shaped dark green leaves; it was under such a tree that the first Egyptian sage had received teachings from the god of knowledge.

'What will your union with Sabni bring us apart from your selfish happiness?'

'Your reproach surprises me, for it is not justified. Don't you see that in buying a precarious peace from Maximin, I would have betrayed the spirit of our brotherhood. Egypt has always been governed by a couple with one and the same ideal. Sabni and I will try to revive a tradition that may well precede other resurrections. You can be sure, my dear sister, that our actions are not inspired by any search for momentary pleasure.'

Ahoure left; her jealousy saddened Isis. It would be up to

the High Priestess to see that it did not turn to bitterness, a fearsome poison for weak souls.

Sitting on top of a huge block of granite, General Narses, as he did every evening, admired the cataract. The tide of the Nile would soon recede; the peasants picked olives and harvested dates, as the sowing of cereals started on those poorly irrigated lands. But the greater part of the grain was destined to go to Byzantium. The small farms in charge of providing food for Elephantine would produce but meagre ears of corn. Just how many people were dying of hunger? Nevertheless, no one blamed the Nile. That land was too beautiful, too pure for human suffering to justify the slightest reproach. Narses was looking for a merciful water whirlpool that would sink him to the bottom of the river.

The General had found a new papyrus roll consecrated to the adventures of a famous African explorer, the Egyptian Hikhouf, whose grave could be found in the Western cliff. Three thousand years later, his legendary exploits were still gripping. Narses unrolled the document and began reading passionately. Delving into paths of an unknown region and firmly guiding an expedition corps organized with care, the hero had come back from distant Nubia leading a cortege of three hundred donkeys laden with bags of gold, ebony, incense, elephant tusks and panther skins. The present the young Pharaoh had loved most had been a Pygmy, who performed zealous dances to the gods of that country on the horizon. How many times had that explorer left home to venture into the unknown, before returning at a very old age to die in his home town? Narses threw the papyrus into the river. He found that this existence of tumults and honours, conquests and glory, happiness and sadness no longer interested him. Was that all human beings could learn?

A strange apparition caught the General's attention. Beyond the last rocks of the cataract there was a man with black skin cloaked in a spotted fur, mounted on some long-necked animal. He stood immobile on the side of a hill. It was an excellent post from which to observe the fortifications on the frontier. When the sun went down, the watchman disappeared.

The Bishop and the Prefect listened to the General's tale.

'A Blemmye mounted on a giraffe,' said Theodore.

'Those people are extinct,' objected Maximin.

'I thought so too. I have written reports on the subject.'

'Are you sure this was one of them?'

'I'm afraid so.'

'No doubt a lost survivor.'

'The Blemmyes used to send a watchman before attacking.'

'Our forts are unconquerable. An army three times as strong as ours would fail.'

'What if we are mistaken?' suggested the Bishop, irritated by the Prefect's self-assurance. 'How many battles have been lost due to a leader's vanity?'

'Are you doubting my worth?'

'If an attack is being prepared, we should protect Elephantine.'

At this point, General Narses felt he must intervene.

'We are no doubt worrying for nothing. The experts feel sure that the Blemmyes are incapable of putting together an assault corps. Nevertheless, I will inspect our fortifications.'

Such a decision comforted Theodore. He no longer feared these invaders from the South; they were fearless adversaries of Christianity and angry about no longer having access to Philae. There was a shrine there to their god from whence they had been kept these last twenty years.

Narses greeted his superiors and took his leave. Maximin eyed Theodore scornfully.

'Do not criticize me, I will not allow it.'

'My only concern is with my mission.'

'Do you think you are capable of changing my mind?'

'Isis will never marry you.'

'She no longer has a choice.'

'You're mistaken. She will never give in to blackmail.'

'Will she sacrifice her community?'

Theodore had asked himself that same question a hundred times.

'The Rule of the temple guides what she does . . .'

'Those are just words! It is the very existence of Philae that is at stake here.'

'I will prevent you from going too far,' said the Bishop gravely. 'That pagan sanctuary no longer exists legally! If you revive it and provide it with renewed splendour, the Christians will revolt against you.'

'Do you realize what you are implying?'

'I'm saying, be in love, Maximin, but do not offend Christ.'

The Prefect kept his cool. Absent-minded, he walked towards the cabinet full of papyri and consulted a document with a distracted eye.

'I want to know what is going in on that community. We need to have a spy there.'

'The law forbids Philae to welcome new adepts. If we send someone, they will become suspicious and expel him.'

'Sabni is a rebel and a plotter.'

Theodore himself feared his friend's initiatives. The Prefect's idea was not wholly uninteresting; to have an informer inside would prevent a lot of unnecessary aggravation.

To the north of the cataract, at some distance from the temple, Mersis took advantage of the first hours of the morning to slap the water with a long pole and jump some fish into his net. He had just trapped a super perch when movements in the water signalled the approach of a swimmer. He recognized Sabni as he gripped the prow of the boat to rest and keep his head out of the water. The captain continued to fish without looking at his friend.

'There has been disquieting news. A Blemmye was spotted near the cataract.'

'Really?'

'Narses is carrying out a thorough inspection of the forti-

121

fications. And there's another danger: Maximin is spreading rumours about his forthcoming marriage to Isis. The bishop is being bombarded with protests. Be careful, Sabni. You are the only real obstacle between the Prefect and the High Priestess.'

'In more ways than you could imagine.'

Chrestos did not leave anyone in peace. The older brothers had to endure his questions and try to answer them. He drew even the lazier adepts out of their drowsiness and forced them back to work. Little by little, the stimulus he brought was emulated and each adept set out to justify his place in the community. Brothers and sisters exchanged ideas, questioning the meaning of the symbols, studying the walls of the temple where the ancients had engraved the principles of wisdom. From the top of columns with capitals in the shape of the goddess, Hathor smiled. November, when harrowing the fields started, was an enchanted time. The low flood season had passed and life went on, as sweet as melting dates. The librarian's pregnancy progressed without any difficulty; Isis prayed every night to the divinities that watched over childbirth.

Philae was recovering confidence in its faith. The adepts had neglected a treasure that they now recognized as being of inestimable value. Had the goddess ever failed to protect them from a hostile environment? From an enemy who after boasting victory now seemed to lose its virulence?

Isis praised Sabni's lucidity, and yet insisted on the visible renewal of the community. He, however, refused to fall prey to optimism. The High Priest, more than any other member of the community, must give thought to the future of the temple.

22

The carrier pigeon alighted on top of the western pier of the first pylon. Chrestos was responsible for fetching the bird. It brought a message from the Bishop: the mother of the carpenter brother was dying. If the latter so wished, authorization would be granted for him to leave the island and go to the woman's deathbed. Some soldiers would wait on the bank to escort him. He would be forbidden to speak with the population.

Neither Isis nor Sabni had any objection to this procedure. Very disturbed, the carpenter went straight away; the pigeon would serve as his safe-conduct.

The militiamen forced him to wear a brown tunic and to don a woollen skullcap that hid his baldness. They did not take him to his mother's house in the poor quarters of the town but to the Bishop's house, where he entered by a side door. Thanks to the speed with which the operation was carried out, no one identified the visitor.

When he was brought before the prelate and the Prefect, the carpenter panicked. Was this some kind of trap? Theodore assured him that his mother, aged eighty-four, was in good health and still managed her farm herself. He made the adept, who was intimidated by Maximin's cold stare, sit down on a folding chair.

'We wish you no harm,' guaranteed the Prefect, 'and we need your help.'

These words flabbergasted the brother.

'I've heard a lot about you. It seems you are an excellent carpenter and render remarkable services to the temple even if they are not given their due value.'

The adept nodded.

'Why do you stay in that community?'

'It is my family, I was brought up there.'

'Have you been initiated into the great mysteries?'

'No, Isis forbade it and Sabni approved her decision.'

The brother immediately regretted confiding in profane people. But the High Priest and his companion carried responsibility for his rancour.

'If you were not the follower of an impious cult, I would gladly have employed you; you would have become rich.'

'Material wealth does not interest me. I love Philae.'

'Do you not love life even more?' asked the Prefect.

The adept became very pale.

'If that is so, speak. Otherwise, my soldiers will have to kill an escapee who disturbed law and order.'

'What do you want from me?'

'Information on your community.'

'Philae is born again. Even the most discouraged are daring to hope again.'

'What kind of activities do you practise?'

'We tender to the temple, present offerings, worship the great goddess . . .'

'Do you plot against the Emperor?'

'No, of course not!'

'Who encourages you?'

'Sabni, Isis and also . . .'

His brothers had often chastised the carpenter for his loose tongue. Once again, he had spoken without thinking. The Prefect drew close and placed his hands on the shoulders of the adept who felt as if he had been gripped by the claws of a bird of prey.

'And also?'

The carpenter had sworn he would keep silent. By betraying his oath, he was condemning the community to oblivion. But how could he resist torture?

His suffering would not save the temple. Others would confess; his sacrifice would be in vain.

'A peasant was admitted into our midst. His enthusiasm is contagious and it has brought us hope for the future.'

'What is his name?'

'I don't know.'

The Bishop promised himself he would find out who this runaway was. By welcoming him, Philae had committed a fault to be taken advantage of.

Maximin paid no attention whatsoever to such a detail. The information he wanted was of another order.

'Is Sabni plotting a subversive move?'

'The High Priest's sole preoccupation is the temple. He is a hard and uncompromising man.'

'Are the brothers ready to rebel against him?'

'They would not dare. Nobody challenges his authority.'

'What about Isis?'

'Isis . . . She does not dispute his decisions.'

Maximin noticed that the brother was ill at ease, he could see he was not telling the whole truth, trying to conceal an important fact. His fingers gripped his shoulders violently. The carpenter repressed a scream.

'Such pain is nothing compared to what you will have to endure if you continue to lie. Isis and Sabni hate each other, don't they? She wants to marry me and he is against it!'

'Yes . . . he refuses.'

Even in the heat of his passion, the Prefect retained his perception. He could see that the adept was confessing what he wanted to hear. He slapped him. The carpenter cried. Theodore looked away.

'Take this man out of my sight.'

'I cannot stand much more of this . . . if he does not speak, I will strangle him.'

The prisoner understood that the Prefect's fury was genuine. To keep quiet any longer would be suicidal.

'Sabni and Isis were married according to custom. By crossing the threshold of their house united, they became man and wife.'

Maximin released the man. Momentarily, he felt like smashing his fist deep into the weak face of the adept.

'Return to the island. You will be our spy there.'

The carpenter backed out of the room, bowing. To have survived that ordeal seemed the most wonderful reward.

'That marriage has no legal value,' declared the Prefect. 'but Isis has betrayed me. Philae and Sabni will be punished. The Christians will be avenged, Bishop. You will enjoy your victory, and I will submit the woman I love to my law.'

Ahoure filled the silver vase with water from the Nile and poured it over the hands of the adepts. The precious liquid came from Nun, the god who personified the primeval waters, the ocean of energy in which the whole universe bathes. The earth was but a hillock emerged at the dawn of time when the creator, born of himself, had pronounced the first word. Each Egyptian temple recalled that origin, re-enacted during the rite of dawn.

Ahoure presented the vase to the High Priestess and evoked the decisive moment when the heart of the Principle was made conscious by his son, Life, who reunited his extremities and rendered them mobile. He, the unique, brought his body to life thanks to the magic of the word and placed in each being's soul the desire to share, through the initiation into the mysteries, the eternity of that moment.

When the community was greeting the sun by elevating towards it their purified hands, Chrestos called out to Sabni.

'Why has the ritualist forgotten me?'

Ahoure turned sharply towards the young man.

'Be quiet, neophyte.'

'What grave fault have I committed to be thus neglected? I have a right to know!'

126

'Such impudence deserves to be punished! I request the permission of the High Priest to chastise the offender severely.'

Chrestos did not lower his voice.

'I am a brother like any other and request only what is my due. If injustice reigns in this temple as it does in the profane world, then it must be banished immediately.'

Furious, Ahoure reached for the stick that the carpenter was offering her.

'On the ground, you rebel! When your back has tasted this master, your vanity will be less arrogant.'

Chrestos gave Sabni and Isis an imploring look. Neither intervened to stop the gesture of the ritualist. The young man tightened his lips and clenched his fists. Stretched out on the floor, he received five blows but did not utter one cry.

The ointment eased the pain. Sabni massaged Chrestos's left shoulder, still swollen.

'My body does not worry me. But why did you not defend me against such injustice?'

'The impulsive person resembles a tree that grows too quickly and whose young leaves are thrown on the fire before the branch is cut. The silent one matures, acquires its green colour, and its fruits are sweet; the shade it gives in the garden is pleasant.'

'One cannot always keep silent!'

'It is painful to stay silent when faced with unjust words, but it is useless to argue with the ignorant. To reply to their arguments would only cause discord, for their hearts cannot bear the truth.'

The young man's eyes lit up.

'Then you admit that the ritualist made a mistake! She is neglecting her duty . . . that ignorant sister. I will never speak to her again.'

'You must not be pretentious because of your knowledge, Chrestos. One should consult both the ignorant and the sage,

127

for no one attains total mastery. The excellent word is more hidden than the green stone; nevertheless, you will hear it from the mouth of the most humble, those who serve the temple, giving their whole being without expecting anything in return.'

'That is not Ahoure's case!'

'Don't make such peremptory judgements.'

'You cannot be that blind . . . not you!'

'Do you despise me?'

Embarrassed, the young man lowered his head.

'No, but that sister . . .'

'The adept who wishes to attain the great mysteries has to confront with an open heart the harshest trials. It is in the heart of the community that you will undergo these, not in the outer world. Forget criticism, rancour and rebellion to prepare yourself to live through them.'

23

From the top of one of the highest watchtowers, the guard noticed two black-skinned people wearing feline skins. They moved forward through the meandering of the cataract with incredible agility, jumping from rock to rock until they were perched on a block of granite around which the waters twirled. Forewarned, Captain Mersis identified the scouts observing his defence line.

'Blemmyes!'

They kept a good distance, out of the reach of any arrows. It was useless to send a detachment; by filing along the banks, they would have alerted the enemy who would just vanish without being intercepted.

For more than two hours the Blacks scrutinized the stockade and the small forts that guarded the entrance to the province of Elephantine. Then, as quick as the wind, they disappeared.

Mersis immediately prepared a report in two copies, taking it to his hierarchical superior, Bishop Theodore. The latter went to the Prefect, whose office was cluttered with accounting tablets.

'Everything is ready, Bishop. This time, Philae will not escape unscathed from this ordeal. I promise to inflict great suffering on the island.'

'There are more urgent matters.'

'Who says so?'

'Read this.'

The report from Captain Mersis was clear and concise.

'Yesterday one, today two, tomorrow a whole army . . . the Blemmyes are preparing to attack us.'

'The fortifications will dissuade them. Let them go on observing. If these savages have any sense, they will give up the idea.'

'The news will spread quickly and the people will panic. You should order an inspection of the troops and organize some parades.'

Although insolent, the Bishop's suggestion was reasonable. Maximin put aside the accounts of the province and fulfilled his role as military chief. He visited the barracks, showed up on the battlements, talked to soldiers, presided over a parade and marched at the head of a detachment through the streets of Elephantine. This demonstration of strength and confidence reassured the people.

If the Blemmyes were crazy enough to attack the city, they would be exterminated.

Sabni took a broken bedstead to the carpenter. Ever since his return, the artisan had a sad look about him.

'Could you mend this?'

'I don't know.'

'Is your mother still very ill?'

'She is fading away and hardly recognizes me; no doubt I will have to go and see her again. Show me the object.'

The carpenter seemed shy.

'Did you meet the Bishop?'

'Me, whatever for?'

'Theodore knows that the adepts have left their blood relatives to find their spiritual family. Usually, they never look back. Why that strange initiative, if not to question you about the secrets of the temple?'

Furious, the carpenter threw the bedstead on the floor.

'Would you dare accuse me of treason? I have sworn to observe silence, but I still have feelings, unlike you. By submitting to that famous Rule, you have forgotten about kindness. You have become dry, implacable. No one loves you, Sabni. When you come to understand that, it may be too late. As for me, I am innocent.'

'The word of a brother is sacred; no other justification will be necessary.'

The carpenter silently vowed to obey the Prefect. Otherwise Maximin would eliminate him without hesitation. As for Sabni, he would never hurt an adept.

Ill at ease, the High Priest left. If he suspected a member of the community of treason, was he not proving to be unworthy of his function? But Philae was at war and the High Priest could not afford to be naïve. The enemy was no longer content to attack from the outside.

What a heavy burden he was carrying . . . How could he not completely trust people he had been living with, side by side, for so many years?

The Bishop asked his secretaries to carry out an administrative inquest on recent incidents involving runaway peasants. The results were disappointing; the police reports only mentioned small offences, the breaking of agricultural tools, the theft of an ass, and the annulment of a complaint by a merchant named Apollo. There was no mention of a runaway. The internal security officers consulted did not give any further details. Their chief, captain Mersis, had only one prisoner in his jail: a farmer accused of causing damage to his neighbour's orchard. He admitted having interrogated Apollo and said he was too drunk to be coherent.

Theodore thought the behaviour of this important member of the community rather strange. Therefore, he asked to see him.

Tense and surly, the merchant stood motionless at the threshold of the Bishop's office.

'What kind of a complaint did you wish to lodge with the police?'

'I was drunk.'

'Why?'

'For the pleasure of it . . . not everybody is an ascetic.'

'Do you have children?'

'Four. Two boys and two girls.'

'Are they old enough to work?'

'They lend a hand from time to time.'

'Has any of them run away?'

'God spare me such misfortune! My family is a close-knit unit.'

'God protects the just. Pray continue to supply us with excellent figs.'

Apollo was happy to get off lightly. Seeing him take off in such a hurry, the Bishop was convinced that he was involved in some shady business. Perhaps nothing to do with the runaway youth. Nevertheless, he would look into it further.

Around the main well, Ahoure gathered about ten sisters who, without being hostile to the High Priestess, were sensitive to the persuasive charms of the ritualist. While filling the vases with fresh water, they protested that the circumstances of their life were becoming more and more difficult. One of them declared that she was afraid of what the future might bring. How were they going to fight against a Prefect who was all-powerful and who would not tolerate the existence of rebels, especially if he had the support of the Bishop. Ahoure advised that they should trust in Isis's will of iron.

'Sabni's intransigence is a threat to us. He is too young to guide a community like ours; that is why power has gone to his head and deprived him of his qualities. Soon, he will become a tyrant, he will even forget the rituals and submit us to his demands. We must all be aware by now that the High Priest is waging a battle against the Bishop. Philae's fate matters to him only in so far as the temple plays the role of a fortress and the brotherhood that of an army.'

'Such a small group against hundreds of soldiers? That is unbelievable!'

'Sabni could not care less,' said Ahoure. 'To defy Theodore is a victory in itself. That we may be reduced to slavery or deported is not important to him. He will sacrifice all of us to his passion, and when the moment comes, he will abandon us to the Bishop's reprisal in exchange for his own freedom.'

The terrible words proffered by the ritualist troubled the sisters. The most reticent among them proclaimed the integrity of the High Priest, his sense of duty, his rectitude that no fault could sully.

'I'm not accusing him of duplicity,' protested Ahoure, 'but of vanity and folly.'

'What do you suggest?'

'Let us converse discreetly with our more experienced brothers. If some of them share our worries, we should see more of them and try and think something out together.'

That very evening, after the meal, the carpenter and the ritualist talked under Trajan's pavilion. Oblivious of the sunset tinting the grey slopes of the cliffs with pink hues, they eyed one another with suspicion. Up until that moment, no adept had ever plotted rebellion. They were aware of starting something that would generate open conflict with the High Priest. That brother's face, full of hatred, and his cold stare frightened Ahoure. She regretted having taken the initiative, but it was too late to retreat.

'Sabni is a braggart,' declared the carpenter. 'He believes we are like cattle, always passive, that no one will cross his path. If we resist him, he will leave the island and convert to Christianity with the help of his friend Theodore. The High Priestess will have no choice but to marry the prefect and Philae will be saved.'

Ahoure thought the plan excellent. The brothers and sisters that the two conspirators took upon themselves to bring together would form a cohort capable of deposing Sabni and guarantee the future of the temple.

*

Chrestos caulked a barge, following Sabni's instructions. Then they raised a new mast carved from the temple's last log of cedar.

'The sun has just risen over the horizon . . . Is it really necessary to work so early?'

'The sage gets up early to create, said our fathers, and the fool to cultivate his restlessness. The latter does not want to listen and lives from what makes one die. As soon as the rite of dawn is celebrated, a new world is born. If we are lucky enough to contemplate its beginning, what does fatigue matter?'

'I do not want to become a fool and am determined to remain safe and sound of hand, mouth and heart, as the Rule requires; but I want to get to know everything, to possess your qualities, those of Isis and those of the whole community!'

'Be careful with greed, Chrestos. It is an incurable evil. It vilifies people, makes the closest of friendships bitter, distances the master from his disciples. The greedy no longer have any abode and they lose eternity.'

Troubled by the reprimand, the boy looked to the work he was assisting.

'Is it ready to sail?'

'Not yet. We'll have to check its balance and tailor the correct rudder.'

'The rudder . . . Does it not have the same name as Maat, the ruler of the universe?'

Sabni felt intense joy, although he was careful to conceal such feeling. Chrestos felt the need to link the hieroglyphs so as to discover the depth of meaning in them. Few adepts had followed the path so swiftly. But vanity was lurking, looking out for the neophyte, and to give him full marks would do him a disservice.

'You're right; a boat is also the celestial one which serves to carry divine powers on their voyages into invisible space. No one guides it, the rudder is the eye that discern the right path.

In it we navigate this world. The celestial Philae appears to stand still but in reality it moves with the waters. In you, Chrestos, the rudder is made of the heart and the tongue; may they be in harmony, otherwise you will flounder.'

'I will prove to you that the boat of the temple is my flesh and my blood.'

'Are you being pretentious?'

'Destiny is smiling on me. I will grab the opportunity with both hands and hope to unveil the great mysteries hidden behind the sanctuary doors.'

'They are not attenuated; your eyes would not bear their brightness. That is why community life educates your eyes and amplifies their vision.'

'Will it take long?'

'The duration will depend on you.'

'Several years?'

'For some, it takes for ever.'

'For ever? I would rebel!'

'That would be useless. Passions do not cross the threshold of the covered temple.'

'If I was your son, would you be more indulgent with me?'

'Much stricter.'

'How unfair! Do you distrust me?'

'As much as the others.'

'But they are our brothers and sisters!'

'You will be praised for your goodness, and punished for your weakness. The community would not forgive any error of mine, and justly so.'

'Why are you so hard on yourself? Is fraternity not the bond that helps us resist the assaults of a profane world?'

'It is one thing to be an adept, another to be High Priest.'

'I don't understand . . .'

'That's natural, Chrestos. My function implies solitude.'

'Are you not forgetting Isis?'

Sabni went on board the boat and checked the fastening at the foot of the mast.

135

'Are you trying to see into my heart?'

'I am your disciple and I have a right to know all that concerns you. If you do not really love Isis, why did you marry her?'

Sabni smiled.

'Don't worry, I do, my brother.'

24

Harrowing the fields was finished and the villagers harvested the last olives. The Bishop celebrated Christmas in a church that was too small for the enthusiastic population. Were people coming to celebrate the birth of Christ or with the intention of fighting for the presents the bishopric gave away on such occasion? Trying not to push his enquiries too far, Theodore, indifferent to the Prefect's excitement, was content to observe this display of peaceful forces.

From each house emerged women, children, old people, the sick and the infirm; they invaded Elephantine, where the healthy men sang canticles loudly. There was almost a fight when the army distributed bags of wheat to the populace; itinerant musicians soothed the spirits. Despite the noisy human chaos, God prevailed.

Maximin had a cold. His head was enveloped in a perfumed cloth and his feet rested on a cushion. Behind him a brazier gave out a pleasant warmth, an appreciated comfort in this cold season when the large southern city was flogged by gusts of glacial wind. Boatmen refused to navigate on a Nile prey to violent convulsions.

Despite these inconveniences, Maximin was pleased with himself. He had not worked in vain: thanks to a series of restraining measures, he would improve the province's tax system. From now on, no one would be able to escape taxes, direct or indirect. Levies and duties would be exacted on individuals, land, professional activity, sales, inheritances, journeys and landed and movable property. The group would pay for those who were bankrupt. In exchange, the State would guarantee the proper operation of the post, the maintenance of public buildings; it promised to pay for the keep of a permanent garrison and for the employees of the Bishop. Admittedly, this reshuffling of the economy meant a list of about one hundred taxes; but their precision would please the Emperor. With his support, Maximin would have a free hand and defeat Theodore.

The Prefect invited him to dine. The prelate ate little and refused wine.

'You don't know what you're missing. Wine is the best remedy against the cold.'

'Has your health improved?'

'The fresh air is invigorating.'

'I have examined your fiscal plan: it is crushing.'

'As much as your own. The Emperor wants results.'

'May I remind you that the Nile flood was almost non-existent this year?'

'Land, be it suitable for cultivation or not, has to be taxed. Only one evades this law: Philae.'

Theodore was afraid of this verification. By classifying the temple in the category of sterile terrain, he had spared it heavy taxation.

'I have established the sum the community owes us, including arrears and fines.'

'They will not be able to pay.'

'They will have to evacuate the site and the High Priest will be imprisoned for fiscal fraud. I will examine the case of the High Priestess. Once free from the burden of this pagan clan, she will come to her senses.'

'You're wrong. They will resist.'

'How? The fiscal agent will show no mercy. And that agent is you.'

*

For the Love of Philae

The Bishop had to wait for a week before the wind died down. To the Prefect's impatience, he replied that he did not want to risk the lives of a crew. At the beginning of January, a boat reached the holy island and brought back Sabni. The High Priest was wearing a heavy linen coat and had put on sandals made of papyrus bark. Wool curtains dressed the windows of the office of the prelate, who was warming his hands on the flame of a lamp.

'The island has been declared land suitable for cultivation by Maximin. You owe me a large sum, Sabni.'

'You managed to prevent such a menace five years ago.'

'This time, the Prefect is here in person. I am forced to obey him. If I refuse, he will send the ecclesiastic funds to Byzantium and the province will be ruined.'

'Can you not get rid of this Maximin fellow?'

'You're the subversive, not him.'

'The temple has only a meagre income.'

'Then you must leave the island so that the agricultural labourers can cultivate the land.'

'Will the Prefect dare send his troops?'

'I'm afraid so.'

'Why such unrelenting persecution?'

'He wants to marry Isis. Your community is an obstacle between Maximin and his bride.'

'That man is insane.'

'He is madly in love. He will first use the law, then cunning and finally force.'

'Will you defend us against him?'

'I desire the ruin of Philae, Sabni. I have never pretended otherwise. If the Prefect's strategy results in abolishing what remains of paganism, I will be his ally.'

'That is the Bishop speaking. What does the friend advise?'

'Convert to Christianity and work by my side. Maximin is God's instrument. His action means that your senseless adventure is coming to an end.'

Sabni dwelt on the Bishop's words before a cabinet full of

papyri organized in compartments. He remembered his conversations with the young Theodore, who was passionate about law, and who had willingly shared his knowledge with his friend.

'If Philae belongs to the category of arable land, then I am considered a farmer?'

'Exactly.'

'Consequently, I can recover the old possessions of the temple that constituted its exploitable domain: fields, vineyards and gardens.'

'If one applies the letter of the law, you are right. That aspect has fortunately escaped the Prefect. Otherwise the taxes would triple.'

'Well, let them triple then.'

'What absurd fight are you getting into now?'

'Maximin wants a confrontation, he will have it. The Prefect is a passing official, the temple is eternal.'

When he again set foot on the holy ground of Philae, Sabni felt both relieved and anxious. Relieved because only the peaceful realm of the temple could restore the serenity that his fellow humans had tried to destroy, but anxious because he was issuing a blind challenge. In a month they would be expelled. Brothers and sisters would cling to the columns, trying in vain to resist soldiers who would throw them on to boats that would take them to the emptiness of the world beyond Philae.

Isis was waiting for him at the landing quay. The sun slid over her figure-hugging dress. He took her in his arms and closed his eyes, hoping that the contact of her body and the sweetness of a summer evening would chase away the demons.

'Is it so serious, my love?'

'The Prefect is imposing the statute of arable land on Philae. We owe taxes, levies and surcharges both for the island and for its old dependencies. The sum is considerable. When we are declared insolvent, we will be deprived of all our goods and forced to abandon the sanctuary.'

For the Love of Philae

'Couldn't we ask for a loan?'

'All the wealthy people are Christian and obey Theodore. All we can do is prepare the brothers and sisters for the cruellest destiny.'

Isis and Sabni walked by the temple, passing beneath the image of the great goddess crowned with a vulture's carcass, symbol of the universal mother, surmounted by a solar disc rising between two horns. In her right hand she held the sceptre that made the earth flourish, and in her left the key of life which opened the world of the gods to the adepts. The powerful walls were reflected in the blue waters. The High Priestess stopped in front of a low relief sculpture: the Pharaoh was hitting a ball with his stick, a symbol of the evil eye. In his clenched hand he held a rope binding four figurines of enemies, incarnations of the malefic powers ready to emerge from the four cardinal points.

'As long as the sky rests on its four supports and the earth is stable on its foundations the divine light will appear as the sun. As long as the flood comes when it is due, the soil will nourish its plants, as long as the Northern wind blows when it is time, the deaconates will perform their task and as long as the stars shine there will be some joy, the ultimate pleasures of the mind, and we will not have to leave.'

'If you should decide to give yourself to Maximin to save the temple, I will kill him.'

She caressed his forehead.

'Do not worry. I will never belong to him. The love I give you, no one can take; there is another way. We will pay the taxes.'

25

It took a whole evening to convince Sabni. The High Priest refused stubbornly to cut into the patrimony inherited from the ancestors. Isis managed to show him how the Prefect, believing he was ruining the temple, was offering it renewed prosperity. If the law placed Philae in the centre of an exploitable domain, why not take advantage? Many peasants would be happy to work for the benefit of the holy island. By using its own resources it would depend neither on the Bishop nor on other unreliable favours. The taxes had to be paid; then they had to pray to the Nile so that an excellent flood was produced, fertilizing fields and gardens.

The High Priest gave in; he was attached to the past, whereas Isis opened a way to the future.

After the dawn ritual, they gathered the adepts in front of the monumental gateway.

'Due to the Prefect's decision, the temple is again considered the owner of arable land. Philae will be rich again, if it can settle its debts to the Emperor. The community does not have a single silver coin, but is rich in precious objects and antique furniture. I propose that we sell these to the antique dealer.'

The carpenter protested.

'Do you have the agreement of the High Priestess?'

'Whichever of us addresses the community conveys the other's thought,' said Isis.

142

'Will we have to part with the ancient papyri?' asked the librarian.

'No, they are the very soul of the temple.'

'So is the furniture,' protested one of the brothers.

'You can refuse our proposition,' admitted Sabni. 'In which case, the army will divest us of everything and expel us from the island. In the eyes of the state, ten murders would be better than to commit fiscal fraud.'

'We have stolen nothing!'

'The prefect thinks we are not in order with regard to the State.'

'That's enough arguing,' intervened Chrestos. 'If the community has chosen Isis and Sabni, it is to guide it. They decide and we obey.'

These words put an end to the protests. The brother who guarded the quay went to his house, from whence he brought out a wine jar with a narrow neck and curved handles; it had been a favourite object with one of Ramses II's cupbearers. The cook emptied his coffers full of precious crockery, among which the most beautiful items were some gold goblets embellished with blue lotus petals and some gold cups ornamented with feminine figures smelling a lotus. On the pavement were now amassed silver basins, bronze lamps, perfume-burners in copper; all fashioned by artisans of genius. Isis added the treasure legated from her predecessors: mirrors made of gold and copper, ointment vases sculpted in lapis-lazuli and obsidian, perfume flasks made of glazed sand and soda in green and bluish colours, combs decorated with giraffes and a bowl in porphyry dating from the reign of Cheops.

One of the sisters burst into tears. Isis comforted her.

'When we are wealthy, we can buy back our goods.'

When Sabni disembarked in the early afternoon, he was surrounded by soldiers who took him to Captain Mersis, who in turn alerted the Bishop.

143

The High Priest asked permission to come and go freely between the island and the province territory. His status as landowner gave him the same rights as any other inhabitant of Elephantine. Theodore had no objection. Sabni would be like any citizen, especially since he gave up all provocation by renouncing his white priestly robes, in exchange for a simple brown tunic sewn on both sides and tied with a belt.

'What are your intentions, Sabni?'

'I mean to pay my taxes. Is that not the first and main duty of the Emperor's faithful subjects?'

'Who found the solution . . . you or Isis?'

'Her genius surpasses my talent.'

Theodore smiled.

'Are you trying to be clever with one of your oldest friends?'

'The Rule demands that I tell the truth, even to an enemy.'

'When will you understand . . .'

'I have understood and it pains me as much as you.'

'What can this new manoeuvre bring you?'

'Respectability, Monsignor.'

Sabni went to see the antique dealer, a Lebanese who had set up shop in the Southern capital two years earlier. His stores in Alexandria and Byzantium were famous. In them he had accumulated treasures that had belonged to the pharaohs, on offer to high-ranking collectors keen on exotic goods.

A small, dark man with shining eyes, the trader welcomed the Egyptian cautiously.

'Who sent you?'

'My name is Sabni.'

'Would you be . . .'

'The High Priest of Philae, yes.'

'I have nothing to sell.'

'But I have.'

The Lebanese thought he must be dreaming. Some rich clients waited anxiously for the fall of Philae, convinced that the temple was full of masterpieces and rarities. But the last pagan community erected such an impregnable barrier between the sanctuary and the world, that even the most skilful trader desisted. To converse with the spiritual mentor of those rebels, in his shop, seemed unreal.

'Have you brought a choice item?'

'Come with me.'

'Where?'

'To Philae.'

'I have to tell my assistants . . .'

'Alone.'

'My security . . .'

'I vouch for it personally.'

'Just me, on my own before the brotherhood, on forbidden territory and peopled by demons . . .'

'Dozens of very precious objects await you there.'

The Lebanese merchant did not hesitate long. If Sabni was telling the truth, here was the biggest opportunity of his career.

'When?'

'Right now.'

'Unfortunately, no one is allowed on that island. If the Bishop . . .'

'You're misinformed. Why would a simple agricultural domain be cut off from the rest of the province?'

During the whole journey, the antique dealer remained tense. Fear knotted his gut during the boat crossing; would the soldiers intervene and throw him in prison?

There were no incidents. Full of wonder, his heart pounding, he touched the stones of the quay. What he saw was beyond his wildest expectations. On tresses made of palm fibres were placed a large quantity of antique objects that doubtless came from the temple's treasure.

The High Priestess, whose beauty was legendary, impressed the Lebanese. No Oriental woman could rival her. Added to the delicate features of her face and her splendid figure was a vivacious intelligence that was obvious from her eyes. The

145

antique dealer had to exercise great self-control not to fall on his knees before Isis and venerate her like a goddess. His inherent business sense saved him from being overwhelmed with ecstasy as he gazed over those shining marvels.

'Are you . . . selling these?'

'To whoever bids highest,' said the High Priest. 'If we find the price you offer insufficient, we will look for another buyer.'

'That will not be necessary! Between honest folk, an understanding is always possible.'

By experience, the antique dealer knew that in transactions of this importance, the first to give a price would be the loser. The occasion seemed so exceptional that he threw aside his usual caution. The aficionados would throw themselves on these extraordinary items and try to outbid each other to buy them. So he quoted a sum that was half market value. Isis increased it by a quarter. The antique dealer examined the objects, criticizing the quality of the wood, the finish of the paint or the archaic style of the ensemble which the court at Byzantium would hate. The High Priestess knew the taste of the collectors. They explored the regions of the Empire looking for antique masterpieces to amass in cellars or in provincial villas.

After a long day of negotiation, a compromise was reached to the satisfaction of both parties. The antique dealer would make a fortune and the temple would earn an unexpected sum, at least enough to guarantee one year of financial independence.

Sabni took the merchant back to Elephantine and interrupted the enthusiastic compliments he was receiving. The High Priest's difficult mission did not end there. Preoccupied, he made his way to the tax centre where a despot reigned: Philamon, the second deacon. He had recently been appointed chief tax collector after a long career as a zealous civil servant. Having recently made it to the hierarchical top, he had discarded his rivals by implicating them in corruption scandals. A firm believer, Philamon was a short, skinny man, nervous, almost bald. He loved God and numbers and hated all the rest. According to him, the Lord expressed himself by tax codes and the numbers were righteous; anyone who did not pay up deserved to be sent to prison, to the galleys, or to their death. The rich existed for one reason only: to pay. When the bishop, at the behest of the Prefect, had sent him a dozen tablets and as many papyrus rolls regarding the new tax rule for Philae as an agricultural domain, his heart had leapt with joy. He could not tell if the Christian or the tax collector in him rejoiced the most. On a piece of clay, he had set out three columns: the first, with the names of the elderly brothers and sisters, whose maximum penalty could only be exile. The second, containing the majority of the adepts, who would be condemned to forced labour, and the third with just Sabni's name. The High Priest would not escape torture and would be judged for offending the emperor, refusing to pay, rebellion and fraud.

Isis was not on the list. As a future convert, she would be placed under Maximin's protection. Philamon was keen on observing the exact procedure. Each adept would be entitled to a charge drawn up according to the rules before being handed over to Captain Mersis, in charge of carrying out the arrests.

The tax collector sampled the figs given by his friend Apollo. How could he refuse the gifts offered by amiable citizens, content to be so well administered? Money did not interest Philamon. He owned only a modest house and a field of wheat; to serve the State was what mattered. God could show clemency to a sinner, but he was not allowed to spare a fraudulent taxpayer.

When the soldier on duty at the entrance of the tax office, a rather fetid building in the centre of town, announced a visitor by the name of Sabni, he made the soldier repeat the name. The tax collector thought that it would be a namesake of the High Priest, wanting to complain about heavy taxation. He would be sent away with a supplementary penalty.

The man entered. His stature impressed Philamon: tall, well built, the taxpayer did not seem troubled. Usually, those who came in the door had difficulty hiding their anxiety.

'Who are you?'

'My name is Sabni.'

'Profession?'

'Landowner.'

'Where is your property situated?'

'Philae and its dependencies.'

So that was him all right! The pagan dared to defy the administration, on their own premises. Was this folly or ultimate provocation? The sanction would not vary. Since the High Priest had come this far, Philamon was happy to do him the service of informing him verbally of the important amount due and added that he had a month to pay, a delay that was not negotiable.

'That won't be necessary,' said Sabni, putting down a bag of money on the floor. 'Here is what I owe the Empire: this year's taxes, charges, arrears and fines. Does this bring me up to date?'

On his knees, the incredulous tax collector counted the money coin by coin.

26

During the weekly inspection of the troops, General Narses felt bored. The discipline to which he had dedicated his existence hung round his neck like an old mistress. In this month of February, as preparations for the Harvest started, Elephantine fell into a reassuring slumber. The Blemmyes had not reappeared. A pale sun, barely warm enough to heat the residence of the Prefect, shone. The Prefect himself felt tied down by his own law. Forced to write a report to the Emperor concerning the financial situation of the province, he explained that General Narses's request for a transfer made it impossible to try any expedition into Nubia, even though it would actually be feasible to cross the cataracts. For several days now, the Bishop had been giving him the cold shoulder. Due to his mistaken strategy, had he not given Philae its legal status back?

Whereas Isis remained in the temple, Sabni frequently went to his lands to remunerate the peasants, who were only too happy to work for the holy island.

Maximin had just ruined years of effort. The pagans emerged from their anonymity; already some Christians were being influenced by Sabni's strong personality. Without any proselytizing, the High Priest had already won many people's good will. Some young people manifested the desire to know the Rule of the temple. What Theodore had so feared, his dreaded nightmare, was actually happening. Sabni, God's adversary, was becoming his most dangerous enemy. Like a weed, paganism was spreading with a vitality greater than before.

Philae's reigning couple had the necessary authority and power to, little by little, turn the situation to their advantage. From being oppressed, Philae was moving towards victory.

The Prefect dreamed of Isis. The Bishop prepared to counter-attack. Narses kept a rather careless eye on his soldiers, while dreaming of the privileged moment when he could be alone, on his rock, contemplating the cataract. Despite this mood, an anomaly caught his attention, so he questioned Captain Mersis.

'Are any men missing?'

'About twenty.'

'Why?'

'They're down with fever or stomach aches.'

'Is there an epidemic?'

'We don't know yet. The doctors are examining the sick men.'

This information troubled the General. He remembered African campaigns during which dysentery had decimated entire regiments. The men died a horrible death after having lost all their body fluids.

'What is your opinion, Captain?'

'I am worried.'

'If other cases occur, I want to be informed immediately.'

He took up his command post again. This evening he would not contemplate the cataract.

The first to wake, Isis and Sabni went through all the rooms of the temple, after celebrating the dawn ritual. Each day the holy island was more beautiful, more radiant.

Their happiness and the intensity of their communion was born out of these stones with smiling souls. The voice of the ancestors dwelt in the corridors where the couple often stopped, mindful of the silence created by centuries of offerings. The love that bound them to the heavens and to the earth grew with the vitality of the mornings and the sweetness of the evenings.

In the courtyard, between the two pylons, the carpenter had gathered together about twenty brothers and sisters. Pressed against each other, they formed a compact and hostile group. As agreed with the leader, Ahoure was not among them; she was copying a ritual and kept apart from the conflict so as to preserve, in the event of failure, the trust of the High Priestess.

Isis and Sabni stood still at the top of the steps leading to the entrance of the room with the columns.

'What do you want?' asked the High Priest.

'We are not in agreement with you. We feel that to sell our goods is a disgrace. We wish to remain out of the limelight; to fight against the Prefect and the Bishop is an endeavour that is too dangerous.'

'We had no choice,' reminded Isis. 'The temple is emerging from isolation.'

'That is what we wanted to avoid,' said the perfumer sister. 'We wanted to grow old in peace, away from the hatred of the Christian populace. You and Sabni are forcing us to fight and wage a battle we know we have lost before it begins.'

'That is not true,' objected Sabni. 'By trying to strangle the temple, the Prefect has offered it a means of survival. To remain closed in on ourselves would have been cowardly.'

'What do you know about courage?' said a musician whose hands were deformed by rheumatism. 'You're too young to be High Priest! Whereas we have endured too much suffering as it is.'

Isis sat down on the steps. Nothing in her attitude betrayed irritation. Sabni did likewise; with a gesture he summoned the brothers and sisters to move closer. Some decided to stand.

'What do you suggest?'

'Let us go back to our old statute,' demanded the carpenter. 'Let our goods be returned to us and let them forget about us.'

'You know very well that is a utopian dream,'

'Not if you really want it.'

'Why all these useless regrets?' asked Isis. 'To hide from reality is a fault against our Rule. We must use the fate the gods are sending us for a good purpose.'

'This is not about the gods, but about the prefect! Do not drag us down a path with no escape. Our community should lay low for a while.'

'That is how we subsisted for many years,' admitted the High Priestess. 'But that period is past. Who could possibly reject Philae's renaissance?'

'We would,' said the carpenter's allies.

'If you persist in your destructive intentions, we shall leave the community,' promised the carpenter.

When they were alone, Isis and Sabni joined their hands. This attack from their own people hurt them. How could they condemn the men and women with whom they had gone through so many trials? How could they judge them? They were free to chose and could go back to the world whenever they wished.

'None of them have crossed the threshold of the great mysteries,' said Sabni. 'Is it possible that the brother carpenter is trying to stir a rebellion so that he can find out what the power formulas are?'

'That would be a guaranteed defeat. I fear a greater evil. Our brother is forgetting that not only are we a human group worried about its posterity, but we are also a community at the service of the divine principle. If we shun spiritual adventure, we are condemning ourselves to death.'

'The carpenter knows that. He is one of the more discerning adepts.'

'In that case, the poison of treason has invaded his soul.'

Sabni grew pale. Isis was verbalizing the accusations that he was afraid of admitting.

'You're right. His allegiance is no longer to the temple, but to the Prefect and Bishop.'

'Do you have proof of that?'

'None. That is why I propose that we call another meeting of the Council of the Rule.'

'Who do you wish to name as your assistant?'

'The librarian. Let us leave the ritualist out of this; she would not tolerate the carpenter's insolence and would show no pity. We have to find out the truth and, if he has strayed, we should try and bring him back to the community.'

'Therefore, I will not summon Ahoure. If this is just a mood or a temporary rebellion, fraternal love will appease our brother.'

An arrogant carpenter, with the shadow of a beard, in profane clothes, came before the judges: Isis, Sabni and the pregnant librarian. Isis prayed to Maat, the goddess representing the universal Rule, to enlighten the way for her faithful followers, by opening their hearts. The accused felt no emotion hearing the words that had, in the past, touched his soul. His position had become untenable and he had but one option: to become so odious that he would be rejected and substantiate the birth of internal insurrection, thereby justifying his departure from the island in the eyes of the Prefect. In this way, he could not blame him and would have to find another spy.

'Do you plead innocent or guilty?' asked Sabni. 'Are you conscious of having violated the Rule?'

'I don't care. You and your companion are leading the community on a disastrous path.'

'Yet you did not raise your voice against our nomination.'

'That was yesterday. Power has gone to your heads. You believe in the resurrection of Philae. That's folly! I refuse your authority. I have decided to leave the island, but I will not depart alone. Many among us share my opinion and prefer reason to dementia.'

Outraged, the librarian wanted to protest, but Isis bade her to be silent.

'My designation as High Priest is at the root of this revolt,' judged Sabni. 'Under Isis's wise government, no protest was made. There is a simple solution, my brother: I hand in my resignation and you take my place.'

'I refuse that post.'

'I am ready to entrust you with it,' declared Isis. 'Carry out that which we aspire to and we will obey you.'

'Leave me in peace!'

'You're lying to yourself, my brother. What demon has enslaved you?'

'I am trampling on your Rule . . . banish me!'

'Are you forgetting your calling to the point of detesting your brothers?'

Without further ado, the carpenter left the room where, on the pavement, shone the Golden Cubit of the goddess Maat, the elements of cosmic harmony on which the temple's measurements were based.

27

Isis and Sabni consulted with each of the adepts seduced by the carpenter's arguments. Ill at ease and hesitant, they insisted on their views. The High Priest was greatly disappointed. How was it that these beings who had devoted their life to the temple were now ready to deny and betray their vocation? The same excuses were repeated again and again: the fear of fighting against too powerful an opponent, the desire to grow old in peace, away from conflicts. For them, Philae no longer existed. They dreamed of returning to Elephantine, to see their families again and enjoy anonymity.

Neither the sweetness of Isis nor Sabni's firm stance convinced the rebels to go back on their decision. Frightened, the carpenter went to the library where Ahoure was working.

'Matters are taking a nasty turn.'

Angry, the ritualist broke her pen.

'Sabni refuses to give in, then!'

'He proposed that I take his place.'

'And you refused?'

'It's too risky.'

'You feel you're not up to it, is that it?'

'Yes, indeed. What do you expect? Problems, crushing work, that's what that post means. We have to flee this island, Ahoure. Our plot has succeeded; several adepts will accompany us and we can go back to leading a normal life.'

'You included?'

The carpenter hesitated.

'I love Philae, no doubt more than Isis and Sabni, but there is a time when one has to give up on outdated traditions. We are enclosed in a dream; let's accept the reality of the times we are living in and forget this temple. Hurry.'

She kept her eyes on her papyrus.

'I cannot.'

'Do not be obstinate. One after the other, all the brothers and sisters are going to abandon the couple who govern them. Soon, Isis and Sabni will be at loggerheads. Do you feel it necessary to watch such a spectacle?'

'Get out of here.'

'Ahoure . . .'

'You are a useless fellow and a coward. I was wrong in choosing you for an ally. I shall not make the same mistake twice.'

Sheepish, the carpenter went to join his companions.

When the boats carrying those who had gone back on their word were already distant from Philae, Chrestos shook his fist at them.

'Traitors, I curse all of you!'

'Try to understand them,' recommended the High Priest.

'They are the most infamous creatures! The great goddess welcomed them with all her love. I can forgive the Christians and my enemies, but not those traitors.'

'New beings follow the path that leads to the doors of the great mysteries,' said Isis. 'Do not venerate the past in a naïve way; even in the most glorious times, the way of wisdom then was as narrow as it is today.'

'We are at war. A deserter deserves to die.'

'Our role is to give life, Chrestos, by continuing the divine work.'

'May they be cursed, all the same,' murmured Chrestos.

The adepts threw themselves into the arms of the soldiers who had observed their crossing. Some announced their immediate conversion; others, incapable of betraying their oath, just stated that they would be joining their family and no one would hear any more of them. Hiding his role as leader, the carpenter mingled with the group.

The militiamen were initially surprised by these demonstrations of friendship, then they reacted brutally. With their spears they pushed back the adepts. One of the sisters fell, wounded in the belly. Many brothers had their arms and legs lacerated. The carpenter tried to interfere, but one of the brothers hit one of the soldiers. This aggression was repressed with the utmost violence. Chained, the rebels were taken to the main fortress. Three died on the way. Their bodies were thrown into abandoned irrigation canals, full of foul-smelling mud where the carcasses of asses and cattle were decomposing.

When Captain Mersis saw the sorry cortège come into the sandy courtyard, he immediately understood the extent of the disaster. Half the community had put themselves willingly at the mercy of an enemy whose degree of violence they could not begin to imagine. The soldiers declared that they were attacked by an organized band of brigands. Mersis followed the rules and threw them into a dungeon where they would stay for a fortnight before going into forced labour camps in Asia along with the next convoy of deported convicts. Even if some of them survived the trip, they would eventually die in the mines. Incapable of moving, dragged by two old adepts, the carpenter brother could not stop crying.

Theodore prayed to Christ, implored Him to enlighten his spirit and to show him the way. After such a catastrophe, how could he save Sabni? The Bishop knew that his friend carried in his bosom a truth that merited preservation. Once the layers of mud and illusion were removed, it would be a triumphant faith. God was entrusting him with the task of bringing a pagan

157

priest into the light of true faith. Could there be a more noble, a more exalting vocation? Sabni had the stature of a great prelate and was a natural leader. Side by side, the two men would be as complementary as the Twins of the zodiac; they would be up to any trial. But, he had to free Sabni from his self-imposed imprisonment, which meant breaking up that community that still bound him to that accursed cult. The Prefect's folly had become a decisive weapon to serve the cause of the Lord.

Maximin wrote Isis his tenth letter, imploring her forgiveness. He tore it up, like the nine preceding ones, not caring about the expensive papyrus. How could he explain to the High Priestess that the stupidity of a carpenter was responsible for such misfortune? By using the services of a spy, the Prefect did not mean to jeopardize the community, although he did wish to destroy it to deliver Isis from the magic spell that imprisoned her.

Maximin was lost in his own thoughts. Finding it unbearable to remain in his office, he asked to see the Bishop. Theodore received him coldly.

'You probably detest me.'

'Are you satisfied with your initiative?'

'How could I foresee that this carpenter would lead a revolt?'

'A rebellious group made up of the old and the sick . . . Who would believe such a far-fetched story? Your spy was terrified and tried to escape in the company of the weak people he was able to convince.'

'Are you blaming me for a few unimportant corpses?'

'I am prepared to hear you in confession.'

Maximin, disturbed by the Bishop's gaze, understood why this man governed a province and would, tomorrow, reign over the whole of Egypt. He did not have to raise his voice to give an order and be obeyed.

The Prefect knelt. At that moment, he believed in God. His

presence radiated through his follower. The Prefect's lips trembled, and he murmured his faults.

Isis and Sabni passed Hadrian's gate and went down to the Nile. The cold of winter was giving way to spring, the first flowers would soon blossom decorating the holy island with red, blue and yellow colours. The young people took a walk on the riverbank, still humid with dew. With every step they took, they confirmed the reality of this sacred land, abandoned by half the community.

The day before, Isis did not have the courage to continue writing the ritual meant to favour the return of the distant goddess. Sabni delegated various tasks, but many activities would not be completed. The temple would now be short of qualified artisans; without a carpenter, how would they ensure the maintenance of the furniture used for rituals, mend the beds and the clothes chests? Sabni would learn the necessary skills, already familiar with the rudiments of such craft. He would teach Chrestos who would know how to make the best of such lessons.

'I cannot stop thinking about the departure of our brothers and sisters,' confessed Isis. 'I keep seeing their faces, remembering their joys and their sorrows, the trials we went through together, their gradual discovery of wisdom. I can still feel their sincerity, the strength of their commitment. They broke down, in a moment's weakness. They will be back.'

'Do not count on that.'

'Why?'

'Mersis has sent a message. But I would like to spare you . . .'

'Speak.'

'Do you really want to know? It will only cause you more suffering.'

'I hate suffering; our people have lived for happiness. But I refuse to lie low.'

'Those who left us are either dead or in prison. The official

159

reason was given as a revolt against the army. Even Mersis can do nothing for them.'

Isis cried softly in Sabni's arms. The sun warmed the couple, who had sat down by a tamarisk bush; the desert wind started blowing, the acacias swayed. A deep peace reigned over Philae, heir to a golden age when each being greeted the rising light before thinking of himself.

'You must leave, Sabni.'

'Are you sending me away?'

'The Prefect will pursue you with his hatred, the Bishop will demand your submission. You are in danger, here. Go north, gather the faithful who are scattered, rekindle their hope. Only Philae's High Priest can fulfil this urgent task'

'My place is by your side, at the head of the community who designated us to guide it. The body must live according to the heart. Today, Philae is the heart of Egypt, the one that beats according to our tradition.'

'Since that is so, I will defend Philae and embody the strongest bastion and an insurmountable dam to protect the community. The last adepts will double their energy and will become as fierce as wild animals. Let's take advantage of the fact that we are so few and become even more coherent. We will breathe one breath and be nourished by one power.'

'This temple is the abode of the goddess whose name you bear. To obey her fills me with a transcendental joy whose secret only you hold.'

Isis put her head on Sabni's shoulder.

'How could I express the love I feel for you? It is more infinite than the sky, more fertile than black earth, more radiant than the stars.'

Their lips met, their bodies embraced and love united them beneath the pink shade of the tamarisk.

28

In the corner of the square, there were baskets overflowing with fish, peas and watermelons. Alongside, figs and dates and a dozen wine jars were placed on mats. In the middle of such victuals, the young Chrestos was jubilant, carrying a terracotta platter laden with round breads.

'What's happening?'

'This food comes from our domains! Two peasants and a fisherman brought them. Just say the word and we can have a banquet.'

'What would you like to celebrate?'

'The departure of those traitors! They should never have been allowed inside the temple. By banishing them, the goddess purifies her community and opens up a new path. What does it matter that we are so few . . . Now, we are as one. That was the price for preserving our integrity.'

Neither Isis nor Sabni replied. With the passion of the neophyte, Chrestos had obliterated the past. Devastatingly whole, he despised nuances and embraced the harshest reality without regret.

'So, it is the birth of a new community that we will celebrate by pouring light into our cups.'

General Narses rounded off his verbal report with a pessimistic conclusion: the epidemic was spreading. In Elephantine, neither military doctor nor general practitioner

161

had proved able to check its spread. There were already about twenty soldiers dead in the main barracks alone. With each day that passed, new cases appeared; a disease that would soon spread to the rest of the population. Something had to be done to halt its expansion, otherwise both the army and the Bishop's men would be decimated. Who would then guarantee the town's safety? Admittedly, the Blemmyes had not reappeared, but the danger was still there, latent, hidden behind the rocks of the cataract.

'I will celebrate a mass and publicly plead for Our Lord's help,' promised Theodore.

'I would not advise that,' objected Maximin. 'In case God does not hear, ask each Christian to pray to merciful Jesus for help. Then neither you nor the state compromises their authority.'

'The populace calls for another solution,' said Narses. 'They say "call in a woman healer".'

The Prefect was indignant.

'We are not going to meddle in black magic again!'

'The people say that Philae's High Priestess has powers that were granted her by the goddess. She managed to avoid a similar plague a few years ago. Is that not correct, Monsignor?'

Reluctantly, Theodore granted that it was so. But he strongly objected to resorting to Philae. This would only revive the kind of superstition the people still cherished. The prefect did not disagree, but how could he resist the opportunity to see Isis again? He ordered Narses to ask the High Priestess, leaving her free to decide. If she refused, he was to refrain from pressing her.

The Bishop breathed a sigh of relief: Isis would not accept leaving the holy island to help the enemy.

'Your boat is ready, General. Four rowers will suffice.'

'They can stay on land.'

'You mean to go alone?'

'I know how to oar.'

To the surprise of the officer and the soldiers, Narses lunged into the river heading towards Philae. He wanted to roam those sacred waters over which white herons and ibises with huge wings flew. He navigated calmly towards the temple, that divine fortress built on a rock emerging from the ocean of energy, father and mother to the universe. As he approached, Narses became more and more enthralled. What inspired architect had dared conceive such splendour, at once so austere and attractive, those luminous stones so strong and yet so ethereal, a sanctuary conceived as a vessel ready to sail to heaven? How could one live anywhere else but on this Holy island, sanctified by the rays of the sun and the breath of the wind?

The watchman of the quay ran to warn Sabni of the approach of a vessel containing just one man. Evidently this was no invasion, so the High Priest did not warn the community. The rower stopped a few yards away from the bank and stood up.

'I am General Narses,' he announced in a strong voice.

'And I am Philae's High Priest. What do you want?'

'I request that the High Priestess come to Elephantine to cast out the epidemic that has stricken the barracks.'

Sabni's first thoughts were for Captain Mersis, a man prepared to put his life in danger for Philae. Even if just for his sake, Isis would be willing to intervene. The behaviour of the General intrigued the High Priest; his expression, of a captivating gravity, betrayed great lassitude. Who would have recognized in this placid sailor the captain responsible for so many massacres? He did not dare set foot on the goddess's territory and fixed his stare on the esplanade crowned with the façade of the first pylon, as if his gaze wandered where his legs would not.

'It is up to the High Priestess to decide,' said Sabni.

'Hopefully you will be able to convince her. It is a desperate situation. I shall wait for a reply.'

Isis was dictating to Ahoure a sentence about the eye of the sun swallowing up the serpent Uraeus, whose fiery breath held back the forces of the underworld. Sabni interrupted.

'Excuse my intrusion: General Narses begs you to use our healing methods to save his army, which is at great risk. No doubt they are afflicted by dysentery. The "Terrifying One" is raging and has struck our enemy with her pestilent breath.'

'We must invoke celestial help . . . We cannot abandon Mersis! Such an exceptional being. Does he not deserve every sacrifice?'

Isis went to the northern side of the pylon and meditated by the western wall, where the ritual to appease Sekhmet was depicted; the terrifying goddess that the community of cosmic powers endowed with the ability to spread illness and punish humanity for desecrating the world by neglecting to celebrate the rites. The High Priestess read the text quietly and reminded herself of the healing formulas.

Narses had not moved. From the height of the landing pier, Isis addressed him.

'Are you telling the truth, General?'

'Lying is foreign to me and I vouch for your security on the territory of Elephantine.'

'You are my adversary and an enemy of the temple.'

'I thought I was, before discovering the cataract.'

'Have you changed your mind?'

'My outlook, rather.'

'Isis has enlightened you.'

'I am a loner; my path vows me to silence, not to any religion or community. My arm is tired of destroying. My men suffer; only your science can heal their distress and counteract the demons with sharp teeth.'

'If I heal them, they will become soldiers again.'

'Under my command.'

'If you receive an order to attack the holy island, will you obey?'

For the Love of Philae

'Do you understand that I would not betray my word as an officer?'

Isis went back to the first pylon. She sat beside Sabni, who advised her against this adventure; by aiding the adversary, she might be considered a traitor by the adepts. The High Priestess refuted that argument. If she succeeded, the fruits of victory would be laid at the feet of the great goddess. Once the hatred and rivalries ended, the brotherhood would enjoy the people's esteem again. As in those happy times when every-one knew that a doctor from the temple would come to the bedside of the most needy without expecting remuneration.

From the laboratory, Sabni selected a statue in black granite; it represented a priest holding serpents in his hands, stepping on scorpions, his body covered in hieroglyphs. With the help of one of the strongest brothers, the High Priest carried this strange figure to the boat, where it was loaded before Sabni and Isis boarded.

After crossing the waters, the soldiers refused to touch the stone devil. Narses himself had to lend the High Priest a hand to get the statue on to a chariot; then the cortège made its way to the unusually silent main barracks. Corpses were being hastily buried, beyond the camp perimeter.

The statue was put in the middle of the courtyard, where the parade that had been programmed would not take place. The High Priest stood by it, whereas Narses took Isis inside the officer's quarters. She drew back, hit by an unbearable smell of pestilence. The pained look on the General's face gave her the courage to go forward. The sick were laid out on straw beds. Most were dirty; some male nurses were trying to make them drink some water. The High Priestess examined the infected soldiers one by one, putting her right hand on their forehead and her left on their belly. Twice she pronounced the terrible diagnostic: 'An illness that I know but that I cannot vanquish.' In all other cases, she would try to heal. She was able to pronounce that most reassuring of sentences: 'An illness that I know and that I can overcome.'

165

'Take them outside, near the statue.'

'The sun will kill them.'

'On the contrary. Please obey me, General, or I'll go back to the island. Every man has to be washed and their clothes burned. Show me where the camp's pharmacy is.'

In there, Isis found the necessary ingredients to prepare her remedy against quartan fever and the intestinal infection: a potion mixed from silphium juice, myrrh, *Physostigma venenosum*, hemlock, hellebore and opium. She mixed the substances in a flask and obtained a solution which she then poured on the statue. The liquid became impregnated with the magic texts proclaiming the victory of light over the demons, the carriers of suffering. Sabni collected the precious brew, and while he administrated a potion of it to the patients, Isis chanted the verses of an ancient rite.

'May they be identified with Horus, the divine son, and preserved from every ailment; may the great goddess deliver them from the male death that attacks from the right and the female death that attacks from the left; may the vessels linked to the heart diffuse energy into each limb expelling the accursed fluxes.'

The High Priestess demanded that the simple soldiers should also be brought to her, and she gave them the same treatment, then she asked for all the sick men to be carried into the stone buildings where the windows were open but veiled so that the air circulated in restful obscurity.

'Let there be no more noise, these men need to sleep.'

Narses gave his orders; the barracks were silent. Isis hypnotized each unfortunate man until they fell into a deep sleep, she massaged their hands and the back of their neck to chase away the evil forces that had taken over their bodies; some fled like simple shadows, others resisted.

By the time the sun had set, the High Priestess was exhausted. The general offered Isis his bedroom. Sabni spent the night leaning on the statue, which the soldiers observed with a certain disquiet. They wondered if their safety

For the Love of Philae

depended on this disturbing figure, this stone medicine man from another world covered in incomprehensible signs.

When evening fell, none of the soldiers presented acute symptoms any longer. Already the rumours had spread in Elephantine, soon to spread through the entire province: the goddess of Philae had vanquished the epidemic.

Captain Mersis was careful to maintain a distant, almost indifferent attitude, but his furtive smile was the sweetest of rewards for Isis. General Narses persuaded Sabni to accept, as a gesture of thanks, about one hundred earthenware jars full of wine. Footsoldiers carried the healing statue, which was touched in passing by dozens of passers-by; many shouted out the name of Isis and acclaimed the High Priestess.

In front of the pier were the Prefect and the Bishop. Maximin took a step towards Isis; he had prepared a speech, but at the sight of her he was struck dumb.

'Why did you save your enemies?' asked Theodore.

'The soldiers ensure the security of landowners. We are grateful to them.'

'You performed pagan rights that are officially banned.'

'My remedies work; as for this statue, it is just a reminder. Why see the devil everywhere? Nature is part of God's work; thanks to plants, we can heal the most terrible illnesses. When the magic of the hieroglyphs is added to their virtue, the medication becomes even more effective.'

Outraged, Theodore turned away, but not before noticing a glint of irony in the eyes of the High Priestess. Another success like this and she would be mocking Christ.

29

Spring triumphed. As soon as the sun came out, the fresh morning air gave way to a sweetness that penetrated the skin like a balm. Each morning Isis took a walk with the librarian, whose pregnancy would soon run its course. Philae was experiencing moments of unexpected happiness. Sabni was taking care of the temple's land on which the peasants worked with growing enthusiasm; the spectre of hunger and poverty grew distant. The High Priest suffered from devoting too much of his time to material chores not conducive to meditation, but he was happy to see that serenity was once again gradually filling the hearts of the adepts. After so many years of uncertainty and worry, the temple, again part of the established order, played its role as castle of the soul that no one dare lay siege to.

The Prefect went through phases of exaltation and neurasthenia. He detested himself and decided to go to the island no matter what, then hesitated and fell into inertia. He had left all matters of state in the Bishop's hands. Without Isis, his days had no meaning. To know that she was so near and yet be unable to join her, could there be a more diabolic torture?

There was no word from the Emperor. Not a single message from Byzantium since the arrival of the conquering army in Elephantine. Either court intrigues were keeping him busier than usual, or he had decided that Maximin was in disgrace.

Such a turn of events would surely result in the appointment of a more powerful administrator to govern the province.

The Prefect had almost forgotten about the gold of Nubia. The love of an inaccessible woman was causing him to ruin a brilliant career. Was he not behaving like a stupid youth, mesmerized by an illusion?

Maximin summoned Narses.

'Prepare an expedition corps.'

'How many men?'

'About thirty, with a scout. The Bishop will provide him.'

'Mission?'

'To surmount the first cataract and progress south by the caravan road. To question the natives and locate the gold mines. As soon as they return, we will lead the army.'

'So you will be coming . . .'

'Did you have any doubts? I will be by your side and we will bring back heaps of gold.'

Three days after the departure of the expedition corps, the scout returned. Seriously injured in the shoulder, with an arrow tip still stuck in his flesh, he died one hour after having reported to General Narses how the soldiers who made up this reconnaissance force had been exterminated. Thanks to experienced boatmen, the soldiers surmounted the first cataract without suffering any losses. During a whole morning spent tracking, they did not meet a soul. When they paused for the first time, at the foot of a dune, they came face to face with dozens of black warriors armed with lances and clubs. Despite valiant efforts, the infantrymen did not resist for long. Although each struck down several adversaries, the horde of assailants grew incessantly. Obeying orders, the scout fled to report back to headquarters. With the fortified walls in sight, he thought he was safe; the arrows flying out from the top of the ramparts certainly dispersed his persecutors, but one of their arrows, as powerful as it was accurate, did not miss its target.

'Blemmyes,' said the scout, breathing his last, 'hundreds of Blernmyes.'

Maximin was terrified. The Nubian gold seemed to be becoming inaccessible. His army would not be able to exterminate a large, mobile and truly ferocious army.

'Let us reinforce our defences,' proposed the Bishop. 'Let your men and mine join forces to make the frontier even more insurmountable. I am sure the Blemmyes are going attack, sooner or later.'

'I am not so sure,' objected Narses. 'They are masters in their own territory and they prove it to us in the most barbaric fashion. The Emperor will not send regiments to pacify this lost, forsaken region. The Blemmyes have reached their objective.'

'God willing.'

Theodore waited until he was alone with the Prefect to point out something that was even more disturbing than the victory of the Blemmyes: the devil was eating its way into the soul of the people of Elephantine.

'Isis's intervention was disastrous.'

'She saved many lives.'

'She also troubled many weaker spirits. Many important people are now suggesting that the system of donations to the temple should be revived. In exchange, the High Priestess would become the head of the corporation of medical practitioners and teach the ancient ways of healing. About a dozen young men and women have asked to enter the community. They have been arrested and I have had them deported to the north, but others claim vocations.'

The Prefect's face lit up. If Isis accepted this new post, she would have to live in Elephantine. He would see her every single day, invent hundreds of ailments for himself, and complain of a thousand incurable and unbearable illnesses that demanded constant care. Fortune was again smiling on him; therefore, he enthusiastically supported the request from the dignitaries.

'You're misinterpreting the situation,' said the Bishop. 'The real faith, in some souls, is a flickering light that the wind of paganism could well extinguish. The powers of darkness are using that woman to destroy Christ's message.'

'Isis is all love; there is no darkness in her.'

'She serves the devil's cause. And so do you.'

The serious tone of Theodore's voice made Maximin shudder.

'That means . . .'

'That means that I am threatening you with excommunication. The emperor entrusted you with a mission: to bring back the Nubian gold and to close down the last of the pagan temples. Not only did you fail, but worse still, you have taken a stand against the Church and against Christ.'

The Prefect did not take the warning lightly; such a measure would condemn him to the loss of all titles and to exile. Nevertheless, he resisted.

'Isis is my life.'

'In that case, let me take action.'

Escorted by soldiers and deacons, the Bishop went to Elephantine's southern tip, where Jewish and Aramaean mercenaries were stationed. They celebrated the cult of Yaho, despite the fact that their sanctuary was destroyed during persecutions that occurred long ago. The triumph of Christianity had given them back, albeit discreetly, their citizenship. However, the Bishop still maintained the ban on a custom that scandalized the inhabitants of the province.

This visit more than surprised the mercenaries. Usually, Theodore crushed them with his contempt. They were the lowest of the low, given the meanest of tasks, and they feared they had committed some fault that would serve as a pretext for some additional chore. However, the Bishop just ordered their leaders to follow him to a closed field where the rams slept.

*

Sabni was making his way to the temple when a peasant warned him that something terrible had happened. The Jews had broken down the enclosure of the rams, a property belonging to Philae since the very foundation of the temple. The animals, still considered sacred by the people, had been taken. In Elephantine, not a single sheep was killed as a sign of respect to the god Knum, the guardian of the secret source of the Nile.

The High Priest confirmed the theft; without wasting a moment, he set off to meet with the Bishop, but had to wait for over an hour in the antechamber.

Theodore welcomed him affably.

'Don't huff so, Sabni. I have been informed.'

'So it is you, you're behind this sacrilege!'

'To kill a ram is no offence to God.'

'By authorizing this massacre, you're harming the soul of every Egyptian.'

'The Egyptians are Christian. The Jewish colony feeds on the flesh of those animals at Easter. They will be slaughtered for the glory of Yaho.'

'Long ago, the populace destroyed their sanctuary to punish the very same transgression.'

'That was in the old days, my friend. Today, Philae no longer governs the province and its power is dead. It no longer inhabits the body of any sacred animal; they are just meat to be eaten.'

'There was stealing and the breaking down of the enclosure: those are grave offences.'

'If it had been so, you could lodge a complaint. I have here a report by the military police. Two trustworthy peasants saw the rams destroy the fence.'

'And chance led them to the camp of the Jewish mercenaries . . .'

'The hand of God, Sabni. He took them there . . .'

'What are your plans to attack the temple?'

'Philae was wrong to emerge from obscurity. Convert,

Sabni, and come and be at my side. I am waiting for you, impatiently.'

The Bishop thought the High Priest hesitated and his eyes seemed to vacillate. Tight-lipped, he turned and left the office.

'The wheel is no longer working,' observed the peasant. 'The iron parts have been damaged. They need replacing; otherwise, there will be no irrigation.'

The man was not exaggerating. The oxen, used to continually turning the great wooden wheel to which they were yoked, seemed astonished to be resting. The sakieh, a mechanism governing the long chain of buckets that filled as they plunged into the water and emptied at the top of their course, had stopped.

'The shadufs are to raise water. Let's make more use of them,' recommended Sabni.

The peasant shook his head. He led the High Priest to the side of an irrigation canal where some long poles were balanced on crossbeams, with a rope and bucket at one end, and a heavy counter-weight at the other. By pulling the rope the peasant dipped the bucket into the water. (Poles were fixed on a fork-shaped contraption which allowed them to swing back and forth. At one extremity there was a terracotta container to fetch the water; at the other end there was the necessary counterweight to straighten the container when it was full.) The forks had been sawn in two, the poles were smashed, the containers broken . . . the vandals had spared nothing.

'Does anyone know who the culprits might be?'

'It all happened at night. Nobody saw anything.'

Each peasant was responsible for his 'shaduf'. On the other hand, the wheel of irrigation belonged to the State. Hence, Sabni set off once again to lay siege to Theodore's office. In the Bishop's absence, a secretary received him, noted down his request and sent the High Priest on to a colleague in charge of the tax roll. The clerk verified that the field existed and asked for a precise description from the owner. The mending of the wheel was not his department, so he took Sabni to the civil servant in charge of irrigation. He in turn asked many technical questions, noting down the answers. The wheel itself was also legally registered, which the official readily recognized. The supply of spare parts, however, was the responsibility of another department. This department was located in the northern part of town. There the High Priest was seen by an old Greek, who was particularly finicky; after a long conversation, he specified that he only dealt with wooden spare parts. If it was a matter of replacing the iron parts, as Sabni insisted, he had to go to the arsenal and contact an officer. Sabni decided not to give up and insisted with the soldiers who tried to ignore him. After being finally admitted to the office of the military supply corps, he was not given a chance to state his case. All metal supplies, even for civilian use, had been suspended given the state of alert. Unacceptable, the request was not even registered.

Hoisting the sail of the boat that would take him back to the temple, Sabni was angry. So that was how the Bishop had decided to destroy Philae; depriving it, little by little, of the subsistence materials that the Prefect had made available. Without fury or violence, the most pitiless of wars had started. Some months earlier, he would have felt desperate; but now the love of Isis had given him strength. He had tasted happiness and would not relinquish it.

30

The baker pounded the grain in a mortar and sifted it, imploring the gods to watch over Philae. When he realized that Isis was standing still beside the oven, he dropped the conic mould that always received the dough of the first bread of the day.

'Why does the presence of the High Priestess scare you so?'

'I was just surprised . . . you never come here.'

'Think of a better explanation, my brother. Not a week goes by when I do not inhale the delicious smell of your bread and your cakes. Your eyes are shining with a vague light: they lie.'

The baker trembled.

'I am worried, like all adepts . . .'

'The carpenter, was he not your best friend?'

'His disappearance was a cruel blow.'

'You were always together. Why did you not follow him?'

The baker lowered his head.

'Was it fear of a hostile world,' asked Isis, 'or the refusal to betray Philae? I wish to know the nature of your soul. Is it in harmony with the temple, or is it lost in the dark waters of resentment?'

The baker picked up the mould and cleaned it.

'I have hated Sabni, for he asked too much of us. He's a young man, and yet he treats his older brothers like children and does not ask for their advice.'

'What advice would that be?'

'To give up and conform. In Elephantine, we would

Christian Jacq

simulate a conversion and we would hold secret meetings to worship Isis. The great goddess would surely be satisfied with such devotion. Are we not incapable of keeping such a vast temple whose very existence draws the wrath of the Bishop down on to our heads?'

'I can remember a time when you were more pugnacious. The carpenter and yourself repudiated the slightest concession to the Church and declared that you were ready to fight.'

'We were young then.'

'Is there not another reason? The fact that you were both denied initiation to the great mysteries?'

The baker lifted his eyes.

'Our seniority gave us the right to know.'

'That is not so, and you know it. Only the perfection of your work and the knowledge of the sacred language can open the ultimate door.'

'That is true . . . but how could we accept stopping midway in our quest?'

'Only you are the master of that destiny. By your actions, you acquire a place for yourself in the temple's hierarchy and you chose your nourishment.'

The brother sifted the flour once more to obtain the fineness required.

'I have accepted my limitations; now, my hatred is gone. Grant me the joy of staying in the community until my last breath and of participating in the work according to my capacity.'

'If that is your wish, fashion your happiness like hot and crusty bread.'

The face of the artisan changed. Under its apparent weakness, a new conviction was apparent.

'I must tell you, High Priestess.'

Isis feared new transgression.

'Neither you nor Sabni realize how much the community loves and venerates you with all their hearts. The trials we have suffered have made us more mature and have made us appreciate what we have; please believe in us as we believe in you.'

176

*

The Bishop consulted the list of missing people: about a dozen farmers had run away, unable to pay their taxes, and three sons who had beaten their drunkard boatman father. They had been caught and put in prison; the Prefect would judge them when he thought appropriate. Indifferent to public affairs, he remained a recluse in his house, dreaming, meditating and composing poems to Isis. In the evenings, he drank until he was completely inebriated.

The Bishop was now sure that Maximin had gone completely mad. How could the love of a woman degrade a man to such an extent? The people, with an imagination that was as fertile as it was naïve, thought him bewitched. Theodore thanked God; through Isis, the Lord was aiding his plans. As complete master of the province, the prelate would succeed in ruining Philae. He would exile the High Priestess and save Sabni.

The Bishop was in the habit of reading all the documents that were addressed to him: interminable lists of taxpayers, common people or important landowners, accounts of decisions taken by the managers of commercial associations, bank administration reports, short messages written by his spies who mingled among the people and listened in on discussions. By neglecting nothing and memorizing each detail, day after day, he was in on every secret his subjects concocted. That was the role the good Lord had assigned him, He knew the heart of all his creatures.

The description of a party held at Apollo's house intrigued him. The bishop noticed that the report omitted one of the fig merchant's sons. Very proud of his success and growing fortune, Apollo had invited many friends along with their children. Several of Chrestos's frieds, for whom the youth's absence was conspicuous, had asked after him and been astonished that he was not at the party. Apollo had replied that his son had left for Lycopolis, where his grandfather lived. Theodore would check this. All he had to do now was to find out whether anyone named Chrestos had indeed presented

177

himself at any of the city's toll points between Elephantine and Lykopolis.

During the first week of March, the twenty adepts resident on the holy island prepared the harvest according to the ancient custom. After celebrating the ritual of the lifting of the cosmos, thanks to which the breath of life circulated between heaven and earth, they implored the solar power hidden in the body of serpents. These, by gliding in the fields and sliding through cultivated land to go and find dark holes to shelter in, brought bounty to the ears of corn. The cobra goddess, the one-who-loves-silence, heard the secret prayers of the harvesters. Thanks to the availability of shadufs, repaired with whatever was to hand, water was not scarce.

Everywhere, chanting voices could be heard. The old tunes and refrains contained many allusions to the old gods and to the benevolent spirits hidden in the ripe blades of wheat. These were times of hope mingled with fear, fear of a bad harvest, fear of the plundering carried out by the numerous day labourers who came from the north. At night, peasants armed with forks defended their goods. Sabni kept them company in their vigil. After the sabotage of the great wheel, they feared some other misdeed.

Philae gave in to a sense of euphoria. In a few days, the librarian's child would be born; Chrestos was making great progress in his study of the sacred language; Isis perceived a wonderful fervour in the adept's spiritual practice. They were now a more coherent community, free from idleness and sluggishness; they followed the path leading to the one and only god celebrated since primordial times in Egypt.

Sabni would have loved to remain among them, under the protective shade of the temple's columns. But his duties came before pleasure. By ensuring the protection of the field, he was preserving the very existence of the temple. He dreamed about the day Chrestos would be ready to replace him, when he would be just one of the brothers again, concerned only with offerings to the goddess and the purity of the ritual.

Numerous gold-coloured sheaves of wheat were assembled
and loaded on to donkeys that transported them to the village
square.

The State would take its part and calculate the taxes due on
the amounts attributed to Philae. Before taking his place at the
head of the procession, Sabni ordered the sheaves to be carefully stacked; during the winter they would make excellent
fuel to heat the pipelines in the water rooms.

A noisy crowd of landowners and peasants assembled
around the village square; the tax collector Philamon ordered
some small wooden stands be erected where, protected from
the sun, the clerks proceeded to register the sheaves of wheat
and calculate the taxes due. Nine trips were necessary to bring
the totality of the harvest. Whereas many of the farmers,
victims of the insufficient flood, had a sad look about them,
Sabni was happy to see the fruits of his generous land.

The tax inspectors were, as in previous years, exasperatingly
slow: not a grain was to escape their vigilance. Released one
after the other, the sheaves were returned to the back of the asses
that were directed either to the granaries or to the private barns.
While nibbling onions and bread, Sabni waited patiently in the
company of other landowners. With the sun setting, the produce
of his field was still stuck in the village square. The scribes were
going to have to hurry if they were to finish before nightfall.
Soon, near the deserted improvised offices, there was just Sabni
and another farmer who had a few patches of land. Worried, the
High Priest addressed the tax collector, who was putting away
his things and preparing to leave.

'I would like to know how much my taxes come to and take
back my share of the harvest.'

'What is the name of the landowner?'

'Philae, as you well know.'

Philamon said a few words to the scribe who was in a hurry
to leave.

'No taxes are due. You have only to pay for the rental of the
asses.'

'But that is incredible . . . My harvest is abundant!'

'Yes, indeed, but it is all reserved for the army.'

'You must be mistaken.'

'I've been doing this job for twenty years and have never once made a mistake.'

'Philae is private property. Ask the Prefect.'

'If you have a complaint to lodge, come to my office tomorrow.'

The tax offices opened at dawn. Already there was a queue outside; many complaints would be lodged and very few acknowledged. When it was Sabni's turn, the inspector consented to consult his colleague who had given the order to send the temple's harvest to the barracks. Without providing any explanation, he vanished and came back a few minutes later accompanied by Philamon.

'My subordinate has committed a blunder,' admitted the tax collector.

Sabni breathed a sigh of relief.

'Do you wish to lodge a complaint against the administration?'

'When can I have the wheat?'

The tiny man bit his index finger.

'Well, that's the problem . . . It will be extremely difficult.'

'And just why is that?'

'Your harvest has already been stored in the military granaries. That means it now belongs to the army. An Episcopal decree would be needed, countersigned by the Prefect, to transfer it back.'

'You will sign that decree, Theodore. You, a man of God, cannot condone injustice.'

'Don't lose your temper, Sabni. It is said that adepts of Isis never lose their cool, not under any circumstances.'

'You want to starve the temple and force us to leave it, even at the price of committing the kind of illegality that you have fought against.'

The Bishop looked Sabni straight in the eye.

'God is above human laws.'

'In the time of the pharaohs, He was their foundation. Your God justifies the malfeasance of his servants all too easily.'

'Your vision is limited; it only goes as far as the temple walls. The time has come to break them down for your own salvation. But I have signed the decree that will give you back your property. If you no longer trust me, take it yourself to Maximin.'

'He will chase me away like a mangy dog.''

'You are a respectable citizen who pays his taxes. No doubt you are right to mistrust Maximin; he is unpredictable. Come back tonight.'

During the afternoon Sabni wandered in the alleys around Elephantine, quenched his thirst in a tavern, walked by the riverbanks. He mingled with the people and heard conversations in which the name of Isis the healer was often invoked. According to them, she was the only one who could ensure that the water would rise, so that next flood would be plentiful. There was also talk of a massacre that occurred when a band of scouts went south to locate the gold mines and were decimated by the Blemmyes; thus the proclamation of a state of emergency and the strengthening of the fortifications.

At the end of the day, Theodore ushered Sabni into his office. On the table was the decree with the bishop's seal.

'Maximin refuses to sign. Philae's wheat remains the property of the army. You will receive compensation.'

'When?'

'As soon as the budget of the province is settled.'

'What date?'

'Perhaps at the beginning of next year, maybe later. The work of the accountants is slow, for it has to be exact. They cannot afford to make any mistakes, or they will suffer the consequences. Furthermore, the Prefect awards compensation with interest. Delicate procedure, Sabni, especially at a time when the army's financing takes priority.'

31

Troubled and disappointed, the High Priest crossed the silver waters with difficulty. Hidden inside the disc of the full moon, Osiris's sacred hare would favour births and renewed energies; Sabni asked for the strength to row and keep his cadence until he reached the holy island.

More powerful and determined than ever before, Theodore was not going to let up on his prey; by despoiling the temple, he condemned it to suffer famine. The Prefect was but a puppet in the hand of a prelate who realized that although Isis had only a few adepts, she was gaining ground. Little by little, she seduced the more reluctant spirits and thus Philae was becoming dangerous.

Fnally, Sabni reached the quay.

Broken in body and spirit, the High Priest tied the boat and fell exhausted on to the stone ledge. No sooner had he lain down than Isis was helping him up.

'Come quickly, our sister is giving birth.'

They went into the door of the first pylon and took the passage leading to the birth temple. Seven sisters, symbolizing the seven aspects of Hathor, bent over the cradle of the newborn, to grant him their favours, forming a circle around the childbearing mother. They rhythmically beat a drum and chanted a hymn to the newborn king, son of Isis and Osiris, with whom the newborn was identified.

'The High Priest should bring the potter's wheel.'

For the Love of Philae

Sabni took the precious object from the treasure room. It was used by Knum to mould the world every day and create beings. Forgetting his exhaustion, Sabni followed Isis who, by manipulating a block mounted on a rolling mechanism slotted into a mortise, liberated the access to a small room where the sisters took the librarian. With sideways pressure, the High Priestess made the stone slot into a void in the wall and hid the entrance.

Two sisters helped the future mother stand above a bed of hot stones from whence came a perfumed smoke. Isis poured water mixed with aromatic calming substances. A sweet light filled this closed sanctuary where, at the beginning of time, the great goddess had appeared as a woman who could be perceived as a black or pink woman.

The delivery was slow and painful. When the birth actually happened, they were forced to acknowledge that the child was stillborn. Isis fainted.

The librarian died a week later, overwhelmed with grief. The father lost his mind. Sabni stayed by his wife's bed; for a long time, she refused to accept reality.

Destiny was proving too cruel; the announcement of the birth would certainly have been received with enthusiasm in Elephantine, in the entire province and even the whole of Egypt. Sabni's tenderness healed the High Priestess of her despair. Refusing to be crushed under the weight of such misfortune, he conveyed his determination to her. If she faltered, the whole community would be lost. Isis overcame her grief; when she gathered the sisters together, she managed to inspire them with renewed joy. Philae had lost a child, but had still gained Chrestos. Youth was not deserting the temple after all.

Even though the sun had vanished into the realm of shadow, its warmth remained. The sweetness of the evenings that the adepts spent in the gardens surrounding the temple were full of the rhythm of poems and tales read aloud. Isis and Sabni went to bed last, after having contemplated the moon and the stars.

'We will soon run out of wheat. Why are our storehouses still empty, considering we had such an excellent harvest?'

'The Bishop and the Prefect have requisitioned all our goods. There is not a blade of wheat left. We should be compensated, but our complaint will be lost in the labyrinths of the administration.'

'Will we be deprived of nourishment?'

'Tomorrow, I will return to our fields. With irrigation we will have another harvest before the flood; no civil servant is going to take that away from us.'

Soldiers were guarding the approach to the field. No peasant was working on it, despite the need for the land to be ploughed and drained.

'Requisition?' Sabni asked a sentinel.

'Access to your land is open.'

'Where are the labourers?'

'I don't know.'

'Why this show of force?'

'I do not know that either. We have received orders to keep guard. The rest is not our business.'

'Where is the officer in charge?'

'He has gone back to camp.'

It was in Elephantine, in the Bishop's offices, that Sabni obtained the answer. Due to the forthcoming flood, Theodore was taken up with clearing the main canals and mending the dikes so that the waters could be directed to the storage basins. Therefore, he had sent quite a number of state employees to carry out an assignment that would take at least two months; to fill in cracks, to clean out the right-angle corners; all required intensive labour.

Among those agricultural labourers told to leave off their usual work were those who depended on Philae.

'The Bishop will see you now,' announced the orderly.

He guided Sabni into a small interior garden where Theodore cultivated medicinal plants. Kneeling, he was watering some sage.

'You have taken all my employees.'

'Necessity makes law.'

'Have other owners been equally castigated?'

'What does that matter?'

'Do my protests have any chance of succeeding?'

'None. Requisition is a legal act and to serve the State is an imperial duty.'

'You're preventing me from reaping a second harvest.'

'I am caring for the welfare of the people in general by improving the province's irrigation system. Is that what you are reproaching me for?'

'You're serving your God, Theodore.'

The Bishop plucked a weed.

'I want the happiness of Elephantine. Its inhabitants must co-operate; Isis and her adepts are no exception.'

'What do you mean?'

'To raise the dikes to a good height, I need many men. The inactive ones will no longer lay about doing nothing, starting with the inhabitants of Philae.'

'How can you, an ecclesiastic, express yourself in such a way? No priest will leave the island. Are you not aware that we work at making divine energy circulate and rendering it perceptible on this earth?'

'There are no longer any priests in Philae, only idlers. If they wish to eat, they have to work.'

'You're ruthless.'

'I have no choice, Sabni. Cease this Calvary of yours, renounce your ways and follow Christ. You will know the greatest bliss.'

'A coward and a traitor . . . Would you have him as a friend?'

'God's mercy is infinite. Your past will cease to count.'

Theodore stood up and took Sabni by the shoulders.

'Don't force me to take measures that are even more restraining.'

'I have no choice either.'

Sabni did not conceal anything from the community gathered together in the courtyard situated between the two pylons. Philae had only vines left, and arid land that produced some very poor quality grain. Thanks to the sale of ancient objects, the temple had some silver coins to purchase wheat, dried fish and fruit. The High Priest would go into town and negotiate.

'Your face is too well known,' said the unguent specialist, a grumpy old man whose voice was seldom heard except during liturgical chants. 'The cowards will refuse to sell you victuals. The Bishop must have threatened them with the worst of financial penalties if they trade with the temple. I will go. I have not left the island for the last forty years. My old friends are rich and respected, they own land and herds; I will get the best prices and rent donkeys and boats.'

'The soldiers will question you.'

'When they understand what is going on, it will be too late. I will embark on the desert side and will reach Philae by the north. No one uses that route.'

Isis interfered.

'It's too risky.'

'I have made up my mind. I have always obeyed and kept quiet, this time I will impose my will because it is in accordance with the Rule.'

'Is that for you to judge?'

'The High Priest must preserve the community both internally and in regard to the outer world. Let him delegate this last function this once and I will confront the profane world. In three days, I will be back with the victuals.'

Isis looked at Sabni. He nodded his approval. The unguent specialist saluted him and walked with assurance to the quay.

A very skinny sister, with a face that resembled the blade of a knife, stepped forward.

'I am leaving with him.'

'It is wiser for our brother to act alone; your health is fragile.'

'You don't understand, Isis, I am taking advantage of the trip to leave the community; life between these walls has become too ruthless. The Bishop, the Prefect and the Christians hate us. They are going to see to it that we starve to death and abandon the island.'

'You have sworn to dedicate your life to the goddess.'

'She no longer protects us from the vindictiveness of our enemies.'

'Remember what happened to those who ran away.'

'I am not running away. I want to survive. They made the mistake of leaving in a group. Alone I will not be noticed.'

Sabni gripped Chrestos by the wrist when he saw he was about to lose his temper. The sister turned to the pylon where the Pharaoh, represented as a giant, terrorized his adversary.

'This is but legend. Soon, it will be a wreck. In less than a century, humanity will have forgotten that a temple was even erected here. Our heroism is ridiculous and vain; you should all follow me.'

She ran to the boat that the unguent specialist had just boarded. Isis closed her eyes and stood close to Sabni.

When she opened them, a gentle joy took hold of her, softening her disappointment; no one had followed suit. No one had followed the sister with the sharp face.

32

From the square that preceded the first pylon, Sabni admired the Western portico whose capitals sang the sacred glory of nature. Dazzled by the sun, he took refuge in the shade of the columns and through one of the windows of the peaceful fortress gazed out into the deep, strong azure of the waters. The temple seemed increasingly vast for this handful of adepts who had chosen to anchor their lives to the island. The vast esplanade, the courts, Hadrian's portico, the room with the columns, the venerable Throne, the library, the laboratory, the treasure, the crypt and the priests' quarters had been built for a large community.

Isis laid her hand on Sabni's chest.

'It's no use torturing yourself. Our destiny is in the hands of the goddess. We are but the clay and straw with which she builds the work dear to her heart.'

'How can I not think of the past? There is so much strength in us, so much desire to bring the spirit to life . . . what is the reason for this decline? Why is this world running towards its ruin?'

'Perhaps because it is all illusion.'

'Are you forgetting that which is set down in our Book of Enlightenment:

"I will destroy what I created. This country will return to its primitive estate. It will return to the waters from whence it emerged. I am what will remain with Osiris for company,

*when I am once again transformed into the serpent that man
cannot know and that the gods cannot see."*'

'You only see the dark side of the prophecy. For he who is
resurrected in Osiris, eternal life is unveiled. It is our role,
Sabni: to prepare for resurrection throughout our lives. As long
as the wisdom of the great mysteries is passed on, the spirit will
radiate forth. Our tradition is the very future of humanity.'

'Theodore is starving us.'

'He is forcing us to awaken our most secret energies.'

He took her in his arms.

'Are you indestructible, Isis?'

Their bodies were in harmony. United in each other, they
were one being. A ray of sunlight delineated a relief sculpture
depicting a sacrifice and bathed them in its warmth.

A cry for help pulled them back out of their ecstasy.
Leaning out over the battlements, Sabni caught sight of a
struggling swimmer clinging to the remains of a raft. The High
Priest ran to the quay and dived in. Within a few strokes he had
reached the drowning man and dragged him back ashore. The
community quickly gathered around the newcomer; when his
lungs had cleared, he recovered his breath.

'Who are you?'

'My name is Khonsu and I worked in one of the Bishop's
farms; I ran away, I cannot pay the required tax any longer. If
the soldiers catch me, they will send me to a labour camp.
Please grant me your hospitality, hide me!'

'Were you followed?'

The sound of a trumpet echoed in reply. Two barges packed
with armed men were heading to the holy island; the rowers
made haste.

'Who denounced you?'

'My nephew. I made the mistake of trusting him. The
Bishop will probably give him a good reward.'

Theodore did not tolerate this particular crime; it meant that
a certain amount of land would remain uncultivated and
abandoned; too many governors were guilty of laxness.

'Please protect me,' implored Khonsu.

'They will search the island.'

'Not the temple! The army is afraid of Isis.'

'We are subject to a Rule,' reminded Sabni. 'If you want us to die for you, pledge your life to Philae. Become an adept and we will shed our blood to the last drop in your defence.'

Terrified, the peasant saw the boats draw up. From one, Captain Mersis alighted; he ordered his men to stay put.

Sabni went forth to meet him. They met in the middle of the great square.

'I am so happy to see Philae again.'

'I am glad to see you again, Mersis: we are not allowed to greet each other amicably.'

'This is a serious matter: you know the law. I must return with the fugitive.'

'I must safeguard the existence of a brother.'

Mersis scratched at the scar on his right cheek.

'I was afraid you would say that. I will be forced to arrest you all and declare the island officially occupied by the army.'

'We will refuse to follow you.'

'I will not raise my sword against you.'

'You will have no choice.'

'I would rather turn it on myself.'

'God forbids you to do so. It is only He who can reclaim our existence.'

The old soldier held back his tears. He would like to kill that runaway bastard and take back his corpse.

'I want to speak to Khonsu.'

As if he had read the captain's thoughts, the High Priest placed himself in front of the peasant, beside whom stood Isis.

'Are you an adept?'

Khonsu trembled.

'No . . .'

'Have you vowed to become one and offer your life to the great goddess?'

The peasant looked at the High Priestess, at Sabni and Captain Mersis.

'No! I am a Christian and believe in the one true God!'

Suddenly Mersis gripped hold of his forearm and pulled the truant over to his side.

'In that case, you rascal, you're coming with me! You have a long confession to make for having dared touch the soil of this pagan temple. Did you not know that this is Hell?'

With an iron grip, Mersis dragged the fugitive to one of the barges, where he was immediately put in chains.

Sweating profusely, the captain came back to speak to Sabni.

'Isis is watching over us. That criminal will be handed over to justice.'

'If he had consented . . .'

'A revolt has broken out in Memphis. If the rebels knew that Philae continues to celebrate their rites, their ardour would be redoubled. North and South must be united, Sabni, as in the old days. Send a message; become the spiritual leader that Egypt is calling out for.'

Theodore set aside the reports that the guards on the frontier between Elephantine and Lycopolis had sent him. Not one had mentioned the passage of a youth named Chrestos. His father, Apollo, had therefore lied.

The Bishop would dig further later, for a serious incident had occurred requiring his immediate attention: in Memphis, the old and prestigious capital of the pyramid builders, a fanatical cult was announcing the apocalypse. Its members claimed that, due to sins and impieties committed by the Christians, the end of the world was drawing nigh. The Byzantine police were experiencing difficulty in controlling the rioters who, luckily, were scattered into small groups. One of their more absurd requests was that there should be freedom for all cults. If by chance they were to learn that the Philae temple had not been definitively closed, the movement could but grow.

191

Why did God submit his faithful servants to such trials? Incidents of paganism were continually being ignited, demons believed banished forever raised their ugly heads again.

A lukewarm believer would have accused the Lord of indecision; but a bishop saw in these tests a means of reinforcing the faith that had been spread throughout the whole world.

Theodore had to act to save Sabni's soul from being possessed by the devil.

Chrestos was inebriated with the quality of the night that bathed the temple. While the adepts slept, including the old guardian dozing on his rod, the boy went and lay down by the riverbank, opposite the small island of Biga, domain of Osiris's eternal silence. In Elephantine, the Elders still spoke with a respectful fear of the mysteries that characterized the union of the god and goddess. From the beginning of Egypt and the ascension to the throne of the first pharaoh, the lips of the initiates had remained sealed. None had lifted the veil over the ritual whose stages marked the resurrection of Osiris, judge of humans and archetypal survivor. Now, Chrestos knew the greatest of secrets: the infinite love of Isis, capable of breathing life into the heart of death. To discover the god, one had to experience the goddess first.

On his left, a shimmer of light intrigued the young adept. Was it a falling star, reflected in the water? When the light flashed again, this time by Nectanebo's kiosk, he knew beyond any doubt that someone was flashing a lamp.

Moving noiselessly, he soon identified the sister who was occupied with this strange task: Ahoure, the ritualist. She sent signals, repeated at regular intervals. Chrestos, after observing the opposite bank, from where no response was forthcoming, intervened.

'Who are you trying to communicate with?'

Surprised, Ahoure dropped her lamp, which was quickly swallowed by the dark waters.

'Are you spying on me, you rascal? On Sabni's orders, I bet!'

'Do not insult me, sister, just answer my question.'

'Why should I?'

Chrestos took a step towards her .

'Would you dare raise your hand to strike me?'

'I have an aversion to traitors. Speak or else.'

The fury of the young man was evident. The ritualist took his threat seriously.

'I could not sleep.'

'And the lamp?'

'Without it I might fall and hurt myself.'

'You know these rocks better than I do.'

Ahoure started to cry.

'You cannot possibly understand.'

'Try me. Your sincerity will open my spirit.'

'Each night, I try and communicate with those who have left. Their absence is unbearable to me.'

'We don't know if they have been imprisoned or deported?'

'I refuse to believe that. If only one had managed to escape, he would try and warn us and I would see his signal.'

'That is an illusion you must not hold on to.'

Ahoure seemed very moved.

'The sisters who have gone were my best friends. Without them, the temple seems so empty. The Rule demands that I overcome my pain, but I cannot. You're so young, how could you possibly understand?'

'You yourself have stated what your duty is.'

33

The Byzantine post was functioning far from effectively. Letters were lost, delayed, delivered to the wrong destination; errors multiplied. The clerks in charge of selecting and forwarding the mail often refused to work; some gave meagre tips to beggars who delivered in their stead and lost the mail on their way to the destination.

The launderer brother, who volunteered to carry a message from Sabni to Memphis, decided to capitalize on this situation. Proclaiming the spiritual sovereignty of Philae would rekindle the fire of the ancient faith; he would rally Memphis, the towns of the Delta and reanimate the desire for independence that burned secretly in the heart of every Egyptian. Sabni assembled the community and read them the text addressed to the rebels in Lower Egypt:

'You are not isolated; the great goddess will inspire you. On the holy island, a community survives devoted to the worship of the ancestral law, maintaining the eternal tradition.'

Sabni proposed to meet the head of the rebels in the small village of Fayum.

The launderer pressed the precious papyrus to his bosom, sealed with the emblem of the temple, bearing the face of Isis between the sun and the moon. His suspicions were raised when, on arriving at the northern exit to Elephantine, he noticed an unusual number of soldiers around the post and along the frontier itself. Each traveller was being thoroughly searched and had to answer a series of questions. The brother asked a donkey trader: 'What's going on?'

'The bishop has forbidden any exchange of letters between the province and other places. The army intercepts the letters and arrests bearers considered subversive.'

The launderer slipped out from the mill of people queuing to be inspected and retraced his steps. Nervous, he bumped into a granary clerk who vehemently shouted at him. The incident drew a soldier's attention.

'You there! Come here.'

Terrified, the brother took flight. Happy to have identified a suspect, two soldiers gave chase. They quickly caught up with him. Out of breath, he tore the papyrus and destroyed the seal underfoot. He had just finished destroying the message, when a violent blow to the head struck him unconscious.

With the patience of one used to handling numerous documents, Theodore put together the torn pieces of the scattered papyrus. He had no trouble identifying the seal of the temple and Sabni's beautiful handwriting, closely resembling the beautiful penmanship produced by the best scribes of the Ancient Empire. Its flow, the fruit of long years of rigorous training, reflected the original form of the hieroglyphs. The Bishop was happy for the opportunity to reread that language, both abstract and carnal, in which symbols became words. It was justly called 'the word of the gods'.

'Daydreams,' exclaimed the Bishop, furious with himself. The launderer brother was dead, his neck broken. Nobody could blame the soldier for obeying orders, all the more because he was choking at birth a plot against State security. According to the fragments of his letter, Philae's High Priest was sending out a call for sedition. Theodore now had proof against him of exceptional severity, grounds for a terrible punishment. His vigilance was certainly preventing serious trouble, such as civil war, for example. It would bring him reward and promotion: the Emperor would entrust the prelate with the government of Upper Egypt before calling him up to occupy a higher position in Byzantium.

Through practice Theodore would become versed and refined in the subtle art of intrigue, gaining appreciation from established master strategists.

He fought with himself all night; the man of God and the friend battled within him. By encouraging rebellion, Sabni was trampling all over his trust; by claiming spiritual legitimacy, he was acting with the determination of a martyr. To understand, to revolt, to forgive, to sign the order for the arrest . . . Theodore hesitated, decided, and went back on his resolve. No celestial inspiration came to his rescue as to what he should do.

In the morning, he called his secretaries.

'I have examined these fragments: they contain nothing of interest. The whole is incomprehensible; a private matter it seems. You will note down that the death of that individual was accidental. An enquiry would be pointless.'

The Bishop burned the papyrus fragments. Sabni had nothing more to fear. God had protected him.

The unguent specialist drank fresh beer in a tavern near the market entrance. He did not feel too tired, despite not having slept for two days running. Everywhere he had been most welcome. His status as a priest of Isis did not trouble his old friends; a benevolent interest was awakened in them. Since the adept was prepared to pay a good price, why not sell him the goods he required? That the pagan temple should prosper as a consequence was something beyond the realm of commerce. Therefore, he was able to assemble the victuals, the animals for transportation and the light boats. A peasant and two boatmen were well paid, and would help him return to the island.

When the patrol stormed into the small café, kicking over a table on their way, the adept felt a lump in his throat. They were moving in his direction. He had never known fear. He did not lower his eyes when the police addressed him.

'Are you one of Isis's priests?'

'Indeed.'

'Are you the specialist in making unguents?'

'I have the honour to be that person.'

'Have you been in Elephantine for the last two days?'

'Why would I deny it?'

'Then you must follow me.'

'What am I accused of?'

The policemen's face bore a sarcastic grin.

'Of having seduced and raped a Christian woman.'

'At my age . . . that's absurd!'

'Pleasure is not a question of age. Get up and do not try to run away.'

The brother obeyed.

'Who is the woman?'

'Are you making fun of me?'

'What is her name?'

'To protect her honour, it cannot be mentioned.'

'Have you seen her?'

'She lodged a complaint with the Bishop and described you in detail . . . She is no longer young, but still attractive with a curious face, as thin as the blade of a knife.'

The holy island was cut off from the rest of Egypt. A message from Mersis told Sabni of the tragic death of the launderer brother and of the suppression of postal exchanges. The Memphis rioters could not learn of Philae's community and their rebellion would dissolve in internal dissension. The dream of a great rebellion that would set Egypt on fire was coming to an end.

Another disastrous piece of news saddened the adepts. The unguent specialist has been arrested for raping a Christian woman and condemned to be stoned. As he was considered a pagan who refused to deny his faith, the old form of punishment would be revived.

'I will see the Bishop and plead for his pardon,' said Isis.

'He will humiliate you,' objected Sabni.

'I will kiss his hands if necessary. The life of a brother is at stake.'

Theodore welcomed the High Priestess with deference. She wore a light green linen tunic and almost no make-up. Her bare feet shod in sandals decorated with pearls, she was a living testimony to her royal lineage; in her, queens and High Priestesses continued to live.

'I felt certain that you would come.'

'So you know the nature of my visit.'

'The complaint has been accepted by the Prefect's office. A special court condemned your brother. In that domain, I have no power whatsoever. The law is the law; such a serious crime must be punished without mercy. I believe the pharaohs were not indulgent with rapists, is that not so?'

'Who believes that an old man committed such folly?'

'Too many years spent on the island have turned his head. Recluses sometimes falter when their senses are awoken from deprivation.'

'You are master of the province. Our ancient laws forbid that one of God's creatures should raise a hand to hurt another.'

'A pagan is a creature of the devil. That terrible act proves it.'

Isis realized that there was no way she could turn the Bishop's heart. So she pretended to submit to his wishes.

'What do you wish to accomplish?'

'That you leave the island and separate from Sabni.'

'Will the life of our brother be spared?'

The Bishop did not reply. He let Isis interpret his silence.

'May I see him?'

'His cell is not the most comfortable. I doubt that a woman of your rank . . .'

'I must see him.'

*

Huddling in the corner of the damp cesspit where he had been locked, the unguent specialist hummed the chant of the Aurora Borealis constellation. When the river had to be forded at its shallow point, the chant ensured the immobility of the crocodile and all the malevolent spirits hiding just below the water's surface. As soon as he saw Isis, he knelt before her.

'Do not stay here: you must keep a better memory of your brother.'

'Allow me to save you.'

'What is the price of my existence?'

The High Priestess told him.

'Too high. I am an old man and look forward to the supreme rest; of course, I would rather die on the island. But does even the greatest sage choose his fate? Do not dishonour me by giving in to the Bishop's demands.'

'Do you know . . . ?'

'About the stoning? I fear the suffering, but it will be brief: my head will not resist the stones for long. To see Theodore triumph would be a deeper and crueller wound than any death. I don't think I have ever asked anything of the community since my admission; unfortunately, I have contributed to its bad fortune by failing in my mission! What does torture matter; I ask that you save Philae.'

'But the life of a brother . . .'

'. . . is not as precious as that of the temple. Thus commands our Rule. Your role is to preserve the spirit and transmit it. All my life I have served it faithfully: why should I betray it at the moment of my death? We will meet again in the heavens.'

Isis kissed her brother, whose face was stained with dust.

34

There was no doubt. Ahoure was lying; she was trying to contact the enemy and keep the Bishop's soldiers informed on developments within the community. But why had the opposite bank remained dark? No one responded to the traitor, as if she was addressing the void. Suddenly he understood: the other light would only shine on the eve of the assault!

Chrestos should have rushed to tell Sabni and reveal the whole affair; but something held him back. To inform on someone displeased him; if he were mistaken, he would have sullied a sister. From the moment they met he had disliked Ahoure, and from then on they had had numerous confrontations. It was up to him to vanquish his enmity, to silence his profane feelings and to gain the ritualist's trust.

This resolution made him burst out laughing: what vanity! Chrestos thought he had discovered a plot, whereas Sabni was not so naïve as to ignore the actions of a sister; if he tolerated her behaviour, it must be because of its innocuous nature. Crazed with pain, lost, Ahoure was searching for her past.

The ritualist was on her guard. From now on, she would no longer light her path with a lamp. Making sure that nuisance Chrestos was not spying on her, she would only light the lamp by the water. The boy was capable of hiding behind a granite block or a column; therefore she would take precautions before signalling her presence to the sister with the face like a knife blade who would, sooner or later, come to meet her and announce that the way was finally clear. Ahoure no longer knew anyone in Elephantine; her ally would find her lodgings and work, and tell her the quickest way to conversion and how to tackle the population, so as to pass unnoticed.

The stalwart ritualist was terrified. To leave Philae filled her with dread; she knew the slightest pulsation of the island. Outside that universe, a myriad of dangers threatened her. She felt unable to confront them alone. Contradictory feelings beset her; on the one hand, she longed to regain the profane land; on the other, she hung on to the temple. The absence of her friend caused her anguish, but all the same, she was afraid of what her reappearance would mean. The imminence of her definitive exile made her recall the wonderful hours she had spent in the company of the young Isis, still carefree about her destiny; by the side of the future High Priestess, the days were full of joy and light. If it were not for this marriage with Sabni, the sanctuary would have sought refuge in obscure peace, away from passions and wars.

To stay on the island seemed madness. Therefore, every night, Ahoure agitated her lamp with the intention of reaching out to her liberated sister.

The sister with the face like a knife blade left Apollo's bed. Normally the fig merchant preferred younger women, but that one had clung to him like a leech, using all the weapons of seduction, from languid looks to lascivious posture. A good trader did not neglect a good opportunity; but, all things considered, Apollo thought he should have discussed the price before the transaction. His impulsive character was not always to his benefit.

'How much do you charge?'

'I do not want any money.'

Apollo frowned. This woman was not a courtesan.

'I . . . I have no intention of seeing you again.'

'I want you to help me leave town.'

'That is not easy. Soldiers guard the roads and check identities.'

'Give me a false name and send me with a convoy of merchandise. I ask nothing else of you.'

'Who are you?'

'Someone of no importance. And you are a rich trader with a warm heart.'

'What if you got me into trouble?'

'I will not breathe a word to anyone, you have my word. I swear you will never hear of me again.'

'By Christ?'

The sister hesitated.

'I swear by Christ.'

Even if the woman was to claim she had shared his bed, this would in no way affect Apollo's commercial reputation. In Elephantine, everyone knew that the fig merchant had a rampant temperament and that he did not pass up on itinerant women, even Nubians. But this one, her distinguished manner, made him ill at ease. Incapable of pleasure, she was play-acting, a charade as sordid as it was clumsy.

Apollo thought it wiser to denounce her to Mersis. This would increase his prestige with the Captain. Sooner or later the rough soldier would be promoted and remember services rendered. The next time he delivered fruit to the barracks, the merchant would propose that the Captain share one of the perquisites of the profession.

Mersis arrested the sister that very night. Terrified, she climbed on to the wall of the terrace and tried to throw herself off; a soldier managed to grab on to her leg and made her kneel, trembling, before the Captain.

'What is your name?'

She hid her face in her hands; Mersis grabbed her by the wrists and saw her face.

'A sister from Philae,' he whispered, vexed. 'What are you doing in this brothel?'

'I . . . I was looking for a rich man.'

'What for?'

'To help me leave town.'

'On your own?'

'Of course.'

'I don't believe you.'

The sister looked at him and her face became even more pointed.

'Do you think that I intended to find an escape route for the community? I could not care less about the community! It stole my youth. No one recognized my talent. I could have been a doctor, a ritualist, a High Priestess . . . Instead, Isis assigned me menial tasks. And that idiot, Ahoure, who counted on my help! I am running away on my own, do you hear, completely alone!'

Horrified, the Captain handed her over to his men. She threw her arms out to him, imploring.

'Don't abandon me. I am beautiful and tender . . . Enjoy my body and grant me my freedom!'

Mersis put his hands over his ears.

Two days later, the sister with the face like a knife blade crossed the border of the province, chained to the chariot of an officer headed for Asia. Just before the first stop, she threw herself under the wheels and was killed instantly.

At the hour when the sister died, Ahoure was waving her lantern, peering into the darkness.

Mersis verified the oars and the state of the hull. Strange mission, indeed! Subordinate officers could have carried it out, but orders from General Narses had to be carried out without question. When the General looked at him, the Captain grew troubled. The accusing eyes of the great soldier, whose illness did not affect his authoritative power, predicted catastrophe.

Mersis had been denounced.

'Rest assured, Captain, no one knows, except myself.'

'General . . .'

'Don't lie to me, please, it would pain me. So you are an ally of Philae's and you risk your life to save a temple that is unequivocally condemned. So, you remained pagan?'

'No, I'm a Christian. I believe in one God, all-powerful, in the resurrection of the body and in paradise; but my God is love, tolerance and goodness. Why should He require the destruction of a community devoted to what is sacred, of a sanctuary where the principle and rites of creation that celebrate our tradition are celebrated?'

'*Our* tradition . . . you are a strange Christian. I understand you, Mersis. I have seen her too. Not a woman, but Philae's High Priestess. Egypt and her mysteries are expressed through her. She has charm, not of a devilish nature, but like the warm light that bathes a summer evening. She conveys peace of the soul and awakens unknown senses, a desire for the universal principle, and a thirst for the heavens and the sun. You, the disciple of Christ, are still in love with the great goddess.'

Narses alighted from the boat.

'I envy you, Mersis. Every part of your being feels the magnificence of this land where you were born. As for me, I am beginning to discover it. That is why I contemplate its place of birth: the cataract. In a few centuries, we may be able to talk.'

'General, how did . . .'

'How did I know? You committed no fault. It's all my years as a leader of men, Captain! My eyes observe everything. I instinctively watch every man. A strange attitude, peculiar behaviour . . . that is what strikes me. It often betrays an unease that I have to dispel in order to maintain the morale of the troops, now my only concern. I observed you when Isis was healing the sick. You did not contemplate her as a soldier, but with the deference of an adept. Be careful, Mersis and may the gods protect you.'

The General plunged the oars and sailed away from the river-bank. The heart of the Captain was in flux for a long while.

35

Inside the sanctuary, Sabni contemplated the wall relief that depicted Isis, with huge open wings, rescuing Osiris's body from death. Still imprisoned by a shroud, the god lifted himself up; from his mortuary girdle, his hands emerged gripping a sceptre whose extremity represented the animal head of the god Seth, his brother and murderer. Thanks to the breath of the celestial woman and her magic power, light triumphed over darkness.

The sculptor had given Osiris's spouse fine features and a placid countenance, resembling those of the High Priestess. Was she not the reincarnation of the goddess whose name she bore, responsible for reviving the community?

As well as marital love, the High Priest felt admiration. Where did Isis find the courage to face the enemy, other than in her knowledge of the divine? She forgot herself to preserve the community from despair. The High Priestess was animated by a communicative joy; in her presence the world smiled. Brothers and sisters went about their tasks, as if no event would ever trespass into the fortress of the soul, as if no misfortune would ever enter the temple.

Chrestos took on ever more duties; he baked the bread, washed the ceremonial robes, and manufactured unguents. He worked too quickly, burnt and tore, but the cult ceremonies took place with their characteristic nobility, and the divine presence never lacked daily offerings.

Sabni climbed the stairs leading to the top of the first pylon; Isis, her arms crossed, her hair swept by the northern wind, looked out at the rocky island of Biga, the sacred territory where Osiris rested.

He put his arms around his wife. Contact with her perfumed skin gave him a feeling of indescribable happiness. Mingled with his desire was veneration for the radiant being that animated this woman's body modelled to perfection by the divinities. The midday sun burned down violently on to the water and the riverbanks, isolating the temple, rendering it inaccessible. For centuries, this wonderful light had defended the sanctuary; no army had ever penetrated it and its walls stood unguarded by any warrior. The eternal mason, Imhotep, had drawn a magic circle around the island. Honoured in a small sanctuary, to the south of the Euergete door, he was the creator of the first monumental work of Egyptian civilization, the step pyramid at Saqqara, and the last, the temple of Philae. For four thousand years, one architect, reincarnated from generation to generation, had built the eternal abodes.

At the couple's feet was the domain of the goddess Isis. After the large courtyard filled with sunlight came the columned room, dimly lit by skylights; beyond, the venerable throne shone irrespective of the interior lighting. The eloquent stones beckoned the spirit to ultimate wisdom and took it beyond the threshold separating the apparent from the real.

Sabni's luck was almost excessive. Loved by an exceptional woman, elevated to the highest religious post, he worked on the island of all origins, close to the great goddess, bathed in the sweet shade of wisdom. Distant from a time of war and hatred, he celebrated the rituals in a preserved space, repeated his predecessors' gestures with the certitude in his heart of performing important work for the future.

His cheek against hers, he felt the strength contained in Isis. Her transmission of the Rule was like a pure emerald, untarnishable by even the deepest pain.

'What do we have left, Sabni?'

'A plot of poor land on the hill. I had neglected it until now. An old peasant works there; I will employ another.'

'The Bishop will requisition them all.'

'I will take care of the harvest myself.'

'Your status as High Priest . . .'

'Will the High Priestess authorize me to feed the community?'

'Forgive me. Sometimes, I forget the limitations imposed on us.'

'We own a vineyard; everyone knows that the grapes contain the blood of Osiris and no one will dare touch it.'

'Let us fight, Sabni. Theodore is an implacable adversary who has acquired considerable power; he wants to separate us, that is the price of his triumph.'

'In that case, he will fail.'

Apollo was stuffing himself with mashed bean purée and warm beer. When business went well, his appetite doubled. He had hired some farmhands on a daily basis at low prices. At the end of the summer, he would finish building a new farm and, in five or six years, take his place among the notables of Elephantine. His career had been truly meteoric, for the son of a nobody. Apollo used the keys to success: lying, tricking and stealing without getting caught. The new religion suited him fine. Didn't God forgive the sins of those who confessed them? Every night, Apollo confessed his faults and implored God's forgiveness. Once a year, he granted a priest a complete confession and several kilos of figs. At peace with his conscience, he had the feeling of being a perfect citizen and an excellent Christian.

His caretaker dared interrupt his meal.

'I demand to be left alone when eating.'

'The Bishop . . .'

'What about the Bishop?'

'He's here.'

'Where?'

207

'He's inspecting a hut at the far end of the orchard.'

'You must be mistaken.'

'It is him.'

Incredulous, the merchant consented to go and see for himself. When he saw Theodore inspecting the shack, assisted by several soldiers, he held his breath.

'Monsignor, you . . . In my modest house . . .'

'I'm looking for your son.'

'My son . . . which one?'

'Chrestos.'

'He's gone to Lycopolis.'

'You're lying, Apollo. Chrestos has not left the province.'

'I swear to you . . .'

'Don't commit the sin of blasphemy. Where is he hiding?'

'I have no idea. I wanted to make a soldier out of him, he refused and rebelled. I am not responsible.'

'Would Chrestos have taken refuge in Philae?'

Apollo kept quiet.

'Did you encourage him to adopt the pagan religion?'

'On the contrary! I am a good Christian! Have I ever missed Sunday mass?'

The Bishop took Apollo by the arm to the middle of the orchard, far from indiscreet ears.

'Your son has forsaken his family to join a satanic brotherhood. By not denouncing him, you have committed a very grave fault.'

'But I did denounce him!'

'To whom?'

'To Captain Mersis . . . but I was blackmailed.'

Theodore showed no emotion. However, the information was surprising: so Philae's ally was one of his most trustworthy and senior soldiers. Should he be immediately arrested? It was better not to act on impulse and think of the best way to use this new weapon that providence had put into his hands.

'You have to leave, Apollo.'

'Me, leave, but why?'

'Because you are accomplice to a crime: to keep silent about a runaway condemns you to having all your property confiscated.'

'Mersis was the one . . .'

'Forget that name. Never pronounce it again. With a recommendation from me, you can go and settle in Faiyum. I will take care of the sale of your land and send you the proceeds.'

'I was born here and . . .'

'If you refuse my proposition, I shall have to proceed with charges against you.'

Vanquished, Apollo lowered his head.

'Trust me. If you keep silent, you will enjoy a happy old age.'

'And Chrestos?'

'Forget about him too. As from today, he no longer exists.'

As Apollo, with tears in his eyes, was leaving Elephantine with all his belongings, the Prefect addressed an appeal to the Bishop. Half drunk, Maximin implored Theodore to proclaim *urbi et orbi* that Isis had converted to Christianity. The young woman would thus escape, no matter what happened, the fury of the Church. Her reputation would be ruined and the pagan community would collapse.

Theodore listened patiently to the Prefect's peroration but did not give in. The faith would tolerate no concessions. Maximin continued to plead his cause. Isis was no ordinary woman; the church must grant her this favour. Faced with another refusal, he offered the prelate a part of his fortune, but Theodore did not falter.

Back in his palace, the Prefect drank wine and lay on his bed; on the ceiling he envisioned Isis's face. Her lips moved, she spoke to him, but he could not hear her. The Prefect stood up and reached out, trying to touch his beloved; the moment he thought he had reached her, she vanished.

'Isis, do not reject my love!' screamed Maximin.

36

Skin and bones, wearing a stinking sheepskin, the hermit emerged from the pagan tomb where he had chosen to live. From the top of the western bank, he contemplated the island of Elephantine, the course of the Nile and, on the horizon, the accursed site of Philae. For thirty years Paul, the hermit with the feverish eyes, had inflicted penance and mortification on himself, and fought the devil so ready to appear in dreams or in a woman's body. He could hardly sleep and was devoted to destroying the figures of goddesses, who shamelessly exhibited themselves on the walls of impious tombs. He constantly protested against the existence of the last of the devilish temples, but found no echo in Theodore, a bishop whose tolerance bordered on complacence, though recently his tremendous power was showing signs of faltering. Paul had been designated spokesman for his fellow Christians and priests of the province. They liked his ardent faith and his desire to pluck out evil by its roots. Leaning on the knotted cane with which he smashed the heads of serpents, he was thinking that the grandiose landscape, so ideal for meditation, was only on loan from the Lord, and that the true believers would wage a real war against the enemies of that Lord-on-High.

The earth was dry and cracked, but the harvest would yield some food for the temple. How could a small, poorly located field of barley produce more? Assisted by two peasants who had escaped the requisition, Sabni worked hard. A magnificent view compensated his efforts. Seen from up on the hill, the holy island resembled a ship whose prow was composed of a huge block which obscured the sacred centre. There, the divine power remained forever inaccessible to human understanding. On the left, the colonnade at the entrance was preceded by an obelisk. On the right, Trajan's kiosk sheltered behind a group of palm trees.

At noon, Isis appeared on the summit of the first pylon, her white silhouette crowning the green of the trees. She hailed Re, the hidden light in the solar disc at the apogee of its course. The whole community repeated the words pronounced by the High Priestess, a salutation addressed to the cosmos for the last four thousand years. In the distance, the ochre mountains sealed the horizon.

The High Priest worked even harder; the barley was of such mediocre quality that no one would even think of coveting it. The adepts would have to make do.

There were only three or four days of toil left; once the blades were cut, Sabni would tie them in sheaves and transport them to Philae.

Under a tepid sun, Sabni climbed the hill at a regular pace. The day before, the two peasants had declared that they would refuse further co-operation. Threatened with denunciation, they were afraid of arrest. The High Priest was not disturbed by this; at the end of the morning, the work would be done.

A few metres from the field, he stopped dead. Goats and sheep had broken down the fences and trampled over the harvest. Some latecomers were savouring the last blades of barley. Sabni cried with fury. This time compensation would have to be granted.

'Your cause is just,' granted Theodore. 'You can lodge a complaint against neighbouring farmers; if you set it out well, the owners of the animals will pay you double the price of the expected harvest.'

'Will the Prefect preside over the court?'

'Too small an affair. It falls within the ecclesiastical jurisdiction.'

The inhabitants of Elephantine knew it only too well. The Bishop held court when he deemed appropriate. In just one day, he examined more than one hundred cases. Well before dawn, a long queue of plaintiffs grew and many of them would never have the chance of presenting their woes. Theodore, like the other bishops, dealt first with major cases of a civil nature: the appointment of local magistrates or village principals, the promotion of civil servants, the release of prisoners, the readjustment of taxes; then, in the time he had left, he dealt with minor disputes.

'When will your court be sitting?'

'When a sufficient number of files require my intervention.'

'I am in a hurry, Theodore.'

'Make a donation to the church, it would expedite my decision.'

'Your laws are not the same for everyone. If a rich man commits a transgression, he is spared your rebuke; if it is a poverty-stricken one, a severe penalty is inflicted, unless he dies before the trial. It is monstrous to have to pay for justice to be done.'

'In Byzantium, it is said that a lawsuit easily exceeds the terms of human life and that it can go on eternally. The justice of God does not prevail on this earth, I admit. If you want to improve our lot, accept conversion and come and work by my side. You would make an excellent judge.'

'When will your court sit, Theodore?'

'Perhaps in the autumn, after the flood.'

Meditating on his rock, General Narses felt more and more estranged from the army and its demands, although no one reproached him for neglecting his duties. Increasingly, Philae

212

occupied his thoughts. At another stage of his life, he might well have requested admission into that community that the Emperor had ordered him to exile. An Emperor so distant and so silent that he no longer seemed real.

Egypt was not easy to conquer. Successive invaders, Asians, Assyrians, Persians, Greeks, Romans, had had to submit to its laws; whoever wanted to reign over it had to undergo the initiation into the mysteries of royalty before wearing the pharaoh's double crown. Moribund, tradition survived in its rituals and symbols. Byzantium and Christianity had imposed other rules; they were mistaken and would pay a high price for their error.

Narses would not have to carry out his orders: Philae was ruined. It had deposited silver pieces in the Bishop's treasure, after the arrest of the unguents specialist, its staff had been requisitioned, its wheat had been diverted for the profit of the army, their land had been rendered infertile . . . famine drew nigh at the temple's door. Once its reserves were depleted, how would it nourish itself?

That slow death served his purpose well. He did not feel the slightest need to intervene against that holy island, where he had almost known serenity, and he would be content to watch it from afar, dreaming of a bygone wisdom and entrusting his thoughts to the southern wind; which a breath would take them to unexplored shores.

Maximin was overjoyed. Since he had renounced his challenge to the Bishop's authority, he was beginning to hope again. Theodore was really bent on subjugating the temple to his will; broken, Philae agonized over its future. Soon, Isis would be free of Sabni's influence. Thus, Maximin made it his business to inform the authorities in Elephantine that soon the High Priestess would renounce paganism and become his wife.

Theodore did not intervene. By making a fool of himself, the Prefect had lost his last shred of respectability. Without uttering a word of criticism, the Bishop looked on as Maximin fell into a sink of sin from which he would never emerge. The Emperor's envoy had been wrong to consider the province of Elephantine a promised land and had underestimated its ability to bewitch people; whoever failed to keep a grip on their spirit and prevent it intermingling with those of the river, tamed by neither its steep containing banks nor the rocks of the cataract, was condemned to losing their mind.

Captain Mersis felt nervous. From the vantage point of a great tower built of pure brick, he looked out over the great South. He did not believe the Blemmyes would strike again. They were strong and they had seen enough of the weakness of Byzantine troops to know that they were no menace. Having lived under the threat of extermination for so long, the Blemmye people could live in peace for many years to come, and there was no reason to undertake a foolish adventure where thousands would perish.

During the evening meal, an officer whose cousin worked at the indirect taxes office mentioned a rumour that had been persistently doing the rounds: Theodore was planning to enforce a tax on medium-sized ships and would demand a detailed inventory both from private citizens and from institutions. Immediately, Mersis thought of Philae. That new tax would be unbearable; Sabni should get rid of the most cumbersome vessels as quickly as possible.

The soldier scribbled down a message and, at sundown, gave it to a messenger-pigeon. The bird took off towards the temple. Mersis was relieved; Isis and Sabni would know how to prepare for this kind of attack if they were informed in time of the adversary's intentions.

From the terrace of his house, the Bishop watched the pigeon take flight; his archers would bring it down over the hills. The false rumour propagated by the prelate had spread like wildfire, ensuring the traitor reacted fast. Mersis was indeed one of Isis's adepts. Before inflicting the punishment he deserved, Theodore would use him for his own ends.

Now, Isis had no more allies. She would confront Christ's representative alone. If the High Priestess became the prefect's slave, the magic wall that stood between God and Sabni would come down, no matter how. Theodore had to guide the pagan fraternity to the true faith so that the will of the Lord would be done. He went forth in peace along his straight road, an instrument in the hands of the Architect of all worlds. With the definitive disappearance of the Pharaonic religion, a new world would be born and Philae must not hamper its expansion. Just one coherent community was more threatening to Christianity than thousands of scattered pagans. All it needed was a leader. A couple such as Isis and Sabni would be ideal to restore vigour and force to the ancient cult and prove it essential. From the beginning of time, Egypt had asserted its vocation as mother of all Civilizations. Repressed, humiliated, enslaved, it continued to produce ideas that fashioned the future. That is where the infinite power of this Holy Island came from. By its prayers and the celebration of rites, Philae guided the heart. Theodore did not underestimate the danger; the weaker the community became materially, the stronger the spiritual brotherhood grew.

The combat the Bishop waged with the High Priestess was fought on an invisible realm; although she was being besieged, she retained one single efficient weapon: Sabni's love. He was the one that had to be destroyed, before victory could be attained.

Beneath the shade of the tall slender palm tree, whose smooth trunk pointed up into the deep blue sky, Isis read the hymn to Hathor, composed by Philae's first High Priestess. Nature's aridity stopped at the edge of the garden, where, since spring had begun, it was delightful to bask in the sun filtered through the palm leaves. Sabni brought her fresh water, figs and bread. Relaxed, she seemed almost carefree.

'Theodore believes we are defeated, without resources.'

'He is too discerning to make that kind of mistake,' objected

215

Sabni. 'He fears you. As long as we are together, he will persecute us.'

'Egypt has suffered many a tyranny, but its faith has survived. The Christians want to root it out and eradicate it from men's memory. Theodore does not behave like one of God's humble servants; he demands a truth that is total and definitive, the one that will reveal Christ to him and on which he will build a new world. For that truth to emerge, Philae must disappear.'

Sabni shuddered. Was Isis announcing the end of the community?

'Do not worry, my love. Whoever invades Egypt will be chased away or rot here. No matter how many centuries it takes. Our message is immortal because it was not born of man's mind, but expresses the secret of the universe; and the Bishop knows it.'

'He was a true and loyal friend.'

'He still is and he is waiting for you, Sabni. You are tearing his soul apart; if he spares the community, it is thanks to you.'

'I will never share his beliefs; he knows that.'

'Doesn't his God accomplish miracles?'

He sat by her and caressed her feet.

'How are we going to feed the community?'

'When we no longer have any bread, we will go down into the crypts. The access has been walled in for two centuries; my father gave me the plan.'

'What do they contain?'

'Later, an urgent task calls me: to render homage to Osiris.'

37

Isis approached the small island of Biga, Osiris's sacred territory. Only Philae's High Priestess could set foot on it. It was there, under an immortal acacia tree, that the god's tomb lay hidden; until the extinction of humanity, he would wait for the coming of his spouse, holder of the resurrection formulas.

Isis climbed the stone steps, went through a door framed with texts of welcome and passed before the statues of glorious New Empire pharaohs whose *ka* resided near the great god; beyond commenced the forbidden realm where no man, sage or ignorant, rich or poor, was allowed to enter.

She pushed the bushes back, and took a path that led into a tamarisk wood. Planted there was an effigy of the Blemmyes' god; he held a gazelle in his left hand and a bouquet with his right. Lord of the secret territory side by side with Osiris, he was called the 'good traveller', companion of Re's daughter, queen of the solar journey open to the souls of the regenerated.

Going forth very slowly, Isis took care not to make any noise; Osiris demanded silence. He did not tolerate any chanting, no sounds of flutes, harps or drums. Around the tomb stood three hundred and sixty five altars; on each of them, the High Priestess poured a little water. Thanks to that libation, each day of the year became a sacred reminder of the Osirian sanctuary and carrier of the rebirth that was also the sun's emergence from darkness. Then she approached the stone sarcophagus, half buried in a domed mound.

Alone with herself, she dialogued with the spirit that moved above the burial site and, during the new moon festivals, took the form of a bird of prey with a human head. The noise of its wings woke Osiris. Isis did not ask for help or utter supplications; pity, despair and personal prayer would have demeaned the cult. She ran through the words of empowerment, the nourishment of Osiris's soul. They revealed the secret nature of the god, sun of the night, principle of incessant mutations. In the voice of the High Priestess generations of adepts spoke, united in the act of making an offering to the god.

At the prow of the ship that took them to Elephantine, Isis and Sabni reread the strange assignation to appear before the Bishop. Theodore had opened his court much earlier than usual, according to an unusual procedure. Normally, an official messenger would announce the event; the Bishop was not in the habit of convening his plaintiffs in this way.

To their great surprise, no queue had formed along the whitewashed walls of the building, guarded by two soldiers at the entrance. At the end of the empty room the prelate and the Prefect were enthroned. To the left of the latter, bent over his desk, a clerk was ready to take down the report of the court session. The doors closed behind the couple.

'Will the reparation be granted us?' asked Sabni, ironically.

'A graver subject worries us,' said the Bishop. 'That is why I asked the Prefect Maximin to be present.'

'Could there be anything more urgent than providing justice?'

'That is my intention. You pay taxes as the owners of the site designated as Philae; owners, is that what you really are?'

Sabni was afraid of what would ensue.

'All possession of land rests on a judicial act; my secretariat has examined the census and there is no mention of Philae. Therefore, the island is no one's property. As it is escheated, that land belongs to the church.'

For the Love of Philae

The attack took the High Priest by surprise. Prepared with care, it was launched by a man who was absolutely sure that he would take possession of the Holy Island without any further ado. The jurist enforced the law. No one could accuse him of being inhuman or cruel.

'You are mistaken,' rectified Isis in a soft voice.

'Do you have proof?'

'Would you like to examine it?'

'It is imperative.'

'It will take a few days.'

Maximin did not take his eyes off her; he had expected a long speech, outrage. Yet Isis remained very calm; and this made her all the more attractive to him.

'We accept,' he concluded.

The clerk noted that the matter was to be settled by another hearing.

Three days later, a large retinue presented itself at the court. Chrestos and the sisters had remained at the temple; the brothers helped Sabni carry the document promised to the Bishop, a heavy stele made of limestone taken from the depths of a crypt. Depicted on it was the goddess Maat, incarnation of the Rule of Life, facing Thoth, the god with the head of an ibis. Taking the dictation from the celestial female, he wrote a text in hieroglyphs.

'Here is the proof that Philae belongs to the gods and not to men,' said Isis.

The clerk put down his quill. Not only was he paid by the line, but he was wasting his youth trying to learn Greek and Aramaic to write bans, contracts and wills. To read hieroglyphs was not within his duties.

The Prefect stood up and approached to examine the surprising property act. Thus could he stand close enough to Isis to breathe in her perfume.

'No one knows that language. How can we judge if this testimony is valid?'

219

Christian Jacq

Sabni watched Theodore. Was the Bishop going to confess that he could decipher sacred Egyptian texts?

'Translate,' he ordered. 'You, clerk, register the declaration.'

The High Priest read each sentence, spacing them out.

'This temple is like the firmament in all its parts. It was built by the Pharaoh by order of the Principle, creator of all things and is permanently renewed to shine like the horizon. At the end of the construction, the master mason gave the building to its master; on this site resides the great goddess, Isis.'

The clerk consulted his tablets. As a notary, he had to apply the strictest law. That is why the bishop had summoned him, so that no one could ignore the proceedings and the judgement be stamped with the seal of rectitude.

'Occupation equals possession. Does someone who answers by the name of Isis occupy this site?'

Smiling, the High Priestess came forward.

'Are you the heir and do you authenticate this act?'

Isis nodded. The Prefect was torn between the desire to take her in his arms and strangle Sabni; he hated that Egyptian who stood between him and his happiness.

'Perfect,' declared the clerk. 'This stele will be deposited in the archives of the registry; next time, bring a more manageable copy.'

Sabni and Isis bid farewell to the Bishop, who remained impassive.

The harvest was completed in haste; the hired hands worked on the threshing without rest, in a hurry to finish before the beginning of the flood. The fiery June sun inflamed the hills of Elephantine. At the temple, Sabni imposed rationing. This did not upset any of the adepts, except Chrestos, who had a voracious appetite. For at least two months, they would have plenty to eat.

Before the midday ritual, Isis and Sabni bathed naked at the foot of the small temple dedicated to Hathor, opposite the eastern cliffs. To swim alleviated tiredness and preserved the

220

body's youth. They did not go far from the shore, dived under water, brushed against the fish and, under the protective gaze of the goddess of love, gave themselves up to tender, fevered games. Isis, with her skin dripping with water pearls, resembled the shining star of the New Year. Sabni kissed the flower buds of her breasts, caressed the bush of her sex, and drank from her inebriating lips. It was too sweet to embrace his beloved, to be nourished by her eyes, to see her bathed in light and to unite with her under the protection of an acacia tree! Did love not sow emerald and turquoise in the sky to create the constellations?

Lying on the ground against each other, eyes half-closed, they savoured these instants of pleasure, feeling sheer delight in existence itself.

38

Chrestos devoured the papyri in the library. Medicine, astrology, geometry, mythology . . . No subject sated his curiosity. He read the hieroglyphs with incredible ease, as if the sacred language was natural to him. Under the guidance of Sabni and Isis alternately, he disciplined his thinking, differentiating knowledge from wisdom. 'The danger,' said Sabni, 'is to accumulate notions without living them. Forget, experiment, and formulate according to your heart, never according to your fantasy.' The young adept slept little and refused to rest. The heat did not bother him; the material chores did not tire him. He felt he had centuries of wisdom to study, thousand of years of initiations to go through. At night, on the roof of the temple, he asked Sabni and Isis many questions. They were more than parents, their family was real, with self-elected members.

In mid-June, Chrestos crossed the threshold of the room with the columns. All the adepts had recognized his capacity to comprehend newly revealed mysteries. Before the eyes of the marvelling boy a fabulous event took place. According to the time of the year and the hour of the day, the rays of light, filtered by the skylights, lit a detail of a column, a divine figure, and a portion of text. Chrestos had to make sense of the separate elements, and work out why some remained in the shade; he would become familiar with the laws of the gods and perhaps understand how everything worked. For now, everything was handed to him; all he had to do was to wander in this labyrinth of symbols and hope to find its centre. He started with great zest.

Since his failure, Theodore seemed to take no action. In reality as the time of the flood approached, he was overwhelmed with bureaucratic work. Every report by the guardians of the canals had to be carefully examined. In many places, the requisitioned peasants had accomplished their task carelessly. If the flood were not sufficiently abundant, the irrigation would be badly directed. The food reserves were coming to an end. Even the army's granaries would soon be empty. The Bishop went out to inspect the dikes himself, to see the emplacement of the boundary stones, encourage the inspectors to keep the peasants under tight reign.

Everywhere, discipline was becoming lax. Philae, Chrestos, Captain Mersis . . . The prelate did not forget them for one moment, but he relegated them to the back of his mind, for his overriding concern was with the survival of the province.

Among the many offerings to the cult was the gift of wine for the gods. At Elephantine, like elsewhere in Egypt, the vine possessed a sacred character; the Christians recognized the symbolic value of the juice contained in the grapes and did not destroy the vines of the temples. When saying mass, the priest likened it to the blood of Christ, just as the adept of the old religion recognized it as the blood of Osiris.

Hence, Sabni was stunned to find that Philae's small vineyard had been ransacked by vandals: the shoots were cut down to the ground, the earth turned over and salted, the pole of the irrigation machine smashed to bits . . . When the three last jugs were emptied, the High Priest would no longer be able to fill the cups of wine he lifted, in the naos, towards the face of the statue.

There was a cross planted in the middle of the vineyard with the name of Jesus engraved on it. Its shape was similar to the

Ankh, a symbol of life in the sacred tongue. On one of its branches hung a piece of jackal skin, declaring the action as being the work of those monks occupying the tombs of the nobles and artisans. There, they destroyed the sculpted faces of women, incarnations of the devil, decapitated statues and burned the walls or covered them with plaster. The Bishop had trouble keeping them under control. Hesitant, they dared not enter the town, where the soldiers heckled them. For a long time, their dream had been to destroy Philae.

The colour of the water changed, becoming more opaque and darker. Isis swam back to the bank. When Sabni joined her, she was offering her body, anointed with jasmine-perfumed honey, to the sun.

'Our last swim before the flood.'

The High priest kneaded some damp soil with the tips of his fingers.

'It will come late.'

'It's too early to say. But it's true, the water will be muddier.'

They tried to reassure themselves, but the signs were unmistakably foreboding. They indicated that Egypt would be subjected to a year of terrible famine, when the famished hyenas would raid people's houses for food, and that could be only the first of seven catastrophic years, condemning half the population to die from starvation If the peasants suffered a shortage of food, they would no longer be able to illicitly make their small donation to the community. The army would confiscate the totality of the harvest.

'Won't Theodore accuse you of practising black magic?'

'The people will not listen to him. I am not worried about myself, but for our old people; a prolonged fast will wipe them out.'

'Be patient. Let us wait for the flood to begin.'

Narses' army had become accustomed to the delights of

Elephantine. Due to their enforced rest and given the impossibility of heading forth into Nubia, the general had, with the Prefect's approval, doubled wine rations, increased pay and leave. The Blemmyes were forgotten and the Byzantine soldiers frequented the taverns and the market where ivory, spices, panther skins and other exotic products were sold. All these were the object of crude bartering. The town's brothel was always full. For the miserable who could not pay the price, cheaper, amateur prostitutes came to the rescue. Narses pretended not to know; his only worry was that an abundant flood would cover up his rock and he would be unable to meditate before the cataract.

The Prefect could no longer banish Isis's face from his mind's eye. He had thought of asking the Bishop to exorcise him, but decided that it was preferable to live with this intolerable pain than risk losing those eyes, lips, and cheeks, even if out of his reach.

In the antique shop, he had discovered an anthology of poems adapted from ancient Egyptian; the verses evoked meetings between lovers in a shaded garden, away from curious bystanders, near a pond filled with fresh water where they bathed after having sworn eternal love. How could he refrain from fantasizing about a naked Isis, gliding in a bluish ripple of water?

In these enlightened, sensual texts, Maximin admired the respect shown for the beloved; this rare feeling made passion seem like the most resplendent gold. He, who had always been so contemptuous of women, would bow down before Philae's High Priestess; this obedience of heart elevated his soul. If Isis refused, he would not conquer her by force, but slowly open the way to her trust. He would have the patience of granite. If people took him for a madman, he could not care less.

Isis guided the boat up to Biga, where she would offer Osiris a libation of the milk that a fisherman had brought to the temple during the night. Some merchants, aware of the destitution that had befallen the community, were not afraid to help. Theodore had not published any edict forbidding the population from trading with Philae, but each person knew the risks involved: arbitrary arrest and deportation. Luckily, the rounds were less frequent; many soldiers were in charge of supervising the cleaning of irrigation basins and not even able to stop the peasants summoned to do the work from fleeing.

While Isis was tying the boat, a black face emerged from the water. The man, athletic with frizzy hair, swam slowly towards her and kept a respectful distance.

'I am a Blemmye priest. Please accept my people's token of veneration and my own. I know that only you can walk on the soil of Osiris's island. Therefore, I will keep my distance . . .'

'What do you want?'

'To know if the Christians have violated this most sacred land.'

'They have respected it.'

'Also to know if the chapel and the statue of our God are intact.'

'Be reassured.'

'Finally, to know if your person is safe from any aggression.'

'I am in no danger.'

'I will take those tidings to my King.'

'Are you to attack Elephantine?'

'We venerate Philae's High Priestess. She is above wars and human strife.'

The Blemmye disappeared, swimming away underwater. Isis walked towards the altars, pensive, to pour the offering of milk on them.

39

Sabni paused before the enigmatic figures of the small chapel near Hadrian's door, opposite the island of Biga. Chrestos identified the sun and the moon surrounded by stars, and the pillar engraved with an eye evoking the resurrected Osiris. He wondered about the meaning of the figure squatting inside a cave encircled by a serpent.

'That's the spirit of the Nile,' said the High Priest. 'His power is hidden in the bowels of the earth, immersed in an ocean of energy. The figure holds two vases that contain the terrestrial and the celestial fluids. Only their marriage will create a good flood: in the stars, we shall read the destiny the earth has in store for us: the moon will unleash it, the sun will stabilize it.'

'How can I describe my joy to you, Sabni? I feel at home in this forest of symbols. It's paradise for me to be surrounded by the language of the gods, the mysteries of the temple and the warmth radiating from these columns. Sometimes I am afraid I might lose this treasure if I am unable to move beyond it into a more ordinary life.'

'Follow your passions in your life: no riches are worthwhile if you ignore what you desire. He who is guided by it cannot go astray.'

'I want to make those stone images speak; to test my words on the scales of truth.'

'If you listen well, your words will be good; to listen with an open heart is a wonderful thing for your path: it results in perfect love. The words of the master properly heard by the disciple will bring fulfilment. God loves he who listens, and hates him who does not heed. You will possess your heart if you listen to it, and you will speak words of truth.'

Chrestos did not miss out a single word. The teaching he received became his flesh and blood.

Theodore's calm was only apparent. He hid a growing disquiet from the eyes of his subordinates. There were signs that the coming flood would be even less abundant than the previous one; the province was rushing headlong into disaster.

The prelate would be forced to implore help from the Emperor and ask Byzantium for victuals; forgetting the Nile's capricious nature, the capital would blame the Governor's lack of foresight. Not only would the flood be late but it would not be sufficiently bountiful to deposit silt over the thirsty fields. Despite the Bishop's efforts, the bad news was soon sweeping the streets of Elephantine and the surrounding countryside. The anguish grew; Theodore was astonished to find the Prefect looking thrilled.

'The people are unanimous, Isis must intervene. Only she can make the waters rise by celebrating the great ritual of the flood.'

For Maximin, this meant being close to Isis for several days.

'I refuse.'

'Do not be so stubborn, Bishop! I am offering you the best solution. If you celebrate mass in vain, how many Christians will lose faith? It is impossible to run the risk. If the High Priestess fails, the mob will destroy the temple. And I will keep Isis here with me.'

'And if she succeeds?'

'People will acclaim her for a time, then they will forget. You will have face a tempest, but you will find a way of attributing the miracle to Christ; Egyptian divinities have not performed any for a long while.'

*

The Bishop had resigned himself to the idea: it would be up to him to convince Isis. She would refuse to see the Prefect and would not listen to any envoy. To go to Philae was humiliating for him, but on the streets of Elephantine, the name of Isis was on everyone's lips. Was the healer not a magician whose power knew no limits? The seers foresaw a flood so weak that not even a blade of wheat would grow. The famished would attack the weak, the poor would assault the rich. The waters of the Nile would be tainted with blood.

The Bishop's boat drew up to the quay where, having been warned by the watchman, Isis was waiting for him. Her long white dress shone in the sun.

'I greet the High Priestess of Philae.'

'May the great Goddess protect her subjects and render their earth fertile. Do you wish to come into the temple?'

'I am forced to ask for your help.'

'Could it be that you believe in our magic?'

'Not at all.'

'Yet it has proven effective a thousand times.'

'Do not fool yourself with your own legends. The people simply need to believe in miracles.'

'Yet you are convinced that the flood will fall short and you wish to use methods that you disapprove of. Why?'

'To avoid famine is my sole concern.'

'By imposing my presence, aren't you insulting Christ?'

'My dialogue with God does not concern you. Will you help me?'

'I also want this province to prosper.'

She descended on to the boat and sat on the prow, with Theodore on the stern. The rowers proceeded rhythmically.

'A simple offering will not suffice. I have to consult the archives of the temple of Knum.'

'Are you forgetting that it has been destroyed?'

'It's true, the fanatics reduced it to a miserable pile of rubble; rumour has it that you saved the papyrus of the House of Life belonging to the sanctuary.'

Christian Jacq

'That is a daring assertion.'

Wearing his long red dress with the collar enhanced by a gold trimming, Theodore was fighting one of the hardest battles of his career. Although he fought to calm his feelings, this woman put him ill at ease. He could not subjugate her. It was as if the will of God had met an indestructible barrier.

'You can read the hieroglyphs, the wisdom of Egypt is your nourishment, and mine. Our tradition is based on wisdom and not on knowledge; that wisdom is expressed in texts that you respect. You, Monsignor, are not a destroyer.'

'Do you need those papyri?'

'You and I both desire an abundant flood. Without the formulas, my voice will remain ineffectual.'

The archives of the House of Life were properly ordered in the basement of the Bishop's house, where no one was admitted. Theordore had saved the great part during the fire because of a sentence so often read in the teachings of the Ancient Empire: 'Cherish books as you cherish your mother.' The Bishop dreamed of a vast library containing all the writings born of the land of Egypt from the very beginnings of civilization. To propagate the new religion, was it not necessary to know the errors of the past?

Moved, Isis touched the venerable papyri covered with columns of hieroglyphs, drawn by the priest of Knum at the time when the sanctuary had been enthroned on the island of Elephantine. Among them there was a text signed by Imhotep himself. It contained the words that would compel him to lift his sandal and liberate the flood.

'You should give us back these documents, Monsignor.'

'Don't count on it.'

'Are you afraid we might use them against you?'

'You overestimate yourself. I am not afraid of your little community. What could it possibly do against millions of Christians?'

'Testify to faith and prove that the number of followers is secondary.'

The feast of the sacrifice to the Nile gathered together the population of Elephantine and a great number of peasants who had come from their villages. Thousands of eyes followed the gestures of the High Priestess, who threw into the river two jugs of sweet wine, milk, oil, spices, sixteen wreaths of flowers, sixteen cakes and sixteen palms. Then she went down to the river and entered the water up to her knees. She collected some fresh water in a gold vase consecrated to Isis. Her voice could be heard chanting the glory of the goddess, celestial dew and eye of the sun. In the heart of the Christian city, pagan prayers were uttered dedicated to the birth of the flood.

Seven days after Isis's intervention, the level rose quickly. The waters swirled upwards, covering the reeds and the sandbanks, then climbed up over the banks. The great flood, joyous and fierce, distributed the fertilizing silt, spreading it out over the fields. The valley became a lake from whence only the dikes and hillocks on which houses were built stood out. That countryside, temporarily immersed in what seemed the primordial ocean it had once emerged from, was a fascinating and sublime spectacle. A boat sailed among reeds, an oar floated by a plough, the labourer became a sailor, and a shoal of fish swam at the feet of a herd of cows. The great inundation, the gold of the poor, brought jubilation to all living beings. Everywhere there were festivities, songs and dances.

When the waters of the river had covered Egypt, the villages were surrounded by groves, palms and fruit trees emerging like green islands in the heart of an immense sea. Many barges navigated on this comfortable route. Each person visited a relative or a friend. Until the time when the Nile waters subsided, there would be rest and joyful celebrations.

From the lips of boatmen were born songs praising the glory of Isis, the magician, capable of transforming poverty into prosperity. The river obeyed her, just as it had obeyed the pharaohs. The deacons tried to explain it all away, saying that the beginning of the flood had been badly interpreted and that the High Priestess had simply taken advantage of a natural phenomenon, but nobody listened. Why should they do without the powers of a High Priestess whose acts engendered happiness? Even among the most fervent Christians, there were murmurs that the Bishop should be more tolerant. Didn't the ancient religion venerate a unique god, who manifested in various forms, and did it not give Christianity the model for the Holy Trinity? Some brought up statues of the deities that had been kept in their basements or buried near a cemetery, placed them back on their domestic altars and prayed to them. The image of the serpent goddess, She-Who-Loves-Silence, protector of harvests, was unearthed.

On the West bank, monks who were furious about the growing prestige of the High Priestess tried to set fire to those still intact tombs of the explorers of the great South.

Some fishermen stopped them, and threatened to break their backs and beat them with their oars.

The turn events were taking came as no surprise to the Bishop. Happy to know that the province had been saved from starvation, he was content to replenish the reserves of victuals and draw some lessons from his defeat. His friendship for Sabni was leading him astray, drawing him away from his sacred mission. His role consisted of imposing the true faith and not of listening to his inner feelings. For a long time, both in the West and in the East, the cult of Isis and Osiris had been Christianity's formidable rival. In a century when the Church thought it had plucked evil out by its roots, it threatened a rebirth in the very place where the great goddess had its most prestigious and venerable sanctuary.

Philae was ruined, bloodless, exhausted, and yet it triumphed, due to a couple who grew in strength as they overcame difficulties. Sabni would never convert; tomorrow he would be the head of a religious movement that would soon become an insurrection against the Emperor. Egypt would not

renounce its genius, or its independence; it would always
believe that time is but an illusion, Christianity a moment of
madness and that its eternal tradition was where true wisdom
lay.

The man Theodore most loved had become his most
dangerous enemy. The Bishop did not have the right to cover
over his tracks: what God demanded of him, he had to
complete without faltering.

40

When the waters, in the middle of August, reached their highest level, the harvests began. When the flood reached its ideal height of sixteen cubits, Isis drew passionate praise. At the time of the council of dignitaries, usually very keen on approving the Bishop's decisions, they proposed that some measures should be voted for in favour of the community: compensation for lost harvests, attribution of arable lands and a vineyard, delivery of blocks of sandstone and granite for repairs to the temple. One insolent creature even dared to ask for an inquiry into the torture somewhat rashly inflicted on the unguent specialist.

Theodore refuted all these demands firmly. Refusing to take no for an answer, the notables requested an audience with the Prefect. Maximin spent most of his time sailing around the temple trying to catch a glimpse of Isis when she climbed to the top of the first pylon. During a brief interview with the notables he listened attentively, but did not know what position he should take. To favour Philae was to reinforce Sabni's power; to fight the Holy Island would mean displeasing Isis and losing her for ever. The Prefect sent the notables back to the master of the province.

The people were muttering angrily. Sabni, whom neither the police nor the army questioned, knew how to speak to them. Without uttering invective or complaints, he just evoked the material difficulties of the temple. Theodore's name was never mentioned. The High Priest only asked for a little justice to be done.

Some women silenced a priest who was reminding everyone loudly and clearly that the pagans were outlaws. Roughed up and thrown to the floor, he had to scramble for safety. The following day, boats carrying bread, fruit, vegetables and wine delivered their loads to Philae; Isis thanked each member of the convoy. Back in Elephantine, they praised her beauty.

Some of the Bishop's spies were beaten with sticks, his secretaries thrown out of public meetings, while some traders began protesting against the taxes imposed by Theodore.

The notables called on Sabni to represent them before the prelate, broadening the scope of their claims; soon they would be trying to influence the administration and the army. Narses refused to take any measures and waited for orders. Maximin became a recluse in his own house; Mersis had trouble containing the anger of his men, jealous of those under Narses and avid for the same privileges. If the master of the province did not react very quickly, he might well lose his Bishop's throne.

Nevertheless, it was a placid man who received the High Priest.

Theodore seemed detached, almost indifferent, as if he had already renounced power. His office was in perfect order.

'What have you come to announce to me, Sabni?'

'Are you conscious of having lost face?'

'Humiliation does not scare me at all.'

'Would you consent to going back to being an ordinary priest?'

'Why not, if God so wishes?'

'What about you, do you wish it?'

'I love this province and want its inhabitants' happiness. As long as the Emperor does not send me away, I will govern. Would you be coveting my place?'

The High Priest burst out laughing.

'That is exactly what will be asked of you, if paganism

prospers; Elephantine will want Isis to be its magician and her husband for its guide.'

'Don't be cynical, Theodore. I have no administrative skills.'

'I do not believe in your innocence; are you not fostering a rebellion?'

'I ask that justice be done for Philae; you must know that I have not implicated you in any way.'

'I know, but the result is the same. You and your community are ruining my work and dragging innocent people along to suffer a repression whose violence you cannot begin to imagine. The Emperor will not tolerate a pagan insurrection. I tried to protect Philae by making its existence go unnoticed; by way of gratitude, Philae incites rebellion and hurls poor wretches into the abyss.'

'We would have died of starvation. Your generosity was a clever way of stifling us.'

'You're very defiant.'

'You are a Christian and wish to convert the whole world.'

'Christ demands it.'

'You are fostering a mediocre religion; the backlash will be terrifying. Two or ten centuries from now, millions of men will slaughter each other in the name of the absolute truth that each believes he possesses.'

'Derisory apocalypse: the message of Christ will engender fraternity.'

'He favours war and darkness.'

'Your mysteries of initiation are revealed to an elite: that is the greatest of injustices. That is the reason ancient cults are doomed to disappear. Why should the divine be reserved for a chosen few?'

'Human beings are not equal. Whoever wants to be initiated must detach himself from this world without denying it and while preserving its beauty. It is up to each adept to cross a succession of thresholds, to go towards the transcendent presence revealed in the naos. No one will ever be able to explain life. That is why the cult does not chatter; the rite does not dissipate the mystery, but places it in the heart of the initiate.'

'Simple souls cannot understand your words; nevertheless, they too have a right to God. Christ was born to bring a universal faith to men; it will not be reserved to a few adepts. Your mysteries will die out in the course of time.'

'A religion that started in historical time will die. Although Christianity seems to be on top now it carries in it the seed of its own end.'

'A baptized man knows eternal life, for he participates in the resurrection of Christ.'

'Before resurrecting in Osiris, the adept faces judgement; only those who have not entered into communion with the Sacred Principle die.'

'Do you not know redemption and charity?'

'It is not essential to believe, but to know.'

Theodore offered Sabni a cup of wine.

'This is truly a strange situation. The people love Philae, they detest me; if you knew how to make use of their anger, you could overthrow me.'

'I have no intention of doing so.'

'That is a fatal mistake: time is against you and public opinion fickle. When they realize that nothing has changed, they will trust me again and reproach you for your weakness; your friends will become your opponents.'

'Give Philae the means of living in peace and allow us to welcome new adepts.'

The hint of a smile animated the Bishop's face.

'Haven't you broken the law enough already?'

Sabni did not answer.

'Be careful, my friend: this is my last warning. I can no longer spare Philae; you must convince Isis to close the temple. The community must disperse.'

'Why so much rancour?'

'You know very well: in my place you would do exactly the

237

same. After Isis's exploits, Philae can no longer escape in anonymity. The island is a menace to Christianity.'

Sabni reflected. The Bishop, animated by final hope, considered him earnestly. Shaken by his friend's intransigence, at last becoming aware of the risks, would the High Priest renounce his outdated vocation?

'Those are just words,' said Sabni. 'You admire Philae, it is part of you. Without it, the province would seem empty and barren.'

The Bishop did not protest.

'I will return to the island. Protect it, Theodore. The world needs it.'

41

Only the tip of the rock emerged. Using the current with skill, Narses reached it without collision. Despite warnings, he insisted on navigating on his own; each day he managed the oars better and grew familiar with the currents whose dangers so attracted him.

The cataract disappeared under the waters; the frontier of Egypt, drowned, became invisible.

The General regretted nothing: not the fierce combats, not the dead, not his sword stained in blood. The defeat that he had feared so much had come from the burned rocks, the ochre land and the ocean emerging from the great South. The desire to conquer vanished, he was learning contemplation. Until the end of time, he would be content to fill his eyes with light, with water and rock. Accepting this defeat was his greatest victory.

Why are we perishing in the dust? asked the young recruits taken from their families and their villages. Narses was not their confessor, nor their spiritual adviser, but it was to him that they addressed a last protesting look, a silent cry against the Emperor, against himself, against a humanity that was in love with crime and violence.

He no longer assigned any tasks for his idle army to carry out. His lieutenants maintained vague discipline. No one bothered to see to the upkeep of an arsenal that was worth a fortune. Captain Mersis was furious: the epidemic was reaching the barracks. If the elite corps were idle, the mercenaries, less well paid, would follow their example.

In the old days, the General would have restored order and team spirit in a matter of days; if the world was evil, to collaborate with the status quo was akin to high treason. The cataract would seal his fate.

Narses was not interested in the Bishop even though he was in dire straits. For a week now, the people had been sullying his name. But instead of taking the lead of the movement, Sabni had retired to the island to celebrate rites that would ensure the fertility that the flood would bring there. Disappointed, his most ardent supporters criticized his lukewarm attitude and gave up the idea of attacking the Bishop's residence.

At Sunday mass, not one of the faithful was missing. Every one noticed the Bishop's calm demeanour. Wasn't that proof that he was in control of the situation and that the army, on his command, would crush any attempted rebellion? Only Theodore, Narses and Mersis knew that some of the men would not obey. Those from Byzantium because they refused to get involved in civil war; the Egyptians because they would not want to kill their own.

During the celebration of the sacrifice, the Bishop had difficulty breathing, but delivered the message. Like his subjects, he was expecting Sabni's arrival. He would throw open the church doors, claim his title, demand recognition of the traditional cults and governorship of the province. The Christians would acclaim him, Elephantine would be jubilant, and the soldiers would swear allegiance to Sabni. An enthusiastic army would march to the North and with forced marches would reach Memphis. Alexandria itself would not resist for long.

Sabni did not come.

Offering the body and blood of Christ towards heaven, Theodore's interpretation was that God had saved him from a humiliating loss of face and reminded him that his most sacred duty was to vanquish paganism.

For the Love of Philae

*

Sabni cleaned the low-relief sculpture with a damp cloth. The Pharaoh, placed under the protection of a row of cobras, received the blessing of Thoth and Horus, who held out above his head two golden vases from which emerged the symbols of imperishable life, in the form of the Ankh cross. By baptizing him, they conferred him with the unique legitimacy of creative powers. Thus demanded the spirit of Egypt, indifferent to human quarrels and to History itself. Tomorrow, when a pharaoh returned to these lands, it would suffice for him to read the texts, and animate the scenes revealed on the temple walls to relive the fire of primordial times, passed down from ruler to ruler.

'You're worried,' said Isis.

'I am wrong not to take more direct action.'

'Are you considering deposing Theodore?'

'To take power seems essential. If we don't govern, we will remain exiles in our own land.'

'You're right, but it is too soon. Your followers would drag you into a war that would be lost before it even started and innocent people would die because of you. It is our soul that you would lose in that adventure. Our adepts are our only army, our only strength lies in our thoughts and the fact is we are not ready for we lack unity, the most decisive of weapons.'

'Do you fear another betrayal?'

'We must make the community as pure as the purest gold so that its brilliance can transform human nature into a true corner stone of the temple. As soon as we achieve that, you can guide the ship of State.'

'Will it not be too late?'

'Let us make the time, Sabni; and now we should concentrate on teaching the Order; in it we will find all the answers.'

The elegant boat glided with ease on the dark waters of the flood. The boatman who handled the square sail was the best sailor in Elephantine.

At the end of this month of August, enlivened by a northern wind whose sweet breath did not lessen the scorching heat, he had the honour of transporting the Prefect and the Bishop, who sat in the shade of a canopy.

Nervous, Maximin supped down glassfuls of new wine. If he had known how to swim, he would have gladly plunged into the waters that mingled with the horizon. The Bishop, oblivious to the heat, savoured some grapes.

'Could you please explain the reason for this interminable leisure trip?'

'Patience, Maximin. Can't you enjoy the magnificence of this scenery? If you wished to commune with the soul of my country, this is the place where you would understand its nature.'

'You're not a poet, Monsignor. Every action of yours carries intention. I demand to know what you have in mind for me?'

'The situation is so delicate . . . don't paint an even bleaker picture.'

'Are you expecting insurrection?'

'We have just about avoided one.'

'Sabni?'

'He's just proved that he is not a warrior leader: an unpardonable mistake in the eyes of the population.'

'Where are you taking me?'

'Near the cataract. It's the only place where we can talk with Narses.'

The General, whose boat was moored to a pointed rock, stood up when he saw the ship approaching. What fool dared interrupt his meditation?

When the Bishop called out to him, he did not react, despite the fact that the Prefect's presence intrigued him; something serious must be behind this expedition.

Theodore and Maximin paused on the narrow platform; the three men looked like strange bipeds seemingly walking on water, lost in the flood.

For the Love of Philae

'This place is fascinating,' recognized Theodore.

'It requires solitude and silence.'

'So sorry to be breaking them, but an official document arrived yesterday from Byzantium.'

The Prefect gave a start.

'You should have told me immediately.'

'Nothing for you to worry about; the Emperor accepts your explanations regarding the Nubian gold.'

'No reproaches?'

'None.'

'What about . . . Philae?'

'He assumes that the problem is settled and awaits your return.'

'That confidential document was addressed to me and you had the impudence of reading it!'

'The Emperor wrote to me requesting that I take the necessary measures; you shall consult the decree in my office.'

'A decree! That means . . .'

'That my decisions are as good as law and you are to obey my orders without argument.'

Therefore, Maximin was now just a high official without any power. The Emperor was not dismissing him from his post, but he was entrusting the Bishop with the authority to govern the province. Once back in Byzantium, the ex-Prefect would occupy an honorary position, probably very boring, far away from Isis, distant from this impossible love that had become his reason for living.

'The Emperor has taken another decision: he accepts General Narses's request. He is appointed permanent chief of Elephantine's military force and placed under my command. When he retires, he will receive a house and some land.'

The General embraced the Bishop. Overwhelmed with happiness, he felt as if his missing arm was still his, and jumped around with joy like a child. He the veteran, the unvanquished soldier, the bravest of the brave, was being disowned by the army and confined to this obscure province!

He was judged senile or impotent. By granting him his nonsensical request, by relegating him to this miserable post at the far end of the Empire, his rivals were rid of him, pleased to condemn him to a definitive exile. Those who despised him could not possibly know that their disdain presented him with the most precious treasure.

The muddy waters attracted Maximin; according to legend, those who drowned entered, without judgement, into Osiris's kingdom. To die meant being deprived of Isis's gaze. Perhaps she would take pity on a fallen man, who had now but a title devoid of power. Elephantine, at the world's end, used up conquerors, blunting their weapons, deadening their claws. Neither he nor Narses had escaped. At this point, to go back to Byzantium would be the ultimate humiliation! To have to endure the sly smiles of the courtiers, the venomous expressions of consolation uttered by his colleagues, the sniggers of former subordinates: he would only be able to bear these trials if Isis was by his side.

'Would you do me a favour . . .?'

The Bishop interrupted.

'It's time to think about your departure; pack your belongings and tell me how many donkeys and camels you need. An escort will accompany you to Alexandria.'

Narses was not listening. The cataract belonged to him. From now on, he would no longer return to the barracks. He would put up a shack on the riverbank, near the rocks assailed by the whirlpools, he would no longer speak to anyone, and he would abandon his soul to the current. He would be thought mad and forgotten.

'Our collaboration begins this very day, General.' It took Narses several seconds to realize that the Bishop was addressing him.

'I am no longer a general.'

'You still have a year's service and you will serve it; otherwise I will have you arrested and exiled. A high-ranking officer like you knows the price of insubordination.'

Narses looked at his beloved cataract.

One year . . . One whole year before enjoying this every second, away from vile humanity. To obey, not to question, to act like a puppet.

'I am at your service.'

Theodore welcomed the general.

'We will carry out excellent work. Get one hundred men and boats ready.'

'Nubia, again?'

'Certainly not. This operation must remain secret and it will be your responsibility. Captain Mersis must not know about this.'

42

Isis rubbed with sand the finest bronze vase in the temple, shaped like an udder and decorated with the outline of the goddess of the firmament hidden inside a tree. On the background of the precious object, the sun emerged from beneath a lotus flower.

The High Priestess intended to fill it with water from the Nile; she descended the steps of the nilometer when she heard screams coming from Biga. Isis hurried to see what was happening and, from the riverbank, watched Narses's soldiers raid the sacred land of Osiris. Armed with pikes, they encouraged each other by shouting while trumpets played to celebrate the deed. Sabni was already pushing a boat into the water when Isis stopped him from climbing in.

'Put that vase back in the temple's treasure,' she demanded.

'I will fight.'

'The rule forbids you from going to Biga.'

'You cannot confront that mob on your own.'

'I have nothing to fear.'

Left with no alternative, the High Priestess paddled relentlessly; she saw the mercenaries head into the woods and violate the secret of the god of pure water, who rested in the mysterious hillock. Here, he merged with the goddess who brought into being what his heart had conceived, and from their marriage, the flood was born. Never before had a lay person dared disturb the serenity of this place.

246

Two mocking soldiers wished to help the young woman disembark.

'Hey, beautiful, we're not getting overly friendly, are we?'

'I am Philae's High Priestess. Get out of my way and leave this island immediately: otherwise I will place a curse on you.'

The soldiers, who had heard of her magical powers, were impressed by the severity of her tone and retreated. The arrival of the Bishop's ship renewed their impetus. The youngest dared grip the wrist of the High Priestess.

'She's just a woman. Look, I've taken hold of her.'

Jumping out of the boat, Theodore struck the impudent man with the back of his hand.

'She insulted us,' he cried.

'Keep an eye on my boat and stay where you are,' he ordered.

With her body barely covered by her white linen dress, Isis confronted the Bishop.

'Recall your drunkards! Biga belongs to Osiris.'

'Osiris is dead and will not come back to life; the island is the property of the State.'

'Respect the mystery, I beg you.'

Theodore, ignoring the High Priestess, went towards the woods. The expedition corps was cutting down the trees and destroying the altars. A tall, bearded giant attacked the statue of the god of the Blemmyes. He shattered the gazelle and a clump of limestone shattered the head, bringing down the pagan effigy. The 'good traveller' ended his voyage laid out in the ochre dust, under a tamarisk that was soon felled with a hatchet.

The High Priestess did not linger around this sad spectacle; in the centre of Biga an even more horrendous drama was being acted out. General Narses was climbing on to the hillock that protected the sarcophagus of the god. With the help of two strong soldiers, he managed to force the lid to swing open.

'Stop!' cried the High Priestess.

'It's no good,' declared Theodore. 'They are acting on my orders.'

247

Christian Jacq

Isis could not hold back her tears. The vandals threw down the sarcophagus lid and proceeded to destroy it with blows; the stone resting-place was now scattered, mutilated blocks.

'The tomb is empty,' verified the Bishop. 'Your false god never did exist.'

Isis had sat down inside the kiosk of Nectanebo I, the builder and warrior who had left the imprint of his desire for independence on the last Egyptian dynasty. Above the floral capitals, Hathor smiled.

'My intervention was useless,' she confessed to Sabni. 'Biga has been desecrated and ransacked, it is in ruins.'

The soldiers had laughed, glad to be able to release the aggression they had repressed for so long! Elephantine resonated with the noises of their victory.

Some people who had long been converts sprayed their heads with dust to mourn Osiris. This time, the ancestors' religion really was living out its last hours; how could one pretend, from here on, that some power protected the Holy sites?

'No fortified wall protects Philae from the Bishop's attacks.'

'You are the protection,' said Sabni. 'Your mere presence will deter Theodore.'

Isis remembered the attitude of the Bishop on Biga; he had defended her against his soldiers. Why did he show her such respect, if he hated her?

'Let us say that the Bishop attacked a deserted island.'

'We cannot do that,' said Sabni. 'Everyone knows the importance of Osiris's sacred territory. Theodore made no mistake in his target. The two islands are but one: Biga desecrated, Philae weakened. If our last magic barrier crumbles, the destruction of the temple will be inevitable.'

'I cannot accept that.'

Isis took Sabni's hands in hers.

'Philae is intact: that is the only reality our community must hold on to.'

'We must be prepared for a new offensive. Theodore wants to corner us into closing the temple ourselves and running away.'

Isis smiled once more.

'In that case, the destruction of Biga was useless.'

The head tax collector, Philamon, was not a good sailor. To step into a barge was enough to make him feel queasy. Nevertheless, he had to go to Philae's pier to make an inventory of the medium-sized boats that the temple possessed. He reminded the priest who observed him that there was a special tax on this type of vessel and that it was obligatory to declare it. Sabni declared that he was ignorant of the existence of such an administrative ruling; the penalties were quite high, payable within one week. Philamon did not listen to the High Priest's protests; he was in a hurry to leave and asked the boatman to hasten his rowing. Before reaching terra firma, he vomited.

Sabni wondered why Captain Mersis had not warned the temple; perhaps the pigeon service was not working. Not to pay meant to be deprived of a means of transport. Isis proposed that they should abandon the majority of their flotilla and keep just one cargo boat and a small barge. The tax would be reduced to a minimum.

'Let's visit the crypt,' proposed Isis.

A sliding stone gave access to the long rooms with very low ceilings. Sabni had trouble getting in; his torch lit up several ritual objects in gold and silver, used in splendid ceremonies that took place in the olden days. Vases, incense holders and statues slept in the dark.

'We don't have the right to sell them. They are the foundation of the sanctuary; without them, it will crumble. Tomorrow's communities will need them.'

Isis closed the first crypt. In the second were the remains of a barge; rebuilt, it would allow the community to travel to the world beyond.

The third was almost empty. It contained the ornaments of a High Priestess: a gold necklace, a pearl necklace, rings and bracelets.

'We'll bargain with this treasure.'

The necklace the High Priestess was offering as payment for the taxes and the fines embarrassed the head tax collector, who was even more bothered by having to calculate how much they came to, given that Philae had given up almost the whole of its flotilla. On what basis was he going to establish a sum? After a number of calculations that were not unfavourable to his own administration, he quoted a sum total. Isis did not contest it. Philamon valued the necklace by its weight in gold, using one of the rare scales in Elephantine that was not rigged. He accepted that the community was in order, pointed out that the use of a barge, even a modest one, that was not declared for tax purposes would entail a prison sentence and issued a receipt providing a precise description of the two vessels remaining to the temple.

Isis crossed the streets of Elephantine at sundown. She walked quickly, indifferent to the spectacle of the street. Some tramps thought they recognized her, but no one addressed her. The High Priestess had moored her barge on the southern tip of the island, not far away from a miserable village where some Nubian families who had converted to Christianity lived in cramped conditions. The flood often carried away their beaten earth huts.

Like a vessel lost in a red ocean set alight by the last fires of the day, the city made the High Priestess nostalgic. While advising Sabni not to get involved in a military adventure, Isis did not forget that the pharaohs had never become detached from their earthly reality. The temple, even if it was on a nearby island, occupied the heart of the city. If its high walls rendered initiation inaccessible to the lay population, it was to mark the frontier between curiosity and a desire for knowledge. From the centre of the sanctuary emerged the great joy of the heart; if the temple and its community did not succeed in re-conquering the land beloved of the gods, who would remain to do it?

Isis pushed back a branch of tamarisk. In front of her boat stood the Prefect.

43

'Don't be frightened. I only wish to speak with you . . . I have waited so long for this moment! Listen to me, I beg you.'

There was no trace of arrogance or defiance in this man with a drawn face; on the verge of old age, Maximin had found the ardour of a juvenile supplicant lover once more.

'Unfortunately, I can be of no help to you,' she said softly.

'Yes, you can . . . you can understand me, lend a meaning to my suffering, enlighten my darkness!'

He spoke for several minutes without catching his breath, explaining that he was merely a puppet prefect and that the Bishop had total power now. He could not even issue an order or sign a decree. The last privilege granted him would be a drunken escort, powerless to defend him against highway bandits. Theodore was sending him to a solitary and dishonourable death in the dust of a country road.

Isis sat down on a half-buried block, the vestige of a destroyed chapel. Nightfall was coming quickly; on the immense lake, the silvery sheen of the moon succeeded solar golden hues. The orange disc was plunging into the horizon, where it would face the demons of the netherworld before its morning resurrection again came up the sandy hill. If it was ever vanquished, and refused further combat with the giant serpent, humanity would fall into the great sleep.

'What I feel for you, Isis . . .'

'Be silent.'

The Prefect was indignant.

'No, I do not want to be silent any longer! It is by being entrapped in silence that I have lost my dignity in everyone's eyes. I am a rich man; I still have property in Byzantium.'

'I am pleased for you.'

'You refuse to listen . . . Theodore will destroy Philae and deport the members of the community. I will no longer be here to defend you. The Emperor has sent for me; I have to leave.'

'May you have a pleasant trip.'

The last rays of sun mingled with the lunar clarity suffused Isis's figure with pink and white hues, effacing the thin veil of her light dress and outlining the contours of her perfect body, an irresistible attraction for a love's passion. Fire burned in Maximin's words and hands.

'If you stay in Philae, you are condemned. Come with me; I will teach you to love me, you will build a chapel and pay homage to Isis. The Emperor will not know.'

'Aren't you forgetting Sabni?'

'He thinks only of himself and uses you to secure his power over the community; he is a conspirator and a coward, incapable of defeating the Bishop.'

'Isn't that an apt description of your personality?'

Maximin lowered his head.

'I have thought only of you and neglected my position . . . But that is how it should be. Politics and power games no longer interest me. I dream of an immense garden, full of trees in bloom where you would walk by my side, by a beautiful lake of leisure where you can bathe, of a sumptuous palace where, adorned like a queen, you would receive our guests. All Sabni has to offer you is poverty and despair.'

'He is the one I love with all my heart, a love that lives at the heart of the temple.'

'Not a stone of that temple will remain standing.'

'I am convinced of the contrary. Philae will defy the centuries and tire out time itself; as long as the northern wind blows, as long as the sun emerges from his mother's celestial womb, the temple will shine and the immobile island sail the river.'

'You're mistaken. Didn't you understand Theodore's warning? Biga was the final stage before an attack on Philae.'

'The Bishop thinks he has killed a god and violated a Holy Land, whose disappearance, he thinks, will plunge us into desperation; he will continue to harass us, but will respect our existence.'

'He's changed. Sabni has become his worst enemy. And you . . .'

'Am I so worthy of fear?'

'You incarnate the love of the goddess. Only Christ's love should reign over the world.'

'Love cannot be decreed, not even by a dogma. The more the goddess Isis is maltreated, the more she will hide in people's souls. When the moment comes, her glory will blossom like a flower with an inebriating perfume and the pilgrims will return towards Philae.'

'It's a dream.'

'You don't know Egypt well. From the moment of its birth, it has borne the brunt of jealousies and desires for conquest. Many peoples have wished they could occupy our land, unveil the mystery of our temples and steal the secrets of our eternal abodes. Some thought they had been successful and floundered in their own nightmares. Today, the Christian armies reign over the world; their religion tries to smother our tradition. Dangerous adversaries threaten them and covet our fertile delta and the Holy valley of the Nile. Tomorrow, perhaps we will suffer the yoke of a Bedouin or Arab faith; the disappearance of our civilization will be proclaimed and it will be said that our gods are dead. Yet, they will only be asleep, prisoners of a long winter.'

'Neither you nor I can wait for an illusory spring. Let us grab happiness; leave this place with me!'

An ibis spread his gigantic wings and flew over the waters, disappearing to the west. The spirit of the Pharaoh was incarnated in it, on its way to the celestial abode to celebrate the gods in the company of his brothers. Isis stood up and walked towards the boat.

'Your sincerity moves me, but I am not the woman you imagine.'

'You are here, near me . . .'

'The temple is my homeland. I would perish if I left it. Go back to Byzantium; tomorrow you will know another love and this will all be but a memory.'

'There isn't an ounce of my being that has not been consumed by your presence; you have no right to abandon me.'

'Farewell, Maximin.'

He took hold of her hands.

'Come with me.'

'It is impossible.'

'I will satisfy all your desires.'

'I have but one desire: to serve the great goddess.'

'Your universe is foundering in darkness. Do not stay on board a sinking ship; in Byzantium, you can be free.'

'True freedom means not having to choose. The Rule of the temple has granted this to me.'

'No one loves you as I do; I can offer you the most fabulous destiny.'

'I wish for no other than that of Philae.'

'Do not reject me.'

'What did you expect?'

'If you do not love me, Isis, I will be forced to kill you.'

'You have lost your mind.'

'And then I will kill myself. We will at least be united in death.'

With a promptness and a violence that surprised Isis, he reached out to strangle her. The High Priestess resisted, but Maximin, crazed beyond control, gripped her throat ever tighter, mumbling incomprehensibly. Isis stopped struggling. Her last thought flew out to Sabni, just as she felt darkness overwhelming her.

A burning feeling ripped her chest; she no longer felt the prefect's hands at her throat. Someone helped her up; she gasped in the deliciously fresh night air and set eyes on her saviour: the Blemmye she had met near Biga.

'I felt your life was in danger; that's why I kept you in view.'

'May Isis grant you strength and health.'

'Who is this wretch?'

'The prefect Maximin.'

The Blemmye spat on the inert body.

'Is he . . . ?'

'Whoever dares raise a hand to strike Philae's High Priestess does not deserve life. Is it true that the Bishop's soldiers have violated the sacred territory of Osiris?'

'My protests were in vain.'

'Was the tomb desecrated?'

'Biga lies in ruins.'

'Has the statue of our god been destroyed?'

'The vandals spared nothing.'

The black priest trembled, as if his body was suddenly overcome by violent fever. Arms outstretched, his face raised to the clouds, he uttered a deep shattering scream that came from the depths of his race before plunging into the Nile.

Isis came closer to the corpse, which lay on its back, eyes open. With her index finger she traced the cross of life on his forehead, his lips and his heart.

44

Stunned, the water-carrier set down his burden. What he saw filled him with horror. What crime could that man have committed to be subjected to such torture? So moved he could hardly utter a word, he knocked on the window of the workshop nearest the barracks. The owner, upon discovering the flayed body hung head down by the fortified wall, woke his wife and children. When dawn gave way to sunshine, hundreds of Elephantine inhabitants were crowded around the barracks' main gate. The spectacle of suffering fascinated them. The conversation became animated; each person had an explanation: rape, murder, blasphemy, plotting . . . But why expose the scoundrel in that way? One woman recognized him; she alerted her husband who was keeper of the cemetery. He broke the news to his cousin, a fisherman; he in turn warned one of the adepts who was fishing near the temple's embankment.

One hour later Sabni pushed through the crowd and reached the front.

'Mersis! Oh no, not you!'

Though his body was lacerated by whiplashes, the captain still managed to move. 'Mersis,' Sabni shouted, 'I'm here!'

The tormented creature struggled desperately to open his eyes. Blood trickled from his mouth.

'This behaviour is unworthy of you, Theodore.'

'Mersis is guilty of high treason. His peers have judged and punished him.'

'I would not fight in that way.'

'Elementary prudence requires it, Sabni. When I notified him of his guilt, Mersis did not deny it; he was aware of the risks. If he had arrested a traitor like himself, he would have shown no mercy.'

'How long have you known the captain belonged to the brotherhood?'

'What does that matter? He is paying for his crime. You no longer have an ally.'

'Mersis does not deserve such an infamous death; he has served his country with devotion.'

'Not his country, Philae.'

'For the love of your God, Theodore, untie him and let him die in peace. It is you who speak of pity and compassion; Egypt does not like cruelty.'

'Clemency? So be it! Be at the temple of Knum before sundown.'

In Narses's presence, the Bishop addressed the soldiers gathered in the courtyard of the barracks. He reminded them that their main duty was to defend Christianity against its enemies and that traitors like Mersis would be punished and exposed before the eyes of the mob.

The body was untied, placed in a shroud and transported to the cemetery of the ram god. When Sabni leaned over him, Mersis needed courage even to breathe, as such faint breathing made his heart race. On his way to the realm of shadows, he had lost the use of words. Sabni sustained his head throughout the agony, although the Bishop remained in attendance.

'A pagan cannot be buried in a Christian cemetery; use this empty terrain.'

With his bare hands, the High Priest dug a grave and put the corpse of his brother in it, before covering the pit with blocks of granite. Mersis would sleep beneath the material that had helped build the temple of Knum.

The Bishop pronounced one of the formulae for extreme

unction; Sabni was astonished. 'This pagan has paid for his sins here on earth. It is now up to God to forgive him: His mercy is infinite.'

Theodore pretended not to be responsible for the tortures inflicted on Mersis. Informed of his treason, the Byzantine officers had voted for exemplary punishment to which the Bishop could not object. But who had thrown them the captain, if not the Bishop himself, using denunciation and rumours?

Sabni felt guilty about his friend's death. He should have insisted that he left the barracks and fled north.

'Mersis would not have obeyed you,' objected Isis. 'He was as obstinate as he was brave. Don't give in to self-pity.'

'We are completely on our own now.'

'We are a community.'

Sabni engraved Mersis's Egyptian name, 'the son of the hoe', on a stele erected between the pylons. He would live there with the brothers and sisters who now lived within the realm of light they had emerged from. Each morning the sun lit the hieroglyphs, the immortal element of their being. Chrestos cleaned the tools and swept up the limestone fragments.

'Should we fight against Narses's army?'

'No, Chrestos, against fanaticism and injustice. They are the really dangerous adversaries.'

'I do not fear them.'

'Don't be presumptuous; they have vanquished the most experienced forces.'

'With your help, I will resist.'

'With the help of the whole community; do not under-estimate the weaker and less intelligent; they have virtues you lack. In each you must discern the quality that helps in the construction of the invisible temple.'

'Didn't you teach me the meaning of the inaccessible?'

'It will show you the path to the sanctuary.'

'And that will lead to the great mysteries?'

'The key is fraternity, not just the simple affection uniting the adepts, but the union of the whole brotherhood with the celestial powers. Do not neglect the small chores; when you carry out the most humble task correctly, you are living with rectitude and you will become a receptacle for divine love.'

The young adept knelt down before the stele. Sabni had a wonderful hand; his style of engraving was worthy of the greatest of sculptors.

'Who taught you to write?'

'Isis's father. I wasted hundreds of limestone fragments before being able to set down a beautiful hieroglyph; then I learned to carve the stone to inscribe the form on it. Often I thought the High Priest was going to beat me: he grew impatient with my clumsiness. When I saw that he was brandishing the stick, I ducked; but he aimed well. I tried to do better; when I understood that I served the Rule of the temple and that that meant eternal life beyond the personal, a love of life that surpassed and encompassed my own life, my hands became skilful.'

Chrestos waved the mallet and the scissors.

'What if I tried? There are some worn stones behind Trajan's kiosk.'

Sabni hesitated.

'You don't trust me.'

'There is one tool missing.'

'I will find it for you!'

'Bring me a stick.'

The adolescent moved back, burst out laughing and ran towards the monument where he would join his master; irrespective of the beatings, as long as he was participating in the sacred work.

The corpse of the Prefect was only discovered three days after his death; the police interrogated the inhabitants of the Nubian village, but failed to find any clues regarding the circumstances leading to the dramatic event. Then a scapegoat was found, thanks to a denunciation: a Jew, accused of stealing a short while before. The accused did not survive the torture for long, and given the gravity of the crime, he was impaled in a public square. Theodore wrote a detailed report addressed to the Emperor, deploring the tragic disappearance of the Prefect; he further mentioned the organization of an official funeral and regretted that the extreme heat would not allow for the body to be sent to Alexandria. Therefore, Maximin was buried in a place of honour in the island's cemetery.

Narses built his hut. When he spent his first night there, eyes fixed on the stars, he swore to forgo sleep to be able to gain more time to enjoy these fantastic visions. After the adventure in Biga, it seemed the Bishop wasn't planning any other military operations: therefore the General had left day-to-day duties to four officers, two Byzantines and two Egyptians who had taken on the responsibilities usually assigned to Captain Mersis. From their first meeting, open discord had set in. The soldiers, receiving contradictory orders, had executed none.

The August sun was so hot that the daily rounds were left off. Deserted, the top of the fortified walls seemed to doze in the sun. Two metres below, the waters of the flood shone.

On the rock above the cataract, the general hummed an old song often heard in the streets of Elephantine.

'The good North wind brought the fresh breath of
    life and made the river fertile;
The South wind helps the flood issue from the
    cavern of the primordial sea, to feed the country
    and fill the altars with victuals;
The East wind lifts souls to the stars;
The West wind waters the sky, to make the earth's
    fruits resplendent and its flowers bloom.'

Throughout the hours, the seasons, the years, Narses would enjoy the company of the winds.

Christian Jacq

*

The baker bit into the long bread he had taken from the oven.
The adepts would be pleased with him; such quality nourishment would suffice to fill the bellies and free the energy
indispensable for thinking. The ka of the bread, its subtle
power, was included in the vast forces that united the star to
the stone. Therefore, according to the Rule, the role of the
baker was not inferior to that carried out by the ritualist.

An overwrought ritualist, who used to be so haughty that
she did not deign to enter the temple's oven room, was afraid
of suffering from the heat.

'Have you finished?' asked Ahoure.

'Just one more loaf to go.'

'It can wait, I can't.'

'An unfinished task is a defeat for the soul.'

'Do you trust Sabni?'

Normally, the ritualist was not as direct. The baker's lively
eyes, contrasting with his heavy features, questioned his sister.

'He's leading us to disaster,' she stated. 'If he had taken
power, we would have known better days; his procrastination
condemns us.'

The baker turned to face his oven.

'Ambition, vanity, the need to plot . . . human beings will
never change. If the gods decide to destroy the race, the
universe will not weep.'

'Help me banish Sabni and become High Priestess,'
implored Ahoure, 'I will know how to negotiate our survival.'

The smell of baked bread filled the baker's nostrils.

'It has taken me forty years, sister, to discover but one virtue
and practise it: obedience to one true master. Thanks to that,
the destructive fires within me have been extinguished and I
can finally enjoy the peace I was looking for. Isis and Sabni are
greater than us because the heavens predestined them for their
task; admit this truth and stop tormenting yourself. To be
satisfied with fulfilling one's duty is the sweetest happiness.'

262

45

The raw sky, the ochre of the dunes, the lively green of the palm trees, the black rocks and the golden light composed, with the calm water, an idyllic paradise untainted by any human presence. Beyond the chaos, the deserts of the great South and the African solitude watched over the cataract with the same motionless gaze that General Narses cast out at the landscape. From dawn to dusk, he savoured every moment; feeling that every hour was sweeter than the last. He would not put a ceiling on his hut, so as to be able to contemplate the night.

Now he knew. The enemy was movement. Only stones, in their inertia, fulfilled the highest ideal of wisdom. Insensitive to the hope and despair felt by animated beings, the stones ignored the insipid variations of desire. In the heart of the rock lay the truth.

Ever since he fought his first combat, the General had doubted that the path ever came to an end or that there was a purpose to existence; nevertheless, each step took him closer to that solitude made of water and granite. It was not by chance that his experience ranged from battlefields to heaps of corpses, from assaults to exploits, from conquests to massacres.

How wonderful not to wish for anything any more and to renounce all desire! No illusion answering by the name of pleasure or suffering had gone so far. Detached from the past, deprived of a future, Narses himself was becoming like a mineral.

The attack took him by surprise. The two men had swum underwater. Armed with knives, they lunged on Narses who, with his right arm, grabbed one of the blacks by the throat. If he had not been amputated, the general would have been able to fight them off. He saw the blade thrust into his left flank and was unable to protect himself. It penetrated his ribs and drove onwards into his heart. Narses died standing, his eyes fixed on the cataract.

The Blemmyes threw the corpse of their first victim into its waters.

The black warriors had waited for the beginning of the flood's retreat, a period of whirlpools and currents, to slip into the natural canals whose form was very familiar to them. They used the papyrus canoes that fitted just two men. One paddled while the other emptied the vessel of the water that gradually seeped in as it moved quickly across the water. They took advantage of the turbulence, of the flux and reflux, they dodged in and out of rocky formations against which many a ship had floundered. Hurling themselves forward at full speed, they reached the first small fort by midday. The sun blinded the only watchman on the lookout, who had his back to the river. The Blemmyes pierced him with their arrows before he could sound the alert and decimated the small group asleep under an awning.

The raid continued. The canoes ploughed into the river so violently that it looked as if they would capsize. But their prows re-emerged before plunging back en route to their target, Elephantine's fort. Hundred of boats ended their race right down below the watchmen doing their rounds. Helping each other up, the assailants reached the top of the fortifications, which the level of flood had made effortlessly accessible.

The screams of the aggressors finally awoke the garrison.

The soldiers fell over themselves in grabbing their bows and swords and tried to protect themselves with their shields from the showers of stones and arrows raining down on them. The black warriors attacked with a frantic fury that scared even the hardiest soldiers. Already, the walls were on fire. Jumping from the height of the battlements into the barracks' courtyard, the Blemmyes handled hatchets and clubs studded with nails with incredible dexterity. Hacked-off heads and members bloodied the soil. A Byzantine officer who tried to organize resistance was immediately stoned.

Those who managed to escape abandoned the fort and dashed towards the stables, where they fought hand to hand until there was a counter-attack by the Byzantine expeditionary corps, whose force halted the Blemmyes. A furious charge led by troops armed with long pikes made the Africans retreat. Crossing the flames that were ravaging the barracks, they withdrew to their canoes.

A second band of assailants attacked the market and the poor quarters. The black warriors massacred the merchants, stole victuals and set on fire public buildings, which no soldier was guarding.

The raid had lasted less than an hour, sparing only Philae.

Women and children hid in caves. The able-bodied men put out fires and collected the wounded. On everybody's lips there were murmurs, but one thing was certain: the Blemmyes would be back.

With Narses gone, Theodore had taken the army in hand. He had only about a hundred soldiers left, too few to withstand any further attack. All that remained of the fort was calcified debris. Rebuilding it would have taken too long; therefore the Bishop ordered the planting of stakes on the banks, with sharp points turned towards the Nile. Rows of archers were stationed behind these. Hidden behind bushes, they would delay any landing. Hastily, the soldiers taught volunteers the use of arms.

Would the Bishop witness, helpless, the fall of Elephantine

and the destruction of his work? For the first time, he rebelled against God. He considered consulting the forbidden oracle of Knum the potter, who responded to human pleas. He stormed into the labyrinthine ruins, and felt surrounded by demons whispering to him to abandon his service to Christ and return to the religion of his ancestors. Behind a gigantic naos made of pink granite lay the fragments of the wooden statue that the priests used to carry into the great court where the consultants met. To the questions asked, the god replied 'yes' or 'no' by nodding his head. Was it necessary to assemble all the dispersed members, redress the hieratic personage, and interrogate him? The Bishop hated himself. With angry kicks, he smashed the hand of the potter, carved in sycamore.

He, Theodore, was the sole person responsible for this massacre. His benign attitude had engendered disaster. Philae had attracted the Blemmyes, who were like destructive insects. Philae had killed the Prefect Maximin and General Narses. Now the Bishop was face to face with Isis and Sabni; no obstacle stood between them. The war would become ever crueller. Sabni, in the midst of chaos, would not be spared. Theodore had warned him: when would he understand that he should flee that accursed brotherhood?

After Sunday mass, the Bishop addressed a sermon to the population gathered in the atrium. To almighty God, he asked for strength to fight the invader. From the Christians, he demanded courage and discipline. Elephantine was not lacking in arms or fighters. If she desired, in the depths of her soul, to survive misfortune, she would know how to defend herself.

He did not expect a solution from the message he had sent off to Alexandria explaining the situation and calling for help. To gather troops and send them to the southern frontier would take too long. It was better to depend on oneself. If their second assault failed, the Blemmyes would not return for a while.

Theodore brandished General Narses's sword. On it, he swore in the name of Christ that he would save the province.

About ten shaggy monks broke through the crowd. Leading them was a creature so thin that his bones threatened to break through his skin. With feverish eyes and a strong voice, he called out to the Bishop.

'Why don't you tell the truth?'

'Are you accusing me of lying?'

'I bear the name of the apostle Paul and I live in a pagan temple that I have purified with fire. The hermits have recognized me as their spokesman. We know how to fight. We have faced wild beasts in the desert. Those black warriors do not frighten us. Give us arms and we will exterminate all pagans!'

The people shouted their approval. In the present circumstances, Theodore could not neglect any allies. He accepted. Assembled, the hermits formed a formidable cohort.

'You're not telling the truth,' continued Paul, 'because you're omitting the true culprit: Philae! It is to take revenge for the violation of Biga and the pagans that the Blemmyes have attacked us. The assassins are Isis and her clique. Philae must be destroyed!'

The other hermits echoed this request. Then a woman shouted. Her husband and children joined her, soon to be echoed by ten, a hundred, then a thousand families. Theodore shouted down the painful concert.

'If we attack Philae, the reaction of the Blemmyes will be terrifying. The chapel of their god is built on the island, placed under the protection of the High Priestess. If she is hurt or the sanctuary damaged, they will set Elephantine on fire and bathe it in blood. Let us worry about our own safety first, then we can think of Philae.'

Despite its passion, the crowd acquiesced. Paul, feeling it would not follow him, tried another angle.

'Let's stop issuing rights of passage to that pagan community! Let them die of hunger on that devilish island. The Blemmyes will have nothing to blame us for.'

267

'You're forgetting the law. They are landowners who pay taxes. They have a right to buy and sell.'

Theodore's argument found an echo in quite a few present. Whoever paid their taxes could not be treated as pariahs or slaves.

'Philae offends God and those who serve Him.'

'You're right,' admitted the Bishop, 'I will take the necessary measures. The most urgent is to reinforce the town's defences and to prepare it for a new assault. As soon as the blacks are vanquished, we will take care of the pagan temple.'

The hermit smiled. The prelate had made a commitment before the assembled Christian community; when the moment came, he would not be able to go back on his own word. And the moment would come, since God fought side by side with his own.

Chrestos had cleaned the workshop.

'Here are our weapons,' he said to Sabni, presenting him with tools. 'We will fight.'

'Theodore will not attack Philae. The chapel of the African god protects the island.'

'For how long?'

'For as long as the strength of the Blemmyes is superior to that of the Christians. The Bishop has sent a message to Alexandria to ask for additional troops.'

'When will they arrive?'

'When the flood decreases, at the beginning of the winter, maybe never . . . Is the Emperor really interested in such a distant province? If he neglects us we are saved. The Blemmye menace will stop Theodore from destroying us.'

'What if you took up your stick again? I feel like sculpting and my back is strong.'

While the High Priest and his young brother went to the southern part of the island, where Chrestos, sweating profusely, continued his sculpting practice, Isis and her sisters were putting the little temple dedicated to Hathor in order.

That was where the ritual dedicated to the return of the distant goddess would be celebrated. They freshened the colours of the capitals, cleaned the columns and relief sculptures of the dust brought by the sand-bearing winds. Serene, almost jolly, the High Priestess read the text she was perfecting.

The future of the community depended on its power. If the goddess heard their call, she would return to those burnt lands and bring to the temple the mountain gold of which the flesh of the gods was made. That the adepts should be nourished by the imperishable was the main prerequisite without which no work could be done.

Beyond the island, the war raged. Once again, men were killing each other in the name of their faith. On the holy island, no one raised their voice. At dawn, the figure of the Pharaoh engraved on the walls became animated and pronounced the words confirming the divine presence. Isis raised her hands in a gesture of prayer. The temple vibrated.

46

On that 10 September, the New Year festivities were reduced to a distribution of grapes. No one had the strength to commemorate an event that had ordinarily been celebrated with strong libations. Everyone lived in anguish. The Bishop had received no reply from Alexandria; therefore, he had decided to send a second messenger. Instead of using the river, he would go by land along the banks of the Nile, because at Lykopolis, in mid-Egypt, there were pirates who attacked boats and bands of brigands who stole from travellers. A man on his own would fare better than a detachment of soldiers, whose arms were coveted by the robbers.

The Nile was retreating lazily. It had deposited the precious layer of mud on the land. The peasants were being trained in the handling of arms under the strict supervision of Byzantine instructors. The hermits had come out of the desert and the tombs, and were continually in town calling people to combat. Thanks to them, Elephantine was acquiring the morale of a victorious party; even if fear knotted their guts, the desire to slay pagans grew.

Posted at the edge of the cataract, the sentinels would signal the appearance of the Blemmyes. By the end of September, not even a tracker had been sited. Fears began to die down. Theodore continued to reinforce the defence system. Many rows of stakes, very close to one another, would prevent access to the banks. To come on shore, the Blemmyes would have to sacrifice hundreds of men, without the slightest hope of success.

Weary of listening to the hermit's importunate singsong, the traders proposed the market be reopened. The Bishop granted their request. On the stalls were piled dry fish, cheeses, onions, pigeons, poultry, flour, wicks for lamps, pottery, spices and other merchandise whose price had risen considerably. Inflation, which the Bishop had managed to contain during the period of peace, was now on the rise: thirty per cent on wheat, fifty for the wood and oil, and one hundred per cent for the meat. The state of emergency justified it. Tomorrow, Elephantine might be completely destroyed. Whoever wanted to enjoy life should not succumb to stinginess.

Conversations stopped dead when Sabni put in an appearance at the entrance of the market where he gave alms to the poor. After selling the pearl necklace to a sheep breeder, the High Priest intended to buy some vegetables, garlic and summer figs. As he approached, the clients moved away. When he asked the merchants the price, they did not reply, declaring thus their refusal to speak with a stranger. Sabni insisted. An emaciated individual with a dirty face came running towards him brandishing a knotted wooden stick.

'Go away, son of the devil! No one will sell you food!'

Sabni ignored the fanatic and addressed the traders.

'I am not begging; keep your charity for the Christians. I have silver pieces.'

'Whoever accepts them will be cursed,' screamed Paul.

The High Priest turned to the hermit.

'A man of God does not raise his voice. You are less noble than a beast screaming like that. If you were my disciple, you would soon lose your taste for commotion.'

Sabni took hold of the stick with which Paul was threatening him and broke it in two pieces.

'Doesn't your religion teach you not to be violent with your fellow men? God's order to Moses was "Thou shall not kill". Don't you respect his commandments?'

'It's certainly not a pagan who will teach me about the true faith!'

'It does not matter who teaches you. What is important is what you take in. Your ancestors are the same as mine: Egyptians who respected men because they venerated God. Human beings like you should be carrying heavy loads side by side with donkeys.'

The hermit stepped back. He could tell the High Priest was very angry and was afraid of his strength.

'Don't touch me, you pagan! The people will defend me.'

'I would not sully myself.'

The merchants and some idlers surrounded Sabni. A cheese-seller pointed at him.

'You and the Blemmyes are together. It's because of you that they massacred and burned.'

'Slander.'

'The hermit saw Isis making a pact with a Blemmye. Can you deny it?'

'I do deny it.'

'If our wives and our children wanted to find refuge on the island, would the doors of the temple be open for them?'

'No profane person can enter. It's the Rule.'

'The Blemmyes possess a chapel there. You would welcome them with joy. That's more proof that you are accomplices.'

The circle became tighter. Some picked up stones, others knives.

'Philae guarantees your survival, Byszantium starves you and would sell Egypt to whoever makes the highest bid. Only the temple will preserve your unity and the country's independence.'

These words spread confusion. Many thought exactly that.

'The Blemmyes will kill us,' suggested a butcher.

'What do you propose?' asked a breeder. 'Does anyone have a solution?'

In the eyes of the inquisitor, there was a ray of hope that

Sabni did not wish to encourage. He must not foster or lead a rebellion.

'When peace returns, we will rebuild Egypt. Philae will be its heart.'

'You encourage dissension,' accused the hermit. 'Those who listen to you will be chastised, like that traitor Mersis.'

The memory of that torture paralysed those who were taking the High Priest's side. He made his way through the crowd and walked straight on.

The small temple of Hathor was reborn; its bright colours enchanted the eye. The sisters rediscovered flutes and tambourines and repeated cadences and melodies. Chrestos cleaned the wooden masks that the adepts would wear throughout the celebration of the ritual. They would pray to the mistress of dances and chants, to the gold of the skies, to the lady of drunkenness who would reveal to them the love that linked the different worlds.

Saddened to have returned empty-handed and to spoil the joy of those who were preparing the feast, Sabni waited for the community to disperse before telling Isis that he had failed.

'If we can no longer buy victuals, then someone will do it for us.'

'Who?'

'A banker.'

Three banks managed the funds of the inhabitants of Elephantine. The most important belonged to the church, the second to a Byzantine financier and the third to a Greek. The latter, like his peers, collected taxes destined for the State, changed money, lent sums at usurer's rates, undertook currency transfers and other more private affairs. By amassing a fortune before establishing his business, he had respected one of the musts of the profession: to be rich in order to become a banker, so as to become even richer. The Greek, who was not as strict as the Bishop and more astute than the

273

Byzantine, did not hesitate to lend his name when the fee was worth it. With a blotchy complexion and his corpulence hidden by a white tunic, he dedicated his leisure to gourmet pleasures.

He examined the necklaces, the rings and the bracelets that Sabni was proposing.

'Very beautiful items. Do you want a loan?'

'I would like to sell them.'

'I will give a lower price than an antique dealer would.'

'Never mind.'

'How do you intend to invest your money?'

'You can take care of that.'

'Rest assured. I will make it yield a profit. You'll be very pleased with my services.'

'You will acquire victuals on my behalf.'

'That may be a delicate operation . . . and it will entail expenses.'

'You will calculate them.'

'I can also deliver, very discreetly, but . . .'

'Add those expenses too.'

The Greek bowed. The temple would be a good client.

As soon as Sabni had left, he entrusted the bank to his assistant and went to the market. The farmers whose assets he managed would grant him considerable discounts, which would increase his benefits. Busy calculating his profits mentally, he bumped into Paul.

'Out of my way, hermit. You smell.'

'Just a moment, Greek. Would you by any chance be planning to help Philae?'

'Business confidentiality.'

'Whoever aids the pagans will be considered a traitor and perjurer in my eyes. Do not defy me and respect the will of the Lord.'

At the beginning of October, the Nile receded. The olive and date harvest started. As the temple had not received any

For the Love of Philae

delivery, Sabni went to see the banker. Elephantine, sheltered by fortifications that were daily reinforced, was being reborn from the ashes. The houses that had been set on fire were rebuilt in brick, masons were mending the walls of the barracks. The Blemmye menace seemed to be fading away.

'I was mistaken,' justified the Greek. 'Those jewels were worthless.'

'Are you refusing to negotiate on my behalf?'

'Of course not . . . but I would need real treasures. It is said that Isis's temple is full of gold; the beauty of the statues is praised. No doubt the crypts contain precious objects; if you bring me those marvels, you will have food.'

'Have you taken leave of your senses?'

'A banker has to live according to the times.'

'You're the slave of the Christians.'

'Prices vary in accordance with needs. Today, a pagan must pay a high price to survive. And my profession is more dangerous than one would imagine.'

'Give me back the jewels.'

'What jewels? If you had entrusted me with them, I would have given you a receipt. If you doubt my good faith, we can go to the courts. Do not even think of roughing me up, I have police protection.'

Sabni thought about happier times, when the tables full of victuals were consecrated by the pharaohs before being offered to the great goddess. With its wealth the temple had been able to ignore worldly concerns, live according to the Rule and transmit its spirit.

'Osiris condemns thieves. Perhaps Christ will show more leniency.'

275

47

Chrestos, who was up to his waist in the water, caught at long last a Nile bass. The moment he held it up, victorious, a kite hawk swept down and snatched the fish from his hands. Carrying its prey in its beak, the predator, indifferent to the fisherman's protests, disappeared off into the blue sky.

Furious, the adolescent smashed the water with his fist, producing a silvery splash.

'Should an adept lose his temper in that way?'

The boy blushed, confused by the sudden presence of Isis.

'I was fishing for two hours and still ended up empty-handed.'

'That's no excuse.'

Ashamed, Chrestos returned to the riverbank. The gravity of the High Priestess intrigued him.

'I'm not very good at leisure, I prefer to study.'

'Have you deciphered the texts on the columns?'

'They're difficult, but I do not despair. If Sabni helped me more often, I would make progress quicker.'

'There is perhaps another way.'

Chrestos followed Isis who, in the middle of the day, took an unusual route. She went up the rather steep staircase that led to the temple's roof; ordinarily, the adolescent only went there at night to study the movement of the planets and the location of the stars. The High Priestess took him towards the corner, where there was a small chapel with closed doors. Chrestos

276

had already noticed the existence of the strange sanctuary that nobody went near except Sabni. To ask questions seemed inappropriate. In an uncertain manner, he felt that it contained some of the temple's closest secrets.

Isis opened the bronze lock. The young adept trembled, certain that his destiny would be sealed inside.

'Go in, look around and meditate.'

As he became accustomed to the half-light, he could closely examine the relief sculptures that decorated the walls; they illustrated the stages of Osiris's resurrection: through the love of Isis he was able to leave his tomb and enter immortal life with her. She bore him a son, Horns, whose destiny was to vanquish evil and reunite the two worlds.

The High Priestess closed the door to the chapel. Chrestos sat in the middle of the floor and concentrated on listening to the voice of the hieroglyphs, the very words of God. From the signs engraved in stone emanated a soft and reassuring light. Despite having his eyes closed, the adept retained a form of vision.

The small room grew and grew; it took on the shape of an immense boat that travelled on lakes of fire. Wheat grew in azure fields, bathed in an immaterial Nile. Suddenly, he saw the throne of Paradise mentioned in the Sacred books; from its plinth the master letters were born. They used the rays of sunlight to alight on the walls of the temple, or so it appeared. At the very source of the signs, Chrestos's spirit learned to understand the universe.

When the High Priestess, smiling, came to liberate him, the adolescent's life had changed; his life no longer belonged to him but had been assimilated by Osiris. From now on, imbued in his blood, the knowledge of the golden age circulated.

'Isis, you . . .'

'That is the first step on the path of the great mysteries. It contains all others. Make that vision grow in silence and work ceaselessly: whatever you perceive, inscribe.'

Theodore had a decisive weapon to destroy Philae's

fortified defences: Chrestos's presence inside it. It constituted an offence of such gravity that it would result in the condemnation of the entire community. The temple had grossly violated the law by admitting a new adept, a runaway guilty of evading taxes. Without even evoking religious justifications, the Bishop could banish the adepts and put an end to the cult of Isis.

The Blemmye menace had prevented him from taking action. Not only was there the assault by the black tribes, but there was turmoil caused by the closure of the sanctuary. But it was not a normal fear which caused Theodore's procrastination. He believed that Elephantine might resist.

A mysterious force forbade him to strike the fatal blow that would forever ruin the hopes of the pagans, as if the last survivors of an ancient time were under divine protection. His bond with Sabni was not of human origin. Ever since their youth, they had felt an identical attraction to a spiritual life. By separating them to the point of putting them in opposite camps, fate was perhaps teaching the prelate that a measure of error at the heart of truth enhances the light that issues from Christ.

Theodore felt weary. There had been too much conflict, too many deaths, too much savagery . . . How sweet it had been to reflect in Sabni's company and to devote oneself to theological arguments as delicious as fresh figs!

Dogma on the one hand, friendship on the other: torn between two paths, incapable of uniting the two strands, he felt he had failed. In the past, he would have confided in Sabni and asked for his help; today, he decided his own fate, although he felt he was floundering in the swamps of uncertainty. To renounce God . . . the temptation appeared before him, similar to an acacia leaf, sweet and irritating.

The hermits were mistaken when they imposed either conversion or nothingness on the world. The voice of the Master spoke of the warmth of love and not the coldness of hatred. This kind of exalted faith Theodore rejected. He felt closer to the wisdom of the temple and to the resplendent beauty of Isis.

The Bishop did not desire the arrival of a rescue force. It would break the fragile balance that had been established. If Theodore had had the power to halt time, he would have frozen its path over Philae.

Paul pushed a young and beautiful woman in front of him; she went forth against her will. Some citizens had identified her, so they were astonished at the incredible show the hermit was putting on. How did he, the propagator of the most austere canons of the law, accept contact with such a creature? Paul demanded a meeting with the Bishop. A few yards from his house, some vagrants gathered and pointed at the unlikely couple. The hermit made so much noise that the prelate came out of his office.

'What do you want, Paul?'

'Do you know her?'

'She must take off her veil.'

The captive did as she was told.

'Who is she?'

'A prostitute. This she-devil sells her body to whoever pays her the most.'

'She is not the only one of her kind and her trade is legal. Is that why you have come to disturb me?'

'This sinner offers her services to illustrious and very generous clients. Would you like to know their names?'

'They are not breaking the law.'

'One of them is nevertheless infringing the Rule of his temple and betraying his wife.'

'Are you insinuating . . .'

Paul shook the prostitute.

'Confess, you trollop! It's the only way you can save your soul! Admit that Sabni shared your bed and maltreated you.'

The woman just nodded.

'Philae's High Priest, a vile being who wallows in mud . . .

that is the truth. Tomorrow, the whole province will know it and you, our Bishop, will condemn him.'

The High Priestess saw her husband walk to the border of the desert in the direction of an abandoned village; from a run-down cottage came a woman of provoking beauty. She called Sabni who, after some hesitation, joined her. The moment she took him in her arms, scorpions stung the neck of the unfaithful man.

Isis woke up suddenly, feverish; this horrible dream had tormented her to the point of disturbing her sleep. She contemplated Sabni, who was lying on the narrow bed with the back of his neck on a cushioned headrest.

Disturbed, the High Priestess went to the library and consulted a key to dreams, patiently assembled down through the centuries. The scene that haunted her was described there in every detail. It was, therefore, not a simple nightmare, but a dream of clairvoyant power. According to the treaty, it predicted a grim outlook for the man in question. Isis took a lock of Sabni's hair while he lay asleep, and placed it on a gold plaque covered with hieroglyphs; they depicted a prayer addressed to the Saviour, a good genie in charge of modifying sombre destinies.

Isis slipped it under the sleeping man's cushion, hoping that the magic of ancestral words would banish the she-demon.

While the hermit spread his poison in the streets of Elephantine, Theodore talked to the prostitute. She refused to say her name, but he had no trouble getting the information from one of his secretaries. Consulting his notes gave him ample information. This young woman's name was Myrta; daughter of Leonides, an Aramaean merchant who had been ruined by unwise investments. She had been selling herself for a year to help her family survive and took her lovers either in her own bedroom or at Elephantine's northern toll station, where there was a brothel that welcomed wealthy travellers in need of some relaxation. In accordance with the law, she paid her taxes, scrupulously declaring the number of her clients; her accountancy was carried out by her father.

A High Priest, according to non-written law, owed loyalty to his wife. This was all the more true if her rank was that of High Priestess and they formed a symbolic couple, the embodiment of Osiris and Isis. By discrediting Sabni, the hermit undermined the spiritual foundations of the community. To prove the wrongdoing of their leader would dishearten the followers and sully the soul of the temple.

'Did Sabni buy your body?'

'Yes', she replied.

'How many times?'

'Just once. But he struck me.'

'When was this?'

'A week ago. I still have the marks.'

She uncovered her back, which was covered in bruises.

'What weapon did he use?'

'A strip of leather. I want to lodge a complaint. He didn't pay me and owes me reparation.'

If what the prostitute said was true, she would win her lawsuit.

'What was the exact time and date of your meeting?'

Myrta stated these and enlarged on details of the maltreatment inflicted by the High Priest. They checked, and in fact, on that day Sabni was in Elephantine.

'I want to lodge a complaint,' said the woman stubbornly.

The Bishop did not doubt that there was trickery involved. Therefore, he tried to delay the beginning of this lawsuit, which would sully and injure his friend. The inquest carried out by the Bishop's secretaries gathered evidence against him. The keeper of the brothel had identified him and two hermits, who begged at the toll station, and swore that they saw a man throw a leather strap full of blood into the Nile. No witnesses came forward to contradict this.

281

Hermits and prostitutes joined forces to clamour for justice. The harlots threatened to go on strike if the Bishop did not agree to their legitimate request. Theodore questioned himself: had Sabni succumbed to his desire and, disgusted by his own behaviour, taken it out on the girl who might reveal his only too fallible nature? Thinking about it, he concluded that this lawsuit might turn out to be an excellent scheme: Sabni would spend some time in prison, and therefore be spared tragedy and also kept out of the fanatics' reach. Forced to pay a heavy fine, an amount the Bishop had yet to determine, the community would sell their last goods before dispersing. Isis, devastated with grief, would not recover, and would no longer have the strength to face adversity. If there were any incidents, Sabni would be kept well away.

Sabni presented himself on his own before the tribunal. He heard calmly the testimony of the plaintiff. The wealth of details scandalized the audience. Without being asked, Myrta exhibited her back and showed the proof of her accusations.

When the High Priest tried to speak he was booed and his voice drowned. The police had to remove some prostitutes already bordering on the hysterical.

'What are the names of this woman's parents?'

'Her mother is dead. The father is called Leonides.'

'An Aramaean who trades in oil.'

'Do you know him?'

'He is the one who should be judged. Did he not attack a sister who refused to give in to his advances?'

Some murmurs could be heard in the courtroom.

'Did she lodge a complaint?'

'She was told it could not be lodged.'

Although it had just begun, the defence was already crumbling.

'My heart,' said the high priest, 'tells me that I must fulfil my duty and it is my witness. I do not betray its guidance and I am afraid of disobeying its commandments. I reached my present station thanks to its directing my actions. By listening to its teaching. I learned rectitude, and although I know that nowadays mendacity often has its way, it is not a reliable vessel. Whoever obtains riches by using falsehood will be sterile; whoever navigates in its company will not reach port safely.'

'Those are worthy principles,' admitted Theodore, 'but we are in a court of law and we judge facts. Do you recognize them?'

'Does that girl recognize me?'

'Yes, it's you! You raped me and lacerated my back!'

'In that case, describe me in my nudity.'

Surprised, Myrta looked at the Bishop.

'Obey,' he ordered.

'He is . . . he's a man.'

There was an uproar of laughter in the room.

'Speak or take back your accusation,' demanded Theodore.

Myrta raised her frightened eyes and moved backwards to the tribunal wall.

'You're . . . you're circumcised.'

'That is true,' admitted Sabni. 'Our rule so demands; everyone knows that.'

The prostitute tried to run away, but the guards stopped her.

'That woman lied; this is the first time that we have ever set eyes on each other. If we had made love, she would have known that I have a mark that distinguishes me from other men. It was engraved on my flesh when I was initiated.'

Sabni undid his loincloth. Above his thigh, on his groin, there was a cross of life.

48

Dates, olives and grapes piled up on the markets. The Nile retreated. Forgotten were the leisure trips by boat; finished the long days of rest and chattering. The peasants were once again busy, their land enriched by the fertile mud the flood had deposited in abundance.

Isis was worried; soon the temple would run out of fresh victuals. Although Sabni had been found innocent, his reputation had suffered from the lawsuit. Public rumours insinuated that the High Priest indulged in carnal pleasures and had betrayed his sacred vocation. Philae no longer respected the Rule. Had not many adepts abandoned the Rule because of such decadence? It was whispered that many sisters, despite their advanced age, indulged in debauchery.The religion of Isis gave women too much freedom; according to Augustine's recommendations, shouldn't they be wearing veils, instead of provoking men by exhibiting their charm? In order to deal with the temptations that these she-devils inflicted on the most virtuous, it was best to restrict their public appearances.

The hermits' rants, repeated a hundred times, made an impression on the people. The image of a beautiful and luminous Isis faded away like a relief sculpture consumed by the passage of time. Those who had surreptitiously brought vegetables and fruits to the temple stopped doing so, fearing Paul, the Bishop, prison and God's punishment.

Despite Chrestos's efforts, the community was becoming lethargic. After a sizzling summer, most adepts felt exhausted; old age could not hold out against the ardour of Elephantine's sun, to say nothing of the uncertainties of tomorrow. Not that the sick or infirm worried about themselves, but they felt concerned about Philae's future. Would the place where they venerated the Gods and were granted wisdom still be there for their successors?

The adolescent also felt at the end of his tether on occasion, but never discouraged, because Isis and Sabni offered him an ever-renewed energy. His thirst for knowledge was far from quenched: he learned new hieroglyphs, studied a papyrus forgotten in the archives, talked with the High Priestess on the nature of the god Thoth, scribe of the light and keeper of the power contained in the sacred language's every word. In the morning, when he attended the purification of the offerings, the young adept thanked the gods for granting him such intense happiness. He pronounced with Isis the verses of the hymn to the nascent sun, went through the gestures of consecration that opened the mouth and the eyes of the temple with Sabni.

'You will assist the High Priestess,' ordered Sabni, 'and carry the sceptre walking behind her when she goes towards the naos.'

'Me, take your place?'

'Not exactly,' replied the High Priest, amused. 'You will fill in for me temporarily, nothing more.'

'Are you going on a trip?'

'To the north. When the belly is hungry, the spirit grows dull.'

'Isn't it dangerous?'

'Nothing is more dangerous than to renounce.'

'I wish . . .'

'You will stay here, Chrestos. After me, you are the strongest man in the community.'

On the highest step of the pier, in the shade cast by the

obelisk, Isis and Sabni kissed. Both were apprehensive about this expedition into unknown territory, from which the High Priest might not return.

At the northern toll station, the traveller declined to give his identity, paid his due and received a poor quality papyrus to present to the patrol chiefs he would encounter on the road, looking for thieves and runaway peasants. Despite his fears, Sabni wasn't questioned. As soon as he crossed the first village, he rented a camel. The moment he reached the area around Thebes, surrounded by wealthy agricultural holdings, he would be able to acquire provisions in great quantity. Far from Elephantine, no one would recognize him.

The High Priest left the province with astonishing ease. None of the Bishop's scribes followed him; at each toll, he paid without further ado. For a small sum, he borrowed a cargo boat; the boatman advised him to moor in a small village to the south of Thebes, where he knew the mayor. The latter was welcoming and efficient. In less than a day, bags of wheat, fruits and vegetables were put on about twenty donkeys rented for a reasonable sum. The peaceful caravan made its way across earthen paths and, thanks to maritime transportation linking the big towns, in four days reached the province of Amon and Elephantine.

Some customs officers inspected the contents of the sacks. Sabni was afraid that they might keep a part of the cargo, but they were content to make an inventory of the load. The High Priest gave the safe-conduct document meant for the administration's archives to the customs chief.

At the beginning of the cortège was a little man, almost bald, inspecting a donkey. Sabni recognized the head tax collector.

'This beast is foreign to these parts. Show me your rental certificate.'

'I don't have one.'

'What is the name of the owner?'

'A mayor from Thebes.'

'This is extremely serious,' said Philamon. 'According to the rules of the donkey owners' guild, you do not have the right, as a resident of Elephantine, to rent animals from competitors. You will have to pay a fine, to give them a year's subscription fee and pay for their autumn banquet.'

'Can I pass?'

'No. At this time of year, the donkeys of the province are only allowed to carry manure and jars. The ruling at present reserves all transportation of victuals to camels. You are, therefore, in an illegal situation and I am forced to confiscate these fraudulent provisions.'

'I must get them back without delay.'

'The administration will decide.'

'Who exactly?'

'The subject seems quite complex. It is outside my area of competence and no doubt concerns several departments; I must consult some specialists and then study the minutes at the tribunal. There is no doubt that you will be condemned, but under what jurisdiction, that is the question.'

Sabni left. Theodore's spies had waited for his return to set up the most legal of traps; still believing the impossible, the High Priest visited four of the most important members of the donkey owners' guild. The first refused to see him, the second and the third did not have any properly documented beasts and the fourth tried to give him two sick animals, incapable of carrying heavy loads.

Sabni gave up. The guild obeyed the Bishop. With a heavy heart and his body so tired it made him prone to despair, he headed back towards Philae. The place where he usually embarked was no longer deserted.

On the river bank, inside a hut that had been quickly erected, was a civil servant in charge of receiving an exorbitant toll for the journey between the land and the holy island. The attendant gave Sabni a receipt for the payment. He was scrupulously obeying the orders he received from the Bishop.

*

Outside the temple, tapestries made of linen, mats made of braided straw and palm fibres were exposed to the purifying sun; tunics, coats and aprons would benefit from the same treatment. Chrestos cleaned the goatskin vessels where the water was kept fresh; the other adepts cleaned daily and ritual clothes, singing soft melodies whose text praised the charm of the breeze and the sweetness of the days.

When Sabni appeared, just a look sufficed for Isis to understand that he had failed. The silence of the High Priest was clear to the adepts; they interrupted their work.

Ahoure went forward. The baker stepped forward to intervene.

'Let's ask him for an explanation,' she proposed.

'His first words are for the High Priestess. Would you be forgetting obedience?'

The ritualist retreated while Isis and Sabni sat down in the shade of a tamarisk tree.

'I followed you in thought. You were in no danger, but destiny did not smile upon you.'

'Theodore is isolating us. We only have the two barges left; with the heavy one, aided by a good wind, I will sail up the Nile as soon as wind is favourable. It will be easy for me to get to a village and obtain some wheat.'

'The Bishop's sailors will stop you.'

'I must give it a try.'

'Will you manoeuvre alone?'

'I will have to.'

'The community is holding up well.'

'Thanks to you, Isis.'

'Your courage and your will reassure the adepts. As long as you fight, the community will not lose hope.'

'What about treason?'

'It is self-revealing.'

'Look at it. It is walking in our direction.'

Escaping from Chrestos and from the baker, Ahoure challenged the couple.

'We demand an explanation. Has the High Priest found victuals?'

'No,' admitted Sabni, 'and my task seems ill fated.'

'Are we condemned to die of hunger?'

'Not yet.'

The ritualist sneered.

'In other words, we are cut off from the world. The Bishop lets the High Priest go out to prove that he can manipulate him at will. We really must change our attitude.'

The brothers and sisters came closer; Ahoure did not lack haughtiness or conviction.

'What do you suggest?' asked Isis.

'Let's negotiate with Theodore. We should hand him the island, on condition that he allows us to leave the province.'

'Each one of us will fend for himself?'

'Evidently.'

'So you're advocating the dissolution of the community.'

'It shall reconvene elsewhere, in a large town where we will go unnoticed.'

'If we separate,' said Sabni, 'we will disappear. Philae does not belong to us. This is Isis's domain and we will preserve it, whatever the price.'

'I refuse this bravado. I, Ahoure, ritualist of the temple, accuse the High Priest and his wife of betraying the Rule. Accordingly, I suggest that the head of the community be replaced and another orientation adopted.'

Neither Isis nor Sabni objected. At any moment, an adept could express such a grievance.

'Who would be our new leader?' asked the High Priestess.

'That's my responsibility. I have no personal ambition; I only wish to serve the best interest of the community.'

'Do any of us doubt that?'

'I do,' said Chrestos. 'Ahoure wants to poison us from inside. It's her own rule she is imposing, not that of the temple.'

The ritualist looked daggers at the young man.

'My intervention may seem shocking,' she admitted, 'but I am thinking of the survival of my sisters and my brothers. To stubbornly pursue the path chosen up to now is a useless provocation. To be thrown out shamefully, to be beaten, to see the weak die . . . is that what you really want? Theodore multiplies the warnings and we pretend not to hear because we think we are the stronger party. Vanity! Let's admit the inevitable, submit to the Bishop's law and save what can be saved.'

'Sensible words,' said Sabni, 'but our quest goes beyond what is reasonable. For the love of Philae, we will preserve the temple. If a brother or sister disagree, he or she is free to leave. If the community approves of the ritualist as their leader, they can elect her. Isis and I will never leave Philae and will continue to serve the goddess.'

Ahoure looked around. No voice was raised in her favour.

'Go away,' said Chrestos. 'Your soul is as soiled as the hermits' rags.'

Sabni told the young man to be quiet.

'You are our sister,' Isis reminded Ahoure. 'Do you still love our Rule?'

'It has disowned me. Now I can't stay among you, but you will miss me!'

The baker took her over to the bank of the profane world. During the short trip, she looked incessantly at the temple. In hesitating to place her foot on land, her ritual robes touched the water. She then ran to the customs officer's hut, where her dress and the absence of a safe-conduct pass violated the law. She was immediately called and arrested.

Two days later, a southern breeze allowed the High Priest to execute his plan. Once the large white sail was unfolded, he sailed around Elephantine and slipped into a favourable current. At the frontier of the province, two boats filled with soldiers intercepted him. Sabni was unable to produce the required document; a permit to travel issued exclusively by the Bishop's office. As he was incapable of paying the fine, that is to say the price of the boat multiplied by three, he left it with the civil servants and went back to Philae on a papyrus canoe.

The only chance of survival now rested with the return of the absent goddess. The celebration of the ritual required that the exact words be pronounced; any deviation was out of the question. Therefore, the High Priestess would not rush. The community was capable of bearing misfortune and would not harass her; each adept was aware of the indispensable rigour that must preside over the dialogue between the human and the divine. Isis, in her battle against adversity, prepared the weapon that was most difficult to fashion. She was only interrupted by bouts of suffering when she thought of Ahoure, already so far from Philae, weighed down by the chains she bore into exile.

49

On this Sunday, a reminder of the resurrection, the Bishop
celebrated High Mass in the basilica of Elephantine where the
dome, covered in fine gold, shone like a fading summer fire.
Many faithful were unable to enter the sacred site where
Theodore, dressed in red vestal robes, brandished a Cross and
called for the Lord's protection over the province.

A wooden partition separated the sanctuary from the rest of
the church; in its centre was a door masked by a veil. Theodore
lifted it and knelt before the altar, a stone table that came from
the temple of Knum. Every day a deacon brought wine and
bread from the church precincts and placed them on the altar.

'I believe and I will proclaim it until my final breath,'
declared the Bishop, 'that this is the flesh of our Lord Jesus. I
believe his divinity was never separated, not even for a
moment, from his humanity.'

Then he made the sign of the cross with the bread, kissed it,
went around the altar thrice and bathed it in incense. The
persistent odour hit the nostrils of the faithful sitting on straw
mats and carpets. With their heads covered and feet bare, the
notables of Elephantine heard the prelate's powerful voice
transmit the Epistle and the Gospel. At the end of the sermon,
some priests sang a psalm glorifying the love of others. To
harbour hatred in one's heart prevents us from communicating
with God and with our fellow men.

The Bishop purified his hands and prayed for Christians all

over the world, for their enemies and for the unbelievers. He broke the bread, lifted a part of it and announced: 'The saintly to the saints.' By his gestures, he revealed the presence, invisible but real, of the celestial Master whose meal the faithful were sharing, a forerunner of the feast to be held on the last day, to which the just would be invited. Invoking the Holy Spirit, the celebrant drank some wine, consecrated it and said: 'Peace be with you.' After having put a piece of bread in the chalice, Theodore evoked the words of the apostle Paul: 'Every time you eat this bread and drink this wine, you will be announcing that our Lord is gone from us until his second coming. Whoever eats the bread or drinks from Our Lord's cup unworthily will be guilty of profaning the body and the blood of the Lord. Whoever eats and drinks without discernment, eats and drinks his own judgement.'

When he left the sanctuary, the Bishop gave communion to the deacons. The sub-deacons, the readers, the psalmists, the notables, the widows, the virgins and the virtuous women waited for him. Theodore was forced to interrupt the celebration: from the bottom of the church came panic-stricken cries. The ranks of the faithful broke and a terrifying figure came forth with a man's body and the head of a jackal.

'The devil!' exclaimed an old aristocratic woman, who fled screaming.

'It's Anubis!' shouted her neighbour. 'Anubis has returned!'

The greater part of the congregation threw themselves on the ground; some closed their eyes and others ran away. Disturbed, the deacons tried to stop them. The mass ended in total disarray.

Anubis stared at the Bishop for a few seconds, then turned back without anyone daring to attack him. Theodore bade everyone be silent. The deacons lashed at the most excited with rods and threw them out of the holy site to where a frightened crowd had taken refuge.

'It was not Anubis,' said the Bishop categorically.

'But we saw him,' protested some eye-witnesses.

'All you saw was a masked man; the High Priest took advantage of your credulous nature. His temple is not a lair of devils, but a refuge for lost souls. Tomorrow, Christ will convert them.'

Some contradicted the Bishop out loud and doubted him. The prelate evoked the processions, where priests took on the role of divinities, to impress a population avid to witness marvels. Some, ashamed, regretted their ridiculous behaviour. Many were still convinced that Anubis had reincarnated to prove the permanence of the ancient faith. Did not the man with the jackal face interrupt mass without being struck by fire from the sky?

Feeling bitter, Theodore isolated himself in the sanctuary and knelt before Christ.

The sister in charge of the barnyard fed the last goose still waddling around. Hens and roosters still roamed freely, but soon it would become necessary to hunt them down like game. The High Priestess had ordered that meat be served to the ailing adepts while keeping the poultry for the feast of the distant goddess. In the main warehouse, where the food was preserved, Chrestos filtered some olive oil. To economize was crucial, despite the fact that the land was rich in olive trees, but Philae did not belong to the Emperor's Egypt any longer. The forbidden island, cut off from the world, survived by respecting its own laws, even if these were contrary to those of Christianity. The young adept reacted to adversity with a renewed energy that no misfortune could weaken. The gods imposed their trials on Philae to enable the adepts to awaken their most vital energies. While believing that he was destroying the temple, the Bishop was strengthening it.

Sabni stored away the Anubis mask with the treasures.

'How did they react?' asked Isis.

'As I expected: they were afraid. Fear has penetrated their spirit and their wonderful consensus has fallen apart.'

'Will they fear Philae enough to respect it?'

'Anubis has been reborn; he opens the doors to the realm beyond and guides the soul towards paradise.'

'No one respects him outside of this enclosure.'

'To express our faith is the only combat that we can wage.'

'To engage in conflict . . . is not our vocation. To perceive the divine light and give it an abode, that is our role. The power of the ritual is unsurpassed; the process of creation is inscribed in it. When we celebrate, harmony occurs, as at dawn. The distant goddess will return.'

Autumn approached. Already, at sundown, the walls of the temple were painted in autumnal silver and gold. Who would have guessed that the stone vessel of the goddess Isis was sailing on turbulent seas?

Theodore found comfort in prayer. Elevating his thoughts to the Lord, he felt that his role as administrator and head of the army was despicable; his vocation was not to fulfil such derisory tasks. Why busy himself with earthly tasks, when God demanded his devotion every waking moment?

The prelate felt like dropping everything, entrusting the province to its fate. Cowardice . . . the word burned his lips. It would be so easy to forget his fold, to open the door to fanaticism and dialogue with heaven without worrying about the misery and misfortune of others. He, the Egyptian, was the link between the old and the new world because he understood the past and was building the future. Was it an illusion, believing that he could shift destiny? To save Sabni . . . that victory he desired with the ardour of the purest friendship. To fail would be the harshest blow; by inflicting it on him, God would lacerate his soul.

He was surprised to start dreaming of the blessed evening when he would be an impotent and solitary old man, silent under his garden's shaded trees, incapable of weighing on other people's existence. But this was an empty dream in these hours when the fate of Elephantine was being decided along

295

with that of Christianity. On either side of destiny were the temple and the church, The High Priest and the Bishop, Sabni and Theodore.

Power . . . he had not sought it. Insidiously, this fever had taken hold of him; mingling with his thoughts and his acts, his function guided him and deprived him of freedom. Did he not resemble his friend so closely, was he not also forced to obey a higher will?

50

Paul and the hermits were surprised by the Bishop's benevolence: each received a linen tunic, figs and some dried fish. Why pander to them so, after having ignored and despised them for so long? Suspicious, Paul was persuaded that Theodore was trying to buy their silence. A hermit who did not suffer from cold and ate his fill no longer battled for Christ; he lost his nerve and fell into a guilty state of complaisance.

Did the Bishop have any fault to hide? Paul walked the streets, questioned, and searched. He did not obtain any worthwhile information. As he feared, Theodore's existence was not darkened by any major sin. Of course he should have ordered the expulsion of the Pagans and the destruction of the temple long ago, but his recent decisions revealed a very clear hardening of his position, in accordance with his spiritual commitment. To accuse the Bishop of softness would not win him followers.

Paul concocted another strategy. Work and prayer filled the days of the prelate, who rarely left his domain. Therefore the hermit researched the exceptions to this rule, without looking into the official outings. His patience was rewarded: he learned that Theodore had visited a merchant called Apollo. Two days later, the merchant, whose business prospered, had nevertheless left town like a thief, to the surprise of his employees and colleagues. The hermit obtained no

297

explanation for this departure, but learned that one of Apollo's sons, Chrestos, had disappeared. His father had gone to the barracks to lodge a complaint. Paul forced one of the soldiers, who sympathized with the intransigence of God's warriors, to speak. He confirmed the meeting between Apollo and Captain Mersis. Mersis the pagan, the traitor, the accomplice of the worshippers of Isis. Paul was filled with a savage joy: he had finally found the Bishop's weak point.

The church was half-empty. The apparition of Anubis continued to trouble the faithful, to the point of keeping those whose calling was weaker away from the true faith. In the streets, rumour had it that the Egyptian god had put a spell on the walls of the Christian sanctuary and that these could convey a mortal illness. Despite energetic sermons, Theodore did not manage to recover the lost ground.

At the end of a mass during which the chants were sung half-heartedly, the Bishop was confronted by Paul. The hermit requested an immediate interview. From his excited look, the prelate understood that the fanatic had a powerful trump card to play against him.

Theodore suggested that they take a walk in the church garden. Planted with sycamore trees, it gave generous shade to the deacons who read sacred texts before the services.

'What do you want from me, my brother?'

'That you respect the law of God without faltering.'

'That has been my sole preoccupation at every moment. Have I failed?'

'I'm afraid so.'

'In what way?'

Paul's grip on his knotted rod tightened.

'By covering up a criminal affair.'

'What proof do you have?'

'Was Mersis not a treacherous officer?'

'He was chastised.'

298

'Was he not visited by one named Apollo that you forced into exile?'

'That fig merchant preferred to go and make his fortune elsewhere.'

'Did you not force him to leave because of his son Chrestos?'

The Bishop did not reply.

'Everyone appreciates your sense of honour and duty; as God's servant, you reject lies. I am convinced that this Chrestos, son of Apollo, took refuge on the pagan island. A serious violation of the sacred law: the temple is forbidden to welcome new adepts, the penalty being its destruction.'

'What proof do you have?'

'I will get proof. Why did you not intervene?'

'I don't have to justify myself, my brother. The reasons of State are beyond you or me.'

'You love those pagans.'

'I want to convert them.'

'When sweetness fails, force has to work. If you refuse to use it, I will reveal your sin to the faithful; their justified wrath will be unleashed on Philae!'

Theodore imagined Paul as head of the province. In less than a year he would have ruined it. The Christians would fight and ultimately destroy each other. Obscure clouds would gather over Elephantine.

'I have seen to it that the needs of the hermits be met.'

'That is not enough. Somebody's head has to roll. After that, Theodore, you will share your power with me. Together we will vanquish the demons.'

'I have my own conditions too.'

'Are you still in a position to impose them?'

'Without me, you would be but a puppet.'

Paul struck one of the sycamore trees violently with his stick. Alas, the bishop was right! Unlike the bishop, the hermit did not have the people's trust. To direct a faction, even if victorious, would not be enough to overcome his power. He would have to be patient, for a while longer.

'What are those conditions, Monsignor?'

'Respect for human life.'

'Are the pagans human? Your soldiers have killed a few and you have not excommunicated them.'

'Those were regrettable incidents, Paul; we pray for our enemies and pray to God for their conversion, not their extermination.'

'God forgives the sinner who repents and damns the heretic.'

'A head will roll, you said.'

'Justice has to prevail in our province; to acquit the criminal would be an insult to Our Lord. You, his representative, will not permit such infamy.'

'Listen carefully to the most important of my conditions: that head shall not be Sabni's.'

Many inhabitants of Elephantine had gathered to watch the demolition of an old building situated near the office of the head tax collector. The masons chased out a beggar who was its only tenant and demolished the walls. A foreman, whose nickname was 'Shortcut', directed the works with precise and well-timed orders.

Suddenly, he screamed.

The workers put their mallets down. The foreman had just discovered a silver casket and immediately alerted the head tax collector. Philamon came quickly and opened the casket, which was full of gold coins and silver ingots.

'I recognize this treasure,' he declared. 'It was stolen from the bishopric a year ago; I must make an inventory.'

Usually the civil servant worked away from the public eye. This time he operated before numerous witnesses. To steal goods from the Church would be severely punished; Theodore requested a thorough investigation.

'The guilty party left his signature on his crime,' stated Philamon. 'Look!'

He pointed to an ivory bracelet inscribed with Chrestos's name.

The bishop's police looked in vain for the young man to interrogate him. Neighbours and friends identified the ivory bracelet as the one Chrestos had left in his room before abandoning the family house. It was his favourite ornament, a symbol of his past, unworthy of the temple: the name of the owner was therefore beyond doubt. Tongues wagged: from a tender age, Chrestos had been too light-fingered. The stinginess of his father had forced him to commit small thefts. A customs officer gave a precious piece of information: he had arrested the boy once when he was taking home an ivory comb stolen from smugglers. Due to the thief's young age, he had just confiscated the comb.

The deacon in charge of the procedure accumulated over-whelming evidence against this dangerous character. At the end of the trial, performed in the absence of the runaway, the sentence was pronounced: he was condemned to forced labour in the Libyan desert. All that remained was to find Chrestos, throw him in prison and deport him.

Theodore asked Paul for a few days of reflection before ordering 'Shortcut' to spread a rumour suggesting the thief had been seen on the island of Philae. The reflection had proved useless because the prelate could not break the agreement he had made with the hermit. The Bishop implored the Lord. Because he had been unable to destroy Philae, now he was forced to make it suffer. In the middle of all this turmoil, would he be able to save his only friend?

Chrestos would not escape torture: there was no way he could spare him. Paul would demand crucifixion, so that no other adolescent be tempted to embrace the pagan's cause. Even though the method was reprehensible, the ideal corresponded to the demands of the faith.

Theodore still hesitated to summon 'Shortcut'; at dawn, Paul would demand his due. What angel would come from the clouds and take in its wings the soul of a young man oblivious of the rigours of his time?

The guard knocked on the office door, where a lamp had burned all through the night. The hermit did not waste one minute.

'Come in.'

The civil servant introduced an officer from the garrison.

'It's very urgent, Monsignor. Two watchmen have spotted a major concentration of Blemmye troops south of the first cataract.'

51

Paul, furious, shouted at the guard.

'Do you know who I am?'

'That will not change anything. The Bishop is not here.'

'That's not true, let me into his office.'

'If you try to pass, I will have to kill you. These are my orders.'

'Where is he?'

'At the barracks.'

'If you're lying to me . . .'

Though he kept his head high, the militiaman was frightened. Like others, he feared the hermit.

Paul forced open the door of the army headquarters where Theodore was talking with the officers in charge.

'You're not qualified to sit on this council,' reminded the Bishop. 'Get out.'

'Not before you have ordered the arrest of the criminal.'

'We will settle that later. I need every single soldier.'

The hermit's eyes lit up with rage.

'Even if a state of emergency is decreed, do not count on delaying the execution of the sentence indefinitely.'

'That is not my intention.'

'You can be sure that God's warriors will make their demands known.'

*

Certain of impunity, a dozen hermits burned the temple's vines and a field where the peasants were suspected of being the pagan's accomplices. Paul and his troops spread more terror than Anubis had done. The population, after having weighed the threats of the ancient god and the anathema of the new, were resolutely on the side of the most exalted Christians. If the army did not intervene against them, it was because they had the blessing of the Bishop.

The temple's adepts were not dying of hunger. On that peaceful October day when a soft sun transformed stones into gold, the adepts were invited to a banquet. Near the small Hathor sanctuary, they tasted fresh olives and dates, roasted guinea fowl, and savoured red wine or barley beer. The Nile formed a protective screen, bathing the island of the great goddess with its peaceful waters. The pleated loincloths of the brothers and the linen dresses of the sisters shone in their whiteness. Sabni wore a leather apron embroidered with gold and Isis a white dress with shoulder straps. Radiant, the High Priestess asked the elder of the priests to hide his face behind a lion mask.

Thus began the ritual destined to make the absent goddess return from the solitude of the desert. Organizing themselves into a procession, the adepts transported the victuals into the enclosure where the ritual meeting would take place. If the words pronounced during the ceremony were heartfelt, the exiled goddess would join the community. Half the adepts remained prostrated, sitting on their heels; the other half, guided by the High Priestess, went away from the building towards a kiosk where musical instruments were kept.

Sabni began the ritual words: 'We are suffering great tribulation. The light is lost over there on the red lands where nothing grows. The eye of the sun, emerged from his forehead, has fled to the desert to massacre the human beings who sought refuge there, believing they would escape his wrath.'

Chrestos acted as the spokesman for humanity.

'What fault has it committed?'

'It forgot the heavens, betrayed the rule of life, despised what is sacred. Human beings have accused each other. Instead of confronting the gods, they hid away. The sun has distanced itself from the earth. From being creative, its fire has become destructive. Suffering has replaced joy.'

'Who will appease the distant goddess?'

'The community has gone to meet her. Through music, chanting and dancing, it will try to assuage her wrath and bring her back here, to her temple. If it fails, we will perish. The goddess will confuse us with the rebellious ones and her lion's teeth will tear our flesh.'

Across the golden sunset echoed the sounds of the triangular harp, of the rounded drum, of the comet trumpet in the shape of a lotus, of the flute, of cymbals and of rattlers. A noisy cortège played a lively tune, with marked intonations. Two sisters, still agile, outlined some dance movements. The grave voices of the brothers broke into a song that begged the terrifying lioness to accept the community's love. In the old days, a domesticated ape played the lute and a gazelle gambolled before the musicians.

The orchestra stopped on the threshold of the temple, by a figure of the god Bes, a corpulent bearded dwarf with a coarse face. Under the guidance of this ugly initiator, the adept had to discover beauty. Bes's ranting laugh dissipated pain and clarified thick clouds; whoever met him on his path knew that his destiny would be favourable.

The community chanted a slow introverted psalm, imploring the distant goddess to come in peace. When the music stopped, Sabni stood up and faced the adepts.

'Does the eye of the sun shine among you?'

'We have looked for it and we have found it,' answered the harpist.

'Has the massacre of humanity ceased?'

'It will continue as long as the eye does not rest in a sacred site.'

'We have built that place with our own hands.'

Christian Jacq

'Tell me its name.'

'The island of the great goddess. The sun is ever present, day and night, in her sanctuary.'

'Who will assuage the wrath of the eye?'

'I who am the High Priest of the temple.'

'How will you proceed?'

'Through knowledge of the divine nature.'

'What is the name of the eye?'

'The one who creates. The enlightened gaze who engenders beings and things.'

'What is the name of the goddess?'

'The Terrifying One who will become a smile, the beloved distant from our hearts, the birth of the first star.'

'What will you offer her?'

'A banquet prepared specially for her. The adepts will commune in the happiness of reunion.'

'Will you recognize her, if she presents herself to you?'

'Let her deign to reveal herself to the community prostrated before her beauty.'

The members of the orchestra moved away. The lion mask came forward, ferocious. He announced fevers, dysentery, blindness and famine; if he triumphed, a nauseating wind, weighed down by putrefaction would invade the temple.

'I do not fear you,' said Sabni. 'You frighten those who are full of fear. Keep out of the path of the goddess.'

The mask disappeared. Strumming the *sistra*, whose metallic sound scared off the demons bent on hindering her movements, Isis appeared.

A broad red belt ornamented her waist and a green hue enhanced the curb of her eyebrows. Her headdress, the crown with two long feathers framing the sun, lit the way that, from the depth of the desert, led her back to the temple.

'You, gold of the gods and smile of creation, unite with this body of stone. Enlighten it with your boundless love, grant it life, strength and coherence.'

The moment she was about to enter the enclosure of the call,

306

For the Love of Philae

Isis hesitated. Was the ritual being celebrated with the faith of primordial times, did the community deploy the energy of the builders whom the hardest tasks exalted? The priest with the lion mask played a grave melody on his lute; the fires of the sunset enveloped the enclosure of the call with a light from another world. The Terrifying One became The Benevolent One.

Isis went forth into Hathor's abode the moment Sabni lit a torch: fire returned to fire.

'You have come back to your own people. The temple is born again.'

307

52

'We're ready to pay,' said Sabni. 'The High Priestess has placed at your disposal some chest and throat adornments, necklaces and rings.'

'It will not suffice,' replied Theodore.

'Did you not say that everything can be bought?'

'Not justice.'

'Do you dare call "justice" this mockery of a trial?'

'The evidence is there. An assembly of citizens, in which I was not included, has found Chrestos guilty.'

'Therefore, your name will not be associated with the crime.'

'Chrestos robbed and fled. If you do not hand him over to ecclesiastic jurisdiction, the hermits will lead a furious mob and attack Philae.'

'You're asking that I abandon a brother and send him to a horrendous death.'

'He has committed unpardonable faults. In my prison, he will be safe. The wrath of the populace will be appeased.'

'His sentence will be but short! Like the others, he will be deported, humiliated, submitted to forced labour and perish in the mines side by side with children and the elderly.'

'Am I responsible for his corruption? By choosing Philae, he was aware of the risks. Either he goes or the entire community will disappear.'

'Is that really you speaking, Theodore? Can it really be you?'

'No, Sabni. It's the will of God.'

Sabni took Isis in his arms and held her for a long time. The sentence passed on Chrestos would be executed in two days and the High Priest had to hand the criminal over to the police.

'Let us appeal to the Patriarch of Alexandria.'

'Provided we hire the services of a fast messenger, it would be a week's journey . . . and even then we can be sure that the judgement issued by the court of Elephantine will be confirmed.'

'Is there no jurisdiction that could overrule that sentence?'

'None.'

'We will not give in,' said Isis.

'They will come and take us all.'

'What if the great goddess protected us and stopped them from crossing the waters that separate Philae from that perverted world? Let's resist, Sabni. Our freedom is more ardent than fire, even more elusive than the wind. To give in means to be resigned to a fate worse than death: to lose spiritual life.'

On the belly of a scarab, Chrestos engraved a major text; it allowed the just to cross the threshold of the first door to the realm beyond by answering the question of an inflexible guardian: *'My heart is the heart of divine light; you will never cease being alive, always and forever, you will be rejuvenated beyond time.'* Since he had come to work at the temple, the young man was free of anguish, the unbearable weight of his adolescent days. Even when he escaped to the fields rimmed with dams, or hid in the tamarisk bushes or in the sycamore woods, crouched in the swamps full of papyrus plants, he could not find peace. Once on the Holy Island, he no longer felt like running away. From the spirit, who was the true master of this site, he incorporated dawn; that primordial light had become his.

Christian Jacq

Usually, Sabni called him away from his work to come and dine. That evening, it was nightfall that interrupted the sculptor. Intrigued, he cleaned his tools, put the scarab on a block of granite and ran in the direction of the refectory, situated near the temple of Hathor.

Brothers and sisters ate in silence. For the High Priest, the peas tasted like clay and the beer like salt water. Chrestos sat down at his side.

'What sorrow distresses you?'

The adepts stood up, one after the other, and slowly made their way to their quarters. Only Sabni and Isis remained.

'Have I displeased you?'

'You are the hope of our community.'

'Why is everyone avoiding me?'

'Who would dare tell you the truth?'

Chrestos looked around. The blue water shimmered under the evening wind; the walls towered above it with their serene insurmountable mass.

'You will dare.'

'I hate my role.'

Sabni felt the weight of Isis's gaze.

'What am I accused of?'

'Of stealing ecclesiastic goods. The existence of formal proof pre-empted the judgement: the Bishop demands your banishment.''

'What does he have in store for me?'

'At best, life imprisonment. At worst, deportation and forced labour.'

'And if I hide on this island?'

'The hermits and their fanatics will invade it.'

'Do you believe these accusations?'

'If I did I would have banished you from this site myself.'

'What have you decided?'

'How can you question it? We will protect you until our last breath.'

'When will they come?'

310

'Tomorrow, at the hour when the sun reaches the zenith of its path.'

Chrestos put forward his bowl.

'I am hungry.'

Isis served him. The young adept ate with a hearty appetite.

'Your determination will not suffice to detain them.'

'By slipping behind my shadow, you will have nothing to fear. To strike Philae's High Priestess would condemn the aggressor to wander for all eternity. Never in the history of Egypt has such an outrage been perpetrated.'

The young adept looked up at the High Priestess with respect.

'Tomorrow, I will remain at the temple. The day after also, and for all eternity.'

Isis's smile was lost in the dark of the night. Chrestos drank a special beer, reserved for special events.

The grain died in the earth, in the silence of the fertile mud; man had no role to play in this mystery of invariable words. On the threshold of inebriation, Chrestos thought of the hymn of the covered temple, dedicated to Isis, inhabitant of the stars, where the soul breathed hope and defied death.

The adept approached the summit of the first pylon and traced the signs engraved on the walls of the stairs with his index finger. Birds, trees, baskets became animated under the warmth of his hand and accompanied him to the topmost part of the temple.

Chrestos wanted to enjoy dawn like a lamb frisking with joy at the first rays of the resurrected sun. He had a long route before him, numerous doors to cross, and difficult work to accomplish. It was true that his spirit was unfolding; if he wasn't careful, vanity would kill his first efforts. To demand perfection in work without believing in that of man: he would never forget the lesson of the community, purveyor of beings.

Only the total surrender of self, beyond success and failure,

311

awoke a sensitivity worthy of the immortal brotherhood present in the heart of each stone.

No, he was not Philae's sole hope for the future. How could the temple be incarnate in just one individual? On the contrary, by provoking the fury of the Christians, he was a threat to the adepts' very existence. That he was victim of the most odious injustice did not count. His love for the Holy Island dictated his conduct.

Chrestos filled his eyes with the sanctuary, where the light was overcoming the shadows of the agonizing night; soon, Sabni and Isis would enter the naos and peacefully awake the divine power. On this autumn day, four thousand years after the birth of pharaonic Egypt, Philae remained serene, unaltered. His duty as a brother consisted of protecting it, by removing the source of the trouble.

From the height of the pylon, Chrestos jumped out into the void.

53

The tramps, whose numbers grew at every street corner, followed the placid man who carried a strange burden. The High Priest stopped before the Bishop's house and deposited on a stone threshold, under the eyes of the militiamen, the corpse of Chrestos, enveloped in a white shroud. Only his beautiful and serene face was visible.

Alerted by the commotion, the Bishop came out of his office. When he appeared, the crowd went silent. Theodore approached the corpse, knelt down, and raised his eyes to Sabni.

'I did not want this death.'

'He gave his life for Philae. Will no sacrifice be enough for you?'

In the High Priest's eyes there was no hatred, but such burning rebellion no words could possibly express.

'I did not want this, Sabni.'

'Let me bury him according to our rites.'

'No,' screamed the hermit Paul, brandishing his rod.

'A pagan must be burned. Let the body be given to the sand runners.'

The 'corpse eaters', as they were called, lived in the desert far from any dwellings. They buried the destitute and disposed of the remains of criminals and thieves. Sabni hoped to avoid this ultimate humiliation.

'This pagan was judged and condemned,' reminded Paul. 'He must not benefit from any privilege.'

A clamour of approval rose from the crowd.

'Are you going to put up with this barbarism, Theodore?'

'You must submit to the law of God, Sabni. I have to abide by it and see that others do as well.'

'Do not bring God into this infamy.'

'The wave is too violent. I warned you: the ramparts are crumbling. Depart my friend; change your destiny.'

The High Priest did not go back to Philae. Forced to abandon Chrestos's corpse in the hands of a rapacious crowd, he wandered in the abandoned quarries of the western bank. In those desolate parts, devoid of any presence for decades, reigned a stifling heat. The northern wind crashed into the granite rocks whence the master masons of the pharaohs had extracted splendid stones to build temples. The pyramid builders did not hesitate to travel the enormous distance that separated Memphis from Elephantine to carve gigantic blocks there, then transport them North by barge.

Sabni stopped by the unfinished obelisk, the most imposing monolith ever carved out. It had nevertheless remained prisoner because of a fissure that condemned it to stay laid out in the quarry. The Greeks had measured it: forty-two metres long, weighing 1,200 tons. Hundreds of men had laboured here to remove the crust protecting the pink granite, or syene, which was on a par with diorite and quartz and was of exceptional beauty.

In this landscape of barren rocks and interrupted monuments, the High Priest saw the incompleteness of his own adventure. Gone were the quarries, lost was the community who worked for the glory of the Rule. A thick mist spread out over the luminous universe of the pharaohs. A few yards from the pilgrim, a colossus tried in vain to free itself from its mineral shroud; it was Ramses II, carrier of the white crown, holding in his arms, crossed over his chest, the sceptres, awaiting the hand of the sculptor that would free him from matter. Sabni felt like grabbing mallet and scissors and freeing the dead king, proving to him that his eyes could see and his mouth speak. But he gave up, disheartened by the enormity of the task.

On a broken stele, he could still make out an inscription:

'Whoever you are, if you want to fully enjoy what you do, be careful to obtain praise from your god. Then transmit what you can to your successor, leaving your heart at rest.'

This message from time immemorial was meant for him. But he was lying stretched out, like the colossus, in a prison from which he could not escape.

The inscription opened a way, the only one to transmit what he had learned. The High Priest of a community would never be his own master; only his function and the service to the brotherhood mattered. Personal questioning was treason; but in a world deprived of justice, forgetful of the Rule, the heart of man was full of personal questions and worries.

The night overwhelmed him. The colossus seemed to shrink; everywhere gloom pervaded, hostile. In this mineral chaos, the roads faded. Even the most experienced traveller would get lost, incapable of finding his way out of the quarries. Sabni felt the call of the desert, of stones whose only horizon was the cataract, with its foretaste of Africa, sparsely softened by touches of green. Who would have expected to find, in this arid maze, green pastures and golden fields? This solitude, rougher than granite, stuck to his skin like a wet robe. Only the love of Isis kept him from running away from himself and from convincing himself that in leaving the community he would be saving it. It was he, no one else, that was the object of Theodore's reprobation and Paul's hatred. If he disappeared, no one would dream of attacking Philae. True courage would be to step down, and, by recognizing that his mere presence exercised a harmful influence, prove his fraternity to the adepts.

Turning his back on the Nile, the High Priest penetrated the labyrinth. A few more steps and he would become a nomad, free from any bonds, and walk to the far reaches of the great South where rivers threw themselves down into the abyss, where the human race no longer existed.

Bending down, Sabni found at his feet a dead falcon with folded wings. The High Priest dug the earth with a pointed stone and buried the bird of Horus, son of Isis. It had come from the sky and wished to return to the heavens, according to the temple's teaching. The eyes of the bird of prey, standing on the ramparts of the clouds, beheld the summit that was forever hidden. He guarded the sanctuary of the gods, built of light and love, the model for terrestrial buildings.

Encountering the remains of the departed bird whose flight had been broken was like meeting his own corpse for the High Priest; but the eternal all-seeing eye of the falcon showed him the right path.

Radiant, bathed in silvery light, Isis stood on the edge of the pier. The barge berthed silently; Sabni moored it and climbed up to meet his spouse.

'In the world of the gods,' she said, 'nothing happens. They ignore the events to which we are subjected, the moments of happiness and misfortune that move us are to them like child's play.'

'Isis, if you knew . . .'

'The trial of the abandoned stones . . . what High Priest has not been through it? You have come back, Sabni, and I love you.'

54

Isis did not get up; a strong fever stopped her from fulfilling her ritual obligations. As soon as he left the naos where, each morning, the great goddess awoke, the High Priest came back to his wife's bedside. Only she knew the secrets of the art of healing, but she did not have the strength to apply it to herself. Her sudden lassitude worried Sabni.

'Could you prescribe a remedy?'

'My spirit is as weak as my body. My energy is seeping away, like a summer mist over the Nile . . . On the other side, on the West Bank, the goddess will be welcoming. I do not fear her; we have spoken so often, like accomplices.'

'No! You do not have the right to give in.'

Sabni took Isis in his arms and bore her to the small temple of Imhotep, the healer. When human medicine proved impotent, it was necessary to resort to the will of the sage who had entered immortality alive. From the invisible realm, he continued to preserve the beauty of the temple and the integrity of his successors.

The High Priest laid the patient down on the paving stones of the chapel the Romans called the sanatorium; paralysed, a senator had come here to regain the use of his members. After having sworn to keep silent on what he would see and hear, he departed, healed.

'Hold my right hand,' Isis requested.

She had always known that death would abduct her from

Christian Jacq

that side; the presence of Sabni would deter it. With the palm of her left hand turned to the roof of the small temple, eyes closed, with a hardly perceptible breath, the High Priestess listened to the song of the stones. Some came from Gizah, others from the quarries of Tura, from Jabal Silsilah or Elephantine; from north to south, they formed the living fabric of the temples and the sacred sites where the spirit would always shine, even if barbarism tried to overwhelm it with a veil of gloom and ignorance.

When Isis saw Imhotep's hieratic face appear before her, enlightened, she sat up to show deference. Sabni sustained her and her eyes expressed the will to live once again.

Sabni gathered the community and announced that he intended to do some work in Imhotep's sanctuary. The baker recalled that Philae no longer received any materials and that no stone mason would dare work on the island. The High Priest dispelled all doubts and fears; the adepts who were able to handle tools would learn the trade as they went along. Chrestos had shown them the way: they had to show themselves worthy of him. The blocks would come from the past; an old dismantled chapel would be the foundation for the new building. Their ancestors had acted thus; they would follow suit.

The brothers who had despaired due to the death of their youngest member found renewed vigour in this project. Forgetting old age and illness, they went to work under the direction of a demanding High Priest who treated them like apprentices. His toughness, far from discouraging them, gave them renewed ardour.

Isis organized the days of the sisters with similar strictness: from dawn to sunset, they practised rituals, studied sacred texts, made ropes and small copper scissors, prepared meals, observed the sky. Hovering over the first pylon, a falcon in which the soul of Chrestos incarnated watched over the work of the brothers and gave it a certain rhythm by drawing large circles in the sky.

*

The midwife's cry of horror awoke the entire neighbourhood. Not only had the pancake seller died with atrocious convulsions, she had brought into the world a child with a serpent's head. Out of his mind, the father decapitated the infant before crushing his own skull against the wall of his own house. Since the demise of Chrestos, his body thrown to the necrophagous beasts, Elephantine had lived in fear. A series of evil omens plagued the town. The water of two springs, famous for their purity, had become poisoned. Two jackals had entered a wealthy part of town and devoured a small boy. Lightning had struck the church, destroying much of its roof.

Theodore, prodigal in sermons, did his best to calm the population. However, Paul and the hermits accused Philae of unleashing the wrath of God and the fury of the devil; as long as the accursed island celebrated its impious rituals and defied the Lord, Satan would prowl.

The Bishop was no longer in control of the troops; there was no revolt, but no one obeyed any longer. Paul spread a violence that the people lapped up: how long would it be before there were more victims?

The more Elephantine became agitated, the more Philae bloomed in a serenity born of the work undertaken. Even the slowness of the progress simply meant that it was all the more appreciated. The community, nourished by the joint effort, shared each individual victory. Freed from the desire for supremacy, indifferent to time, generous to the point of exhaustion, the adepts discovered day after day unsuspected resources. Scratched hands and painful backs gave the sisters an opportunity to put their gifts as healers into practice. One heart, one will: the community was being reborn.

Theodore had counted on its rapid degradation after Chrestos's suicide. Was it not condemned to disappear, as it was forbidden to accept any other neophytes? Any reasonable person would have admitted defeat. To grant a vote of confidence to a great goddess who let her faithful die out was

319

Christian Jacq

insane. If Sabni managed to free himself from Isis's influence, he would no doubt come to see reason. The High Priestess bewitched him and led him to ruin; caught in the web of that she-devil with an angel's face, he refused to escape.

That is how the Bishop tried to persuade himself of his friend's folly. Nevertheless, his inner voice contradicted him and clamoured an unforgivable admiration for Isis, as well as respect for a woman devoted as he was to the divine. He had to dismiss the most hellish temptation: to admit that the pagan faith could be preserved and transmitted. Granted the revelation of the unique God, humanity was transformed. Having emerged from the darkness of paganism, it made its way to celestial Jerusalem, the paradise of the just. The exalted Paul was not wrong when he accused feminine seduction of being a devilish weapon. Contemplating Isis, intoxicated with her charms, entranced by her goals, her bearing, her way of walking, what Christian would hold out for long against the embrace of the great goddess?

To hide Philae and reject Paul's fanaticism: caught in the grip of this conflict, the Bishop, who had so loved his solitude, bore it with difficulty now. Sabni was lucky to live with a woman he could share his most secret passions with, who dissipated his torments and offered him the sweet complicity of her favours. It was against this fortress that the Bishop's assaults were in vain.

The old chapel was revived as the new sanctuary dedicated to Imhotep, their glorious ancestor. As if their hands had instinctively found a forgotten knowledge, the adepts cut the blocks of stone, matched them and mounted them with an enthusiasm that made up for inexperience. A perfume of eternity floated once again over the temple rooms; the hostile world was distanced, borne away by the Nile, and the rumours from Elephantine were dispelled by the morning light.

'What do you wish for, Sabni?'
'That tomorrow never existed.'

320

'Look at our brothers and sisters: the construction of the temple makes them younger.'

'If only we could trap the light at the summit of the pylon, drown the future in the cataract . . .'

'Hope, my love. Hope, with the power of fire and the patience of water. Wear down time, break it as if it were a stone unworthy of the edifice.'

The clouds of mosquitoes, carried by the warm air, attacked the sleepers and spread fever. No one had forgotten the omens and everyone felt that this abnormal heatwave, which made legs heavy and hearts beat slower, was strange. Only the Bishop was glad of it because it lessened the ardour of the hermits. After having vainly encouraged the populace to ransack the accursed island, they had taken refuge, disappointed, in the tombs of the western riverbank.

The prelate possessed an authority that no one contested, not even Paul, but he hesitated between intransigence and clemency, losing the zest he had once had as a young priest with an aversion to concession. Sabni was his great failure. By converting him, he would have modified both his destiny and the High Priest's; a door would have opened up on to the invisible realm. God would have turned his face towards them. Too many people, too many thoughts and too many rituals stood between the High Priest of Philae and the bishop of Elephantine.

Was God misguiding the world of the future by bidding him to deny the past and destroy the temples? The country of pharaohs, mother of the universe, was submitting to laws without genius, borrowing an ineffectual art and speaking a bastardized language; by becoming Christian, it was losing the fire of its youth and the splendour of its maturity. If Christ were banished from the land where he had taken refuge, what invader would replace him? At the doors of Byzantium, barbaric peoples were preparing to dismantle the Eastern Empire; at Egypt's doors, the tribes of the Arab peninsula

321

coveted productive lands. The Bishop, a witness of the revelation, could not doubt his mission. That the individual was fragile and anxious, the Bishop could not help.

From his terrace, he contemplated the town. He loved it with a paternal tenderness: villas with colourful gardens, small white artisan houses, poor cottages all side by side and bathed in the autumn light, under Christ's watchful gaze. In the animated alleys, people chatted. In the market, heaps of victuals weighed down the traders' stalls.

The shouts of a skirmish did not surprise Theodore; there would be others before the end of the day. Violent discussions occasionally erupted between merchants and buyers. Just as the Bishop was returning to his office, he heard cries that were, in fact, very unusual. A dishevelled woman ran shrieking towards the Episcopal palace.

'The Blemmyes! The Blemmyes are attacking!'

55

The Blemmyes attacked Elephantine in the middle of the day, throwing thousands of men into an assault they intended to be decisive. Drunk on palm wine, the Nubian warriors hurled themselves on Elephantine's fortifications. With their naked torsos, their loins draped in animal skin, the blacks thought they would easily climb the palisade and slip round the sharp stakes set out against them. They quickly realized that they had misjudged the situation and beat a hasty retreat. The Bishop ordered the cavalry to attack the aggressor's right flank, but it only assailed a void: the Blemmyes threw themselves on the ground, hung on to the horses' harnesses, disembowelled them and unhorsed the Christians. Even the most talented horsemen did not manage to trample down their elusive adversaries, who were used to fighting wild animals with their bare hands. Weighed down by extremely heavy armours, the Christians offered a meagre resistance to the Blemmyes.

Despite this defeat, the Bishop did not lose confidence: his defences would hold out against attack. The enemy was very still, silence succeeded the cries. Then his ranks broke as an unusual army made its way forth, a troop of elephants guided by archers mounted on them. The pachyderms, whose trumpeting frightened the population and put the last horsemen on the run, crushed pious folk and stakes alike. Those who were in the way of their inexorable march forward were either pierced by arrows or perished under their gigantic feet.

The survivors retreated in disorder, sheltered by the last line of fortifications, a mixture of ruins of the fortress and blocks that came from dismantled temples. The Bishop, at the head of what was left of his army, would fight to the death.

Between the elephants appeared hundreds of Blemmyes equipped with armours made of attached bronze and steel plaques. The seams left the joints free and made moving easy. Others protected themselves with tunics made of scales that covered them from neck to knee. Their faces resembled those of underground demons that surfaced when the year ended.

Interminable minutes went by.

The Christians trembled; without the presence of the Bishop, there would have been an exodus. The Blemmye army grew unceasingly. The black warriors, emerging from everywhere, gathered for the final assault. A young soldier, succumbing to an attack of nerves, gripped the Bishop's wrist.

'I don't want to die.'

'Put your trust in God.'

'I am too scared!'

'I am frightened too. Our body shies from sacrifice; our soul does not.'

The Nubian troops, finally assembled, kept about a hundred metres from their future victims. The elephants no longer trumpeted. The Blemmyes' High Priest took a step forward; he was wearing a panther skin. With a shaved head and his forehead anointed by seven sacred oils, he held in his right hand a long golden rod.

'Let Theodore, the Bishop, come to meet me.'

'Don't go!' cried the soldiers, gripping the prelate. 'They will massacre you.'

Theodore disengaged himself, then jumped on the heap of stones that formed the ramparts of Elephantine's last defence. His red robes embroidered with gold thread flashed in the sun;

he went towards the Blemmye High Priest and stopped a metre from him.

'You, the Christian, you destroyed the sanctuary at Biga, violated the secret of Osiris and smashed the statue of our god. You despised the mystery of the resurrection and sullied our faith. That is why we will massacre the cowardly and impious people that you govern. The followers of Christ do not deserve to live because they only engender hatred.'

'Submit to the Emperor and to God's law. Otherwise, you too will be slaughtered.'

'You are known as a brave man, Theodore, but you are blind.'

'If your decision is taken, why so many speeches?'

'I am not a bloodthirsty mercenary, but a High Priest whose god lives in Philae. Only the holy island's High Priestess can consecrate my victory over evil.'

Isis welcomed the strange delegation. While the Blemmyes, touched, admired the Holy Island, Theodore spoke.

'You have the destiny of thousands of people in your hands. On your orders, my enemies will destroy Elephantine. This province will become burned land and happiness forever lost.'

'But Philae will be saved.'

'Philae will be saved . . .' repeated the Bishop.

At last, he was witnessing the hell where his weakness and friendship had led him. The magic of Isis did not threaten in vain; her community attracted dangerous forces and would keep the true faith at bay. It was this woman, no one else, who waged the most relentless battle against truth; by making those black-faced warriors emerge, she triumphed.

'Great goddess, mother of God, fountain of life, sovereign of the soul's territory that no one can tread, benevolent magician whose words chase away the demons, hear my plea,' implored the Blemmye High Priest.

'Only your will gives each star its place, nourishes hearts,

325

crowns kings and renders conquests sacred; bless my arm and the sword of my warriors.'

'Whoever follows the path of sages,' answered the High Priestess, 'spends his existence in peace, and is overwhelmed with joy. He grows old in his own town, is venerated in his province, his successors receive his teaching, from generation to generation.'

'Everything is marked with the seal of Isis; nothing can be accomplished without her, both on earth and in heaven.'

'Come to the temple.'

Leaving Theodore in his warriors' charge, the Blemmye followed the High Priestess.

The adepts, wearing white robes, saluted their host. The High Priest greeted each one and then he entered the chapel where his god dwelt; Isis invited him to collect himself. The favour granted him put him in a state of elation; by being associated with the mystery on Philae's pure soil, he renewed his people's most venerated tradition. How right he had been to believe in Isis and hope she would be his people's salvation!

The High Priest forgot time and meditated until evening, absorbing the energy contained in the walls of the chapel, where the memory of his religion survived. When he came out of the sanctuary, he was offered bread and wine.

'Philae will remain intact,' he stated. 'Tomorrow there will not be one Christian left in this province. No massacre will be more joyous.'

'It will not happen.'

Astonished, the adepts suppressed their protests.

Why would Isis refuse the help of powerful allies and the extermination of their enemies?

'The Emperor will not accept a defeat of this dimension,' said Sabni. 'Elephantine is one of his frontiers; he will send an army to avenge his honour and the death of a bishop to proclaim the superiority of Christ. His army will pursue the Blemmyes no matter how far they flee and Philae will be destroyed.'

For the Love of Philae

The High Priest's face darkened.

'What do you wish, you to whom I owe obedience?'

'Make a pact with the Bishop,' replied Isis.

'He will not respect it and will threaten Philae again.'

'Let us dispel that danger by entrusting you with the statues that we venerate. In your country, they will be safe from profanity. The Christians will consider that the divinities have left the island and our community; therefore, they will no longer be seen as agitators. Inactive, the temple will not offend their conscience. We will also be left in peace and shown indifference. This will protect us better than the most powerful armies. Who will live in Philae, except a few old folk nostalgic for the past?'

This vision thrilled Sabni. To give up the cult statues would be a painful sacrifice, but in a century or a thousand years hence, they would come back, just as the distant goddess would return from faraway Nubia. Philae, the silent one, remote from any disputed routes or jealousies, would be free to secretly welcome new adepts and grow in Theodore's shadow, crowned by triumph.

The High Priestess approached the Bishop, who was standing in the shade of a tamarisk tree, guarded by black warriors. He turned his eyes towards her and did not try to hide his disquiet.

'What have you decided?'

'Are you aware that the great goddess bestows life, not death? Philae will remain at the heart of Elephantine and will not be its executioner. Both will be saved.'

'By what magic of yours?'

'By the gift bestowed by the goddess.'

Two heavy ships, with Blemmyes on board, sailed to the holy island while the Nubian army camped before the besieged. The cult statues were transported to the battlefield and hoisted on to the back of the elephants before the mesmerized eyes of the Christians.

327

Christian Jacq

'Philae has given up its soul,' judged an officer.

Theodore remained silent. He watched the pachyderms go, then the Nubian warriors broke rank and, forming an immense line, headed south.

Escorted by about a hundred infantrymen, the High Priest approached the Bishop. 'Tomorrow, at dawn, I'll be waiting for you at the cataract. We will negotiate a peace treaty there.'

The inhabitants of Elephantine cheered Theodore. Indifferent to the deliverance chants and the feast that was already being prepared in the streets, he went back to his office. Could it be that Isis and Sabni had renounced the material aspect of the cult to preserve what was most precious: the spirit of the temple?

56

A month after the Blemmyes' departure and the conclusion of the one hundred years' peace treaty, the Bishop summoned Sabni. They met in his garden, which was bathed in the peaceful incandescence of the end of autumn.

'You and I believe in a principle higher than man; we are both just passing, travellers hoping to discover landscapes where the soul, whose thirst is never tarried, seeks its source.'

'Your god does not laugh, Theodore, but is crippled with pain on a cross, regretting being incarcerated in a human body. You have not followed the path of our ancestors and your religion is the accomplice of a vulgar society that crawls on the ground, undermines conscience, encourages selfishness and destroys the zest of community. It is not progress but rather illness; return to the science of the temple, turn towards the heavens. The daughter of the gods bestows her blessings on this earth and guides us towards the mysteries from whence we emerged.'

The Bishop raised his eyes to the tall palm trees; a soft light bathed the two friends.

'Do you despise me to the point of believing that you and Isis deceived me?'

'There is no statue left in the temple. Even that of the great goddess, who stood by the venerable Throne, now lives in exile with the Blemmyes.'

'I was present at the scene, like other thousands of

Christian Jacq

witnesses. You no longer possess those ancestral emblems, but you will always be a profane community.'

'How can we celebrate rituals without statues?'

'Even if the naos is empty, your hearts will always be filled with the same desire. You have not given in, Sabni; your faith remains intact. Nevertheless, Philae will no longer convince anyone.'

'What can you possibly fear from an agonizing community?'

'That like the alchemist and the phoenix, it will regenerate itself in its own death and prepare new gold.'

'We only wish for silence and contemplation.'

'Your eyes tell me otherwise. You are not a resigned man, but a conqueror who hides his face behind a mask. What are your real projects, Sabni?'

'If you can read my soul, you know them.'

'Forget our reasons for discord, forget the habit I am wearing. Behave like a brother, like the only human being whom I trust totally.'

'Nothing separates us, Theodore, but everything keeps us apart. We do not tread the same path; if the gods are favourable to us, we will meet up at the same port.'

At the end of each mass, Paul besieged the Episcopal palace. The prelate listened to him after having made him wait a long time, increasing his anger tenfold. The hermit, accompanied by his disciples, who had come out of tombs and grottoes, indefatigably demanded the destruction of the pagan temple and the expulsion of the community, guilty of complicity with the Blemmyes. On this November Sunday, Paul's virulence became insulting.

'I demand that you pluck the last roots of paganism.'

'Otherwise?'

'You will have to answer for your procrastination before the patriarch of Alexandria.'

'He does not appreciate the exaltation of certain pious people.'

330

'We, the hermits, are not like the lukewarm believers that would make Christ.'

'To become a hermit implies certain duties. Your followers do not all belong to the army of the Lord. I recognize among them some ex-criminals, failed merchants, mercenaries who have been expelled from the army . . . no doubt they make worrying allies.'

'They believe in God and hate the pagans. Their past does not interest me.'

'I will not tolerate any excess. Do not forget that I am responsible for civilian peace.'

'There is no other peace, but that of the Lord. How can He be satisfied with the existence of a temple inhabited by ancient demons?'

'All that is left is a small community that grows old without disturbing public order.'

'Even if there was but one pagan left, he would have to be destroyed.'

Theodore stood up and turned around to face the hermit. Dirty, with dusty hair hanging down his back, he wore a rancid sheepskin.

'I would like to understand you, you who are my brother in Christ. His followers desire love and shun hatred. If you nourish animosity, your prayers will be reduced to vituperations.'

'Would you be praying for pagans?'

'If God had not changed our souls, we would have remained pagans. Why not implore Him to convert those who still wander lost in illusion?'

'Philae has become an irrefutable enemy.'

'Isis saved our lives. Without her intervention, the population of Elephantine would have been massacred and the town burned down.'

'Devilish trick! What the High Priestess wanted was to save the statues of the idols. You should have stopped these from leaving. From the depths of Nubia, they will continue to spread their slime. The Emperor's army will be forced to exterminate the blacks and destroy those accursed effigies.'

'What do you know about that army?'

Paul struck the floor with his rod.

'It will come! Do you think Christians should be passive? Martyrdom has taught us to fight. We form a chain of believers that goes as far as Alexandria, we run across the deserts so that the church is informed of what goes on here. Tomorrow the Emperor will know and he will act accordingly; you will have to justify your behaviour. You were wrong to conclude a pact with Sabni: he is not your friend but the envoy of darkness!'

'What if you are wrong?'

'He would have renounced false gods and asked to be baptized.'

'Do you not have any compassion?'

'I reserve it for believers who, like Christ, fall on the way and stand up again. Our faith is universal, Theodore. To admit the existence of one single pagan is to betray God. Since you have renounced action you are an accomplice; the arm of the Lord will replace yours.'

57

The restoration of Imhotep's temple was almost complete; Isis and Sabni studied the sculpted programme to render the walls alive and perpetuate tradition. In the absence of statues, the holy images engraved in stone and in the hieroglyphs, animated by the spoken word and the gaze of the faithful, would ensure the permanence of the ritual.

The adepts felt proud; despite the lack of tools and their inexperience, they had managed to carry out the work. By fulfilling the demands of the Rule, they would leave a trace of their passage on earth and a tangible token that would inspire their successors; the chain of revelations was not broken.

With each day that passed, Sabni admired his wife more. Passion opened on to a flamboyant horizon where the High Priestess was enthroned, enveloped by light, in the incandescence of heart and senses. Their union had the perfume of eternity incarnated by Isis in the daily adventure. When the voice from the realm beyond danced in the wind, the features of the goddess emerged on the earthly woman's semblance. That each sanctuary, according to ancient texts, should be heaven and earth, Sabni did not doubt.

It was here on earth, nowhere else, that the pilgrim could know the plenitude he would testify to before Osiris's tribunal, without fearing the devouring female or the genii ready to cut the throats of liars and cowards. Isis had offered him the key to eternal happiness; did she not resemble the goddess hidden in the tree on the Western bank, ready to pour the eternal fresh water that filled the traveller to the infinite with delight?

Philae captured time, Isis made it sacred. The soul did not age, thoughts bore no wrinkles, even the humblest acts shone like summer stars. As the feast approached when Isis would reconstitute Osiris's corpse to make him live again, the community sailed once more in the current of those masons who were able to transmute matter.

Two days before Christmas, the Bishop's boat berthed on Philae; Isis welcomed Theodore. In the prelate's eyes she saw distress.

'You saved Elephantine, now I want to save you. The imperial decree came during the night: Philae's community must be dispersed.'

'The hermits.'

'Perhaps they have already been warned. The Emperor's letter, countersigned by the patriarch of Alexandria, announces the impending arrival of an expedition corps commanded by a Byzantine general.'

'Look at this abode ornamented with gold, with a lapis-lazuli ceiling, silver walls, acacia wood floor, copper doors, a work meant to last for ever: don't you recognize that it belongs to the creative principle?'

Theodore implored the High Priestess.

'Never mind what I may think; it is impossible for me to delay the deadline. Leave the island without delay, I beg you.'

Sabni walked towards them, with a sculptor's scissors in hand. On his apron, there were fragments of limestone.

'I heard, Theodore.'

'If you love her, convince her.'

'Where would we go?'

'My boat is at your disposal. Go south.'

'Take refuge with the Blemmyes? The Emperor's army would pursue us. I was born in Philae and will not run away. This temple was entrusted to the High Priest and to myself; we protect it from suffering, anguish and danger.'

'Each adept will be free to go,' explained Sabni. 'As for us, we will not abandon the sacred land.'

'How can I persuade you?'

'Come with me, Theodore.'

Reticent, the Bishop followed the High Priest. Sabni opened the rooms of the temple, commented on the relief sculptures, described in detail the cult ceremonies and the initiation rituals. He withheld no information regarding his science.

'This dying world is now incorporated in you for ever.'

'A useless treasure, Sabni, because it is contrary to my faith.'

'By transmitting this wisdom to you, I have freed the forces buried in the crypts of the temple. They will become your thoughts, birds with immense wings that will fly to the summit of the sky. You, my implacable enemy, have become my hope.'

Isis informed the Bishop that no adept would leave the island. The community agreed with the decision taken by their superiors.

Theodore understood that more words would be useless; he would try and persuade the Byzantine general to spare the lives of those who were in no way a threat to the Empire's grandeur.

'Do you remember, Theodore, the words of Prince Sarenput, engraved in the western tomb, when he was reborn among the gods:

'I touch the heavens, my head pierces the firmament. I scrape the belly of the stars, and I shine with their light. Overwhelmed with celestial joy, I dance with the constellations?'

In his time, the town was celebrating, the soldiers sang with the peasants, the old people and the children rejoiced.

The High Priest and the Bishop embraced like two brothers. Theodore stopped before Isis.

'No one,' she said, 'reaches the West, abode of the One with no blemish, apart from those whose heart is ready to practise the Rule. There, there is no distinction between poor and rich, for the weighing of souls is in the hands of the master of eternity.'

The High Priestess kissed the prelate's forehead; this kiss of peace burned into his soul.

In September of the year 437, a last hieroglyphic text was engraved in the stone of Philae, a prayer to Isis.

That Christmas of the year 535, Sabni carved the last low relief sculpture of Egyptian civilization; on the lintel of Imhotep's chapel, he drew the master mason's apron and his work. No line was finished, no face emerged from matter.

Inside the small building, the community burned small balls of incense. The perfumed smoke would charm the nostrils of the gods who navigated in the boats of day and night. Perhaps a hand would one day pick up the proper tools and finish the figures that Sabni left imperfect.

When he stepped back to contemplate his work, he felt a feeling of great revolt grow inside him. There was still so much work to be done, so much to experience! Isis coiled lovingly around him; with her hair, she caressed his face.

'The sanctuary will not be dismantled.'

'How shall we stop it happening?'

'I don't know.'

'You're trying to reassure me.'

'I have seen Philae in the faraway realm, beyond our existence. Those lines, that your hand drew on the stone, will not remain sterile.'

Paul thanked the Lord; by alerting the patriarch of Alexandria, the hermits had achieved the result they had expected. Anxious to safeguard his power and not to displease the Emperor, the head of the Egyptian Church had gone to Byzantium to account for the Elephantine scandal. In his wisdom, the powerful sovereign had taken the best decision:

to send out soldiers to exterminate the pagans.

Theodore would, once again, try and save his friend Sabni. Luckily, the messenger coming from Alexandria had been talkative, only too happy to prove his importance; the news would overturn the province's destiny. Informed of the content of the imperial missive, Paul felt invested with a sacred mission and, this time, he would outsmart the Bishop's machinations.

'When will they attack?' asked the sister in charge of meals.

'The moment the Byzantine army crosses the gates of Elephantine,' Isis replied.

'Two weeks?'

'Perhaps only one. In this season the sun is mild; they will force the pace, the infantry will go fast.'

'It's not very long, one week . . .'

Brothers and sisters waited for the moment when the river would be covered with warships; for the festive banquet there was garlic, onion, bread with lotus grains and carobs. The Elders, without teeth, were happy to boil some papyrus stems.

Sabni watched the riverbank where the assailants would embark; he was trying to build up some courage, soon to be dispelled the moment the soldiers' cries resonated.

At the summit of the Pylon, Isis contemplated the dark blue of the oncoming night; then the tender, deep, quiet blue, fading into the oncoming orange, expiring at the boundary of an intense red, dusk's last word; finally, darkness brutally separated from the fires of the day agonized on the curved line of the horizon, the insurmountable frontier between yesterday and tomorrow. The last incandescent glow faded; black and white approached one another, happy to be reunited after a long separation. The tender blue let itself be reabsorbed, the red became a fringe, and the orange expired. What is above and what is below merged in the obscure mesh woven by the Creator to cover the earth.

'This night will be the last,' Isis predicted.

The day had the sweetness of a ripe fruit after the sun had dissipated a few odd clouds. On the deserted riverbank, sand uplifted by the desert wind formed elusive spirals.

Isis and Sabni went down into the only barge the temple still possessed. With the help of a pole, the High Priest distanced it from the pier and slid it into the current. Facing the East, he chanted the morning prayer; his voice vanished into the mountain slopes. Isis drank water from the river, soft to the touch and pleasant to taste, still carrying the freshness of the spring hidden in the rocks of Elephantine. She thought of the happy days when life drifted wherever the Nile went, offering itself to the gold of the dunes and to the whiteness of the sails. When the gods loved to visit the luxuriously green banks, their statues adorned fields and villages where men felt they were hosts to these deities.

'At the time of the pharaohs we walked without fear on these paths, sailed trustingly on the river, talked near a well or a basin, not far from the pastures where the cattle was free to wander. I can see your face, Sabni; you descend from your boat made of pinewood from prow to stern, and you open the house you built. The piece of beef grills, the jar is uncorked, some melodies enchant us. Around us, young girls dance, recite poems, perfume us and decorate our necks with garlands of flowers; they prepare our bed where, once night falls, ecstasy will unite us.'

'That was our life, one thousand years ago . . . A dream lost in the solitude of the country's cataract. Should we really defy the impossible?'

'We have sworn to transmit the mystery.'

'What if you left? Isis, safe and sound, the guardian of the tradition.'

'To separate would be folly.'

'Your life is precious. As High Priestess, you are the future.'

'The future no longer exists. We are left with the present, even if it has a more ferocious face than that of the terrifying one. May the youth of the temple last for ever and we will have served the Rule; the sky is incarnate in Philae.'

'I find the Rule so harsh, sometimes.'

'So do I, Sabni, for we are unworthy of it; that is why there must be two of us.'

'For the love of Philae . . .'

They embraced. The barge, left at the mercy of the current, drifted towards the land of the dead, somnolent under the winter sun. Both thought of their communion on the site of the tomb of Osiris, of that absolute happiness, that the nights and days regenerated.

'Philae is the last temple of a world that our enemies think has disappeared; religions will succeed one another, tear at each other and flounder at the feet of the sanctuary even if the community seems extinguished.'

'Do you desire so much to pass on, Isis?'

'Not for a moment. I want to live a hundred years, grow old by your side and see our brothers and sisters flourish.'

The current changed and brought the barge back towards Philae.

It was not the Byzantine expeditionary corps that, a little before the middle of day, launched the attack on Philae, but a heterogeneous troop made up of hermits, lost soldiers and inhabitants of Elephantine that Paul had driven to the brink of insanity. The hermits had been fasting for four days; the others were drunk. Armed with spears, pitchforks and swords, they chanted psalms celebrating the victory of the Lord over demons.

Paul did not want to relinquish that act of faith and hand it over to a foreign general. It was up to him, and no one else, to crush once and for all the head of the pagan hydra and take over the temple. The Bishop was not warned. When rumours about the carnage reached him, it would be too late.

The adepts were terrified at the sight of the screaming mob; under the leadership of 'Shortcut', it was already invading the square. Ready to fight, the adepts placed themselves behind Isis and Sabni.

The High Priestess had dressed with the ornaments pertaining to her function, a lapis-lazuli choker, a chest ornament composed of seven rows of pearls, silver bracelets and gold rings. The whiteness of the long dress emphasized the splendour of the jewellery.

A hermit brandished a half-broken stick; Isis did not move back. Two brothers jumped on the aggressor, whose attack was interrupted. Two soldiers came immediately to the rescue

For the Love of Philae

and struck the adepts, who fell, their faces covered in blood. 'Shortcut' clasped the High Priestess's wrists with his belt; Sabni tried to free her but was immediately tied up.

When a hermit strangled a bedridden sister, two infantry-men intervened.

'We are here to expel, not murder them.'

'Be silent, you lukewarm spirits! The Emperor wants to purify this accursed island!'

Those who hesitated were hit from behind by wild peasants and were forced to stand aside. The sister was trampled to death. Her death rattles were muffled by the screams of the other adepts, stampeded with blows. The sticks crashed down, again and again, pitchforks disembowelled bellies, swords cut throats. The discovery of a small cult boat increased the fury of the assailants tenfold. They broke the prow and the stern, which bore a sculpted head of Hathor. Paul burned the debris.

Neither Isis nor Sabni were crying. A pain that was simultaneously glacial and burning stopped their tears. Where was the sweet and smiling death promised to sages? According to the teaching of the mysteries, the adept of the sacred magic went out by day and strolled in the realm beyond as far as his heart desired. Soon, the veil would tear and the door open.

'Shortcut' ripped off the High Priestess's necklace; inebriated by his success, he tore the top of her dress. Sabni repelled him with a head butt.

'Don't touch her.'

With his wrists tied, he could not defend her, but there was such authority in his eyes and his voice that the man stepped back.

'You're nothing now, High Priest, and you will answer for your sins before the Almighty!'

Not finding any further resistance, the vociferous troop poured through the rooms of the temple, disappointed not to find any treasure. The more excited spat on the relief sculptures where the goddesses featured. While they defaced them, other acolytes of Paul's burned the masts made of pine from Cilicia, symbols of divine power. The hermits had often dreamed of tearing down those proud emblems.

Helped by a dozen deserters, 'Shortcut' killed off the wounded. A soldier went mad and threw himself into the Nile from the height of the covered gallery where the adepts loved meditating. Paul gave the order to destroy the doors to the sanctuaries and to let light penetrate the obscure rooms.

Suddenly he felt ill at ease. The eyes of Isis and Sabni were riveted on him. He no longer feared them; the magic of the great goddess did not prevent her conquest. The community was devastated; never again would Egyptians celebrate a cult to the glory of false gods, drawn from hellish realms.

Isis put her head on Sabni's shoulder.

'Give me some water, so that its freshness may calm my heart. Turn your face towards the north; it will show us the way. What we have built on this earth will remain so in heaven.'

These ritual words, an appeal to the ocean of energy where the soul drank from a primordial spring, calmed the High Priest. He feared seeing her sullied, disfigured, and not being able to spare her the suffering inflicted. Isis remained serene; she gave him strength to confront the ultimate tests before appearing before the court of Osiris.

Paul walked in their direction.

'Do you repent and implore the Lord's pardon?'

'You are neither God nor his messenger.'

'Poor fool . . . don't you understand the great goddess is dead? Repent, you demented wretch!'

'You're right, Paul; with us disappears a whole world that the gods inhabited, that they made sacred by their presence. It is not a community that you are murdering, but a vision, a temple built thousands of years ago by a communion of thoughts.'

'You will witness the dismantling of the building, High Priest; it will perish just like the adepts, servants of the netherworld.'

342

'You're wrong,' stated Isis. 'It will survive.'

A fellow Christian warned the hermit that the Bishop's boat approached; no doubt the burning of the masts of the pylons, visible from Elephantine, had alerted him.

Paul's victory would be incomplete if the couple escaped divine wrath.

'Bring the community barge here!'

The order was promptly executed; 'Shortcut' forced Isis and Sabni to climb on board the vessel down by the centre of the vast esplanade, between the first pylon and the pier. In the distance, the white sail of the prelate's boat flapped in the wind.

Upon a sign given by the hermit, the soldiers set fire to the improvised stake.

'Untie our hands,' demanded Sabni.

The sword cut the ropes. The High Priest took Isis in his arms and held her close.

'The temple will not be destroyed,' she repeated.

Paul waited for their despair, hoping for a cry of hatred, a curse, a useless revolt; but the couple were oblivious to his presence, to the fire that consumed them. Isis and Sabni kissed, forming one being with Incandescence, born of the dance of fire and the love of the goddess.

The Bishop knelt down by the stake and blessed the tortured bodies, unable to pray. Behind him, Paul burst out laughing.

'The Emperor will be satisfied. You will benefit from my combat, Bishop; you will reap the honours and I will obtain divine praise! What you did not have the courage to attempt, I have accomplished!'

Theodore stood up; with his cross, he struck the hermit. With a bloodied forehead, Paul moved back.

'You have disfigured the Saviour; because of fanatics like you, religion spreads misery and death. No god will absolve your sin. I curse you down the centuries.'

'Thanks to me, Egypt is free from evil; all that is left is to destroy the temple.'

'Philae will remain intact. When the end of time comes, it will contemplate the dawn of the last day.'

'Philae must be completely destroyed. It is the Emperor's wish!'

'I transform this pagan temple into a church; it is here that I will celebrate Sunday mass. Everywhere in the Empire it will be known that God has elected as his abode this most magnificent building.'

Stunned, the hermit curled up, his forehead against the pavement, sullied with his blood.

Theodore, sensing a fleeting shadow, lifted his eyes and saw a couple of wild geese, with gigantic wings; they circled above him before soaring and merging with the light.